She nodded, then hiked a breath.
"So... that's it? You've apologised, and..."

"And nothing," he said. "I ask nothing more from you, than hopefully, one day, your forgiveness."

"All you want is my forgiveness?" She raised her eyebrows. "You came all the way here, just to apologise and ask my forgiveness?"

"No. No, *Querida*," he said. "I didn't come only to apologise, and ask forgiveness. But I thought it appropriate to start there."

"Start there? Start there, and go where, Jake? Where do we go from here?" The tears she'd been fighting broke free. She made no attempt to stop them.

My Own

OTHER TITLES BY DEBORAH SMALL

My Dear One

My Own

Book II
Dear One Series

DEBORAH
SMALL

Cover Design: Victoria Cooper
Deborah Small
Author Photo: Purple Butterfly Photography

First edition

Deborah Small
www.deborahsmall.com

Printed in the United States of America and Canada

First Printing: November 2018

ISBN- 978-1-7753173-3-3

Soul and body,
Forfeit;
Freely given to you.
You are my heart.
You are my own.

—DEBORAH SMALL

For my husband, Darwin,
You are my heart.

And my children, Travis, Melissa, Aric, and Matthew—
You are my own.

Acknowledgements

Many people are owed a depth of gratitude for their direct, or indirect, help in getting this book out in the world:

My husband Darwin whose ceaseless support of my writing career, and willingness to come home after work and whip together supper while I attempt to make word music, makes what I do so much sweeter. Thank you, Honey. You are my HEA.

Beta Readers Kathleen, Mary Ann, and Rita, who offered important feedback and encouragement. Honestly, Ladies, Thank You.

My editor, Eileen Cook, whose questions, suggestions, and comments, all liberally sprinkled with praise, challenged me to reimagine many of the scenes in this book and overhaul it in a way I hope does justice to the hard work she invested in helping me make this story better.

Victoria Cooper, of Victoria Cooper Art, who crafted the cover.

I must also thank Dianne Mackenzie and Roxanne Snopek who, when I agonised about where to start the story, offered to read two different opening scenes—and independent of each other—chose the same one. They also shared why they preferred it, and what made them want to read more, as I hope it does you.

Thank you for picking up this book today. May it bring you as much tearful joy at the end, as it did me.

DS

Part One

A straight oar looks bent in the water.
What matters is not merely that we see things but how we see them.
~Michel de Montaigne

Chapter 1

Want and Need

Douglas, Texas
May 1914

*W*hy won't you let me go with Papa?"

Dianna managed not to sigh, or close her eyes in exasperation, but continued to guide the tiny dessert spoon in her young son's hand to his mouth. Once JJ successfully captured the pea on his tongue and released his pudgy-fingered grip on the spoon, she met her adopted daughter's accusatory gaze across the dining table. Gently, in hopes of dampening Amelia's short-fuse, she said, "We discussed this, Amelia."

Amelia's small chin came up, a defiant mould becoming all too familiar of late. "If I don't go tomorrow, I won't be able to go until next Saturday and all the babies will be born by then. I did everything Papa said to. I finished my homework, and my chores. Tell her, Papa. Tell her you said I could go, if I did everything you said."

Jake, with Dianna on his left and Amelia to his right, shifted, no doubt uncomfortable being boxed—literally—in the middle of a battle he believed unwarranted. Katie, beside Amelia, kept her head bowed, long dark braids dangled over the shoulders of her blue pinafore shifting in rhythm with the slow, careful scrape of her knife and fork, as she sliced the roast beef on her plate.

Truly, they were as different as two sisters might be. One dark and quiet and mysterious as a moonlit lake, the other as bright and charged and quick as a shooting star. Yet equal in their desperate need for security, love, and... structure.

She answered Jake's questioning gaze with a twig of one eyebrow.

So far, he'd kept himself well removed of this, her and Amelia's first test of their fledgling relationship as mother and daughter not yet a year in its maturity. Publicly. In private, he revealed himself aligned with Amelia's position: that she was old enough, and capable enough after six months of riding lessons, to occasionally accompany him on horseback to inspect fences and the ranch's ten-thousand strong herd of Simmental and Longhorn cattle. Dianna disagreed.

She could not fathom exposing a child to the dangers lurking on the thirty-thousand acres that comprised the combined J-D Quarter Horses, and Douglas Ranch cattle operations, especially during calving and foaling season.

Broken bones, lacerations, rope, and campfire burns never mind simple sun and wind burn, frostbite, and saddle chafe... The injuries the men employed year-round to manage the livestock experienced were frequent, if varied. And usually tended by the men themselves. Only the most serious involved the town doctor. Even then, he was a doctor. Not a God. As Jake knew too well. He'd lost his stepfather four years prior to an overprotective Longhorn that misinterpreted his attempts to free her calf from a barbed-wire fence and gored him.

Jake continued to hold her gaze. She widened her eyes slightly.

Clearing his throat, he turned to Amelia. "You are right, Mia. I did say you had to do your chores and homework, before I'd let you come with me. And I'm proud of you for catching up so swiftly."

Amelia bobbed her head, mouth curling in satisfaction, until Jake finished with, "What you forgot, is that I said you could come with me if you had your homework and chores done, *and* your mother agreed."

Dianna ground her molars to contain a tart "Thank you", as Amelia pinned her with a stare. Honey-blonde hair in a single braid down her back and sharp features set with determination, amber-coloured eyes narrowed, she resembled a young lioness set to pounce.

And Dianna the hapless prey.

"You have to let me go, Mama. I did everything. My homework. The dusting. I even helped clean the windows."

"Yes, I know darling, but—"

"You go."

Dianna compressed her lips. "Not often. And I'm an adult. You're only nine."

"Papa went when he was my age."

Dianna choked off an instinctive reply. Noted the flare of satisfaction—victory—in Amelia's gold-flecked eyes.

For the briefest moment she almost regretted her decision, and Jake's agreement with it, to raise their children with the expectation girls were as capable of achieving anything boys were. As deserving of the right to create of their life what they would, without deference to their sex. *Almost.*

This time Jake allowed his expression to convey his thoughts on the matter.

Like Amelia, he watched her, waiting for her to finish wrestling with her conscience and ultimately come down on the side of that which she truly believed: girls were as capable as boys.

Or they weren't.

Katie, too, had looked up from her meal. Only JJ remained blessedly oblivious, babbling his baby talk as he smacked the peas on his tray with his palms. *Bloody hell.*

Dianna forced her throat muscles to convulse once more, swallow the sourness on her tongue.

She'd always hated the taste of crow.

"You haven't anything appropriate to wear, Mia," she murmured. "So, you have to wait until Saturday next, at least, to give me time to fashion something suitable." *And adjust to the idea.*

"I think I can help with that," Jake said. "There's that trunk of my old clothes in the attic my mother sent over. I'm sure we'll find something in there to fit."

Eleanor Douglas had saved a few of the better outfits from Jake's childhood as mementos for her benefit, but passed on the lot to Jake the previous year in anticipation an item or two might prove suitable for JJ. Not quite a year-and-a-half old, JJ was yet too small for most of the trunk's

4

contents. Amelia, however... There was at least one pair of denim trousers Dianna recalled seeing that just might fit.

How convenient.

Amelia had a hand over her mouth, and her eyes so recently blunt with ire, sparkled with awe as she stared at Jake. "I can wear some of your old clothes?" she whispered.

He nodded. "If they fit. I expect the trousers will need suspenders."

Amelia clasped both hands under her chin. "Can I have my own rifle?"

"What?" Dianna looked from Amelia to Jake. "No. She absolutely cannot."

Amelia scrambled to her feet. "Why don't you trust Papa?"

"Amelia," Jake said, his tone weighted with caution.

"It's not that I don't trust your father," Dianna said with enforced calm. "It's that I don't want you to get hurt—"

"Papa won't let me get hurt."

"Yes, I know—"

"No. You don't." Amelia glared. "Because if you did, you'd let me go."

"Amelia. Marie. Douglas." Jake set his fork on the table with enough force to draw not only Amelia's startled glance, but JJ's.

A pea pincered in sticky fingers, he stared at Jake, wariness dimpling his small brow. Dianna stroked his fine dark hair and murmured quiet reassurance as she used her other hand to spoon a couple more peas from her plate.

Jake's next words were soft-spoken, conversational, if his gaze on Amelia unyielding: "You want any chance of going with me, at all, Mia, you best apologise to your mother and then sit and finish your supper."

Amelia pinched her mouth closed, but fire still sparked in her gaze when she looked at Dianna. Katie, poor mite, shrank further as she diced her food to smaller, and smaller pieces, the grate of silver utensils on porcelain echoing the hollow throb in Dianna's throat.

In the first months following her and Jake's adoption of the girls the previous year, both had done as twelve-year-old Katie continued to do: their level best to remain obscure members of the household. Barely speaking. Always awaiting invitation to enter a room. Timid, fearful behaviour not unexpected, given the trauma they'd suffered at the hands of the man they had once called Father. Where Katie remained firmly at arm's length, Amelia's reserve had begun to soften during the past Christmas season, especially after she opened her gift from Jake.

Books, clothes, dolls, music boxes... every fanciful thing a girl might hope for scattered in open packages around them and Amelia and Katie were most awed by the moccasins Jake had made for them to help protect their feet from the cold floorboards, and wooden whistles he had carved, and required them to carry with them always when outside.

"For if you need help," he explained, as he'd looped the leather laces on which the whistles were hung, over their necks in turn, Katie flinching when his fingers brushed her neck. "Voices tire and are never as loud, or as easily heard, as whistles."

The utter astonishment, and genuine gratitude and joy on each girl's face as they admired the rabbit-fur-lined hand-stitched slippers had crushed Dianna's heart, making her wonder if they had ever received more than one gift—or even one—from their father. She suspected not. Especially, after their mother died. Charles Harney had cared less for what he could give his children, than what he might take from them.

"Sorry."

Amelia's muttered apology forced Dianna to discard her morose thoughts, retrain her attention on her daughter as Jake laid a hand on Amelia's shoulder, his large fingers loose. Comfort and support, rather than coercion.

"Look at your mother," he said. "And speak louder. Acknowledge exactly what you're sorry for."

Amelia, her head bowed, slim fingers working the end of her braid, heaved a deep breath and looked up. "I'm sorry Mama for speaking wrongly to you." Rushed, and forced though her words were, they sounded sincere.

Willing a genuine, if faintly wobbly smile as she fought a curious urge to cry, Dianna said, "Thank you, Amelia. It takes a great deal of courage to apologise, and I admire, and thank you for it."

Amelia blinked, and her sulk relaxed. Marginally. "Does that mean I can go with Papa?"

Dianna stifled a laugh at Amelia's bald ploy, swallowed a sob seeing the desperate appeal in her amber gaze, despite the hard set of her jaw.

You remember what that was like, don't you, hiding your true want behind a façade of bravado so he wouldn't know how much it hurt when he said no?

6

Amelia had worked hard to fulfil her responsibilities... *It's not about responsibilities. It's about her want to be with Jake. To spend time with him, because... She loved him. And he her.*

The realisation clenched deep in some part of Dianna she hadn't known existed, raw, hollow, foreign pain, because though she'd been a child in want of a parent's approval, she'd never been a mother, heart-broken by a child's rejection. Her throat tightened, forcing her to draw on her upbringing to maintain eye-contact with Amelia, while denying even a single tear permission to bloom.

This was silly, her feeling rejected by Amelia's show of belligerent allegiance with Jake. It was exactly what she'd hoped both girls would eventually come to feel for her and Jake. Well, not the belligerence. The allegiance. The fact it was happening more swiftly between Jake and Amelia, where she seemed to be rapidly losing any ground she'd gained with the child in the last year, was not hard to understand.

Amelia loved everything to do with the out of doors—horses and riding, wiling hours tossing a lariat at long curved horns culled from a deceased cow and affixed to a wooden sawhorse. Things Jake did every day, though the horns he roped were generally still attached to their owner.

Happy as she was outside, Amelia loathed being inside, bemoaned schoolwork, piano practise, embroidery and crochet, all things she was expected to do, or catch up on Saturdays, so they could spend Sundays together as a family.

No wonder she prefers Jake. And resents me. He represents freedom. I represent everything she despises, and she's too young to understand the difference. Just as I was, when I was her age.

And how did that work out?

Not well. There was good reason she and Jake had chosen to remain in Texas, despite ample reason for them to move their family to England.

Despair, and acceptance, twined a rough knot in Dianna's throat, chafing her voice, "Yes, Mia, you can go."

Amelia, who had opened her mouth the moment Dianna opened hers, perhaps in anticipation of rebuttal, stared. Then she canted a look at Jake, before turning her wary gaze on Dianna. "You mean it?" There was as much doubt, as disbelief in her voice. "I can go? I can go with Papa, tomorrow?"

"Yes. Provided Papa's in agreement?" Dianna looked to Jake.

He held her gaze for the space of a heartbeat, before nodding at Amelia. "Yes. You can come. But—"

"You must listen, Amelia," Dianna said before he could set further conditions, before she had laid out hers. "You must listen to your father, and do everything and anything he tells you, without question. If he tells you to stay where you are, or to come *home*, you do so, immediately. Do you understand me?"

When Amelia looked to Jake, he nodded.

"Your mother's right. Out there—" He indicated the lace-fronted window overlooking the porch and main yard, and beyond miles and miles of rangeland— "I'm the boss. And my word is final. Understand?"

"Yes, Papa," Amelia said breathlessly. "I understand. You're the boss. Out there," she amended with a lowered-lash glance at Dianna.

Dianna willed her facial muscles to remain smooth. "And no gun, Mia. I mean it."

Again, Amelia glanced at Jake. Again, he nodded.

"Not until you're big enough to handle it safely," he said. "Your mother and I will decide when that is."

Amelia nodded. "Yes, Papa."

"Now sit and finish your meal." Jake retrieved his fork. "After supper, we'll go out and make sure Dirk and McGuire know to have King *and* Sonny ready come morning."

With a nod and a happy grin, Amelia slid into her seat, took up her fork, and dove into her supper with surprising alacrity.

Dianna released her breath and lowered her shoulders, as she reclined against the seat back, mildly assuaged to know Amelia would ride Sonny. Of all the horses available to her, the gentle sixteen-year-old gelding was by far the most sensible, and best trained. A perfect mount for a novice rider.

Noting Katie's gaze on her, Dianna offered a reassuring smile, and when Katie looked at her plate, she doled a few more peas to JJ's tray—he'd squished more than he'd eaten—and grasped her fork, careful to avoid Jake's gaze lest she relay the disquiet and disappointment still thrumming within her. She looked down, eased out a silent sigh.

The wonderful beef roast and Yorkshire pudding Mrs. Brown had slaved over all afternoon, and she had anticipated so highly, was all but congealed on her plate. Still, she was starving.

Tucking the tines of her fork under a gravy-soaked wedge, she startled when JJ smashed his palms on the tray and loosed the frustrated screech that indicated his patience for family drama—and being confined three-feet off the floor—was done. Closing her eyes, she inhaled, savouring the rich, succulent, and buttery scents that were the closest she'd come to tasting her food, and popped open her eyes when Mrs. Brown's voice interrupted her pity party.

"Shall I take the wee lord off your hands, Missus?" She stood in the entrance to the kitchen, a clean white apron over her black dress to replace the one made grubby during the day's meal preparations. Her expression was neutrally expectant, her grey hair wound in a tightly controlled bun, picture-perfect example of someone fully prepared to accept—without complaint—whatever reply was offered.

Dianna flashed a grateful smile. "That would be—"

"I've got him." Jake skewered the last morsel of meat from his plate with his fork, stuffed it in his mouth and setting knife and fork crosswise on his empty plate, shoved his chair back to stand.

"Oh, let me, Mr. Douglas." Mrs. Brown started forward. "You stay an' enjoy dessert. I'll bring it right out, and then I'll take the wee man up for his bath."

"Thank you, but I'm done, Mrs. Brown. Dinner was delicious. As usual."

"Oh, well..." Mrs. Brown clasped her hands in front of her, her plump features reddening. "You're welcome, sir."

JJ rocked in his seat chanting "Da, da, da," as he grasped Jake's shirtsleeve with green-slimed fingers in delighted anticipation of achieving freedom.

"Please, Mrs. Brown," Jake said, as he lifted JJ. "Jake, or Mr. Douglas, is fine. No need to stand on ceremony, here."

The grateful smile Dianna thought to give him died on her lips, as he turned away with JJ. Sucking the insides of her cheeks she swallowed a frustrated growl, an awful habit developed of late, acquired roughly the same time Amelia began to display overt signs of resistance to her every word, and Jake subtle signs of withdrawal.

To anyone else, he'd been doting on his son, not ignoring her. She knew better. Knew him.

Knew how often he usually sought her eyes out with his at every opportunity to convey his affection with a wink, or amusingly lecherous leer, especially when words weren't possible, or appropriate, owing to distance, or others being in a room with them.

Tonight, his decision to not look at her when she'd angled towards him, to keep JJ's small dark head between them, had been deliberate. Just as he'd deliberately held her gaze earlier, when Amelia pleaded to ride out with him.

He'd been testing her resolve.

Conveying disappointment.

With her.

In her.

And then, to raise the spectre of the earl, of the lifestyle she'd once lived, where Mrs. Brown's offer to attend to JJ, her use of Sir, would never have been questioned let alone discouraged, no matter how gently... Breathing deeply to loosen the tentacled grip a rare spur of anger directed at her husband had on her innards, she willed a conspiratorial slant to her smile as she captured each of her daughter's gazes in turn, before coming around to Mrs. Brown.

"I believe you mentioned something about... dessert?"

∞ ∞ ∞

He was seated, still clothed, on his side of the bed, his back to her and elbows braced on his knees, when she entered their chamber after tucking in the girls for the night. And the room, which so often in the months since their reconciliation had glowed with lantern light and the visceral warmth of mutual passion, was brittle with silence, lit by a slash of hallway light let in through the open bedchamber door.

Closing it softly, she stood in the darkness, stared at his slumped shape sheathed in a shimmer of moonlight through the terrace doors.

"JJ's asleep?"

He nodded.

"No fuss?"

"No."

Shifting her hands behind her back, she leaned with palms flat against the door. She might have remained there indefinitely, cool air swirling around her ankles and up the inside of her nightdress, toes curled inside her moccasins, if he'd not sighed and lifted his head.

"She's right, you know."

"Who? About what?"

"Amelia. You don't trust me."

She pushed off the door. "That is not true."

The bed frame creaked in imagined relief when he stood to round the foot of the bed, a tall, wide, male shadow that was she not intimately familiar with its owner, might have terrified her.

"Isn't it?" he murmured.

"No. It's you who doesn't trust me." Her throat ached with the strain of withholding sudden—ridiculous—tears. "You're supposed to support me, instead you undermine and insult me—"

"Undermine—insult, you?"

"Yes. The clothes in the attic. The comment to Mrs. Brown."

"I wasn't trying to undermine you. I was offering a solution. And—" He dragged a hand over his mouth. "I'll speak to Mrs. Brown. Ensure she understands I meant no offence and was only trying to reinforce our decision to raise the children like I was raised. Little formality, and more hands-on involvement from us. Something she still seems to struggle with—"

"Of course, she still struggles with it," she said. "Two years ago—and for almost fifty years before that—inattention to proper protocol or the needs of the family would have got her fired. It *did* get her fired. She and Dirk both. They defied the earl to help me."

"I know." He nodded. "I know what they did to help you, how different your lives in England were. And I know they're trying. You're trying. We're all trying." He inhaled. "We agreed this wouldn't be easy, that it would take time to help the girls adjust, help *us* all adjust. No one, least of all me, thought this would be a picnic. Especially considering this time last year I was convinced I'd never see you again. *Had* no intention of ever seeing you again."

"I apologised for that," she said, unable to keep the hurt from her voice.

"I know," he whispered and grasped her cold hands in his warm ones. "I know you apologised. We both apologised. I'm as responsible as you for what happened. Your uncertainty about my feelings, my motivation in marrying you... We both failed then Dianna. You could have asked me, instead of running. I could have told you, instead of assuming you knew. But I corrected my mistake, in New York. I made clear how much I loved you. Do love you. I also made clear my willingness to help you raise JJ, and Katie and Amelia. Be a good father to them, but..."

"But what?" she rasped, her throat rough with guilt, and shame. Guilt, because she'd lied to him about why she'd left. Shame, because she could never tell him the truth. She'd promised his mother she wouldn't. "What, Jake? What am I doing so wrong, that even Amelia hates me?"

"What? No, *Querida*." His fingers tightened on hers. "She doesn't hate you. She's a child—"

"I know." She slipped her hands from his, yanked the collar of her bathrobe closed at her neck. "I know she doesn't hate me. She hates the power I have to make decisions that affect her. I understand that. Understand her anger. She's never been on the range. She has no idea what's out there. What I don't understand, is why you backed her, not me?"

Shaking his head, he sighed. "I'm not playing favourites, Dianna. I'm trying to be what I promised you I would be—a good father."

"And that means being a poor husband?"

For a half-second he didn't move. Then he spun, and stalked to the far wall, braced an arm on the frame of the terrace doors to stare out, his breath audible, angry. Digging her fingers into the fabric of her robe's collar she hugged her elbows tightly to her chest.

She'd blamed the low-level discord slowly invading their interactions in recent weeks on many things: accumulated fatigue after three months of broken sleep inherent to calving and foaling season; pent-up frustration after a long, dark and cold winter that had tested the limits of the children's patience for being confined indoors, and her and Jake's creativity in keeping them amused. Natural discomfiture as they all acclimated to new dinner, and bedtime routines. But this... Whatever this was yawning like a bottomless chasm in the midst of their bedchamber was all of that.

And so much more.

Which you only make worse with unkind, unjust words.

"I'm sorry, Jake." Her moccasins scuffed softly on the oak floorboards as she stepped off the rug, and touched his back that was rigid as hot steel beneath the soft fabric of his shirt. "That wasn't fair."

"You're damn right, it wasn't." He turned. "I'm doing my best to find a balance, here, Dianna. Trying to support you, *and* the children. Something we seem to have very different ideas about. You think because we eat meals together every night as a family, and I back your every decision with regard to the children, and help you read to them and tuck them in at night, that all is well. What you don't see, *pequeña*—" He broke off, turned back to the window, moonlight drawing the taut ridge of his jaw. "What you don't seem to understand, is that they need to trust me, too. To feel safe in coming to me with questions, or requests. To feel safe being alone with me. But... Everything must pass through you first, *Querida*. Everything—"

"Because we made an agreement that we would make decisions together." The indignation in her voice rang faintly hollow.

"We did," he said, his tone more confused than angry. "And every single decision we've agreed upon since was at your initiation. Those ideas you don't agree with never find traction."

"Because I think Amelia is too young to handle a gun? Too small to be out there—" She thrust a hand at the darkness beyond the terrace doors— "with monstrous bulls and, and... rattle snakes?"

He faced her. "She's no younger than you were when you learned to shoot. And she's older than I was when I started riding the range. If she's ever going to learn how to manage out there—"

"I only learned to shoot at her age—younger than her age—because my father—*stepfather*—forced it upon me," she said. "And you... you grew up here."

"She's growing up here, Dianna." His words were gentle. "They're all growing up here. And this isn't the fancy, protected English estate you grew up on—"

"You think I don't know that? It's *why* I don't want them out there."

"But they're going to be out there. They *live* here, Dianna." He shoved a hand through his hair. "We decided together to make *this* their home, instead of the one in England you inherited. A ranch. A *working* ranch. And Amelia *wants* to learn. Everything she can. That includes guns. And monstrous bulls. Rattle snakes and every other danger—and joy—that might be found out there. And if I had my way... If I had my way, she'd learn it all. She'd learn everything she needs to know to protect herself, how to manage in the wild, and keep her wits when in danger. How to appreciate the rain and sun and tolerate the wind. Survive the cold. Katie, too. And JJ, when he's old enough. And this one." He pressed his palm lightly to her abdomen.

She flinched, and backing away, shook her head. "No. You—I—I'm not even sure, yet. There is no way you can know."

He made a sound in his throat that might have been a stifled laugh. "You forget I know you, *Querida*. Know your body, know your heart. And I know you're not usually this... tetchy."

"Tetchy?" She glowered. "Are you implying—"

"That you're emotional? Quick to anger? Less patient, and more obstinate than usual?" He nodded. "Yes. And the last time you were like this was when I met you. I put it down then to you being high-born. High-strung. On the run. But I've learned better. I know who you are when you're not scared. You're gentle, loving—patient—and that changes only slightly the week before your monthly. But this... tetchiness?" He closed the distance she'd put between them, brushed the knuckles of one hand along her cheek. "It's lasted closer to a month, and is far more... intense, than usual. So that, along with my calculation that you're at least two weeks overdue... Yes. I believe you're with child."

She blinked, surprised he kept track of her menses.

But of course, he did. It was one of the things she'd been drawn to in him even when she'd wanted nothing to do with him those first days after he'd made her his unwilling ward, before she agreed to become his wife: his thoughtfulness and ability—willingness—to look past her *tetchiness* to see her. Hear her. When all her life she'd only ever been seen or heard in relation to how well she fulfilled other's expectations, in particular, the earl's.

She bowed her head to his chest, shook it. "I can't be," she whispered.

"I beg to differ," he said, voice tinged with wry humour as he slid his arms around her, tugging her close to his solid frame.

"You know what I mean." She looked up. "We've only just... started. Started living as a family. Ten months. That's all we've had with the girls, and JJ, all of us together under one roof, and now..." *We're at odds. Already unhappy.*

"We'll be fine, *Querida*." He cupped her face in his callused palms. "We'll get through this. One day, one row hoed, one argument—one child, at a time." Thumbing a tear from her cheek, he bowed his forehead to hers. "We're going to have disagreements, *pequeña*. Isn't a married couple alive, that doesn't. But we'll get through it, Dianna Douglas. Because that's who we are. We don't quit. *You* don't quit."

"I know. I know." She inhaled. "This one is... yours. This one will be yours."

"They're all mine, *Querida*," he murmured. "The fact I sired this one, won't change how I feel about any of them."

Her tears fell more copious as he gathered her closer, smoothed her hair.

He never questioned it. Never questioned his decision to wed a pregnant runaway, take on her unborn child, and two more besides, as his own. Never doubted his—or her—ability to overcome whatever they faced. *So much, in two short years.*

Births. Deaths. Lies. Truths. So many lies, and startling truths... No wonder she was tired. Cranky.

Four.

Four children.

Their first, together.

Nosing into the warm cotton of his shirt, she slipped her arms around his waist, grateful he was the only man JJ would ever know as his father. *Thank Heaven.*

It was enough Katie and Amelia would forever live with the scars of their past. She'd not have her son's psyche branded with knowledge of how he'd come to be, and by whom.

"Dianna?" The timbre of Jake's deep voice deepened as he angled to look at her without letting her go. "What is it? Why are you crying? Is it the baby?"

"No."

"You're sure?"

She nodded.

He brushed at the tears on her cheeks. "Are you still angry with me, about Amelia?"

She shook her head. She wasn't overjoyed at the prospect of Amelia jaunting off to ride alongside him and the vaqueros, but she had no cause to be angry now she'd given her consent. To recant would be wholly unfair. She would never gain Amelia's trust, and she'd risk losing Jake's, if she started changing her mind at will.

"I was thinking of... Charlotte." Which was not a lie. Charlotte was at the heart of their relationship with the girls.

"Oh, *Querida*, no," he whispered. "Don't. Don't go there—"

"How can I not? Especially knowing Amelia's going with you tomorrow?" She looked up at him. "She begged me to take care of them, Jake. To protect them. Get them away from *him*—"

"*Querida, s*top," he said firmly. "You musn't work yourself up this way. It's not good for you, or the babe. Or the girls. They need you to remember Charlotte the way they remember her, as their sweet, protective older sister. That's how she *deserves* to be remembered."

"I know. But... she was my friend, Jake, as much as she was their sister. And I... miss her."

"I know you do, *Querida*," he murmured. "I know you do."

Bowing to the gentle, insistent pull of his strong arms, she leaned against his chest, comforted by the solid thump of his heartbeat beneath her ear. "I'm trying to do what she asked, Jake," she whispered. "Protect them. Protect them all. They're just children—"

"Who will one day be adults, *Querida*." His fingers traced gentle swirls on her nape. "And the better equipped they are to manage, whether a rifle, or account ledger when they get there, the better. For them. Isn't that why you want to raise the girls to not use their sex to define their goals, because you want them to believe in themselves? To stand up for themselves?"

"You know I do."

"I do. I also know, no one, not even you, *mi pequeña*, can control everything. None of us can. Amelia will grow up—she's growing up. They're all going to grow up. Whether they get where they're going with what they need to survive depends on the choices we make now: trust them to learn—or fill them so full of doubt and insecurity they can't make a move in any direction to save their lives. Is that what you want, for them to grow into adults afraid to think for themselves, like your father tried to do to you?"

"My father?" She thrust away. "How dare you bring him into this? And he's my *stepfather*, not my father—"

"Stepfather. Father. Whatever he is to you now, Dianna—" He held out his hands, a tall, broad silhouette of helplessness. "He's here. Whether you want him here or not, he's here in every restriction you set upon the children, just as my father is here, in my want to teach them everything I know."

Her heart squeezed at his easy reference to John Douglas as his father. But that was how he thought of the man who'd raised and loved him like a son. While the man who'd raised her...

Twenty years she'd called him Papa. But in the eighteen months since learning he was her stepfather, she no longer knew what to call him. How she felt about him. What she wanted from him. She only knew she wanted to do better than he had, leave no question in any of her children's minds to her love for them. Only... Jake was suggesting she was more like Edward Marshall, than she knew.

Wanted to believe.

"No," she said. "I want them to be *safe*. My stepfather wanted—"

"The same thing, *Querida*," he said quietly. "I hate to admit it, knowing what I do, but I have to, knowing what else I know. Because whether you see it, I do. I *see* you doing it. And I know *why* you're doing it. I also know there is no guarantee of safety. Anywhere. Didn't you believe yourself safe with the man that sired JJ? And again, when you stepped on that ship in Southampton—"

"How dare you—"

"I'm not accusing you of wrongdoing, Dianna." He grasped her hand, held on when she attempted to yank free. "If anything, your fool fa— stepfather is to blame. His rules were so damn stringent, your days so rigidly pre-determined, every move tracked by whatever servant was ordered to watch you that you never learned to develop your instincts, instincts that might have helped you avoid... what happened. Sense that weasel's true intentions. And the ship?

"Its loss, and that of all the people that went with it, is on Captain Smith. The only thing you had control over was whether you got to safety. You're just plain lucky that officer didn't wait your permission, before throwing you in a lifeboat. And I don't want that for our girls, Dianna. For any of our children. I don't want them to rely on another person to protect them. Save them. I want them to be able to think, and act, for themselves, without always having to look to someone else for guidance."

She opened her mouth to retort, but found words failed her. As they often did when he was right.

The earl had sketched impermeable borders in which she and her sisters were to be raised, literally, and figuratively.

17

No venturing out of doors, even on their own land, without a chaperone. Daily regimen of piano and French language practise in addition to academic studies. Long, silent, straight-backed hours wiled through several courses at the dining table consuming polite, minuscule bites of food and teenier sips of water, or wine on the rare occasion he permitted it, whilst he discussed the latest political travesty or triumph, and she and her sisters and mother listened intently on the off chance he might solicit one or more of their opinions.

Oh, how he loved to test his family's attentiveness. Obsequiousness.

It begins with the vote, and next you know, they're demanding to wear the trousers in the home. That will never happen here. Do you understand me, Daughters? Understand, that your place is where you're best-suited, as support and succour to he who will one day keep a roof over your and your children's heads?

Yes, Papa.

She inhaled.

A good head and shoulders taller than her and eight-stone heavier, her husband never, ever, made her feel small the way the earl had. Never took advantage of his greater physical strength, the way the "weasel" had. Though he wasn't a weasel. He was far, far worse.

He was a traitor.

Swallowing, she hammered the lid on the strongbox in her mind where she'd caged the memory of his betrayal, the day she'd married Jake, and made the conscious decision to move forward with her life. A life, as Jake noted, she'd not now enjoy if not for the selfless actions of the young ship's officer who'd tossed her, bodily, into a lifeboat not an hour before the *Titanic* dove to the bottom of the sea when she'd have delayed too long waiting for her travelling companions.

She let the air in her lungs escape. "You're partly right," she said. "I have been too protective. And it's harming my relationship with Amelia. And you." She drew her hand free of his to touch his jaw, splayed her other hand on his chest. "But you're wrong about my motivation."

"How so?"

"My stepfather sought to control me. Shape me in his image of an ideal daughter who would one day become an ideal wife. I seek only to protect Amelia. All our children. And I listen. I listened to her, to what she wants— needs. My stepfather never listened to me. He or Mama. They ignored us girls. All the time. Our wants held as much water as a bottomless bucket.

And eventually, that's what drove me to rash acts that I would regret, had they not ultimately led me here, to you. That still does not excuse their disregard of my feelings. My right to decide whom I would marry."

"No. It doesn't." He grasped the hand she held to his jaw, and turning it, kissed her palm. "And before Katie and Amelia and JJ, I could not have understood why they did what they did."

She frowned. "What does that mean?"

"It means..." He raised his other hand to enfold both her hands, hold them snug against his breastbone. "Now I'm a father, I better appreciate why yours acted as he did—shh," he hushed. "Let me finish. He and your mother wanted to protect you from the wolves that would have come crawling out of the swamp when news of your inheritance broke—ah, ah."

She bit the inside of her lower lip.

"They chose the duke for his wealth and power to insulate you, and protect you—"

"Not me," she blurted. "Themselves. They wanted to insulate their reputations. Specifically, Mama's."

"Yes." He nodded. "They had a large stake in the race. And a powerful son-in-law would have gone a long way to putting a little shine back in any tarnish their images suffered when it came out who your father really was. But you had a larger stake. A much larger stake. And married to the right man, even if you despised him and hated them, but retained your fortune, you were better off than married to the wrong man for the right reasons."

She dragged her hands free of his, crossed her arms. "You think I should have married him? Married the duke?"

"I think," he said, "from my perspective as a father of a son and two daughters in line to inherit fortunes of their own, I better appreciate your parents' reasoning, if not their method. Think to when JJ and the girls are of age to marry... Would you prefer they marry someone in love with them, or eager to get their hands on their future wealth?"

"The duke didn't love me," she said through gritted teeth.

"No. But he wasn't in it for the money, either. You told me, he's rich as Croesus. Had already signed an agreement divesting him of any interest in your inheritance."

"Of course, he did. He has money. It's an heir he needs. *That* was his interest in me." She shrugged her shoulders to loosen them, ease the tension knotting her jaw to near immovability. "Three wives, all dead, and still no children. Without at least one, the Blackburn title goes into abeyance, and all falls to wrack and ruin. The same as any fallow peerage, ducal or no, without sons to seed it."

"You're not a son."

"Because my father, for whatever reason, argued successfully that the Holderness patent allowed for an *assignee* without regard to gender or birth order *or* the title-holder's marital status provided the heir was of the existing title-holder's body. And he had my uncle's cooperation. As heir presumptive, my uncle could have challenged my father's petition and won easily. My father's interpretation went far outside the norms of most patents, and the fact my uncle supported his brother's petition to the Lord Chancellor is as odd as the Holderness patent's wording that even allowed my father to rewrite his will to suit his end. It's almost like he knew he would meet his end before he would make it to the altar." She tugged her arms against her bosom to ward off a chill not entirely caused by the temperature in the room, as she looked out the terrace doors. "Though I imagine he was anticipating a son," she added watching a curve of moonlight glide over the stable's roof. "Most men do."

"Not all." Jake moved behind her, slid an arm around her waist as he cupped her abdomen through the soft layers of her nightwear with his other hand. "Son or daughter, it doesn't matter to me, *Querida*. I'm going to teach this one to rope and ride with the best of them."

She tipped her head against his breastbone, rested her folded arms on his, her gaze on the stable's weather vane, a horse-shaped silhouette turning slow pirouettes in a halo of moonlight like a ballerina in the glow of a single stage lamp.

"Not all men are like you, Jake Douglas," she murmured. "Few are. And none among the peerage. Perceived purity of a bloodline depends on a peer being scrupulous in his choice of bride. And I say perceived, because a peer must sacrifice an heir he knows is his, for one he's certain isn't, if the latter is the one born on the right side of the blanket. The very thing the duke wanted from me, needs most in this world if he's to preserve his ancestors' ducal grip on earthly power, is the very thing that, had he learned of my... condition, would have compelled him to terminate the contract. Had I not severed it first by marrying you. Pride, dear husband," she added primly as she turned in his arms to look up at him, "is worth more than blood, where I come from."

The moon's hazy illumination allowed her to see his tender smile. "You're from here, now, *Querida*," he rasped and lifted his hands to trace his thumbs a slow arc along the ridges of her cheekbones. "And foolish old pride's loss, is my gain."

She closed her eyes, let the veneer of righteous anger stiffening her spine slip away enough to permit her to fit her arms around his waist. "As you are ours," she whispered, and lifted on tiptoe to plant a light kiss on his mouth. "Just promise me you won't take Amelia into *Diablo*."

"*Diablo?*"

She traced an index finger along his collarbone to the divot that marked where he'd broken it in a desperate struggle for survival after he was swept away in a flash flood.

"Ah," he said and clasped his hand over hers. "I learned my lesson, *Querida*. I won't be taking any more greenhorns into *El Diablo*, even the beautiful, courageous ones that save my life."

A silvery frisson of desire rocked her as he lowered his mouth to hers inspiring a tingling cascade of goose-bumps, and damp heat between her legs.

"I only saved your life to save mine," she whispered against his lips, "I had no idea how to find my way out of that canyon. You were my only hope."

"And I thank God every day for your selfishness woman," he murmured as he walked her backward to the bed, pressed her to the mattress and stretched out beside her to nuzzle her neck.

"Take Charlie." She reached for the buttons of his shirt, shivered with pleasure as he floated a hand over her waist and hip, on route to her nightdress's hem. "She'll be good company for Amelia, if for any reason, you need her to wait somewhere."

Roughly a year-and-half old, Charlie was yet an exuberant dog. But like Amelia, she listened well to Jake who had been her primary trainer since rescuing her filthy and bedraggled rib-thin canine-person from a slum in New York City. More importantly, she took her role as the girls' protector as seriously as the girls took their devotion of her.

They had named her Charlie in honour of their sister, and insisted she sleep in their room at night. The three were as bonded as animal and humans could be.

Nothing caused poor Charlie more anxiety, than to have *her* girls in separate areas of the house, or yard. She ran herself ragged trotting between their opposing locations to check on them. But out on the range, with two of her three favourite people in the world to keep an eye on, not to mention miles of grassland to trot and sniff, she would be far less anxious than if she were forced to remain behind.

Jake aided her attempt to shuck his shirt, and settling beside her, rucked her nightdress to stroke her thigh as he lowered his mouth to her nipple, teasing it through the warm flannel, stoking the liquid throb pulsing in her veins.

She raked her fingers through the dense curls on his chest when he lifted his mouth to rasp, "I'll take Charlie. And we'll stay out of *Diablo*."

"Promise," she whispered.

"Mmhm," he moaned, suckling her again, his fingers inching ever higher.

She clamped her thighs. "Promise."

He stilled, then raised on his elbow to look at her, his other hand trapped fingertips short of its goal, his breath ragged.

She caught her lower lip in her teeth, trembling with need, and want to retire with a rousing session of lovemaking their disagreement—the entire painful evening and all that it had dredged up. But she had a responsibility. A responsibility to put aside selfish desire and stand firm on... something. Something in the interest of ensuring her children's safety. And this... This was it. This was her motherly stand.

With a low chuckle, he bowed his forehead to hers, his brow warm, breath smelling faintly of Colgate cream, which suggested he'd brushed his teeth, if not shed his clothes, prior to her joining him in their chamber.

"Yes, *Querida*," he murmured. "I promise. I promise to do everything within my power to keep Amelia safe. To keep all of you, safe. Always."

Chapter 2

Birth, Death and Babies

*D*irk's shirt sleeves were rolled back to his elbows, exposing muscular sun-darkened forearms that belied his true age, all sixty-one years seeming to have collected in the crags and hollows of his weathered face.

"Aye, 'tis a bonny colt you 'ave there," he said, as he wiped his hands with a fist-full of clean straw. "Black as the devil's heart." He let the straw fall, reached for the cheek strap of the mare's halter with one gnarled hand to prevent her swinging her rump when Dianna stepped forward. "Don't know as I've ever seen one so pure of colour as this one."

Which was saying something, given his five decades of experience helping to breed, train, and race some of the finest equine flesh in Britain. And now America. Truly, how did she get so blessed?

Because your stepfather is a fool, and your husband a genius.

Handing Dirk the electric torch she'd held to guide his sight while he'd help guide the colt into the world, she knelt and ran her hands along the foal's long legs, bony ribcage, and small, perfectly formed head.

"He's absolutely beautiful," she murmured. "And you're right. Not a speck of white anywhere."

"What are you going to name him?"

Startled, Dianna looked up. Katie stood outside the stall, her face pressed between the iron bars that formed the upper half of the wall.

"Katie, love." She pushed to her feet, took the torch from Dirk. "Is JJ awake?" She angled a look along the shed row to the open door of the stable.

The sun had risen enough to lift a faint mist off the short carpet of early-spring grass, and reflect silvery-pink along the house's south-side windows and white siding. The smallest window right of those that marked her and Jake's chamber was dark, no glow to indicate anyone had switched on the nursery's ceiling light.

"Mrs. Brown's listening for him," Katie said, "so I could come see if the baby was born yet. And bring you this." She lifted her hands.

Dianna flashed the light on the mug she held, steam curling from its contents.

"Oh, Katie darling, you sweet, sweet child. Come." She opened the stall door. "Come see the beautiful colt Miss Lizzy has blessed us with, which is what we call baby boy horses. Colts. Baby girl horses are fillies. When we don't know a baby horse's sex, we call it a foal."

Ignoring Dirk's grunt of what might have been disapproval, and Katie's flush at her choice of words, Dianna accepted the mug from Katie with a grateful smile.

"Thank you, my darling." She took a sip. Perfect. Milk, two sugars. Exactly how she loved it. Sliding the mug between a pair of iron bars to rest it on the wood frame, she grasped Katie's hand, and angled the torch to guide her path inside the stall.

Dirk kept himself between Dianna and Katie, and the mare, as Miss Lizzy went about her motherly ministrations with practised efficiency. Anyone who didn't know better would never guess she was a new mother as she rasped her pink tongue along the colt's fast-drying coat.

"What do you think of... *Diablo*?" Dianna asked, holding the torch so its peripheral light showcased the colt, and mare's head, without blinding either horse. "Dirk says he's black as the Devil's heart, and *Diablo* is Devil in Spanish."

Katie offered a shy, over-the-shoulder glance, before looking back at the colt, and nodding. "*El Diablo*," she said softly.

"*El Diablo*." Dianna swallowed, eyes smarting with happy tears.

Yesterday she might have shooed Katie back to bed, insisted it was too early for her to be awake, let alone be tromping about a stall helping choose a name for a colt while its mother nibbled the last of the amniotic sac from the straw, before returning her attention to her foal. But that was yesterday.

Her disagreement with Jake had alerted her to this, the need to trust her children. Include them. Educate them. Not just about those things she thought safe for them to learn, but what interested them. That they *wanted* to learn. Because this was the life she'd chosen for them. The one she volunteered to live with Jake after walking away from the life she'd been raised to live, and the one she inherited. She eased out a breath.

James Richmond Ramsay, 4th Marquess Holderness.

It was still surreal to her, even after a year-and-a-half, to know her mother had been engaged to him. Would have married him had he not crashed his new motor carriage and died the evening before the ceremony. How different her life might have been—She dismissed the thought as she laid her hand over the locket shielded beneath her shirtwaist and sweater, where she kept treasured miniatures of her sisters close to her heart.

Had the marquess lived, she'd not have grown up with Lizzy and Lainey. Would not be here now, pondering the beauty and miracle of new life with her daughter as the colt bobbed his darling head about in dazed confusion, snuffling and sneezing as he sought to clear his tender pink nostrils of residual fluid.

Pressing the locket, she imagined her sisters felt her mental hug across the miles that separated them, knew how much she missed and love them.

This is my life now.

This was all their lives.

Birth.

Death.

Babies.

Allowing herself a private smile, she lowered her hand to Katie's shoulder. They'd tell the children in a few weeks, if her suspicions, and Jake's convictions, were confirmed with at least one more missed menses.

The foal tilted his head, shook it, like a swimmer attempting to clear water from an ear, earning a giggle from Katie. Dianna thrilled at the sound.

It was the first genuine sound of delight she'd heard from her. Even at Christmas, when a smile, and heart-felt "Thank you", were the closest she'd come to expressing spontaneous emotion.

Oh, how she wished Jake was here to hear it. But he and Amelia had ridden out in the pre-dawn darkness, pausing only long enough for Jake to return inside the house and rouse her with news Miss Lizzy was in labour.

She'd immediately dressed and hastened out, arriving at Miss Lizzy's stall in time to hold the torch and witness the colt's birth.

The mare persisted with nuzzles and nudges, goading the foal to gather his spindle-like legs, and with Katie softly coaching, he lunged. Crashed head-first into the mare's chest. Undeterred, he tried again, this time succeeding in launching himself upright on long wobbly legs.

"You'll not find what you're looking for there," Dianna murmured handing Katie the torch, before moving to brace the colt and gently redirect his nuzzling quest from the mare's fore, to her hind.

"Hey now," Dirk muttered, rubbing Miss Lizzy's neck to distract her when she laid back her ears, as the colt found the teat. The mare stomped a hind hoof when the colt latched on and started to suckle, little whisk-broom tail switching furiously, but after another firm but gentle reprimand from Dirk, Miss Lizzy relaxed with a resigned sigh. Dianna bit back a smile.

Welcome to motherhood, Miss Lizzy.

"He's so dear," Katie murmured.

"Isn't he?" Dianna said. "Would you like to pet him?"

Katie's awe-filled stare was answer enough.

Taking the torch from Katie, Dianna revelled in the beauty and joy of the moment as Katie caressed the nursing colt from neck to haunch.

Oh, Charlotte, if only you could see this... Tears welled, forcing her to duck her head and dab at the inside corners of her eyes with her shirt cuffs.

The colt broke from nursing and like a four-pillar house of cards, collapsed in the straw. Tucking velvet nose to broom-brush tail in the shadow of his mother's raw-boned body, he fluttered long silky-black lashes, and closed his eyes.

Dianna touched Katie's arm. "Time to let Miss Lizzy and her baby rest, love."

"Aye," Dirk said as he followed them out of the stall. "Birthin's hard business."

"And what would you know of it?" asked an amused voice.

"More an' you, I'm sure," Dirk said smoothly as he secured the stall door.

"I'm sure neither of you know enough," Dianna retorted splitting a glance between Dirk, and the man at the working end of a cart piled high with manure and soiled straw exiting the neighbouring stall. She managed to maintain a neutral expression despite the strong odour wafting from the unwieldy load. "Good morning, Mr. McGuire," she added in a formal tone.

McGuire lowered the cart, touched a finger to his hat. "Morning, Missus. Miss Katie. I overheard the good news. Miss Lizzy produced a colt."

"Yes," Dianna said. "A very fine colt."

"Can he be mine?" Katie murmured and clasped her hands under her chin.

Her first spontaneous laugh. Now her very first request. For anything. And nothing so simple as a book, or particular colour of hair ribbon.

"Uh... he's a colt, sweets," Dianna said. "One day he'll be a stallion. Stallions are... unpredictable. But," she added quickly when Katie's expression fell. "The first filly born is yours. I promise."

"Firelight is due next," McGuire said. "She's a sweet-tempered mare. If she has a filly, it'll be the best filly in the barn."

"Aye, McGuire's right," Dirk said. "Firelight's a bonny horse."

Katie looked between the two men, and then at Dianna. "Firelight is beautiful," she admitted softly.

"A rare colour too, them Palominos," Dirk said.

"Why don't you go with Dirk and check on Firelight," Dianna suggested gently, "while I go in and see how Mrs. Brown's getting along? See if JJ's awake. When you come in we'll have breakfast, and then head over to Grandma Ellie's and tell her the good news about Miss Lizzy's new baby."

With a barely perceptible nod, Katie joined Dirk in moving down the shed row toward Firelight's stall, careful to keep her distance, but adjusting her youthful stride to Dirk's rheumatic gait.

Firelight, a ten-year-old mare, was a lovely horse, calm, sweet-tempered, and forgiving. Like Katie.

"Thank you, McGuire," Dianna murmured once Katie was out of earshot, as she reached for the mug of tea. "You helped ease what could have been a tricky situation."

"Katie's a sweet girl," McGuire said. "I've no interest in seeing her hurt by that red bitch—er, forgive me, mum."

Dianna nodded. Before she could reply, or turn away, McGuire continued: "What I mean is, Miss Lizzy is too high-strung for the likes of Miss Katie. You can't turn your back on her for a second. She's given me a few good marks." He rubbed absently at the back of his arm. "Nah, Firelight's a far better mother for tolerating a sweet lass like Miss Katie who likes her dolls and to pamper the wee Mac. I wouldn't be surprised to see Firelight's baby parading about in one of the wee Mac's old bonnets. Now Miss Amelia, she's not one for taking guff. She'd knock sense into Miss—"

"Er, thank you, McGuire." He was a chatty fellow whose interest in the children, especially JJ who he'd dubbed the Irish equivalent of the small son within days of coming to work for her, often unnerved her.

He'd arrived late the previous fall looking to work with horses. Dirk, expecting J-D Quarter Horses' inaugural crop to start hitting the ground in the spring and in need of more experienced help than Dianna or the young man Jake had hired to muck stables could reliably provide, had tested McGuire by procuring his services to geld a two-year-old colt unfit for stud. McGuire hadn't batted an eyelash.

Forty-minutes later, streaked in blood and horse-spittle, Mac McGuire had signed on as an official employee. Good as he was with horses, he chafed Dianna's sensibilities.

His attempts to engage her in conversation, ingratiate himself into her life like he was a close friend free to discuss matters with her other than the horses and their care was unlike anything she'd experienced. Her stepfather would have fired him his first day for impertinence. Which was probably why she tolerated McGuire. Permitted him greater latitude than he ever would have dreamed of experiencing at Ansmall under the earl.

She wanted to be a different person than the earl. Someone more like her husband who was not feared, but held in great esteem by the men he worked alongside every day. Still, she was fairly certain Jake didn't share details of his personal life with the vaqueros, but confined talk to cattle and horses or things related to cattle and horses.

Drawing a breath, she asked, "How's the training coming along with Spitfire?"

Firelight's two-year-old colt had been at the mare's side when she was purchased a year-and-a-half earlier. He was the same wonderful creamy gold colour of his mother, and Dianna planned to add him to her breeding program. For now, she was preparing him for Quarter-mile racing.

McGuire tilted his hat to scratch above his ear. Sweat dampened his russet-blond hair, testimony to the hard hours he'd already put in that morning. She felt a slight twinge of guilt at her unkind thoughts.

One thing she couldn't fault McGuire on was his work ethic.

"I think we're ready to move him to the snaffle," he said, hooking a thumb in his suspenders. "Another week of ground work, and I'll get on him."

"That's wonderful. Make sure you let me know when. I want to be there, first time he's ridden. Oh, and please have the buggy hitched, and ready to go by ten."

"Aye, I will. Will ye be taking the wee Mac with you?" His moss-green eyes blinked innocently, but Dianna felt a familiar tension spread across her shoulders and up her neck. As if sensing her disquiet, McGuire added, "I promised him a ride around the yard, on his pony."

She willed a smile. "That's very thoughtful of you, Mr. McGuire, but yes, I'll be taking JJ with me. He can ride Sammy later, after we return. He'll like that." And that was the other problem.

JJ was far too young to be riding anything short of a docile lamb. Yet Jake, Dirk, and McGuire each insisted they'd started riding before they could walk. So, the Shetland pony Jake brought home for JJ's first birthday, had become a prized fixture in JJ's daily life.

McGuire tipped his hat. "Good morning to you, ma'am." With one strong shove he started the over-loaded cart rolling.

He wasn't near as tall as Jake, but he was almost as wide, and his muscular shoulders tested the sweat-stained material of his blue shirt. Jake admired his physical strength and horse acumen. Truth told, she respected that part of McGuire, too. It was his chummy behaviour she objected to.

With a last, elated look into Miss Lizzy's stall at the black bundle asleep in the straw, she hastened for the house.

∞ ∞ ∞

"This wee man will be the death of me," Mrs. Brown muttered as she heaved JJ red-faced and thrashing, into Dianna's arms. "'E's a wicked wee temper. Started up the moment I lifted him from his crib, an' he realised neither you nor Mr. Douglas was coming in after me. Reminds me of you, when you were a bairn," she added wistfully. "Makes me feel young again, 'e does."

"Well, I'm glad he has that effect on you," Dianna muttered as she hooked JJ's sturdy legs around her waist and moulded his sweat-dampened body to her side. "Because when he gets like this, he makes me feel as old and worn as one of Jake's boots."

"Aye, well, that's better than lookin' like one, like me," Mrs. Brown muttered. "But yer a few good years from auld age yet, an' I expect ye can manage 'is temper a bit longer than me."

"You're fine, little man," Dianna murmured, jiggling JJ as she smoothed his hair and kissed his brow. "Mama's here. No need to fuss, so."

Mrs. Brown clucked her tongue and shook her head as though she was commiserating with Dianna's plight, but Dianna knew better. Her very proper, Scottish-born English-manor-raised housekeeper, was expressing disapproval of Dianna's lenient manner of discipline.

"Mr. Vásquez was by with the post." Mrs. Brown scooped a stack of envelopes off the hutch by the porch door. "There's a letter come for you from Lady Elaina, an' one from Lord Laxton. One here for Mr. McGuire, too. I hope Miss Elaina has good news about Lord William," she added, frowning. "Italy is much drier, better for them wi' wheezy chests, so it may have helped, taking 'im there."

"I hope so," Dianna said as she accepted the letter bearing the earl's familiar seal. Her uncle's monthly updates on her inherited holdings could wait for evening, after the children were abed when she could concentrate. Or another day altogether. Learning the estimated cost to replace a threadbare floor rug or cracked window was not near as important or urgent as knowing the welfare of her brother. "If anything happens to him—"

"Now don' be inviting trouble." Mrs. Brown returned the remaining envelopes to the hutch. "Last Miss Elaina wrote, Master William was holding his own. Scrambled eggs and toast, all right?"

"Yes, please. Katie will be in shortly. And I'm not inviting trouble." She scratched at the wax-sealed flap, trying to open it without dropping her son. "I'm expressing honest fear. I care deeply for what happens to little William. Not to mention, Mama. She can't risk another confinement—"

"'Ere, let me help." Mrs. Brown slipped the envelope from Dianna's grasp, peeled it open, and handed her the enclosed note.

Dianna scanned the flowing script. "Master William is not yet home," she said, able to speak at normal volume now JJ's shrieks had subsided to gasping shudders with the occasional vigorous nose rub against her shoulder. "But should be soon. Within the month, as he's... much improved!"

"Oh, that's a relief." Mrs. Brown pulled a cast-iron pan heaped with scrambled eggs and buttered toast from the warming oven. "I'll rest easier now, knowing his young Lordship's going to be all right."

"Yes," Dianna murmured. Rest easier, indeed.

She only knew her little brother through her sister's letters, but already she loved and worried about him. Four months older than JJ, little William was far behind when it came to robust health.

Elaina's letters too often conveyed news of a sickly child who'd struggled from his first breath with, as Mrs. Brown characterised it, a wheezy chest. She could well imagine her sister and parents' joy at his improving health, because she shared it. She'd be sick if it was JJ who perpetually teetered between mildly and gravely ill.

Bussing JJ's cheek, she murmured, "Your uncle's getting better, little man. Isn't that grand?"

∞ ∞ ∞

"Shall I drive you over, then?" McGuire asked, not without sympathy.

Dianna suppressed a sigh. "It seems you shall have to, if I'm to get any peace today."

She should have asked Dirk to bring the carriage out. Because the moment she paused to hand McGuire his mail, before attempting to lift JJ up to Katie who was already on the passenger side of the bench seat, JJ reached for the groom screeching delightedly, "Pony."

When she gently explained a pony ride would have to wait for another time as they were off to visit Grandma, JJ promptly launched into a tantrum. Like a writhing Python he refused to be bundled into the carriage, arching away from her towards McGuire so violently, it was all she could do to keep him in her arms.

McGuire clambered into the driver's seat, while Katie moved to the rear of the buggy. Handing JJ to McGuire she climbed to sit next to him, and settle her son on her lap. With a nod to McGuire, they were off.

"Ba," JJ shouted a moment later, pointing to a dark shape stamped against the crystalline-blue sky.

"Yes, love," Dianna said. "A bird. A hawk."

He swung his pudgy finger right. "Tee."

"Yes, a tree."

"Ow," he exclaimed, as McGuire handed Dianna the reins and hopped down to unlatch the barbed-wire-and-wood gate that separated her and Jake's parcel from his mother's ranch.

"Bull, love. A daddy cow."

"Daddy ow," JJ screeched as Dianna, one arm around his chunky frame, clucked to the horse. Once the buggy was safely through the gate, she drew the reins with a soft "whoa". McGuire locked the gate and reclaimed the driver's seat and reins.

Within minutes of resuming the journey, JJ fell silent. Soon he was asleep, his head turned to Dianna's breast. She realigned his cowboy hat, a miniature replica of Jake's, to shield his face and protect his delicate skin from the sun.

"He's a sweet boy," McGuire commented.

"Yes, especially when he's asleep," Dianna murmured.

"Children can be quite a handful at times," he said soberly.

And what would he know about children? Far as she knew, he was a bachelor. He had arrived alone, and not once mentioned a wife or family. To her, at least. Not that that was confirmation they didn't exist. Many husbands and fathers left home to find work.

What did she really know about McGuire, beyond his ability to work hard, and handle horses?

Steadying her bonnet that the wind threatened to tear loose despite the ribbon securing it under her chin, she darted a glance at him.

Square jaw, cleft chin dark with stubble. Lips surprisingly full and nose straight if a trifle short. But his eyes were perhaps his greatest feature. Large and wide set, they were the colour of moss, framed with lashes many shades darker than his hair reminding her somewhat of JJ's eyes, though his were a lighter green.

"Are you married, Mr. McGuire?" The question was out before she realised how inappropriate it was. Lowering her hand, she glanced over her shoulder.

Katie, fortunately, was too engrossed in the birthday gift Elaina had sent her—Wuthering Heights—to notice her mother's faux pas. And McGuire seemed to take no offence.

He shrugged. "No. Never been. Wasn't in the cards, I suppose."

"Suppose? You're hardly past marrying age. How old are you?" She justified the bold question with the knowledge she deserved to know as much as possible about the man who spent so much time around her children.

"Thirty." McGuire flushed, as though embarrassed to admit that at that advanced age he was still unmarried.

"You're plenty young yet," she said. "And you seem to like children. I'm sure you'll marry and have children of your own one day. I've a brother only a few months older than JJ. My father was fifty-two when he was born."

Now what had possessed her to reveal that? Gads, next she knew, she'd settle down to a game of cards with the man and tell him about how she came to be married to a Texas cattle rancher, instead of an English gentleman.

"I know."

She frowned. "You do?"

His flush deepened. "Dirk mentioned something about it, about JJ having an uncle not much older. He didn't tell me how old your father was, but I assumed he was a bit past thirty to have a daughter your age."

It made sense. Dirk and McGuire worked side by side, and shared accommodations at the rear of the stable. She could hardly expect them to confine their conversations to horses and manure. Still, it was disturbing to know McGuire knew more about her, than she him.

"Well, then," she said. "You needn't worry about being too old to marry. You have plenty of time yet for that, and children."

He nodded. "I come from a large family, two sisters and nine brothers. It'd please me to have a brood of my own, especially sons. I expect I'll have to find a good woman first, though."

"Yes. A wife would help matters." She didn't bother to add there was no guarantee he would reap sons from the union, something her stepfather knew too well.

The earl had sired two living daughters, and one son, and buried many more stillborn children. Far as she knew, Mama never visited the tiny coffins, though she had seen the earl exit the family crypt, usually with an empty liquor bottle clutched in one hand, his mouth a harsh slash in his drink-flushed face.

33

"Well, I hope I'm as lucky as your husband and find someone as beautiful to marry," McGuire said.

Dianna stared ahead, her face warm with heat she knew she could not blame entirely on the sun. Perhaps she could learn to like McGuire, after all.

∞ ∞ ∞

The scent of baking pies and murmur of voices filtered through the porch door screen. Dianna rapped on the wooden frame, before opening it.

"Dianna, what a pleasure," Eleanor Douglas, her mother-in-law, exclaimed as Dianna stepped into the warm cinnamon-scented kitchen with its white-painted cupboards and wood-topped counters. "Come dear. Let me take that." She whipped the basket from Dianna's hands, peered inside. "Ooh, mincemeat tarts. What a delight. You have to thank Mrs. Brown for me." After setting the basket on the counter, she glanced past Dianna. "Where are the children?"

"Yes, where are the children Dianna?" Maggie transferred a pie from the oven to a wire rack on the counter. Setting aside the thick pads she'd used to protect her hands, she brushed at the damp red curls clinging to her flushed face. The pink-and-purple-flower patterned apron she wore was cheery counterpoint to her navy-blue white-trimmed dress. "I don't think I've seen you once since your return without at least one of them in hand."

Dianna unlaced her bonnet. Lifting it off with one hand she pointed with the other out the window above the sink to the buggy parked in the shade of one of the outbuildings. "JJ's sleeping, and Katie offered to stay with him. Amelia's out with Jake."

"Yes. We know." Eleanor grinned. "They stopped by to collect the wagon and a roll of wire to repair a fence. Amelia could barely contain herself, she was so excited to be on her first adventure with Jake."

"Yes," Dianna said. "She was... quite eager to go."

Eleanor's smile faded. "You know Jake would never let her come to harm?" The sincerity in her voice almost flushed loose a couple of tears.

"I know," Dianna said. "He's very good with all the children. When they're grown, I hope they truly appreciate how lucky they are to have him for a father."

34

Eleanor's reaction was subtle, a slight shadowing of her gaze as the spectre of the earl passed between them, before she brightened. "And your family, darling? Any recent news of how your little brother is doing?" Her smile bore no trace of ill-ease, so guilt likely added the slight emphasis to Your, Dianna thought she heard.

"Yes, actually," Dianna said. "He's on the mend. I received a letter from Elaina just this morning. Little William is expected home soon."

"How wonderful," Eleanor said.

"Yes, very good news," Maggie exclaimed and swept Dianna into an embrace.

Dianna gasped, surprised by the ferocity of Maggie's rib-creaking hug. She tucked her chin to look down. "What's wrong?"

Maggie released Dianna. "Wrong?"

Eleanor's niece and Jake's cousin through marriage, Margaret Stewart was Dianna's best friend in all the world. After Jake. She was also Dianna and Jake's inadvertent matchmaker.

Margaret and her late husband William had helped secret Dianna out of England on route to Texas where the couple had planned to set down new roots close to William's aunt and cousin, and adopt Dianna's child when it was born thus freeing her return to England. The *Titanic's* sinking sunk all their grand plans.

Margaret ended up widowed and destitute, dependent on her late husband's family for everything until she became the town of Douglas's new school mistress. Dianna, in heart-rending contrast, after a few traumatic bumps in the road, was happily married to William's cousin. *And expecting his child.*

Guilt itched in Dianna, but she refused to scratch it. Maggie would not allow sympathetic regret on her behalf when she herself never wallowed.

Unfair as the hand was that she'd been dealt, Margaret Stewart never complained. Rarely offered any strong public display of emotion. Which made her bruising hug, and wide-eyed Mona Lisa smile, all the more suspect.

"Yes," Dianna said. "You greeted me like I was a long-lost friend you hadn't seen in years, if not decades, when you were by for tea just last week."

A flush filled the pale gaps between Maggie's freckles. Eleanor wore a "who me?" expression. Rosa, Eleanor's housekeeper and Jake's godmother, did not look up from the dough she was gently rolling to pie-crust on the kitchen table, though a corner of her mouth tilted in a private a smile.

Dianna narrowed her eyes. "What are you all not telling me?"

"Not me," Eleanor said shaking her head.

Rosa angled the rolling pin, continued massaging the dough with measured movements, her long braided hair swinging in slow rhythm glossy black against her red blouse. Maggie raised her hands prayer-like to her mouth. Waggled her fingers.

"Margaret Anne Millicent Stewart, let me see that." Dianna grasped Maggie's left hand, stared in stupefaction at the glittering diamond wreathed with sapphires. "It's... beautiful. What—when—"

"Last night," Maggie exclaimed and enveloped Dianna in another breath-robbing hug. "George asked me last night."

"He did? He's here?" Dianna looked around. "I had no idea he was in town."

"He's not. He was. But he's not now." Maggie's flush deepened. "He was here two nights. He stayed at the hotel. We... didn't tell anyone, because I didn't know he was coming. He surprised me. He's between jobs and he... he just showed up. To ask me, and I... I said yes."

George Sweeney was an architect-builder. Maggie had met him a couple of months after her husband's death, when Jake hired Mr. Sweeney to build the house and stables Dianna and Jake now called home. Mr. Sweeney made clear his interest in Maggie almost from day one, but she'd not returned his interest, nor encouraged it, for the full year she was in mourning. The last year their courtship had progressed slowly owing to Mr. Sweeney's frequent absences as he travelled to various states to work on his latest project, and Maggie's reluctance to abandon her new teaching position.

She loved the children. And they her. But apparently, she'd come to love George Sweeney enough to consider trading her children, for married life again. *And perhaps this time she'll finally welcome the child of her own she's always wanted.*

"Oh, Maggie," Dianna said, tears filling her eyes. "This is so wonderful. I'm so happy for you."

Maggie nodded, but her smile faded.

"What's wrong?" Dianna asked. "It's what you want, isn't it?"

Maggie bit her lip. "I... do. But... is it too soon?"

Over two years had passed since the *Titanic's* sinking. What Maggie had suffered as she rebuilt her life as a widow Dianna could only imagine, and though she felt it was time for Maggie to embrace love—and happiness—again it was not her place to say so. She looked to Eleanor, whose brown eyes shone with pain of a similar loss.

"If it's what you want Margaret," Eleanor said gently, "then it is the right thing to do. You mustn't feel guilty. It's not a question of whether you *should* fall in love, but whether you have. Trust your heart. It'll not lead you astray."

"You never remarried," Maggie said shaking her head. "Maybe I didn't love William as much as you did your husband—"

"No." Eleanor gripped Maggie's hands. "Don't compare yourself to me, child. I've been a coward, lacking in the courage necessary to risk love again. But you're much stronger than I, Margaret. So, don't waste another precious moment being afraid. If you love George Sweeney, then by God Almighty, marry him."

The kitchen rang in sudden silence. Maggie stared at Eleanor, no doubt as shocked as Dianna, by her outburst.

"Mama, what's wrong? Why is grandma crying?"

Startled, Dianna turned.

"Katie? Ah... it's nothing. Nothing is wrong with grandma. Those are happy tears. Aunt Maggie's getting married. But where's JJ, darling?" she added to divert Katie's attention, and give Maggie and Eleanor time to pull themselves together.

Katie gaped at Maggie. "You're getting married?"

Maggie's gaze skipped to Dianna, and Eleanor, before resettling on Katie. "Yes," she said, breathless. Then again, stronger, "Yes. By all that I love, yes, I am marrying Mr. Sweeney."

To Dianna's utter shock, Katie ran to hug Maggie. It truly was a day of firsts. Beautiful, miraculous, and blessed firsts.

"We need pie," Eleanor announced. "Pie to celebrate."

"Did you make my favourite, grandma?" Katie asked, breaking away from Maggie to survey the disc-shaped humps under a series of tea towels on the counter.

"Come see." Eleanor raised a corner of one towel.

"Katie dear," Dianna said as the joyful ache in her throat subsided enough to permit her to speak. "Is JJ still sleeping?"

"No. Mr. McGuire took him for a ride on Queenie."

The familiar tension crept into Dianna's shoulders.

She shaded her eyes as she stepped outside and off the porch, heart quickening when she didn't see Mr. McGuire or the old mare that had been Jake's childhood horse, in the yard.

"Where was he taking him for a ride?" she called through the kitchen window, hoping she'd be heard over the clamour of plates and cutlery, and wedding plans already under excited discussion.

"Behind the nursery," came Katie's reply.

The nursery was a wide metal-roofed barn built by Mr. Sweeney and his crew to replace an older smaller version that had burned down two Christmases ago. It housed sick, premature, or orphaned calves and their natural or adoptive bovine mothers, close to the main house for ease of treatment and round-the-clock nursing.

As she hastened across the yard towards it, Dianna tried to tame the rush of anxiety that filled her whenever she didn't know exactly where one of her children was, or with whom. She knew with whom, just not where, and she had to stop being so over-protective. No doubt, she'd find McGuire leading Queenie and JJ in lazy circles in the paddock behind the barn.

It was empty.

"Mr. McGuire?" She peered through a doorway, into the dark recesses of the nursery.

"Not here," a voice called.

"Mr. Vasquez?" Juan Vasquez was the ranch manager, and Rosa's husband.

"No, Pete." Pete Harder, a short, slim man, emerged from shadows into a rectangle of daylight inside the barn's doorway, a grimy spade in his gloved hands. "I haven't seen McGuire, and I've been here all morning, mucking out, when I'm not bottle feeding the orphans. But I can help look for him."

A huge black fly dived at Dianna. She waved it away, consciously resisting the fear kindling in her. "No. Thank you, Mr. Harder. He... can't be far. And your help is needed in there." Turning away, she trotted across the paddock, through the far gate and up the grassy slope behind, toward the range.

Jake claimed cattle were passive creatures, taking exception to humans only when one came between a cow and her calf, or a bull and his harem.

But their size and long curved horns intimidated her at any time. The thought of JJ trampled by the massive cloven hooves—"Stop it," she muttered. "Just stop it."

At the top of the slope, slightly out of breath, she looked around. Hundreds upon hundreds of cows. But no horse or man shape.

A rising wind tousled her skirt, tugged at her hair pins. Brushing a few stray strands from her eyes, she turned a slow circle scanning the grassland. A large shadow made her look up.

Oh, no.

She swept her gaze around again.

Where were they?

There! A figure leading a horse along the wagon track east of the main house.

"McGuire," she shouted, waving her arms. "Mr. McGuire." If he heard her, or saw her, he gave no indication. *Did he realise a thunderstorm was headed their way?*

Hiking her skirts, she ran, buffeted by increasing wind, and yelped when lightning flashed, filling her nostrils with the acrid scent of sulphur. She ducked as thunder boomed and hail immediately descended in stinging torrents.

"Dianna!" Eleanor, one arm hooked around a porch column, waved at her, gestured toward Maggie and Rosa and Katie who were dashing towards the storm shelter.

"JJ," Dianna shouted and kept running, not sure if Eleanor had heard her over the clatter of marble-sized hail pinging off roofs.

She'd experienced Texas thunderstorms before, but this was different. Some primitive part of her brain, the area responsible for survival, screamed at her to seek shelter.

"JJ! Mr. McGuire." She stumbled, gasping as a cramp gripped her side. Pressing a hand to the pain she limped on. "McGuire. Mr. McGuire!"

Something heavy struck her between her shoulder blades and slammed her to the ground.

Dazed, she gulped and gasped, desperate to draw air into her stunned lungs as she fought to get back up. But she was no match for the force pinning her to the earth like a butterfly to a board, while hail pelted her skull and raked her cheeks.

Hands clasped over her head and elbows tight to her ears she tried to meld with the earth as the roaring wind shrieked, and wood, metal, and glass exploded, vicious shards whirling all around her. The weight on her back abruptly lifted off.

Screaming, she clawed at dirt and grass, fighting for purchase as she was lifted by an unseen force and sent spinning, a stringed marionette at the mercy of a ruthless wind.

Chapter 3

What Happened?

ater. She needed water. But the sound that came out of her mouth did not resemble the word in her mind. Thankfully someone understood.

A strong hand slipped under her neck, and a cup pressed to her lips.

"Aye, don' drink too quick, my lady. You'll choke."

Too late. Dianna coughed and spluttered, sucked for breath until the spasm eased and she could sip again, more carefully. The effort drained her. She fell back on the pillow without opening her eyes.

She was in bed? Sick? Injured? Must be. She hurt all over, and Mrs. Brown was there, caring for her. *A fall riding?*

That would explain the dull ache in her bones and sharper throbbing pain behind her eyes. It must have been a nasty spill. The thought of moving again, or opening her eyes, exhausted her. So, she let her mind drift into the grey mist enveloping her.

"Is she awake?" a voice murmured.

"She was. Asked for more water. Then back to sleep she goes." There was a definite note of despair in Mrs. Brown's voice. "Ye sure this is normal, all this in and out?"

Dianna struggled to lift her eyelids, but they were heavy. So, so heavy.

"Yes. Quite normal with any severe concussion of the brain. But the fact she's in and out is much better than if she was out completely. Come. Have a bite of breakfast. We'll check on her later."

Concussion of the brain? Heaven, how had that happened?

Before she could summon the strength to ask the voices faded, and with them, her ability to remain awake. When she again awoke it was to the feel of fingers pressed to her neck.

She angled her jaw away and the same strange male voice from before said, "Good. It's only been a couple of hours this time. How do you feel?"

"Awful," she croaked. With supreme effort she opened her eyes. Closed them again immediately as searing light scored every nerve fibre in her brain.

"Oh, glory," Mrs. Brown said. "She's not answered a question before. Are you awake, my lady?"

"Yes," Dianna rasped. "How else could I talk?"

Mrs. Brown gasped. "Did ye hear that, doctor? She's not just babbling. She's truly awake. I... I 'ave to send for—"

"Not yet, Mrs. Brown," the man said. "Let's not send for anyone, until she can open her eyes, *and* answer a few more questions. I want to know she's regained full consciousness and clarity before I raise anyone's false hopes."

Full consciousness? Clarity?

Gritting her teeth, Dianna forced her eyelids to lift, winced and squinted and blinked until blurred and blinding whiteness resolved to a small but tidy and square white-painted room lit by shafts of sun through a window above her head, and another on the opposite wall.

She stared in confusion at the plaster cast encasing her right leg from thigh to ankle elevated a foot or so off the narrow bed by aid of a leather strap hooked around her calf and attached to a pulley bolted to an overhead beam. Her arms too were in wrapped in plaster-gauze, her right from the shoulder down, and left from below her elbow. Her pale bloodless fingers resembled white sausages.

"What happened?" she whispered. "Who are you?"

The lean white-haired man in a blue shirt, and dark trousers, a stethoscope looped round his neck, smiled. "I'm Dr. Stanley."

A neat woman in a black skirt and white shirtwaist, her silver hair twisted and pinned under a white nurse's hat, handed him a clipboard.

"This is my wife, Mary," he added. "We've been looking after you since your accident. Do you remember anything about it, how you were hurt?"

She licked her lips to moisten them, before managing a faint shake of her head. Mrs. Brown, at the foot of the bed, cast a worried look at the doctor, but he kept his gaze on Dianna.

"Don't worry," he said. "You'll be fine. You've suffered a concussion of the brain and multiple broken bones, but you're well on the road to recovery. If you can manage, I have a few questions I'd like you to answer." When she nodded, he asked, "Do you know your name?"

"Dianna."

"Your full name?"

"Dianna Ellen Louise Marshall." Her voice rasped from her throat like dry corn being husked.

Dr. Stanley glanced at the clipboard. "Your date of birth?"

Mrs. Brown offered a nervous smile and encouraging nod.

Dianna murmured, "December nineteenth, eighteen-ninety-two."

"Your address?"

"Ansmall Hall, Herefordshire—is this really necessary? I'd rather know how I got hurt than answer questions you obviously know the answer to. What happened? Where am I?" Because wherever she was, it was not Ansmall Hall. Perhaps not even England. The sky outside was too blue, the air in her nose too dry, the doctor's voice too... American?

Mrs. Brown pressed chapped fingers to her mouth, her brown eyes wide. The doctor's wife maintained a kind non-committal smile, deepening it to something maternal as the doctor patted Dianna's shoulder.

"You're going to be fine, Dianna," he said. "For now, you must rest. Mary will give you a sedative, and later, after you've slept, we'll discuss what happened."

"What? No," Dianna said, fighting the very fatigue and need for sleep the doctor suggested she needed.

"Yes." The doctor cast a quick warning glance at Mrs. Brown, who looked poised to speak.

The elder woman pinched her lips together, as the doctor's wife popped a pill in Dianna's mouth and immediately followed it up with a glass of water to help her wash it down.

Exhaustion, and the sedative, were dragging Dianna below consciousness before the others finished filing out of the room.

The next morning Mrs. Brown confirmed her suspicions: she was not at Ansmall. Or in England. But in America. Texas, to be exact, having arrived there two years previous where she'd married a rancher, Jake Douglas. They had two adopted daughters and lived in Douglas County, not too far from Dr. Stanley's homestead where she'd spent four agonising weeks in and out of consciousness subsisting on water and broth when she was awake, healing her body when she slept.

"You slept most days," Mrs. Brown told her. "And when you were awake, you asked all the same questions over and over again. Where am I? What happened? Today's the first day you've not repeated yourself, but remembered what was discussed when you were awake last. It's a good thing, the doctor says. Means your brain's healing."

"But it isn't, is it?" Dianna murmured. Because, try as she might, she had no recollection of moving to America and getting married, establishing a business raising Quarter Horses, or of adopting two young girls.

She remembered Mrs. Brown, and Dirk whom Mrs. Brown claimed had left Papa's employ when she left to come work for Dianna on this mysterious ranch. Mama, Papa, Elaina, and Elizabeth, she remembered as well, but not the new brother Mrs. Brown told her would turn two in July. Much as Mrs. Brown told her, Dianna retained the distinct impression the kindly housekeeper left out more. What, she had no idea.

The preceding two years floated in a murky miasma, random images rising when she least expected. Fleeting impressions really, that, when she tried to force them to better clarity disintegrated, shreds of mist dispersing on a swift wind.

She fell asleep to the comforting sound of Mrs. Brown's retelling of her and Dirk's voyage to America, fitful slumber haunted by an urgency of something she must remember. She awoke when Mrs. Brown brought her lunch convinced there was something horribly wrong, more so than her physical injuries or loss of memory. But she had no time to brood, or ask Mrs. Brown what else she needed to know, as Dr. Stanley arrived full of brisk authority. Another, larger man, followed him in.

"Ooch, there ye are, Mr. Douglas," Mrs. Brown said. "Isn't it grand? She's awake. And talking. Lord above, it's a miracle."

He was huge, over six-foot tall with broad muscled shoulders and a chest to match. His pale-blond hair was trimmed short and crimped at the temples, presumably by the band of the hat he held in one large hand. He wore a white long-sleeve shirt tucked into denim trousers, the trousers themselves tucked inside the tops of scarred leather boots. She shivered as their eyes met.

Deep brown eyes flecked with gold fixed on her with a measure of relief and concern, squint-lines etching the sun-darkened skin at their corners. "Dianna?"

His voice was deep, questioning, as if it was he who didn't recognise her. She swallowed.

The man looked to the doctor, who stared thoughtfully at her.

"Do you recognise this man, Mrs. Douglas?" Dr. Stanley asked.

She bit her lip, chest filling with hollow fear as the tension in the room seemed to escalate, every theatre-goer on the edge of their seat in anticipation of the dramatic Opera's climactic denouement. Mrs. Brown offered a faint nod, her plump face soft with 'you can do it' support. Only she couldn't. *She couldn't lie.*

Whoever this man was, whatever she didn't know about him, she knew he would not like her to lie.

Shaking her head, she whispered, "No. I'm so sorry, but... no."

"It's not unexpected, Mr. Douglas," Dr. Stanley said when the big man flinched as though Dianna had flung dung at him. "Loss of memory is not uncommon with injury such as hers." He met Dianna's stare, smiled. "But in my experience, it's rarely permanent. A temporary setback is all."

"You're confident she'll make a full recovery?" the man asked, his gaze on her.

"Yes. With time. And *rest*," the doctor added emphatically.

"She's out of danger, then?"

"Definitely. But it'll be months," the doctor cautioned as the big man moved toward the bed, "before she'll be truly well. Once the casts come off, she'll need time to rebuild her muscles, and during that time I'm sure her memory will recover as well."

"Good." The big man frowned. "Do you not remember me at all?" His voice was quiet, his grip light when he grasped her fingertips. His were warm, callused. An image flared.

"You broke your arm," she blurted.

His eyes widened in surprise, but he nodded. "Not my arm. Collarbone..." He unbuttoned his shirt enough to draw it aside, show her a notch that marked where the bone had healed off kilter. His shirtsleeves were rolled back exposing darkly-tanned and well-muscled forearms covered in hair lighter in colour than the burnished-gold curls of his chest. "Do you remember that day in *Diablo*, how you saved my life?"

Diablo? Saved his life?

She shook her head. "No. I'm sorry. No."

"Don't cry, *Querida*," he murmured and brushed a tear from her cheek. "It'll come. When it does, I'll be with you."

She nodded, though she wasn't sure she believed him. If she could not recall something as important as having saved his life, how would she ever remember other important things, like having married him?

"Oh, *Querida*. My dear one. My love." He bent to gently embrace her. "Thank God you're alive. *Mi Dios*, I couldn't stand to lose you, too."

Too?

Another image floated up, this of a red flower, and white tombstone.

Mi Amor.

"You were married before," she rasped. "Before me."

He stiffened, then eased away, releasing her with obvious reluctance. He sat in the chair by the bed, dark eyes faintly narrowed. "You remember Connie?"

She shook her head. "I... remember a red flower. And... a dove?"

A grievous smile touched his mouth. "Poppy mallow." His voice was hoarse. "The flower. My grandmother's favourite. I planted them around the cemetery on our ranch. The dove I had etched on Connie's stone."

She bit her lip, aching with the pain she had roused in him.

Dr. Stanley touched Mr. Douglas's shoulder, cleared his throat. "Your wife needs rest. If anything of concern arises in your absence—not that anything will," he added hastily when Mr. Douglas twisted to scowl at him—"I'll send for you. But right now, she still needs a great deal of sleep, if she's to heal."

"I'll stay with her, Mr. Douglas," Mrs. Brown said. "I've been here these weeks past, an' know what she needs."

"Thank you, Mrs. Brown." Mr. Douglas stood, his hat caught by its crown in large fingers. "You've done an admirable job here, but your services are deeply needed at the ranch. The house is in ruins. I hired two young women to take your place, and my mother and Rosa help, but they've not your skill. I need your proficient hand, there, to prepare for my wife's homecoming."

Mrs. Brown's small mouth formed a prim 'o'.

Mr. Douglas had cleverly disguised an order in the form of a compliment and the discord it created within the housekeeper was plain, her dark-eyed gaze darting between him and Dianna until, with obvious reluctance, she relented.

"Aye," she muttered, "I expect it'll take me a month of Sundays to get things orderly again."

"I expect it will," Mr. Douglas said. "And I expect you'll have all of a month to do it." He looked to Dr. Stanley for confirmation.

The doctor inclined his head. "As soon as she can walk unassisted, she can leave here. But," he added sternly, "she'll need weeks of rehabilitation to strengthen her muscles, and recover her stamina, before she can return to regular duties."

"I understand. Garrett's here," Mr. Douglas said turning to Mrs. Brown. He waved for her to precede him from the room. "I'll see you out, have him see you home." He stopped, leaned over Dianna and to her utter shock, kissed the tip of her nose. "I'll be back," he whispered.

She forced a wavering smile. "I... I'll be here."

"You have no idea how happy that makes me," he said and grinned.

"You're a lucky woman, Mrs. Douglas," Dr. Stanley said when they were alone. "I've been at this a long time, over forty years. I've seen a lot of anxious husbands whose wives needed my medical help for one reason or another, but none like Jake."

"Jake?"

He nodded. "Jackson Andrew David Douglas. Helped deliver him almost thirty years ago. Been his family's doctor longer than that. Watched him grow up. Stitched up his dog in fact—"

"Pepper."

The doctor hesitated, and then frowned. "Yes. But... I thought she died before you moved here?"

She bit her lip, shook her head. "She might have. I don't know. The name just... popped out—"

"Now don't panic." The doctor settled in the chair, patted her casted arm. "Don't force it, Mrs. Douglas. Your memory will return in due time.

For now, concentrate on knitting those bones. I plan to retire soon, but not until you're up and around, and moving under your own power."

"You're retiring?"

"Yes." He smiled. "My youngest son just graduated medical school. He'll be here in a few weeks to take over my practise, and when he gets here, I'm taking Mrs. Stanley on a long-promised trip to Italy."

"That sounds wonderful," Dianna murmured.

"Not as wonderful as you, getting better." He got to his feet, offered that paternal smile. "Be patient with him, Mrs. Douglas. And yourself. Time heals all wounds." He left, closing the door softly behind him.

When she next awoke, it was to the sense someone was in the room with her. And she was fairly certain she knew who.

The doctor had a medicinal smell about him. His wife too, though hers was tempered with a floral perfume. Lavender soap and wood polish were Mrs. Brown, while this faintly citrus scent mingled with odours of grass, leather, and horse, could be only one person. One, very large, person.

"Are you going to look at me, or lay there pretending I'm not here?"

She opened her eyes. "How did you know I was awake?"

"I've not lost *my* memory, *Querida*." He set his hat, brim up, on the bedside table next to the lamp that tossed his movements in massive shadow on the far wall, alerting her to the growing dusk outside. "I know you, probably better than you know yourself some days. You've never been good at containing your emotions, even when you try. And you have a delightful tendency to turn a wonderful rose pink when you're embarrassed or upset."

"Oh." She felt herself turning a brighter hue and glanced away. "You... don't have to stay, you know. I'll be fine."

He chuckled, but it was a hollow sound. "You're afraid of me."

From the corner of her eye, she watched him run a tanned hand through his wheat-coloured locks. "It's like starting over," he said. "Only this time, I don't know how to break through."

She looked at him. "Starting over?"

He nodded. "You were afraid of me when we first met, too. But then, I knew why. Now..."

"I'm sorry," she murmured.

48

He touched his knuckles to her cheek. "Don't apologise, *Querida*. It's not your fault. It was a tragic accident, and you've suffered greatly for it." His voice hitched.

"Still, I'm sorry," she rasped. "I'm sorry I don't remember."

"Don't cry, *Querida*." He stood to hug her. "Please don't cry."

Only the tears refused to stop.

"I really am sorry," she whispered. "Please, forgive me."

She had no idea why she felt the need to beg his forgiveness. She only knew it felt imperative. Urgent. As urgent as the shadows that haunted her sleep and hovered at the edge of her consciousness when she was awake, turning the marrow in her bones to ice.

His arms tightened around her, and for the first time since waking to the horror of all she could not remember, she felt warm. And safe.

∞ ∞ ∞

Jake crooked an arm. "Lean on me."

"That's all I've done for a month," she said. "Is it not time I stood on my own?" He returned to his—their—ranch at night but spent much of his day-time hours with her, exercising his considerable muscle to ensure she exercised hers, ignoring her protests of fatigue and exclamations of pain as he insisted she push herself.

Her casts had come off a few weeks earlier. Since then, he'd insisted she do four additional repetitions of whatever type of exercise the doctor recommended. When she managed to do as he demanded—gasping, groaning, and sweating the entire time—he immediately demanded two more repetitions. And two more after that. Only then did he let her rest, and only for the time it took her to catch her breath. Then he prodded her on to the next exercise in the regimen.

She would have happily prodded him off a cliff a few times, had she the strength and a cliff from which to launch him. But now, balanced precariously on the edge of the bed, her bare feet skimming the braided floor rug, she was grateful for his tough medicine. Dr. Stanley would allow her to go home when she walked unassisted. Today, after almost twelve full weeks in the doctor's care, she intended to do just that.

"As soon as you're stable, I'll step away. Ready? One, two—"

"Three." She pushed to her feet and clung to his arm as her legs wobbled. He let her hold on, but only until she found her balance. Then he eased away.

She locked her knees, gasped when her calf muscles cramped.

"Breathe, Dianna. See yourself standing tall. Walking tall."

She exhaled, concentrated first on relaxing the cramp and as it abated, she straightened, squared her shoulders, visualised herself walking confidently the short distance to the door. Jake laid a hand on the small of her back, an offer of support, not requirement she move.

Yet.

Heavens, but he was a good man. If she weren't already married to him, she'd want to be.

"I'm standing," she murmured.

"You are."

She eased a foot forward, legs shaky. She took a second step. Then a third, and fourth—

"Well, well, looks like you're ready to go home."

Dianna looked up at the sound of Dr. Stanley's voice and flailed for a hand-hold when she tottered. Jake swept her up in his arms, as if she weighed no more than a small child. Something clenched in her chest, forcing a groan from her.

"Did I hurt you?" He lowered her to her bed, brown eyes dark with concern.

"No." She shook her head. "It wasn't you. It was... I'm not sure. I can't see it, but I can feel it. I thought of you, holding a child—" She frowned at him, glanced at the framed likenesses of their daughters he'd brought and set on her bedside table. "Our daughters? Are they, all right?"

She'd been told Katie and Amelia were at her and Jake's home, overseen by Jake's mother Eleanor and her niece Margaret, whom, along with the children and others on the ranch, had been discouraged from visiting by Dr. Stanley who feared Dianna's damaged recall might cause all involved unnecessary torment, but none more than the girls. So, Jake had brought the photographs, and painted verbal portraits of each girl that she'd used to write them letters, share her progress, offer reassurance she'd be home soon.

Katie was the elder and more serious of the two, Amelia stubborn enough for both. Katie loved needlepoint and to cook; Amelia avoided all hints of domesticity, preferring the barns and horses. But had Jake lied, or obfuscated the truth for fear of setting back her recovery?

"Something happened," she said. "What is it? What's happened?"

"Nothing's wrong. With the girls," Jake added, his voice hoarse, expression bleak. "It's—"

"Time to rest." Dr. Stanley gripped Jake's shoulder. "Your wife needs to rest."

"No." Dianna squeezed Jake's hand. "Jake, please tell me. What's wrong?"

"Nothing," Dr. Stanley said firmly. "You mustn't overdo it, Mrs. Douglas. You will learn everything in time, when you're ready. For now, you must rest. Doctor's orders."

"But—"

"No, buts." Dr. Stanley said. "You, rest. I must talk to your husband and instruct him on your care once you leave here." He towed Jake from the room, leaving behind his wife Mary with strict instruction that Mrs. Douglas was not to leave her bed.

Exhausted from her exertions, and the grinding sense something was seriously wrong, Dianna offered no resistance when Mrs. Stanley insisted she accept a sedative. As she slipped into a medicinal haze she was struck by a numbing realisation: in the weeks he'd cared for her, not once had Jake allowed the doctor to intervene. Until today.

Worse, he let Dr. Stanley lead him out.

"Jake," she whispered, and a heartbeat later, tumbled into darkness.

Chapter 4

I've Got You Now

*J*ake halted the carriage in front of a weather-beaten cabin. Dianna's skin prickled with cold despite the mid-July sun's warmth as she glanced at the neighbouring barn, hazy memory skittering through her consciousness.

Papa? Asleep on the ground? She closed her eyes, tried to freeze the image in her mind, but it was gone, leaving her uncertain if it was a memory. Or recollection of a dream.

She looked at Jake. "This... is our home?"

He shook his head. "You don't recognise it?"

"No. I mean, I sense something familiar. I seem to recall... my father? But... I think it's not a memory, but a dream. I can't imagine Papa would ever come here," she added surveying the grassland surrounding the cabin broken by a burbling brook, and crop of trees far side of the barn.

"He was here," Jake said. "I'll explain, later," he added when she stared at him in surprise. "Hold these." He handed her the reins. "I'll be right back."

The horse tossed its head jangling the traces as Jake hopped down and strode to the cabin's door. He knocked, then clanged a dinner bell. She startled at a squealing sound and turned to find the barn door rolling open. A tall sharp-shouldered man dressed in a brown shirt, and denim trousers, and holding a shotgun, stepped into the sun, his thick white moustache and sideburns knotted in a ferocious scowl as he swept his gaze from Jake, to Dianna, and back.

"What do you want?" he demanded, his voice as deep and gravelly as a well bottom. Before either she or Jake could answer, he added, "Don't tell me you've changed your mind about wanting to be hitched?"

∞ ∞ ∞

Once her initial shock at their host's surly reception eased, and her surprise at discovering Justice JT Wardlaw was Jake's former army CO *and* the man who'd presided at her and Jake's wedding two years earlier—a wedding her father had, Jake explained, shown up to try and stop—Dianna realised she liked him. Very much.

Behind the brusque leathery exterior and sea-blue eyes lurked a keen mind, and dry wit. Not to mention a healthy appetite for shine, as he called the nasal-searing liquid he stored in mason jars.

"So," Justice Wardlaw drawled as he poured a measure, his shrewd gaze somehow divided between her and the glass into which he poured. "You sure you haven't changed your mind about being married to this knot-head?"

"Knot-head?" Jake's voice was dry.

JT Wardlaw cast him an appraising look, as he slid a part-filled glass to him. "Coyote?"

"How about, Jake?" Jake raised an eyebrow. "Just, Jake."

"Just Jake my—"

"Yes," she said biting back a smile when JT winked at her. "I am quite content to remain married to Jake."

"Pity," the Justice murmured. "I was thinking a bit of ribbon and lace would brighten things up around here." He winked again and lifted the jar to his mouth. He was not off on his assessment, at least with regard to the cabin.

A rectangle split in two rooms, a living area and bed chamber furnished with square and sturdy wood furniture, windows on the north and south facing walls, the cabin was spare and serviceable. And like its owner a little rough around the edges. A touch of colour and softness would definitely enhance its comfort.

Jake, his arms on the table and hands clasped lightly around the glass, angled a look at her. "Do you remember JT visiting you in the hospital a few weeks ago?"

"He did? You did?" Dianna split a startled glance between the men. "I...
no. I don't recall that."

"Don't fret yerself," JT said. "Happens to the best of us. I'm always
forgetting something, like my spectacles. Usually find them on top of my
damn head. And at least once a day I get half way to the barn and have to
turn 'round and come back inside, because I forgot what I was going out
for." He tapped the stub of his amputated thumb to his temple. "Good
memory; just real short."

"You're teasing," she said.

His tufted eyebrows lifted. "Am I?"

She laughed, and glanced at Jake, froze when their eyes met, her skin
erupting in warm tingles.

He was beautiful, his face bold and strong, white laugh lines creasing
the corners of his eyes, reddish-gold and black stubble framing his wide
mouth, sensuous and perfect for kissing—She tore her gaze from his,
flustered, and inexplicably shy.

"What do you remember?" JT asked.

She dragged her gaze to his, offered a bewildered shrug. "Everything,
but the last two years."

"Yes," Jake murmured. "She can recall most of her life up to about six
months before I entered the picture. Everything after, has been wiped clear
off her slate."

Dianna glanced at him, stung by a hint of rebuke in his voice. "You say
that like I've done it on purpose."

He didn't answer, but the skin around his mouth tightened. The warmth
in her body drained away.

"You... cannot seriously believe that?"

He shrugged. "It just seems odd, you remember the first nineteen, or so
years of your life, but not the last two-and-a-half."

A surge of adrenaline brought her to her feet. She looked at their host.
"If you will excuse me, Mr. Wardlaw, where might I find the WC?"

JT hesitated, and then hooked his stub-thumb toward the window
behind him. Through it, about a hundred yards out and listing slightly,
stood a weather-beaten wooden privy. She turned to leave, paused without
looking down when Jake grasped her wrist.

"Let go," she said through her teeth. He complied, and, back stiff and knees wobbly, she marched outside. By the time she made it to the privy, she could barely see for her tears.

Did he not understand how odd it was for her? How odd that she was here, in Texas, with him, when what she could remember of her life contradicted everything she was experiencing now?

She'd gone along with him. Gone along with all of them—Jake, the doctor and his wife, Mrs. Brown—when they told her she'd met Jake in England when he was there visiting, fell in love, and ran off to America with him to elope. How she and Jake had made the magnanimous decision together to adopt two sisters from an orphanage in New York. How she'd personally accepted the challenge of building a stable of racing Quarter Horses, while he acted as major-domo of his mother's ranch.

But even as she sat there mutely accepting the story-book retelling of her and Jake's romance, she'd sensed its fairy-tale quality. Suspected that behind the smiles and assurances that she was, prior to the accident, a happily wedded woman and loving mother, lurked a subplot of fiction. Or at least, significant lack of critical plot points. Yet she'd not questioned them. Not questioned how she met Jake. Why she chose to marry him when she had vivid memory of looking forward to her debut, of wedding a peer of the realm. Swanning around Britain and Europe.

She definitely had no recollection of considering America as a viable place to live. It was a rough and unrefined country, full of rough and unrefined people. She had only to open the privy door to confirm that. Which she did, but only to reap the fresh air the coarse and overwhelmingly empty land around her offered. Moving to a square of shade one side of the privy, she dabbed at her eyes with her handkerchief, stared across the seemingly endless miles of grass bowed to the wind's whispers.

She'd been too afraid to question, or challenge the orated story. Because whatever it was the narrators were loath to speak of, it must be awful. Very, very awful.

So, she clung to the romantic notion that her parents' displeasure with and forbiddance of her relationship with Jake, had inspired her cross-Atlantic flight with him to elope. That Papa had followed, too late apparently to stop her from becoming Jake's wife, but in time to end up in an altercation with her new husband. Physical remonstration Jake and the

Justice assured her was initiated by Papa, if finished by Jake, which explained her vision of Papa on the ground.

Jake had struck him. Once. But with enough force to break the earl's nose and render him unconscious. When he'd come around, Papa had immediately decamped for England. Apparently still wasn't talking to her. That, of all she'd been told, was the one thing she could believe: Papa's rancour.

The earl nursed grudges and exacted retaliation even for minor infractions. She recalled many hours confined in her bedchamber for what she now recognised as inconsequential, if not silly errors of judgement on her part. She'd learned to avoid him. Avoid disappointing him. Avoid making him angry. Which was why now, with her limbs intact if not fully strengthened, and her ability to reason improved if her memory still impaired, she could no longer gullibly swallow the syrupy narrative.

She would have never taken up willingly with an American in defiance of her parents, even if by some bizarre chance she had opportunity to meet one. That was something else she remembered, how rarely she and her sisters had ventured off their country estate in Herefordshire.

Mama's fragile health, exacerbated by Papa's quest for a son, frequently kept the countess bedridden, unable to entertain, or go out to visit.

There were no Americans at Ansmall. Near Ansmall. Invited to Ansmall.

So how the hell had she met Jake?

Drying her eyes, she tucked the damp handkerchief in her pocket, inhaled a deep, shuddering, and cleansing breath.

The time for mute acceptance was over. She wanted answers. Needed answers. Real answers.

Honest answers.

Returning to the cabin, she found JT Wardlaw seated on one of two chairs in the shade of the porch roof. He gestured to the empty chair, and a full glass of cooled tea on a small table next to it.

"Please forgive me, Justice, for my outburst," she said. "I—we. We had no right to subject you to such discourtesy—"

"Don't fret yourself, young lady," Justice Wardlaw said. "You subjected me to nothing I haven't experienced a thousand times over. My wife—may she rest in peace—and I had our share of scuff ups. And I preside over dozens more each week in court. Now, just sit yourself down there and take a moment to catch your breath."

She eased slowly to the proffered chair, glanced around.

"He went for a walk." The Justice kept his gaze on the dirt track winding alongside the creek that flowed past his home, as if he expected someone to ride up it.

"A walk?" And left her alone, with a virtual stranger?

JT nodded, his profile meditative. "Most men don't have a problem displaying their anger, but when there's tears need shedding..." He tipped the half-full jar to his mouth.

"Tears?"

Justice Wardlaw nodded, still looking out. "Anger's kept our species alive for centuries. Given us strength to fight wars and spend long months, even years, far from family sleeping alone in the cold with nothing more than anger and will to drag us from our bedrolls on to the battle field where death dogs every step. Like the lion that defends his pride or the stallion his herd, we draw on rage to clash with those that threaten our own." His gaze grew more distant and she knew he wasn't seeking shapes on the horizon, but seeing ghosts of battles fought in another time, in other places. "It's only after," he said softly. "After the battle, after the bloodshed when there's no one left to fight, and no fight left in us, that we finally let ourselves... feel."

"Feel?" She picked up the glass of cooled tea, held it with trembling hands while she tried to logic-out the Justice's homily. "He... Jake. Jake feels threatened because... he's afraid I won't remember. That's why he brought me here." She straightened, stared at the Justice. "He hoped I'd see you, this place, and I'd remember. If not everything, at least marrying him. I'd remember... *him*."

JT Wardlaw dipped his chin fractionally in confirmation.

"But I *will* remember," she insisted. "I'm sure of it. He's my husband. I just need... time." Time, and she would love him again. She was sure of it. "It's frightening, I know. I'm terrified. But I will remember. And he can help me. He remembers everything."

"That he does," JT murmured, and took a drink of his shine. Something in his tone...

Because whatever it was the narrators were loath to speak of, it must be awful. Very, very awful.

"Where is he?" She set the glass on the table and stood. "I need to talk to him. Now. I need to talk to him right now."

The Justice hesitated, then pointed at the barn. "There's a path on the other side, leads to a swimming hole. You'll likely find him there. It's a good place for unravelling worry knots."

Worry knots. Like her memory loss, and Jake's heartache, were so much tangled yarn.

"Thank you," she said, and stepped off the porch into the piercing sun.

A hundred yards past the barn the path disappeared into a nest of trees and cacti. Fifty-yards further along and she was winded, and damp with perspiration when she turned her ankle on a loose rock and fell. She sat for a moment, fighting tears, before finally shoving to her feet and dusting off her gloves. She hobbled on and moments later, hot, tired, and no end of irritated, she broke into a small clearing. The swimming hole was surrounded by thick vegetation and large boulders but for a patch of pea-sized gravel wide enough for one large, or two smaller people, to sit.

"Jake? Jake? Where are you?"

"Dianna?"

She startled when he abruptly loomed over her from the apex of a tall boulder.

"What is it?" he asked. "What's wrong?"

She stared, then scanned him for injury, something to explain the panic clawing up her throat. But he looked as he usually did: Stetson covering his fair hair, cotton shirt tucked into denim trousers, worn leather boots—

What was that, in his hand?

Another hat. A small one, made of straw. A replica of his own, but too small even for her. A child's hat.

A child's hat.

She stumbled, and hunched, brought her hands to her head as pain sheared through it and a roar filled her ears like all the wind in the world had converged inside her skull. Her knees buckled, bile surging up her throat as she pressed her forehead to the ground.

"Dianna?" Gravel crunched as he landed next to her, grasped her. "What is it? What's wrong?"

She moaned as images enhanced by resounding echoes of sound and odour swirled in her mind like an ocean of fish and crustaceans had exploded through a stone dam to drown her.

A handkerchief in her mouth. Strong knees forcing hers apart. Mama ordering her to put on a disguise, leave. A ship. A baby. A boy.

A son.

"No," she whispered. Arms tightened around her. "Don't touch me." She shoved, clawed.

"Dianna. Dianna, look at me." A firm hand clasped her chin. "Look at me."

Maggie. A ring. Diamonds. Sapphires. Wind. Roaring wind. Dirt everywhere. In her mouth, in her eyes.

"Dianna, look, at, me."

"No." She writhed, palms clutched to her head trying to compress it, stop the swelling pain. Whirl of crushing memory.

A nun. Mother Mary. Two hollow-eyed children. One blonde, one with dark hair. Their sister, dying in a hospital bed, poisoned by the fruit of their father's sin.

"Charlie," she whispered. "Amelia. Katie. Oh, Jake. Jake."

"I'm here. Dianna, I'm here." Strong hands and arms gathered her close.

A child. A boy.

A son.

"JJ?" She pushed away. "JJ? Where is he, Jake? Where is he? Why do you have his hat? Why do you have JJ's hat—No." She shook her head when he only stared, his eyes haunted. Hunted. "No. No, no, no." Twisting, she tried to break free, but his arms refused to release her, instead enfolding her, drawing her to him gently as butterfly wings. "Let me go. Please, let me go. It's my fault. It's my fault. I lost him—"

"No," he said, and tugged her to him. "It's not your fault. You almost died trying to save him. From a tornado. There was nothing you could do. You couldn't stop it. No one could."

"No," she croaked, shaking her head.

"Yes," he said, emphatic. "It was an accident, Dianna. A tragic, tragic accident. Not your fault. Not your fault." His voice cracked, chest heaved.

"No." She sagged, and he dragged her on to his lap, buried his face in her hair. Despite the urge to kick loose and run, she turned, and clasping her arms around his neck, held on. Not for herself.

For him.

For weeks he had held it all in. Lived with the loss she'd not remembered—*had not wanted to remember*—unable to find comfort in her arms.

He grieved alone.

Remembered alone.

But not anymore. She couldn't give him back their son, but she could give him comfort. Stroking his hair, she held him while he wept.

"It's all right," she whispered, rocking him. "I've got you. I've got you, now."

Chapter 5

Take Me Home

She held him until the sky darkened to voluminous swirls of charcoal and lavender, and the air bristled with chill. When he lifted his head, something crinkled. JJ's hat. Nestled between Jake's head, and the sunken hollow of her belly. She bit her lip.

Two children. She'd lost two children in one day.

How could God be so cruel, as to steal both her babies at the same time?

Anger roiled. She wanted to scream. She wanted to cry. But she had energy for neither. So, when Jake helped her to her feet, she followed, meek as any lamb, her hand caught in his.

He led her back towards JT Wardlaw's home. The Justice was no longer seated on the porch, and a faint odour of frying bacon and woodsmoke swirled on the air. To her surprise, Jake veered toward the barn. She stopped.

"It's all right," he said. "JT invited us to stay the night. The guest room is in here. Do you remember?"

She did. She also felt the same awkward shyness now, she had felt then. Leg-locking and tongue-tying reluctance to venture in the barn, and past the invisible barrier keeping intimacy at bay.

He gently cupped her chin, tilted her gaze to his. "Do you remember what I told you, almost in this exact spot, on our wedding night?"

She closed her eyes against the remembered shame of what had truly brought them together.

She'd left England, not in a romantic rush to elope with a handsome American, but to foil the earl's plan to compel her into marriage with a man old enough to be her grandsire. An arrangement that would have revealed, at least to the Duke of Blackburn to whom she was unwillingly contracted to marry, the truth she had sailed across an ocean to hide: that she was no longer a virgin. And was, in fact, with child. A child Jake had come to divine was not conceived through a consensual act. And still he'd offered for her hand.

Promised to raise the child as his own.

Never take from her, what she did not give willingly.

She curled her fingers around his strong ones, drew his hand up to kiss the rough knuckles, and looked at him. "You said you wanted a whole wife," she murmured.

"Yes," he said. "A willing wife. Someone who wanted me, as much as I wanted her. I meant it then, *Querida*, and I mean it now." He shook his head. "Nothing's changed, Dianna. I won't accept anything less, than your full and willing heart."

"But that is all that's left," she rasped. "Less than nothing."

"No." He swallowed. "I won't let you believe that. I won't."

She didn't resist as he drew her inside the barn, rolled the door closed. In the white-washed stall converted to a bedchamber at the back she stood beside the brass-bed, head bowed, watching through the dark veil of her hair that had fallen loose of its pins at some point during her hysterics, as he gently hung the tiny hat on a nail in the wall. Anguish swept through her.

She sank to the mattress, wrapped her arms around her middle and stared at the rough plankboard floor as Jake stripped off his clothes, and then, with exquisite tenderness, helped her undress until she stood as bare as he in the cooling air, and more vulnerable for it. Goose bumps flared as his hands travelled the lengths of her arms, before he touched her stomach, which she contracted reflexively.

"I'm sorry, *Querida*," he murmured.

She nodded, tears erupting. He kissed her temple, held her, his cheek resting on her head.

"I love you," he whispered. "I love *you*."

"I love you, too," she rasped.

He eased away, folded back the bed's coverlet. She gasped, and shivered as she slid between the cool sheets, grateful when he joined her to gather her next to his warm body.

"I never should have left him in the carriage," she said. "It's my fault. I should've woken him, but I didn't want to. I was so tired, and he looked so peaceful—"

"Dianna." He hauled her more firmly against his chest. "Dianna," he said again, with more gentleness. "You can't blame yourself. What happened was a tragic accident. You did the right thing, letting him sleep. He needed it. You couldn't know a tornado would come. You couldn't prevent it, or even run from it. I know you tried, *Querida*. I know you tried. Mother told me how you tried to get to JJ. She told me how you ran, and ran—"

"But I shouldn't have allowed McGuire—"

"McGuire had taken him, before you knew he was awake. Don't you think I don't know that? Katie told me. She told me everything, how as soon as she came in the house you went out. They heard you, Mother, Margaret, and Katie. They heard you shouting for McGuire and JJ, trying to bring them back before the storm hit. It's not your fault, *Querida*. You can spend the rest of your life blaming yourself, bemoaning what you should have done, could have done, might have done, and the result will be the same." He dragged in a shaky breath. "He's gone, Dianna. And beating yourself up, won't bring him back."

She tucked her nose in the warm hollow of his neck. "But I want him back. I want my baby back."

"I know," he rasped. "It hurts *Querida*, and there is nothing I can say that will change that. Nothing. You'll hurt for a long time. Sometimes the pain will be unbearable, and you'll wish yourself dead, but you can't give up. I know. It took me years after Connie and baby John died, to accept the fact there was nothing I could do to change what happened to them. They were dead, I was alive, and I hated myself for it. I thought of joining them. Escaping the painful burden of living without them, but I thank God I didn't, because I wouldn't have you. And the girls."

She hadn't thought it possible she could cry more, but tears seeped from her swollen eyes. "I... can't go home. The nursery. The memories—"

"Will be hard," he whispered. "But we have each other. And Katie and Amelia need us now, more than ever. They're just children, and they need us to help them heal. We lost a son, and they a brother, and the only thing we can do now is pull together."

It sounded so easy. And absolutely impossible.

"I made the mistake of withdrawing from everyone and everything after Connie died," Jake murmured. "I didn't ever want to feel that pain again, so I cut myself off from those who loved me. Lived in a land of shadows. Woke up every morning, put my socks on one at a time and pulled on my trousers, tucked in my shirt, drank my coffee, and went out to ride with my troop, but for the life of me, had someone asked, I couldn't have told them what colour my socks were, what section of land I'd patrolled, or even who I'd talked to that day. I was trapped in my mind, locked in the bedroom with Connie watching her die, over and over..." He crushed her to him. "Don't do that. Don't withdraw. We have to help each other get through this."

Her heart and lungs throbbed with the effort of withholding her rage. Grief.

Regret.

She was alive. And she didn't want to be. Not when her son was dead.

Why did I remember? At least now the narrator's lack of candour made sense.

The truth was truly, very, very awful.

"Promise me you won't quit, Dianna. I need you." His arms contracted around her. "The girls need you. We all need you, and you need us."

Katie.

Amelia.

They'd already survived losing their mother and older sister, and the horror that was their father. Blossomed in her and Jake's care. Started to trust, and believe in a different future...

"Dianna?"

She bowed her head to his chest.

"We have to face this together," he said.

She nodded, and whispered, "I know."

He slid his hands in her hair, massaged her scalp with strong fingers. She moaned with the pleasure of it, dipped her chin lower exposing her nape, shuddered as his fingers found and caressed the tender skin at the base of her skull.

"I need you, Dianna," he rasped. He cupped her face, applied gentle pressure to her jaw, until she looked him in the eyes. "I need you," he repeated softly, inspiring in her the same raw want she heard in his voice.

The need to possess the other, escape the pain of mutual loss in the joining of hearts, and flesh.

"Oh Jake," she murmured and pressed her cheek to his rough one. "Please, please make the hurt go away."

Afterwards, lost in repletion and release, she jerked to awareness as his hand slowly trailed up her spine, mustering goose-bumps.

"I love you so much, *Querida*," he said. "So much."

With a sob, she curled into his arms, and he held her, unspeaking, while she grieved for her son, and the future he would not have. "I want to see him," she muttered. "I want to go to his grave."

She drew back when Jake stilled, and wiping her swollen eyes, looked up. "What is it? What's wrong? What?" she insisted when he returned her stare with the hollow look of someone granted a peek into his future, only to see the flickering fires of Hell.

Easing out a breath, he compressed his lips, shook his head. "There is no grave, *Querida*. We... never found his body." He nodded to the pale shape hung on the wall. "That's all we found. All we ever found, was his hat."

∞ ∞ ∞

Dianna sat up, shoved her hair from her eyes. "What do you mean, that's all you found? Where is he?"

Jake dragged himself to a seated position. "That's why Mrs. Brown stayed with you. I was out every day. Juan, Sheriff Boone, every ranch hand I could spare and those I couldn't... We looked. From first light until the sun went down, we searched, and sifted every inch of the ranch, the canyon, a five-mile grid either side of the swath cut by the twister." He shook his head. "We found no sign of him. Just his hat, caught in scrub, three miles from Mother's house."

She leaned toward him. "But if you never found his body, then how do you know he's dead?"

He didn't answer, just reached for her, but she scooted off the bed, charged with hope.

"If you didn't find his body, Jake," she said, "then you don't know he's dead. What about McGuire? Where's he? Did you find him?"

He shook his head. "No. But that doesn't mean anything—"

"Doesn't mean anything?" She reached for her chemise. "If you found nothing to prove they're... not alive, then there's a chance they are—"

"Dianna. We found Queenie. She..." He shook his head.

She bit her lip, closed her eyes. "That... doesn't mean anything." She looked at him. "McGuire could have taken shelter somewhere. With JJ. Maybe he's hurt. McGuire's hurt, or lost—or lost his memory, like I did—Oh, my God. Pete. Pete Harder. Did he..."

Jake shook his head. "He... didn't make it out of the nursery in time."

"Oh, my God." She hugged her chemise to her bosom. "But I... I spoke to him. He... offered to help me. Help me look for JJ and McGuire. I... I told him no. I told him no. Maybe I should have—"

"You shouldn't have anything, Dianna." Jake's voice was stern, his hands warm as he took the chemise from her stiff, icy fingers. "I told you, none of it's your fault. Here," he added in a gentler tone as he slipped the undergarment over her head, helped her fit her arms in the appropriate holes, the way he would a small child. The thought reduced her to tears again.

He hugged her, their bodies melded knee to neck.

"I know it's hard," he murmured. "But you can't blame yourself. What happened to Pete, to JJ, none of it's your—"

"No." She glared up at him. "He's not dead. I feel it. Here." She touched her breast, above her heart. "And I'm going to look for him. Every day. Every day, for as long as it takes. I mean it, Jake," she said when he compressed his lips. "I'm going to look for him, until I know for sure. Until I'm convinced. Until I..." She inhaled. "I just will, that's all."

∞ ∞ ∞

The next morning, she ignored the torment of his silent ambivalence as she surveyed the ground where once there had been a grand house.

The monstrous whirlwind had lifted her mother-in-law's home off its foundation and disassembled it, leaving the structure and its contents strewn for miles. Only the heavy timber doors over the root cellar where Eleanor, Rosa, Katie, and Maggie had sheltered, were miraculously intact. But everything else...

Jake had told her how they found forks and knives, and tiny wooden bits of all that remained of his mother's sideboard embedded in the trunk of an oak tree that, though it had been stripped of its leaves, miraculously

66

survived the storm. Even more amazing than finding utensils and chunks of teak buried in the tree's bark like pellets from a shotgun, was the framed miniature of Jake as a baby, glass cover cracked but intact, tucked in a forked limb, its pewter framed scratched yet whole.

She suspected he told her about the sideboard to reinforce the strength of the storm—strong enough to lift and shatter a piece of furniture so heavy it had required four men to unload it from a wagon and carry it in the house when it was originally delivered—to dissuade her from searching for JJ.

How could a small child possibly survive winds that had tossed his mother in the air like she was a straw doll, snapped her bones like they were matchsticks? But Jake's baby face smiling from an oval frame only reaffirmed in her belief that, like the tiny portrait, her son could have survived. Especially if McGuire had protected him from the worst.

"Are you, all right?" The gentleness of Jake's question seemed out of context with the starkness surrounding them.

Neighbours spared the tornado's wrath had helped clean up. There was nothing save the crumbled foundation, and a blanket of scorched earth where the Nursery had once stood to suggest a tragedy even occurred. That a man had died there.

Jake had told her how he'd taken a few days off from searching for JJ to escort Pete Harder, a bachelor, home to his widowed mother in Kansas. Pete had travelled in style, dressed in a suit and laid out inside a blue-silk lined casket bought by the Ranch. Eleanor sent along a letter of condolence that included a cheque equivalent to a year of Pete's wages made out to his mother. Jake gave Mrs. Harder additional money to cover the cost of Pete's funeral. By the time he returned to the ranch, every scrap of wood, cloth, broken glass and china, twisted length of wire or metal, paper, and other items of human possession, had been collected and either salvaged, burned, or buried. The yard where he'd played as a toddler was as silent and empty as a graveyard.

"I'm fine," she said.

His gaze probed hers. He hadn't wanted her to come here, at least not right away. He wanted her to return home and see the girls, take some time to rest, build her strength, but she'd insisted.

They spent the night at JT Wardlaw's, limbs entwined as though to prevent the other slipping away in the night, and at daybreak, not sure if she'd slept and certain he hadn't, she turned to him. They made love without talking as if afraid the slightest word, would break the peace and security they found in each other's arms. Afterwards, bodies still joined, he held her while she cried.

When she quieted, he left her long enough to gather a basin of warm water and a cloth, returning to bathe her with infinite tenderness, before helping her dress, never once saying a word.

They enjoyed a quiet breakfast with their host who seemed to understand their need for silence, the Justice speaking only when they left: "Draw courage from each other" he whispered in her ear when she hugged him goodbye.

Staring at the enormously wide strip of black earth where the twister had ripped away turf like a razor peeling flesh to the bone, she didn't feel courageous. Only resolute.

"He's alive, Jake. I don't know where. I don't know why I believe it. I only know I'm going to do whatever I can to find him."

He said nothing, but like the night before, she sensed his concern, knew he wondered if the trauma of remembering hadn't damaged her mind in other ways.

Sucking a strong breath, she straightened her spine, silently rebuffed his doubt. "Take me home," she said. "I want to see my girls."

∞ ∞ ∞

As they began the shallow descent to where the lake sparkled, and house gleamed perfect as a pearl, grief and gratitude battled for supremacy of her emotions.

They'd started their married life to the south and east, in a small two-level house built by Jake's great-step-grandfather who'd founded the ranch. The new house and stables were Jake's wedding gift to her. A gift she'd almost lost forever before she received it, when she fled the ranch a month before construction was complete.

"Your father was Viscount Tolle when I knew him."

That was one secret she wished she hadn't regained with the rest of her memories, her mother-in-law's tearful confession in the old house's diminutive kitchen after she'd seen a grainy photograph of the earl.

Jake was away for a few days at a cattle sale, and Maggie in town for the afternoon to interview for the School Mistress position, so she and Eleanor were alone for the first time for more than a few minutes since they'd made their acquaintance. Her stomach still clenched recalling Eleanor's pale haggard expression when Dianna confirmed that the man in the photograph was indeed the man Eleanor thought it was: Edward Marshall, 7th Earl of Ansmall.

Eleanor had started to cry. "Jake doesn't know the truth..."

And he never would, far as Dianna was concerned. From her, at least.

Jake believed his sire the man his mother had married in England and emigrated with to America, a man shot dead in a failed attempt to rustle cattle a few weeks before Jake was born. But Thomas Wilson was not Jake's father. He had been a stand in, a man his mother had been coerced to marry following her misguided transgression with a different man—her twin sister's fiancé—then heir to a powerful earldom.

Now he is the earl, and in control of all that power.

Which was why Jake—and the earl—could not know Jake was the fruit of his mother's transgression, not the result of her brief first marriage.

It was tragic enough Jake believed himself sired by a common cattle thief. She'd not compound his shame by revealing to him he was instead blood son of a man who would never acknowledge him, and who had called him a toerag. Especially when his love and fealty as a son lay with John Douglas, rest his soul, who lay buried on the hillock to the west.

Ignoring the ache of yet one more painful memory, she relaxed her fists and jaw and tilted her head to her husband's shoulder as he drew the wagon to a halt on a plateau three-hundred yards shy of the house.

Not a board or window cracked, nor a tree or shrub around the house out of place. Behind it, the stable was equally whole, while on the slope beyond— She sat forward, pointed.

"Is that..." She looked at Jake.

He smiled. "Miss Lizzy and *Diablo*? Firelight and her filly? All the mares and their foals?" He nodded, and slipped an arm around her back to hug her as she returned her teary gaze to the horses cavorting on the slope, chestnuts and bays, palominos, and greys—shades of brown, red, silver and gold—racing across the grassy hillside like fall leaves chased by the wind. "Your first crop, Mrs. Douglas, in full bloom."

They were beautiful. The entire pastoral scene was beautiful. Surreal. And ever more precious after today, witnessing the bleakness of what was left of Eleanor's home, remembering how her mother-in-law's shame-faced confession had prompted her to leave it all behind.

She felt with her right hand for the silver band on her left, firm beneath the mobile material of her gloves, throat tightening with the memory of leaving it on her vanity with the note asking Jake not to look for her.

If only I'd known then, what I know now.

"Do you remember the day I brought you here, to this house, for the first time?" he murmured.

She smiled, no longer surprised by his ability to sense her thoughts.

They'd been back in Texas less than a day. The children had barely two hours to get acquainted with their new grandmother and Aunt Maggie, and Jake was insisting she sneak out and accompany him on a horseback ride. She hadn't known exactly why, though she suspected he wanted to show her the stable. She'd never dreamed he'd had a new house built, too.

"I was so surprised by the electric lights."

"You kept murmuring, 'Oh, Jake. Oh, Jake'."

"Until you took me outside to the stable and I started bawling like a baby when I saw the horses, and then Dirk and Mrs. Brown. And just when I finally got myself under control, you made me cry again—" She gasped, and straightening, clutched at her throat. "My locket."

"Right here." Jake leaned away and stretched out a leg to reach in his trouser pocket. "One of the vaqueros found it dangling in the branches of a tree not too far from where you were... found." He swallowed. "I had the necklace repaired." He held it up, and when she tipped her head, he slipped the gold chain and locket around her neck, secured the clasp.

She grasped the locket, exhaled in relief when she opened it to find her sisters' images safe within. "Thank you," she whispered and met his gaze. "That's the second time you've given it back to me."

"It's the second time you've come back to me," he murmured.

Tears welled as he slid an arm around her and hauled her close to him, so they sat hip to hip.

Second and last time, for she was never leaving him, or here, again.

"Please tell me I'm not dreaming," she said watching *Diablo* and a cream-coloured foal rearing and kicking at each other as they played.

"No, *Querida*," he said. "You're not dreaming. We're home."

She swallowed, chest aching, because words that should have brought comfort, instead brought pain.

Home was where the heart was. But her heart wasn't here. At least not all of it. Part of it was treading the ravaged trail left by the tornado, searching for her son.

Chapter 6

Into The Darkness

*M*ama!"

Katie was the first out the door, brown braids flying as she charged down the porch steps into Dianna's arms. Dianna clutched her close, eyes hot with tears as she inhaled the sweet scent that was her daughter, chamomile, and aloe soap, overlaid with sugar and spice.

"You've been baking," she said as she drew back, gently brushed a smudge of flour from Katie's cheek, pausing to behold the promise of a beautiful woman in the facial bones under the unblemished skin of the child.

"Cinnamon buns," Katie said.

"Ooh, my favourites," Dianna said.

"I know. Mrs. Brown told me. She said Aunt Elaina's favourite is lemon cake, so we're making that, too."

"That's lovely." Dianna started to look up, expecting Amelia to come out to greet her, and then looked back at Katie. "Making that... too?" The question was barely out of her mouth, when she heard the screened door bang.

"Hello, Dianna. You're not hallucinating," Elaina added as she stepped gracefully off the porch. "It's me." She stopped a few feet away, smiled tentatively, no doubt put off by Dianna's incredulous stare.

Two years had changed Elaina considerably. Gone was the pudginess that had dogged her all her young life, and in its place voluptuous curves, graceful swells and valleys Dianna knew must turn many men's heads, and as many women green with envy. Her pale skin, however, was unchanged. The same dewy white velvet tinged pink over strong cheekbones once hidden under a plump layer of fat, but that now rose sharply from an oval chin to offset large grey eyes rimmed with long lashes the same dark gold as her hair that swung in a graceful bob along the firm set of her jaw. She wore a simple dress of white linen hemmed above her slim white-stocking-covered ankles, and cream-coloured low-heeled shoes. She looked like Eleanor. Could be her daughter in fact—*No.*

Not Eleanor.

Jake.

She looked like Jake.

"Dianna?" Elaina advanced, face pinched with concern, slender hand outstretched. Dianna stepped back, stopped when she slammed into a hard body.

"Are you, all right?" Jake murmured.

Charlie whined and nudged Dianna's fisted hand with her cold nose. Forcing her fingers to unfurl, Dianna ruffled the dog's soft ears, willed her heart to slow.

She needed to get herself under control. Just because she saw the similarities, did not mean anyone else would. Except, perhaps Eleanor.

"Dianna?"

"Yes. I'm fine." She flashed Jake a smile. "A little shocked to see my sister." *Your sister.*

When he held her gaze, she drew on her many years' experience of similar stare downs with the earl, to maintain a noncommittal expression.

"I'm sorry to surprise you like this," Elaina said. "But when I received the letter from Mrs. Brown, I had to come. I had to—"

"Oh, Lainey." Dianna turned to her. "I'm sorry for behaving so silly. I... wasn't expecting you. But I am so terribly happy you're here," she added when doubt flashed in Elaina's eyes. "Come here." The instant Elaina's arms went around her, a rush of homesickness welled so strong it cut off her breath. "Oh, Lainey," she squeaked. "I've missed you, so."

"I've missed you too," Elaina mumbled. "It's been hell back home without you."

With her eyes closed, Dianna could almost smell their childhood mingled with the musky scent of Elaina's perfume, the pungent earth and wood of the forest where they rode their horses after it rained, the waxy odour of burning candles in the hallway that led to their bedchambers, the sickly-sweet fog of their father's cigars permeating the lower floors, heady floral scent of their mother's rose garden in spring.

She ached with longing to go home again, to snuggle in her bed with her sisters and talk about nothing. And everything. Braid each other's hair, or get in a rousing pillow fight. It didn't matter. Just so long as she did not have to have all the answers, or be the one the others turned to. She wanted to be a girl again, free of responsibilities and painful realities. She wanted someone to hold her, and kiss her hurts, make them better. She wanted her mama.

She sagged under the weight of her need, and clung to Elaina, sobbing.

Two years she'd kept thoughts of her mother and sisters reserved, tucked away and brought out only for special occasions, like Christmas and her birthday, and only for the fondest of memories that didn't risk releasing the anguish she felt separated from them not only by geography, but disapproval. She still felt the sting of her parents' rejection, and though Jake's love had done much to heal the hurt, it couldn't close the wound completely, erase the emotional scar she knew she would carry for life.

"Dianna?" Jake touched her shoulder.

She turned toward him, unable to find strength, or want to stop her tears.

"Come," he murmured as he scooped her up, and with apologies to Elaina, carried her inside the house.

"Mama?" Amelia's voice was soft, stricken, as Jake stepped inside the foyer.

"She's fine, Mia," he said. "Just needs sleep. You'll see her in a while."

Mrs. Brown and Eleanor's startled exclamations were quickly followed by questions, and offers of assistance that Jake declined, as he turned up the stairs. Dianna pressed her nose to his neck, embarrassed, yet grateful for an excuse not to face everyone just now.

When Jake lowered her to their bed, she curled in a ball, and grasping a pillow, hugged it tight. Jake smoothed her hair from her cheek with his fingertips.

"I'm sorry," she croaked. "I don't know what got into me."

"Shh," he soothed. "You've had too many shocks to deal with recently. You need rest, and I intend to see that you get it. Sleep now. I'll bring you something to eat, later. For now, I'll make your excuses, and ensure no one bothers you."

She looked at him. "Did you know? Did you know she was here?"

"No. I didn't." He lifted her hand to his mouth to kiss her knuckles, and then smiled tenderly. "But I'm glad just the same."

∞ ∞ ∞

She awoke with a start, disoriented in the darkness. It took a few seconds for the mist of sleep to clear before she relaxed, recognising the warm body, and muffled snores next to her.

She was home, in her bed. With her husband. Her heart pulsed painfully.

He'd not questioned her reaction, but accepted the shock of seeing Elaina combined with exhaustion and mental fatigue enough to undo her. Which it had.

Did Eleanor see it? Even if she did, she'd never admit it. She probably regretted ever having told Dianna.

Jake changed position, and Dianna froze as he slid an arm over her waist, insinuated one of his solid hairy knees between her legs. With a contented sigh, he resumed snoring. She gave silent thanks he'd not awakened. She had no desire to talk. She needed to think. Think about where McGuire, if he was alive and had JJ, would go?

She wriggled, not enough to wake Jake, but enough to cause him to snuffle and roll to his other side, his back to her. She waited many long minutes until she heard his breathing deepen and snoring resume, and then slipped from the bed.

She still wore her day dress. Her half-boots were where Jake had left them on the floor next to her side of the bed. She retrieved them and tiptoed to her wardrobe, held her breath as she reached inside the cupboard and felt around in the dark for what she needed.

The additional clothing clutched to her bosom along with the half-boots, she eased the bedchamber door open and slipped out. Drawing the door closed with a barely audible click, she crept past the girls' room and down the stairs, waiting until she was in the kitchen to exhale, relieved she'd not elicited a questioning bark from Charlie.

Changing in to her trousers, shirtwaist, and pullover sweater, she left her folded dress atop the butcher's block and grasped a pencil and notepaper from the table by the door. Hunched in the moonlight filtering through the window above the kitchen sink, she scribbled a note. Leaving it with her dress she collected a few items from the larder and headed outside, paused in the shadows in front of the stable.

How was she to select a mount and saddle it without disturbing every horse in the barn? The salutatory nickers, and whinnies would wake Dirk. A snort to her right nearly stopped her heart.

She edged toward the round pen where green horses were worked, peered through the rails. The ghostly outline of a pale horse glimmered in the moonlight, shimmering brightest off the flaxen mane and tail. *Spitfire*. Firelight's two-year-old colt. Still in training, but a sensible and calm horse. Best of all, he was saddled. She offered silent thanks to Dirk.

He often left a saddle on a green horse for days, checking periodically to ensure the rigging wasn't chafing or pinching, but not removing the saddle until the youngster no longer raced around the pen, rolled, rubbed against a post, or engaged in other fretful behaviour designed to dislodge the unusual apparatus.

"Horses are prey animals," he'd told her once. "They don't like things on their backs. That's where a predator jumps ye see, an' horses can't fight what's on their backs. Add a tight girth around their middles an' ye got a good fight on yer hands. That's why ya leave it on until they grow accustomed to it, realise it's not hurting a wee bit. Once they get to that understandin', they're no afraid o' the saddle again."

From the looks of it, Spitfire was well used to his saddle. He stood centre of the corral, head down, one hind leg cocked, thoroughly relaxed.

Dianna clucked her tongue as she entered the corral. Spitfire's head came up. She whistled softly, and he trotted up. She made a mental note to give Dirk a raise when she got back.

"Good boy," she whispered, and rubbed his silky neck.

One large brown eye regarded her with equanimity. She glanced around.

No matter how far along he'd come in his training, Spitfire wasn't ready to be ridden without a bridle, or some form of head restraint. To her relief, she spotted a halter and lead rope tossed over a post.

She retrieved them, secured the halter on Spitfire, and looped the rope around his neck, knotting it to the halter's underside, grateful Dirk started all the young horses in a hackamore. The halter and lead would have a similar effect, allowing her to guide the colt's head, and apply pressure to his nose when she wanted him to stop.

Hopefully.

Pushing thoughts of what could go wrong from her mind, she strapped a saddlebag to the back of the saddle, dispersed the contents of the flour sack into it, and opened the corral gate.

She led the colt well out of earshot of the stable and house, and once on level ground where the grass was short and there were no trees, or other obstacles to crash into, she crouched to untie the thin leather strip securing the saddle's stirrups flat against the colt's sides, so they didn't bang or flap. Spitfire's warm underside flinched and quivered, but he otherwise stood motionless, while she released the stirrups, and tucked the leather strip in the saddlebag.

"All right now, boy," she murmured and gave the saddle a wiggle to ensure it fit snugly. "I don't know if anyone's been up on you yet, but tonight I will be, so let's get along, shall we?"

She grabbed the lead rope and a fistful of mane in one hand, inserted her left toe in the near stirrup and in one quick move, hauled herself up and right leg over the colt's back. Spitfire snorted, and sidestepped, but she was prepared.

As the colt pranced, she kept his head turned to her toe, let him turn circles until he grew tired, and stopped. Releasing his head, she rewarded him with a soft murmur of encouragement, and stroke along his neck. The colt relaxed under her.

"What a lovely fine lad you are," she remarked, and pointing him uphill in the direction of Eleanor's former home, she squeezed her calves to his sides.

Spitfire moved out smartly, one ear pricked forward, the other back, listening to her soft commentary as she told him all the wonderful places they would go, and what a perfect gentleman he was.

The optimism and praise seemed to have a positive effect: Spitfire walked sedately to the top of the hill and halted on cue.

She looked back at the house, a large multi-peaked shape, its white siding and porch columns dimly illuminated by moonlight, tall windows glinting with a similar ivory glimmer, like dark eyes following her every move. She shivered, and drawing a breath, rode into the darkness.

∞ ∞ ∞

She knew he was there before his shadow fell over her. She wasn't surprised he had found her, only that it had taken him this long.

"Are they terribly worried?" she asked softly.

"Enough." His tone was harsh.

She sighed, pressed more firmly against the tree trunk at her back, and picked the red bloom growing by her knee. "I left a note."

He grunted.

"I thought you would catch up to me yesterday."

"I would have, but I had to find Amelia first."

"Amelia?" She looked up.

His brown eyes glinted, and not with humour. "She went out after you. Alone."

"What? Me?" She dropped the flower, clambered to her feet. "Good heavens, why? She could have gotten lost."

He grabbed her wrist.

"What are you doing? Let go." She tried to pull free, but his hand was an iron manacle as he dragged her down the hill. "Damn it, Jake, let go." She dug her heels in the grassy slope, but may as well have tried to hold back a coal-fired locomotive. She'd never seen him this angry and her terror grew as he dragged her inexorably toward lower ground, away from the small cemetery at the crest of the hillock and the massive oak tree that stood guard.

She had started out at the remains of Eleanor's house, riding slowly in the dawning light of morning as she scanned the earth for any clue that might lead her to JJ or McGuire. But it proved an impossible task. The earth was pockmarked with tracks, hundreds of hoof prints, equine and bovine. There was no way for her to identify those belonging to Queenie. Still she rode for what remained of the day searching scrubs and washes, peering under shrubbery and into high branches of trees until her eyes watered. She even dismounted to inspect gopher holes, all in the vain hope she would find some small sign her son had been there, or was near. She found nothing, unless one counted a hawk's nest and the bleached skeleton of a calf.

That had given her a fright, the knobby end of a grey bone sticking from the tangled roots of a fallen tree. She pulled it out and dug around, her alarm escalating with each small bone she clawed up. Then she uncovered a skull. A calf skull. But for those few horrendous moments...

Spending the previous night out under the stars wrapped in a single blanket with only Spitfire for protection and company against the coyotes that howled mournful cries had been easy in comparison to the potential horror of finding her son's remains.

She awakened that morning exhausted and achy, but convinced she had survived the worst of her fears. Now, however, the rage emanating from Jake sent icy spikes through her, kindling a dread she'd not felt since leaving England—and the chilling rages her stepfather had flown into when his word or authority was disobeyed—behind. For the first time since she married him, she feared her husband.

"Please, Jake, I'm sorry—"

Halting, he whipped around to face her without relieving his hold on her wrist. "Do you have any idea the trauma you've caused? Do you?"

She nodded weakly.

"Do you really?" He glared. "Do you know what it did to the girls to wake up and find you gone? Or to me to realise you'd run away, *again*?" He lowered his face within inches of hers. "Do you?"

She looked away, hurt, and frightened by the unbridled fury in his eyes. "I didn't run away."

"I've put up with a lot from you," he continued as though she hadn't spoken. "But I'll be damned if I'll accept you terrorising the girls like this."

"Terrorizing?" She scowled. "I told you in the note what I was doing. Where I—"

"You disappeared in the middle of the night."

"Because I knew you'd try and stop me."

"You're damn right I would have stopped you." His nostrils flared. "Did you know it was Katie who found your note? She got up early, to make *your* tea. She wanted to surprise you. I spent an hour with her trying to calm her and convince her you'd be fine. By that time Amelia had run off, and that set Katie on another tangent. It damn near killed me to leave her with my mother and Mrs. Brown—and your sister—crying her heart out—"

"I never meant to scare her," she insisted. "That's why I left the note. Saying where I'd gone and why—"

"You think that makes it okay?" He stared. "First her own mother, then her sister. Why should she believe something terrible wouldn't happened to you?"

She frowned, shook her head. "Her mother and Charlotte died. I didn't die. I went—"

"No, she didn't."

Dianna blinked. "Who didn't, what?"

"Katie and Amelia's mother. She didn't die."

"Yes, she did. Mother Mary told me. Katie and Amelia's mother died in childbirth."

"That's what you were told," he said. "That's not what happened."

She scowled. "What in heaven are you talking about? Mother Mary wouldn't lie—"

"Katie told me." He inhaled. "She cried, and cried, and asked me how come her mamas always leave her behind? I tried to console her. Explained her mama hadn't chosen to leave, she'd died, and if she could, she would still be there to love her. I promised her you'd be back. But she refused to believe it. She told me that her mama wasn't dead. She'd run off with another man and wasn't ever coming back, and her father had made her tell everyone her mother died, because he didn't want anyone knowing his wife had run off and left him."

"What?" Dianna frowned. "That can't be. Katie must be mistaken. What kind of woman would run off and leave her children behind, especially with that monster?"

Jake raised an eyebrow. "Maybe you could tell me?"

She jerked as if he had punched her. "You're not a monster," she rasped. "And I did *not* run off. I told you exactly what I was doing."

He shook his head. "You never should have left."

"I had to." She glared. "I needed to. I needed to look for my son."

"I already searched," he said. "For weeks. Every day for weeks from sun up to sun down. What makes you think you could find him, when I couldn't?"

"I don't know," she cried. "But I had to try. He's my son. I had to look for him."

"He's my son, too—"

"No." She shook her head, anger, humiliation, and grief colliding in a frenzy of irrational fury. "He's *mine*. It was my body he grew in. *Mine*. I laboured to deliver him. I nursed him and changed him, and sang him to sleep. You... You didn't even see him until he was six months old!" If there was any way to take back the words, she would have, the instant they left her mouth.

Jake's face crumpled and the anger blazing in his dark eyes died as his shoulders slumped. He seemed to age before her eyes, the laugh lines around his eyes deepening to creases, grief dragging the corners of his wide mouth.

"So that's how it is," he murmured.

"No." She swallowed. "I'm sorry, Jake. I didn't mean it. He is your son. And I know you love him as much as I—"

"Don't touch me." He flinched away when she reached for him.

She twined her hands together. "I'm sorry, Jake. I am. I was... mad. And that's no excuse. I know. But you must believe me, I didn't mean it. Truly. Please, please forgive me. Please Jake," she whispered. "Please believe me, I didn't mean it."

He stared at the ground, his jaw muscles bunching, hands flexing, and closing in fists. Her lungs ached with the effort of holding her breath, praying he would forgive her, understand it was anguish that drove her to unkind words. *Unimaginably cruel words.*

Unimaginable anguish.

With a strong inhalation he jerked his jaw up, angled his head side to side, stretching corded neck muscles. Finally, after a slow exhalation, he murmured, "Why here?"

She followed his gaze.

The oak tree's green leaves flashed umber and gold in the glow of the midday sun. Only the tips of the crosses and headstones were visible beneath its leafy canopy.

She closed her eyes, recalling the names engraved on the stone markers: *Connemara Rosita Vásquez Douglas. Jonathon Andrew Douglas. Jackson 'Three Bears' Douglas.* Jake's first wife and son lost in childbirth, and his stepfather, victim of a cow's maternal ire.

"I... wanted to talk to her," she rasped. "To Connie."

He looked at her, frowned. She dropped her gaze to her hands she had locked together, heels of her palms pressed so tightly, her elbows ached.

"I... " She swallowed. "I asked her to look after JJ for me." And with the words, the last of her anger dissipated, sucked away in a windstorm of grief.

Her knees buckled. Jake caught her, and she went willingly to his arms, sobbing, so deep in misery she did not at first register his words.

Then the low rumbles in his chest formed a coherent sentence in the air.

"What?" She wiped at her eyes, tilted to stare at him.

"I said," he said hoarsely, his eyes red-rimmed and damp. "It might be too early to ask that of Connie."

"What? Why?" She clutched at his shirt. "What do you know? What do you know, Jake?"

Enclosing her hands in his, he shook his head.

"Not me," he rasped. "Your sister. Elaina. She thinks... She thinks JJ might be in England."

Chapter 7

I'll Be Waiting

Elaina's smile was taut, her porcelain cheeks pink. "I did plan to tell you right away," she said. "But you never gave me the chance. I told your husband."

"I know." Dianna nodded reluctantly. "I... shouldn't have left without..." She exhaled. She'd already apologised, profusely, to everyone, beginning with Katie and Amelia and ending with Elaina. Now she wished only to get to the heart of her sister's incredible assertion. "Please, Lainey. Jake's only told me that you think JJ might be in England, but not how you've come by that belief. Tell me. Tell me why you think that?"

They were all in the parlour, Dianna and Jake on one settee, Mrs. Brown and Eleanor each in a wing chair, Maggie and Mr. Sweeney ensconced on the second settee across from Dianna and Jake. Elaina perched on the edge of a Queen Anne chair beside Dianna. Katie and Amelia weren't home.

After accepting her tearful apology, they'd reluctantly agreed to accompany Rosa and Juan, and Charlie, on a trip to town for lunch and to collect the mail. Jake had given each girl money to choose treats and a book at the General Store, before their return home, a spontaneous adventure ostensibly to keep the girls busy, but Dianna suspected was intended more to shield them from hearing the collective and individual opinion of the adults who remained to share their thoughts on her egregious behaviour.

The only adult who'd not weighed in was Elaina's lady's maid, Ms. Willow, who'd retreated upstairs to the guestroom she was sharing with Elaina.

A tremor shook Lainey's hand as she lifted her teacup to her mouth for a cautious sip. Replacing the cup to its saucer, she set both on the low sofa table, and cleared her throat. "I'm not positive, you realise," she said. "And if I am wrong, Papa will never forgive me, and... I hate to get your hopes up, in case I am wrong—"

"Oh, for pity's sake, Elaina," Dianna said. "Spit it out."

Elaina blinked. Jake squeezed Dianna's knee in silent rebuke.

"I'm sorry, Elaina," she said. "Please, go on. What has Papa to do with any of this?"

Elaina glanced at Jake, question in her eyes. He nodded, cleared his throat.

"Miss Elaina told me she thinks the child her father returned home with from Italy, isn't her brother, Lord William," he said. "That he might..."

Dianna dug her fingernails into her palms.

"She thinks the boy could be JJ," Jake finished.

There was a collective gasp. Dianna stared at Mrs. Brown and Maggie. Their faces mirrored her shock. She turned to her sister.

"What, on earth, is he saying?"

Elaina's clasped hands twitched, her flush deepened. "This is why I didn't want to tell you. In case I'm wrong, but... he's different. Lord William. He's not the same little boy I remember before he went away."

"Not the same little boy, how exactly?" Dianna forced the words out with careful precision to keep from shouting. "And how might that lead you to think he's JJ?"

Elaina's gaze skittered from face to face, before settling on Dianna's. "I didn't. Not at first. You see when Papa and Lord William arrived home, I'd not received the letter from Mrs. Brown telling of the tornado, and how you were barely alive, and your son missing and presumed dead. So, I didn't have any suspicions. I was simply amazed by how big little William had grown. He'd always been so small, smaller than most lads his age, and though I expected he'd grow a bit in six months, I just wasn't prepared for how much." She lapsed to silence, a tentative smile on her face.

"And?" Dianna prompted.

A crease formed between Elaina's eyebrows. "I was happy to have him home, and therefore willing to overlook a few things. He looked very similar, what with dark hair and a little snub nose, if much chunkier and quite tanned. But Papa said he had gained weight and darkened up from Italian food and sun, and I had no reason not to believe him."

"Of course," Dianna said. "But something troubled you."

"Yes. The birthmark little William had. I noticed it was gone. And then there's his behaviour."

"Behaviour?" The question came from Mrs. Brown, whose normally ruddy complexion had paled considerably.

"Yes." Elaina shifted to face her. "William was always such a quiet, gentle child. But the little boy Papa returned home with is a regular hellion. He pitches nasty tantrums when he doesn't get his way. Mama says it's because he's healthier now and has energy to spare. She's so grateful to have her little lord home, she's scarcely questioned the changes in him."

Dianna swallowed.

If what Elaina was saying was true, how was it Mama didn't realise the child her husband brought home wasn't her son? And if he wasn't, could he be JJ? A wave of dizziness alerted her to the fact she was breathing too fast, beginning to hyperventilate. Firm, but gentle pressure on her knee from Jake's hand, warned her to settle. Exhaling slowly, she looked at Elaina.

"What colour are his eyes?"

Lainey frowned. "Eyes?"

"Yes." Dianna widened hers. "Blue like mine and Papa's, or green, like Mama's—"

"Green. But not the emerald colour of Mama's or Mrs. Stewart's," Elaina added with a nod to Maggie. "Lighter, like new grass."

Jake grasped Dianna's hand. She gripped his strong fingers, seeking stability in his callused strength as she fought the icy storm of disbelief funnelling through her.

"He throws tantrums?" she murmured.

"Oh, yes, terrible fits of temper." Elaina nodded. "Shouts, yanks hair if he can get a fistful. That's how I discovered the birthmark was missing. He wanted to go outside to the stable, and ride the pony Papa bought him, but it was raining. I said he couldn't. He started to scream. So, finally I agreed to take him down to give his pony an apple, but when I told him it was time to return to the house, he threw another fit. I picked him up, but just outside the stable, he bit my arm. I was so startled I dropped him, right in a puddle." She rubbed a spot above her elbow, as if feeling the pain of that bite. "He was filthy," she went on, "and I didn't want anyone to know what had happened. Papa had forbidden anyone to take Lord William out in poor weather afraid he'd fall ill again, so I sneaked him up the back stairs to my bedchamber and bathed him myself. That's when I noticed there was no birthmark. There used to be one, about the size of a pea, and colour of a raspberry, above his heart." Her face turned scarlet, and she quickly dropped the hand she had raised by illustration, twining it with its mate, on her lap. She cleared her throat. "I only know about the birthmark, because shortly after William's birth, I overheard his first nurse commenting to our new housekeeper about it, how it was the sign of a bloody death. I was concerned enough to sneak into his nursery and look for myself. But when I asked Mama about it, she said to pay no mind to ignorant superstition, though by the end of the week, she had replaced that nurse with William's current one, a nice girl, not prone to silly notions and blather."

Elaina's smile was more of a wince and her cheeks bright, whether with residual shame over inadvertently drawing attention to her bosom, discomfiture at having revealed information of a personal nature to an audience of veritable strangers, or guilty awareness that sharing her concern with Mama had instigated the original nurse's dismissal, Dianna couldn't tell. Didn't care.

She pivoted to face Jake. "We must go. Right now, to England."

Jake held her gaze without expression.

She pressed his hand between hers. "We must. Don't you see? It could be JJ. Green eyes. Tantrums—oh, Jake, what if it's him? And if it is—" She looked at Elaina. "If it is him, how on earth would he get all the way to England?" She straightened. "Good heaven. There's only one way..."

"Papa," Elaina whispered, her face bleak.

"And McGuire," Dianna added.

"Oh, I can't believe that," Mrs. Brown protested. "Sure 'e's a sly devil is our Lord Ansmall, but certainly he'd not sink so low as to kidnap his own grandson, try to pass 'im off as his own? Why would he?"

Yes, why would he? Dianna stared at the gold-rimmed china tea set on the table in front of her without really seeing it. "There is only one reason he would," she murmured.

"Our brother must have died." Elaina's grey eyes shimmered silver under a veil of tears.

Dianna reached for her hand, gripped it firmly.

"But why?" Jake said. "I mean, I know the man has no like for me. The feeling's mutual. But to take JJ... why?"

"An heir," Dianna said.

Elaina nodded.

"An heir?" Jake looked more confused, than shocked.

Eleanor folded her lips under. Mrs. Brown shook her head, her dark-eyed gaze stern.

Dianna met Jake's bemused stare. "Remember what I told you about the duke," she said. "How without an heir, his title goes into abeyance, and all falls to wrack and ruin? How pride is worth more than blood?"

"So?" Jake demanded.

"So, the earl is a proud man—"

"Proud enough to kidnap his grandson, to save a... title?" Disbelief coloured Jake's glower.

"Not just a title," Dianna said. "The entails. The land, the power... it all goes away, without a son to keep it up."

"Our son?" He turned his glare on Elaina. "If he took JJ, why would he let you come here and tell us?"

"Yes," Dianna said, facing her sister, relieved Jake had found a weakness in Elaina's supposition. "Papa would never let you come, knowing what you know. If it's true."

"He doesn't know," Elaina murmured shaking her head. "I shared my suspicions with no one, especially him. In fact, if not for Mrs. Brown's letter, I would have dismissed my concerns, and carried on like everyone else, idolising the little Lord. But then I learned you might die, and your son was missing. I knew I had to come, not just because of the changes in William, but because I couldn't bear the thought I might never see you again." Her voice caught, eyes filled with tears. She swallowed, exhaled. "It took me weeks to convince him. In the end, I had... I promised him, if he arranged my travel here, and let me stay for as long as you welcomed me, but no longer than one year, when I returned, I'd..." She cleared her throat. "I told him I'd marry whomever he chooses for me."

"What?" Dianna stared. "Whomever? Whomever he chooses? But what if he chooses someone you don't care for, like he did me? Elaina you can't agree to that—"

"I already have, Dianna. It's done." Elaina's fingers were cold, trembling, but her expression unyielding, echoes of her father in the stern set of her chin and mouth.

"Oh, Lainey." Dianna shook her head. "You shouldn't have."

"I did what I had to, so I could come." Her tone was matter-of-fact, without apology or grievance.

Dianna's heart cracked, knowing what her sister had sacrificed to gain permission to come and see her. Closing her eyes on a rush of tears and guilt, she forced her mind to focus on Lainey's' other critical revelation.

Was it possible? Possible her brother had died, and the earl had... She suppressed a shiver as cold from Lainey's fingers seeped into her.

He'd arranged her marriage to the Duke of Blackburn without regard for her wishes, to please Mama. He'd followed her to America, and would have dragged her home and to the altar to wed the duke, had Jake not intervened. Now he'd co-opted Lainey into an agreement Dianna could only pray her sister would not come to regret. But would he be so cruel as to sacrifice Dianna's heart yet again, with another clandestine arrangement designed to keep Mama happy, spare the countess the heartbreak of losing another child, and himself an heir?

"Yes, he would," she murmured and releasing Elaina's hand, looked to the others in the room. "He would do anything to save his name and reputation and protect Mama. They're the only things that matter to him."

"Ooch, ye can't be serious." Mrs. Brown scrambled to her feet, jowls flushed. "I worked for the man over twenty years, an' I know he's a fearsome temper, and thinks of 'imself most often, but... To steal 'is own grandchild? Yer mad to even think it." She looked around the room as if seeking an ally. She didn't find one.

Maggie's freckled face glowed with rage. Mr. Sweeney sat uncomfortably next to her, his attention on the black Stetson nestled on his lap like a big house cat as he smoothed a callused finger round and round the hat's crown. Eleanor, who'd not said a word since entering the parlour, stared at Jake, her face as white as the bone china cup in her hands, brown eyes huge. Even Elaina, ever the family defender, avoided Mrs. Brown's expectant gaze as she fiddled with a loose thread on her skirt. Only Jake had the courage to face the outraged housekeeper.

"Your concerns are valid, Mrs. Brown," he said, "but there's only one way to know for sure if Miss Elaina's suspicions are founded."

Mrs. Brown's eyes narrowed suspiciously. "Aye, an' what's that?"

Jake looked at Dianna. "I'll have to go to England."

No one moved or spoke. The glint in Jake's eye warned Dianna not to contradict his decision.

She nodded. "We'll both go."

His eyes narrowed. The moisture in her mouth evaporated. She thought about taking a sip of tea but dared not look away from him. To do so, would be to concede her will.

"I agree, Dianna," Maggie said. "Better if Jake goes. You're still recovering, and the girls can't be without you again. Jake can identify JJ as well as anyone else in this room."

Dianna opened her mouth to tell Maggie to mind her business, and closed it without uttering a word.

Jake can identify JJ as well as anyone else in this room.

Whether Maggie intended it or not, she'd struck a very sensitive nerve. Dianna gritted her teeth.

Jake was testing her. Wanted to see if she would argue, question his competence by insisting on accompanying him, or if she would trust him to go alone and identify the child, and if he was JJ, return him home safely.

But that would take weeks, almost a fortnight to Britain, and then however long it took to gain access to the child. She could not imagine Papa would allow Jake anywhere near him if he was JJ. And if he was, once Jake got him back, they still had to make the return trip.

She clenched her fists, pressed them on her upper thighs.

A month minimum. More likely six weeks forced to await word on whether to celebrate, or start the grieving process all over again. She stared at her bunched hands, so pale she could see the bones of her knuckles below the skin.

"You—you'll write me, the minute you know anything?" she whispered.

Jake's larger darker hand slid over hers and squeezed gently. "I'll write as soon as I know anything. I promise."

She closed her eyes. "I'll be waiting," she rasped.

Chapter 8

Direct Approach

*I*dling the Model-T he had hired from the innkeeper in Hereford in the shadowed archway of massive oaks that overhung the gravel drive, Jake studied the manor's stone façade, partially hidden by an ivy-covered trellis.

It was impressive. A massive structure of light-coloured stone easily ten times wider and double the height of the white-painted wood house he had had built for Dianna. The entirety of their two-level home in Texas could tuck neatly in one corner of the behemoth she'd grown up in. The same one her stepfather had grown up in, and his father and grandfather, and great-grandfather, and so on.

Did she miss it? This beast of a home and the history, and lifestyle that went with it? The lifestyle she could be living right now?

She shared so little about her childhood with him, and what she did share never failed to stir the pot of resentment towards Marshall he usually kept cold on a back burner—which was likely why she parcelled out titbits only as necessary to explain her reaction to things. About her former home, and the one she'd inherited, she said even less.

"Ansmall is big, damp, and draughty," she'd told him. "Nothing like this beautiful, warm, love-filled home you made for me. Holderness, I imagine, is much the same as Ansmall, cold and lonely."

Cold and lonely, maybe, Ansmall Hall was definitely big. Huge. All that cornicing, and dozens of windows and chimneys to clean and repair, an acre or more of roof... Of course, Marshall didn't get his hands dirty. He had a brigade of servants for that.

"Papa is the seventh earl," Dianna had explained before he left. "His twin brother was stillborn, and his three younger sisters died of pox, before they were of age to marry. Papa was fortunate to be away at school when illness swept through Ansmall and so was spared. But his father, who'd also taken ill but survived, never sired another child. Papa's uncle died without issue, making Papa the last of his line, which is why Mama risked her health so many times to finally provide him a successor.

"Little William, if it's him," she added gravely, "will be the eighth earl, charged with ensuring the viability of the title. If it's not him, if Elaina is right and there is no heir, the title dies with Papa. He won't let that happen. So, even if you know without a doubt the boy you find there is our son, Papa will not let you take him. You must understand this. You can't walk in and demand to see William, or accuse the earl of taking JJ. The only reason you and the sheriff were able to scare him off when he came here for me was because he has no legal jurisdiction in America. Just as you will have none when you get there. Papa is, literally, one of the lawmakers in Britain. More importantly for you to know, he does not like to lose. When he does, he seeks retribution. Which means, the moment you step off the ship on to English soil, he will own you, if he chooses to. So, please—" She cupped his face, her expression no longer cautionary, but pleading.

"Please, Jake, tread carefully. Do not give a hint of your true intent. And if you are able to confirm the child as JJ, you can't just pick him up and carry him out. Every servant there is charged with protecting the heir. If you manage to get him away from his nurse without her knowing—which will be extremely difficult—there'll be dozens more servants willing to die before they'll let you leave with the earl's son, because they know what will happen to them should they lose the heir on their watch. The earl will see them imprisoned for negligence, if not hanged. In fact, if it is him, and you know you can't get him safely away without being caught, send for me. I'll have better luck as the earl's daughter, or as Marchioness Holderness, in provoking an inquiry, if not JJ's immediate return."

Stifling a rise of guilt, he tracked his gaze to the far-right window, one of over twenty he'd counted on this side of the manor. Dianna had given him a verbal blue-print of the manor's layout:

"The nursery is the last room on the right on the first floor—above the ground floor—if you're looking at the manor from the drive. It's furthest from the main stairwell, and closest to the servant's stairs for expediency of hauling up bath water and food, which as you may have noticed children, especially young children, require frequently, if not in great quantity."

If half of Marshall's servants were as efficient and capable as the two he'd fired, and Jake had been fortunate enough to hire, he'd never make it to the nursery. He'd have to make sure the boy was brought to him. How, was another question, and one he hoped he wouldn't need to answer. He preferred to believe Mrs. Brown's assuredness in Marshall's impeachable character—with regard to the kidnapping of his grandson—had foundation, than to know his father-in-law truly was an evil bastard.

Mrs. Brown's loyalty to the man who'd fired her had surprised him. But after further thought, it made more sense than he liked to admit.

She and Dirk didn't work their aged fingers to the metaphorical bone, and look out for the children and Dianna the way they did, for the wages Jake paid them, generous as the money was. And they didn't do it for full Sundays off, either.

Their dedication had nothing to do with pay, or time off, and never had. Their fealty couldn't be bought, because it was priceless, forged with the strongest of all human emotions: love. Not that he could fault them.

He'd crawl naked through a pit of deadly vipers to get to Dianna if she needed him, take a bullet to protect her. The same he would for everyone he loved, though the feeling was most intense for her. Which was why he was here, determined to put aside his acrimony for Marshall long enough to play nice, and get the confirmation he needed, so he could go home and help his wife take those first tortuous steps on the long road to healing.

Swallowing, Jake loosened his death-grip on the steering wheel to ease the pain spiking through his knuckles, as shame rippled through him.

He lacked Mrs. Brown's courage. She had stood up for Dianna by standing up for the man who'd raised her, the sole unifying voice in a room of people prepared to shred the man's character, while he had sat there, silent, unwilling to help validate Mrs. Brown's assertion because he couldn't bring himself to tell Dianna, or any of them, what he knew.

Coward.

The corpse he and Juan had found in *Diablo* three weeks after the tornado, had been ravaged and dismembered by animals and insects, leaving gnawed bones, still partly clothed, scattered around. They'd looked, but not located the skull. Filthy and tattered bits of blood-stained blue fabric clung to some of the ribs. Katie claimed McGuire had been wearing a blue shirt the last time she'd seen him. More definitive was the partially-chewed boot they found with the initials MM carved into the leather inside the boot, about a half-inch down from the top.

Mac McGuire.

Juan had gone for Boone, who'd concluded the body must be that of McGuire. He was the only male in the area unaccounted for.

They scoured the earth around the bones and for a thousand yards in all directions, but found no tiny footprints, no tiny bones. No sign of JJ at all, save the hat found on the upper plateau. Juan and Boone's beleaguered silence as they helped him gather and bury the man's remains had told him what they wouldn't say; what else they had concluded.

In the end, none of them voiced it. They danced around it by agreeing to not share what they'd found, with anyone else.

None of them wanted the women living with the knowledge of McGuire's ultimate end. Even if he had been dead when the animals got to him, it was horrifying knowledge to hold. Better they lived out the rest of their days painting the blanks in the story with joyful memories of a green-eyed boy with plump cheeks and dark hair, who'd met a mercifully swift and painless end... Jake closed his eyes, waited for the tautness in his throat to loosen before opening them again.

That was the only way he could cope, believing JJ had died quickly, and without pain.

Gritting his teeth, he shifted the pedals to set the Model-T in motion.

For Dianna's sake, he'd get through this agonising ~~charade~~ visit with her family. Then he'd go home and help her—help everyone—accept the inevitable. Help them through the grief. Help them move on.

They had to move on.

Halting the auto in front of the manor house, he shut off the engine and swung open the door to step out. Tugging off his gloves, he left them on the seat with his goggles. The quiet thunk of the Model-T's door when he closed it, echoed like a pistol shot. He glanced around.

Manicured lawn. Sculpted hedges and shrubbery. Border gardens full of rich loam bursting with colourful flowers. A three-tiered fountain burbling water to a mat of lily pads in a decent-sized pond. And not a soul in sight.

That was what was bothering him. Besides the impetus behind his being here in the first place. The unnatural stillness and quiet broken only by a tinkle of water and a few song birds.

So accustomed was he to the constant whine of wind over the Texas plains, and the low persistence of cows and calves bawling pierced by the occasional horse whinny and welcome sounds of his wife and children's voices, that hours of train, ship, and coach travel confined with dozens of conversant people, before rattling over a rutted road to reach his destination, hadn't bothered him. But this... hush?

It weighed, exacerbated his reluctance to tread up the stairs and essentially spy on his in-laws. Shaking off his disquiet, he smoothed the lapels of his coat, adjusted his hat, and squared his shoulders.

The best approach was a direct one.

Gravel crunched as he crossed to the front steps, the soles of his leather shoes barely audible on the stone risers. A bronze plaque inset in the lintel above double hand-carved wooden doors looked old. Very old. Its raised image weathered and almost erased by age and decades—centuries—of exposure, though he made out the faint outline of a Knight's helmet and shield. In the centre of the shield was an elaborately scrolled M.

Eight generations.

He rapped on the door. A few minutes later, he knocked again, then noticed the bell ringer and pressed it. After an interminably long time, the curtain covering a window left of the door twitched. Jake stepped back, allowed the viewer to see him.

He had nothing to hide. And in the trench coat, bespoke suit, bowler, and polished shoes he'd acquired on his last trip to London, he looked respectable, if not the gentrified son-in-law of an English lord.

The door creaked open. A tall, sinuous man with a receding hairline kept one hand on the door as he assessed Jake with cool green eyes. "Yes?"

"I'd like to speak with Mr. Marshall."

"His Lordship is unavailable. You may leave your card."

Jake smiled. "No thanks. I'll wait."

The man's pale eyebrows rose fractionally. "There is no waiting sir. Visiting hours are—"

"Tell Ansmall I'm here to see him. And I don't care if he makes me wait an hour, or a week. I'm not leaving."

Three weeks. Damn near three weeks to get to this point after making the decision to go, and he was tired. Damn tired. Too tired to scrape and grovel. Too tired to heed his wife's warning. Too tired to play games. Too tired to be sent away with an if.

He needed to get inside, and get this over with, so he could go home to his wife and look her in the eye, tell her he had done as he'd promised, and verified the child's identity. To do that, he had to rule out the one-percent potential her stepfather had taken their son. If, by some blasphemous miracle, Marshall did have JJ, he'd take him. Scoop him up, and take him home—right after he realigned Marshall's nose. It was the least he could do, considering he'd broken it in the first place.

Jake stuck his foot in the gap before the servant could finish closing the door.

The butler scowled. "Sir, really—"

"Yes. Really." Jake matched the man's imperious stare. "I want to speak to—"

"Who is it, Buckland? Is it my husband?"

The servant—Buckland—narrowed his gaze at Jake, before looking over his shoulder which he had pressed to the door, preventing Jake from seeing the woman who spoke.

"No, ma'am. It's a gentleman—"

"Mr. Jackson Douglas," Jake called out. "Lady Dianna Douglas—Lady Holderness's husband." He had no idea whether her title held sway, but the use of it had a definite effect on the butler.

He staggered back a half-step creating a small opening between his body and the door, through which Lady Ellen Marshall, Countess of Ansmall, squeezed, her face ashen, eyes wide. Jake was more intrigued by the servant's reaction. But as their gazes locked, the butler shuttered his surprise behind a stare as empty and flat as a golf green.

"Dianna?" Lady Ansmall's knuckles whitened as she pulled on the door, forcing Buckland to release his hold or engage in a tug of war with her.

"But Madam," he said.

"It's fine." She opened the door fully, glanced at Jake, before looking past him.

"She's not here, Ma'am," Jake said. "It's just me."

"Oh?" She offered a guarded smile. "How is she?"

95

"Well." He kept his tone neutral. The woman hadn't exhibited a great deal of regard for her daughter's welfare since she'd shipped her away from home. She had no claim to her wellbeing now.

"Why are you here, then?" she asked quietly.

He'd had the better part of almost a month to formulate a reasonable explanation, and was prepared for the anticipated question: "Business," he said.

Ellen Marshall pursed her lips, as though rolling his words in her mouth and deciding whether to swallow, or spit them out. "Business?"

"Yes." He removed his hat, held it in both hands. "We were at sea when news broke that Britain had gone to war. I was on my way to Scotland, to look at Highland cattle to cross with my Longhorns to improve their ability to withstand our harsh winters, but..." He shrugged, and let his hands fall to his sides, retaining his grip on his hat with his left hand. "I decided to make my way here first for a visit, and then head straight home. I booked in to the Poitras Inn in town," he added when she stiffened, to allay any concern she had about his expecting overnight—or longer—hospitality.

She held his gaze, and he sensed some sort of internal struggle, before she stepped back. "Come in, Mr. Douglas. Buckland take his coat."

As the butler, with a faint moue, accepted Jake's overcoat and hat, Ellen Marshall pulled a bell from her pocket and rang it. A spare woman in a black dress overlaid with a white apron appeared almost instantly, as though it was her sole purpose in life to respond to that tinkling sound.

"We have company, Gertrude." Ellen Marshall's tenor was even, authoritative despite a faint tremor of her hand, as she replaced the bell to her pocket. "Tell Cook to prepare Tea."

∞ ∞ ∞

Daylight spilled into the high-ceiling room through numerous windows to sparkle off flower-stuffed crystal vases, and glimmer along the fine dark curves of hand-carved furniture unsettling in its familiarity. The room reminded him of his mother's former parlour, which made sense. She was English, and whether consciously or not, her decorating had reflected her origins.

"Please, Mr. Douglas, do sit down," Ellen Marshall said. "You make me nervous, standing over me that way."

She didn't look nervous. Auburn hair rolled in a wavy chignon and small hands clasped lightly at waist height, the sleeves of her pale-gold gown slipped back to expose tiny wrists and slender freckled forearms, green gaze clear and expression emotionless but for a faint expectant curve of her lips, she looked poised. Petite, but poised. Similar to how his mother looked when confronted with people she was not fond of, but not fond of offending, either. Biting back a smile, he sat.

His mother-in-law eased primly to the opposite settee. "Do you like tea, or would you prefer something stronger?"

He glanced over the feast a pair of servants had laid out: cold ham cuts, roast pork ribs, cakes, cookies, jams, and jellies, amongst other delicacies.

"Tea's fine," he said.

"Milk and sugar?"

"Black."

She nodded and poured out. "Help yourself, Mr. Douglas. It's all very good."

"Thank you, ma'am, but I'm not hungry. Is your husband here?"

"I'm afraid he's not." She offered a practised smile. "He's in London."

"London?" Jake was more disappointed, than surprised. Dianna had said, and Elaina confirmed, that their father spent most of his time in London, coming home on irregular weekends. He'd hoped this would be one of those weekends. "When do you expect him back?"

"Not any time soon, I'm afraid." She arched her eyebrows when he frowned. "The war?"

Jake nodded, oddly relieved to know he'd not have to confront Marshall. "Well, maybe I can meet the rest of the family?"

"Excuse me?"

He smiled, kept his tone matter-of-fact in hopes of assuaging the unease that had sharpened her voice. "Elizabeth, and little William?"

"I don't understand." She curled her fingers into her palms.

He shrugged. "I thought since I'm here, it'd be nice to get to know my wife's family. I brought photographs of our daughters." He tapped a pocket of his suit jacket.

"Uh... This is so unexpected." She fumbled in her pocket. That's when Jake remembered the bell.

"Dianna asked me to make time to visit, ma'am," he said. "She knows little William was sick. And she misses her sister. I promised her I'd bring back word—" A flutter of movement drew his gaze to the window behind Ellen Marshall.

The girl instantly ducked out of sight. He returned his focus to his mother-in-law who seemed not to have noticed his momentary lapse in attention, or conversation. She stood.

"I'm sorry, Mr. Douglas, please forgive me. But this is really not a good time." She shook the bell. Buckland materialised before Jake could rise to his feet. "See Mr. Douglas out," Ellen Marshall said. "Then advise Elizabeth it's time for her piano practise."

"Please ma'am," Jake said hoping to appeal to her maternal instincts— if she had any.

She still hadn't mentioned Dianna, or what she'd suffered, though she must know what had happened given he'd written to tell her, and her other daughter had pledged her future for the right to visit Dianna and comfort her. Quelling a rise of anger, he knew would not endear her to him let alone gain him extended welcome in her home, he willed a congenial smile.

"Call me Jake. And I'd appreciate if we can make time to get to know one another better, so I can bring word back to my wife." *Your daughter.* "We suffered the loss of a child recently, and I think it would help her to heal if I could assure her that her baby brother, and the rest of her family, is well."

"The wellness of another person's child does nothing to ease the loss of one's own, Mr. Douglas," she said harshly. "Nothing."

Her bitterness surprised him. He'd thought her heartless, un-motherly. But the kind of callousness lacing her tone developed from repeated chafing of an emotional wound, numbness developed to protect, like a callus. Perhaps she wasn't heartless, so much as heartbroken.

"Knowing those you love are safe," he murmured, "can make your own suffering easier to bear."

Emotion flickered across her face, external confirmation of a raging internal storm. She inhaled.

"Madam?" Buckland said.

Jake's fingers twitched with an urge to strangle the officious butler.

Ellen Marshall jerked, as though drawn back from the edge of a steep precipice, and exhaling, inclined her head. "Good day, Mr. Douglas," she said. "Buckland will see you out."

"Can I come back tomorrow?"

"Goodbye, Mr. Douglas."

"Jake," he said. "My name's Jake." But she was already departing the room, her steps quick, back stiff as she proceeded up a flight of stairs, while the horse-faced butler ushered him out like a sheriff escorting a criminal to lock up, reinforced by two other male servants. Moments later, Jake stood beside the Model-T at the end of the drive peering past tree trunks and other greenery to glimpse a corner of the house, and part of the lawn.

He'd arrived believing his father-in-law innocent of anything more than being a miserable son-of-a-bitch. Now he believed Miss Elaina might not be wrong. Worse, he suspected his mother-in-law was not an unwitting beneficiary of Edward Marshall's maleficence, but an active participant.

He had to get back inside. But the butler had positioned himself at the front door after seeing Jake out, long arms crossed, dour mask of a face designed to deter all but the blind, while a couple of groundsmen materialised out of the surrounding landscape bearing shovels and hedge shears like guns-at-arms—Jake spun around. Smiled.

"You must be Elizabeth."

She narrowed her eyes. "How do you know my name? And why are you spying on my house?"

"I'm not spying. And I know your name, because I've heard a lot about you. I'm your brother-in-law, Jake Douglas."

"The stinking yank my sister married?"

He swallowed, then gestured toward the manor house. "Aren't you supposed to be practising piano about now?"

"I hate piano," she muttered. "I'd rather learn how to fence or fire a pistol."

"Come to Texas for a visit, I'll show you how to do both." Though he was sure she meant sword play, a day or two of stringing barbed wire would take Miss Uppity down a notch. Or two.

Her scowl deepened. "What makes you think I'd want to visit you?"

He shrugged. She planted a small hand on her hip, or at least on the approximate location of her hip bone. Her brown riding habit fell in a straight line from the sharp points of her shoulders to the ground, echoing the straight slant of her nose that she somehow managed to gaze down as she looked up at him.

"Why are you still here?" she demanded.

"I came to visit. Was hoping to speak to your father."

She dropped the hand, snorted. "Even if he was here, he wouldn't speak to you."

"Why is that, do you suppose?" Jake asked.

"Because he thinks you're a stinking yank."

He rubbed a hand over his mouth. She definitely took after her father.

"Maybe you can help me?"

Her green eyes narrowed further. "Why would I help you?"

He took a breath, reminded himself she was a child, a rude child, but a child just the same. "Actually, it's not me you'd be helping; it's your sister, Dianna."

"Dianna? She's here?" She looked around, as if expecting Dianna to pop up from the other side of the Model-T.

"No, I'm sorry—"

"Then why say I would be helping her?" She glared. "I can't help someone who's not here, can I?"

"You're right." He held out his hands in an expression of defeat. "It's me who needs help. But I shouldn't have asked you. You're obviously too young to—"

"I'm not too young."

He forced his tongue against his teeth. She'd actually stamped her foot. "Dianna and I have two daughters close to your age," he said. "Katie and Amelia. You remind me of Amelia, feisty, smart, and very capable."

"Why isn't my sister with you? Is it true you kidnapped her, and are holding her hostage?"

"What?" He scowled "No. Where—"

"That's what my father says. He said you poisoned her mind, turned her against us, and that she won't ever come home again. And it's all your fault." She glowered. "I hate you. You took my sister away and I hate you for it. You need to leave."

Was Marshall that vindictive? That unforgiving of his stepdaughter's decision to marry against his wishes that he'd poison the rest of the family against her?

Apparently so, if Elizabeth's accusation and complete dismissal of Jake's mention of her cousins was indication. She despised him, and wanted to pretend Katie and Amelia didn't exist.

Just like her father.

Striving for calm to ensure he didn't live up to whatever malevolent image Marshall had painted of him, he said, "I'm not interested in hurting anyone. I certainly didn't kidnap your sister. I came here to visit. To get to know my—" He broke off, distracted by a woman's shout and a child's high-pitched squeal.

Straining to see past the shadows and trees lining the drive, he caught sight of two figures before they vanished out of view: a small dark-haired child running as fast as stubby legs could fly, a dark-haired young woman dressed identically to the maid Gertrude, in pursuit.

The boy was about the right size, and colouring...

"Take another step and it'll be the last thing you do." Buckland appeared from behind a massive oak ten-yards up the drive. The groundsmen also came out of the trees, spade and shears still present and accounted for.

Every servant there is charged with protecting the heir...

"Lady Elizabeth," the butler said, his tone as formal and correct as his gaze on Jake was cold and threatening. "Her ladyship requests your presence in her sitting room."

Jake glanced at his sister-in-law. She smirked.

"We're not your anything, Yank," she said. "So, best you go and not come back." With a sardonic twist to her smile that reminded him of Marshall, she turned away, her long copper-coloured braid brilliant against the deep brown of her jacket as it swung in time with her steps.

Seeing no immediate alternative to leaving, and fairly sure if he tried to stay, he'd end up with spade-shaped bruises if not shear-sized puncture wounds, Jake leaned over the Model-T's door to double-check the parking brake before reaching through the steering wheel to adjust the spark, throttle, and key, before rounding to the front of the automobile to churn the crank. The roadster chugged to life.

Jake flicked a glance up the drive as he returned to the driver's seat.

That was JJ he'd seen. Had to be. Because no matter how angry his father-in-law was at him for breaking his nose, or estranged his wife from her parents, common decency and civility should have earned him a short visit. Instead, he'd been given the bum's rush. Insulted and threatened to boot.

He tugged on his gloves.

Tread carefully.

Hitting the foot pedals, he launched the auto on to the road, spraying gravel from the tyres as he turned the roadster towards town.

∞ ∞ ∞

The creak of a floorboard heralded Elaina's arrival. Her expression was a mixture of concern and annoyance. More annoyance than concern.

Dianna stood, laid the stuffed bear in the empty crib. The rocking chair moved briefly, settled into stillness, echoing the silence and sense of loss that filled the room.

"Has the post come?"

"Yes," Elaina said. "And no, there is nothing to report, other than it's time for you to come down. Making everyone wait, especially Katie, is not only rude, it's unkind."

"Wait?" Dianna closed her eyes, touched a hand to her forehead. "Katie's recital."

"Yes. Her recital." Elaina's words were clipped.

Opening her eyes, Dianna offered a bleak smile. "I'm sorry. I... forgot."

"I don't mean to be callous, Dianna," Lainey said. "But your forgetfulness of almost everything but the post's delivery is becoming a real problem. You know Mr. Vasquez promised to deliver anything from Mr. Douglas immediately—"

"I know," Dianna said. "And I'm sorry. It's just..." *I should have gone with him.*

Elaina touched Dianna's cheek. "It's hard on all of us, Dianna. But he's only been gone little more than three weeks. Most of that, travel. The best any of us can do, while we wait, is to go about our lives as normally as possible. The girls need things to be as normal as possible."

"But there's a war on over there, Lainey. There wasn't when he left, but there is now. And I still don't know anything about—"

"Stop it." Elaina's usually doe-like grey eyes hardened to wolf-like intensity. "Stop wallowing. Stop dithering in what-ifs and have-nots. You are a mother. A wife. A hostess. You have a house full of people downstairs who go on every day having lost... someone. Your own mother-in-law mourns her husband and your husband's former wife and child, and now worries for her *son*. As you fret about yours. But she's not hiding behind a wall of self-pity. She's down there doing your job, looking after your guests. Your children. So, stop chasing and snapping at shadows, and step

102

into the light of what you have here right now. In this house. This moment. That's all you've got, Dianna. This moment, and the next, and the next. Quit charging into a future that hasn't happened yet, especially when all you seek to find there is... God-awful!"

Dianna inhaled, closed her hands in fists. Elaina hardened her expression, offering no quarter. It was like staring down the earl again, only this time... This time Elaina was right. Dianna was not alone in her suffering. Katie and Amelia mourned their baby brother, Mrs. Brown her beloved little Lord, and Eleanor her grandson. Now they all hung on tenterhooks awaiting word from Jake.

But she was the only one hiding, feeling sorry for herself.

Easing out the breath almost strangling her, she nodded and rasped, "You're right, Lainey. You're absolutely right." She swallowed, hard. "I'm sorry. Let's go."

Katie's eyes lit with joy—and relief—and Charlie, lying beside the piano stool, thumped her tail, as Dianna took her appointed seat next to Eleanor. Eleanor clasped Dianna's hand, gave it a gentle squeeze. Dianna blinked away tears.

Her mother-in-law was the only one who seemed to understand, who did not hold her to some arbitrary schedule of healing, but respected her need to grieve at her own pace.

Katie started out slowly, finding the keys hesitantly, but with barely audible encouragement from Eleanor, she found her rhythm.

The delicate melody of Chopin's *Nocturnes* filled the room, bringing more tears to Dianna's eyes. When Katie moved on to Beethoven's *Moonlight Sonata* Dianna's tears dried as her heart thundered and blood thrummed. Katie followed up with a minuet, that danced in Dianna's soul lifting her heart, before she transitioned to Mozart's *Requiem*. As the last mournful chord echoed, Dianna stood with everyone else to clap wildly.

Katie slowly rose from the piano bench to face the assemblage, and flushing furiously, dipped a shallow curtsy. As the applause died away, Dianna grasped her up in a hug.

"Oh, Katie, dearest. That was beautiful! You have such talent."

"Only because Grandma taught me," Katie murmured ducking her head.

"No dear. Because you took what I taught you and made it so much more." Eleanor grasped Katie and kissed her cheek. "Many people can read and write, but few have the talent to tell captivating stories. You, my dear, are a masterful story-teller."

"Oh, Grandma, you're exaggerating," Katie exclaimed.

"No, she's not." Maggie swooped in to give Katie a hug. "I attended the London Symphony many times. Never have I been so entertained as today. And to think, it's only been a year since you saw your first piano—" She broke off, and turned toward the foyer, as Charlie's bark overrode the door chime's fading buzz.

"I've got it Missus," Mrs. Brown said and waddled hurriedly from the room.

"Quiet, Charlie," Dianna said. "Keep her here, please Katie," she added as she followed Mrs. Brown.

Everyone was here. Eleanor, Maggie, Mr. Sweeney, Mrs. Brown, Rosa... even Juan and Dirk had taken time out from their chores to attend.

Mrs. Brown's voice filtered down the hall: "I'm sorry, Miss, he's away just now. Do you have a card? I'll see he gets it—"

"Don't lie to me you old hag. I know he's here. I heard the music. You don't have a party going on and the big man about the house not be in attendance. So, don't just stand there. Go get him. Tell him he's got company."

"Don' take that tone with me, Missy—"

"And don't you be taking that tone with—"

"Excuse me," Dianna said. "Can I help you?"

The buxom woman with dirty-blonde hair, her face flushed and perspiring, turned her scowl on Dianna. "Who are you?"

Dianna barely kept her smile fixed. Sensing the woman came prepared for—in fact expected—a battle, she touched Mrs. Brown lightly on the arm. "Would you be so kind as to fix our guest a glass of lemonade?" Dianna looked at the woman. "Or would you prefer sweet-tea?"

Surprise slackened the woman's jaw. She recovered quickly, thrust her chin forward. "I don't want nothin' from you. It's him I want. Where is he? Where's Jake Douglas?"

"Is everything all right, Dianna?" Maggie's voice rang with concern, and mild threat. Dianna glanced over her shoulder, and stifled a groan.

Everyone from the parlour was grouped in the foyer staring curiously—or in Maggie's case, hostilely—at the stranger.

"Please, everyone," Dianna said. "Go back to the parlour. I'll be but a minute—"

The woman pushed past Dianna and Mrs. Brown, stood with her dimpled hands fisted on the hips of a faded blue dress at least a size too small, and ten years out of date.

"That's far enough." Dianna moved in front of the woman, a sharp surge of adrenaline dispersing the lethargy that had plagued her for weeks as she stared at the woman in disbelief. "What do you think you're doing? Who *are* you?"

"Oooh, aren't we the fancy accented la—dy." The woman sneered. "All hoity-toity and full of herself. Think this was your house, instead of his." She made his, sound like a snake hiss.

"That's it." Dianna stabbed a finger toward the door. "Out. Out of—"

"Carmen?"

The woman froze.

Dianna looked around as Eleanor broke through the group, halted next to her, her gaze on the newcomer. "Carmen Carlotta Boone?"

The woman's eyes widened.

"It is you," Eleanor said. "But... everyone thought—your father—" She brought a hand to her mouth, seemingly overwhelmed by the reality of the woman's identity. No wonder.

Jake had told Dianna about Carmen, how she disappeared the same night she failed to seduce him, her clothes abandoned on the bank of a creek swollen with spring runoff. After a lengthy search, it was assumed she had drowned, her body swept away by the current. More than a dozen years later, and here she was, loud, obnoxious... *alive.*

"What are you doing here?" Dianna said. "Why are you looking for my husband?" *And where have you been the last fourteen years?*

"Your husband?" Carmen Boone arched an eyebrow. "Well, isn't that a snort? Me, and you, sharing the same man."

Dianna ground her teeth. "What do you want?"

"Never you mind, Fancy. My business is with the Mister."

"What business?"

"I said—"'

"I heard what you said," Dianna said. "But as my husband is away, and will be for quite some time, you have a choice: explain your presence here, or leave." *And never come back.*

105

"Aye, ye heard the lady." Dirk shuffled forward. "Ye'll speak yer business, or go, but we'll 'ave no more nonsense 'ere today."

Though no one else moved, the mood in the room shifted. It was like the others projected the whole of their being, a united energy that enclosed Dianna, Mrs. Brown, and Eleanor, in a protective shield, while forcing the strange woman out. Even Charlie emitted a low growl, and Dianna was relieved to note she was restrained by the collar by both girls, using both hands.

After a nervous glance at the dog, Carmen raised her chin. "You can't make me leave. I have every right to be here." She jammed two fingers in her mouth and whistled.

Dianna winced at the piercing sound. Frowned when a bulky boy stomped up the porch steps and stopped, his head cowed, hunched shoulders straining the threadbare fabric of his shirt he wore with cuffs unbuttoned to accommodate thick forearms. His hands, presumably equally large, were shoved deep in the pockets of his patched trousers. His scalp glowed with sunburn beneath a pale burr of blond stubble. His nape and blocky ears were similarly red, though Dianna suspected more with embarrassment, than too much sun.

Carmen Boone shot Dianna a snide look. "As the mother of Jake Douglas's *son*, I have *every* right to be here."

Chapter 9

Don't Make Me Leave

Mrs. Brown's gaze glimmered with foreign animosity. Though appreciative of her loyalty, Dianna found her presence in the kitchen troublesome. The tension exacerbated the mid-August temperature stifling the room. And there was no hope of resolution to Carmen's vexing announcement with her and Mrs. Brown eyeing each other like a pair of territorial bears squared off over a section of prize spawning grounds.

Carmen could not possibly hope that anyone would believe her ludicrous accusation? But unless Dianna could discover her motivation in making it, there was no way to discredit her.

The boy was big, and fair, like Jake. And Jake was a teenage boy at the time of the child's conception. Some people would be more than happy to lay responsibility for the child's existence at his door, including the child's grandfather.

This could not be happening. Not with Jake gone and unable to defend himself. Not when he and Sheriff Boone had started to allow years of open hostility to fade to unofficial indifference.

If Sheriff Boone knew—but he must? He must know his daughter and her son were in the area. How else did they arrive at the ranch, if not via the town's train station? The sheriff's office was only a couple doors down from the arrival platform.

"Mrs. Brown," Dianna said politely, but firmly. "Would you be a dear and help Elaina escort the girls and Charlie upstairs? I believe Amelia has a book she was assigned to read over the summer she's not finished, and school starts Monday. Katie has a cross-stitch she can work on."

Mrs. Brown flattened her lips. With one last glare at Carmen Boone, she slammed through the swinging doors, her voice a decibel shy of a bark as she called to Elaina and the girls over the clanking of piano keys that suggested Katie was attempting to teach Amelia the scale, advised them they were to go upstairs per the mistress's order.

Exhaling, Dianna faced Carmen Boone.

Carmen's sweet-tea remained untouched in front of her on the table. Her son, slouched on a chair beside her had downed his, along with at least three butter tarts consumed whole. Beside Dianna, Eleanor's ramrod posture belied her carefully neutral expression.

"Is your tea all right?" Dianna asked. "Can I get you something else? Water, or—"

"I don't want nothing from you," Carmen said. "It's that bastard I—"

Eleanor shot to her feet, glared at Carmen with savagery Dianna would not have imagined possible was she not witnessing it with her own eyes.

Carmen raised her hands, slid from her chair, backed away from the table. "I'm sorry, Mrs. Douglas—"

"You will not speak of my son in such terms," Eleanor said through her teeth. "No matter, your opinion of him."

Bobbing her head in agreement, Carmen said, "Yes, ma'am. I apologise. I... I'm just... trying to protect my Jimmy."

"Jimmy," Dianna repeated, trying the name on her tongue the way she might a new food.

Carmen glared at her. "What of it? It's a good name—"

"I never said it wasn't," Dianna said. "My father's middle name is James. As is my son's."

Carmen's plump cheek twitched in a ghost of a smile. "We have even more in common then, don't we?"

Heaven, forfend. But afraid of reigniting Carmen's hostilities, Dianna nodded. "Apparently we appreciate some of the same things." This induced a smile from Carmen. Jimmy retained the same sullen expression he'd carried into the house.

It must be horrid for him, sitting by while his mother talked trash about the man she alleged was his father. She knew she would hate it. Much as she abhorred her stepfather's behaviour at times, she would not tolerate someone besmirching his reputation. It would feel dangerously close to a personal attack. Which was why she never spoke ill of Katie and Amelia's father. He truly was a bastard. But he was their sire, and to track his name through the mud, was to smear them with the same soil.

"Jimmy," she said. "Would you like to go outside and see the horses? There's an apple tree around the side of the house. If you pick a few, Dirk will show you which horses you can give them to."

Jimmy glanced at his mother. Though nothing in his face changed, Dianna thought she caught a glimmer of hope in his eyes. Blue eyes. Like his mother. Jake's eyes were brown, as were Eleanor's. But not Jake's father. His eyes were blue.

Ice blue.

Dianna forced a smile as she looked at Carmen. "Would that be all right, if he went out and fed apples to the horses?"

Suspicion, like insects, skittered across Carmen's face. Dianna kept her smile pleasant, without expectation.

If she read Carmen Boone correctly, the woman was obstinate and controlling. She would not do, nor allow her son to do, anything that was not her idea. From Jimmy's demeanour, he had learned that lesson a long time ago, which explained his abject silence. No expectations, no disappointment. How heart-breaking.

"Fine," Carmen said with martyred resignation. "But see you don't touch nothing not yours," she added sharply to her son. "Do as you're told, or you'll be sorry. You hear?"

The boy nodded without raising his head. Dianna looked at Eleanor, whose barely perceptible smile indicated she understood what Dianna wanted.

"Why don't you come with me, Jimmy," Eleanor said. "There are probably a few apples on the ground we can take to the horses."

Without comment, gaze on the floor and hands deep in his pockets, Jimmy slouched out after Eleanor. Dianna waited until she heard the front door open and close, and the tread of shoes down the porch steps, before turning on Carmen Boone.

"Sit." She pointed to Carmen's vacated seat.

"I won't—"

"This is my house, and you are a guest." Dianna arched an eyebrow. "If you want to stay another minute, you will sit, and talk like a reasonable human being. If you don't, I'll order my men to pick you up and carry you out. I'm sure your father will be more than happy to receive you in his office, considering he's believed you dead these last years."

Carmen paled, and glanced around, as though she feared Sheriff Hank Boone would burst from one of the kitchen cupboards, confirming Dianna's suspicion.

The sheriff had no idea his daughter was in town. Because if he did, and he believed any of the drivel she was trying to sell, he would have beat her to the front door with every intention of forcing Jake to take responsibility.

Dragging in a silent breath through her nose and praying for the umpteenth time she would hear something from her husband soon—like he was on the way home with *their* son—Dianna poured a fresh glass of sweet tea.

Seeming to gather herself mentally, Carmen sat. Scowled.

"Now," Dianna said without malice, raising her eyebrows. "Why don't you tell me the truth? What really brought you here to lay false allegations against my husband?"

∞ ∞ ∞

Carmen hiked her chin. "I'm here 'cause my Jimmy's entitled to his father's lot."

"Your son is entitled to nothing here," Dianna said. "Jake is not his father. That much I know to be true. If you care to tell me the real reason you're here, I'll see what I can do to help."

"You know that much to be true, do you?" Carmen smirked. "I was there, right there, and Jake between my legs getting more pleasure than I'm sure you've ever showed him."

Dianna barely managed to keep her revulsion for the woman from showing on her face. "I take it you're declining my help, which means we're done here. I'll show you to the door."

"You'll show me my son's room."

Dianna narrowed her eyes. "You can leave under your own power, or I'll have someone assist you."

"I'm not going anywhere—"

"Mama?"

"Amelia, darling. What are you doing?" Dianna asked without looking away from Carmen. "You're supposed to be upstairs with Katie, and Mrs. Brown."

"Mama?" Carmen glanced past Dianna. "She's yours... and Jake's?

Amelia ran in and threw her arms around Dianna's waist. Dianna kept her gaze on Carmen as she offered Amelia a reassuring hug. "Amelia, darling, this is Miss Carmen. Sheriff Boone's daughter."

"Pleased to meet you, Miss Carmen," Amelia said shyly.

Carmen stared at Amelia.

"Miss Carmen has to leave now," Dianna said. "But her son, Jimmy, is outside with grandma looking at the horses. Could you run and tell them that Miss Carmen is ready to depart, and for Jimmy to come in?"

Carmen laughed, a scoffing bark that Dianna ignored.

"Go on dear." She gave Amelia a gentle push. "And hurry."

Amelia dragged herself away from Dianna, and with one last baleful glance at Carmen, dashed outside. Dianna glowered.

"Get out."

Carmen uttered a derisive laugh. "I told you, this is as much my house as it is yours."

"You heard the mistress." Mrs. Brown stumped into the kitchen. "Get out. Your kind isna welcome here. You're foul-mouthed and stinkin' up me kitchen." She grasped Carmen by the elbow.

Carmen punched her. Square in the mouth.

Mrs. Brown recovered from the shock before Dianna. With a throaty growl she grasped Carmen by the hair and yanked. Carmen shrieked and grasped Mrs. Brown's muscled arm with both hands.

"Let go, you old bitch." She kicked, but Mrs. Brown, without loosening her grip on Carmen's hair, moved her lower body out of reach with surprising agility.

"Stop," Dianna shouted. "Stop this nonsense at once."

Neither woman heeded her.

With an inhuman snarl, Carmen launched herself at Mrs. Brown, and both crashed to the floor. Attempting to intervene, Dianna received a smack in the nose.

Rearing back, hand to her face, she blinked to clear the tears that bloomed in response to the stinging pain. Housekeeper and uninvited guest writhed on the floor, fists, and feet flailing. It would take more than her to stop them.

She raced out on the porch. "Juan! Dirk! Garrett!" She had to scream their names a few more times, before Dirk and Garrett finally appeared around a corner of the stable. "Help!" She pointed to the inside of the house.

Garrett was past Dianna and galloping down the hall, before Dirk had crossed the yard. Dianna turned and followed Garrett.

"The kitchen," she said when Garrett paused in the foyer.

It wasn't until they burst through the butler doors that Dianna realised why Garrett had hesitated: there'd been no noise to guide him to the scuffle.

Mrs. Brown was sitting on the floor propped against a cupboard dabbing blood from her nose with a corner of her apron.

"Mrs. Brown." Dianna knelt to touch the elder woman's cheek. "Are you, all right?"

"Aye, Missus." Mrs. Brown offered a wry smile. "It takes more than a tramp like 'er to best me." She moved to get up, stopped, and nodded. "Think I'll bide awhile, if ye don' mind Missus?"

"Of course not," Dianna said, and looked around. "Where's Carmen?"

Mrs. Brown indicated the back door. "I tried to stop her." She opened her hand to reveal a clump of blonde hair. Repressing a shudder, Dianna looked at Garrett.

"Go quick. Get Doc Stanley. And the sheriff," she added as Garrett whirled to leave.

"Juan already went for the sheriff," Garrett said. "But I'll get the doc."

Dirk burst into the kitchen and immediately flattened himself against the wall as Garrett pushed past him. Shock erased the age and consternation on Dirk's face when his gaze locked on Mrs. Brown.

"Beth." He shuffled over and gripping the counter to aid his descent to one knee, clasped Mrs. Brown's hand in his. "What happened?"

"Nothing serious," Mrs. Brown murmured.

Nothing serious?

Shaking her head, Dianna shoved to her feet and twisted on the tap water to dampen a clean dishcloth. She gave it to Dirk who gently applied it to Mrs. Brown's cut, just as the doors opened again.

"Good Heaven," Eleanor Douglas said. "What happened?"

"'Twas the slatter—"

"Jimmy," Dianna blurted silencing Mrs. Brown as the boy loomed behind Eleanor. "Ah, Mother Eleanor, would you... would you take Jimmy—

and Amelia, " she added when Amelia pushed in next, "to the parlour? I'll bring refreshments."

"What's going on?" Elaina and Katie and Charlie crowded into the room. Before Dianna could reply, Elaina's gaze landed on Mrs. Brown. "Good, lord." She stared at Dianna as though she blamed her for the housekeeper's dishevelled condition.

"I'll explain, later," Dianna said tersely. "For now, can you help Eleanor escort the children—and the dog—to the parlour, and keep them there?"

Momentary chaos erupted as Eleanor and Elaina convinced the three children to move to the other room. Amelia protested verbosely, begging for inclusion in the adult drama. Jimmy remained quietly stalwart as his eyes travelled the room, eventually stopping on Dianna. A glint of resentment sparked in his eyes before the shutter of indifference slid into place. Shoulders slumped lower than ever, he gave to Eleanor's hand, let her guide him from the room.

Dianna exhaled, and pointed. "Amelia, go."

With an exasperated huff, Amelia stomped out, Elaina on her heels to ensure compliance. Dianna crouched in front of Mrs. Brown, said to Dirk, "Help me get her to her room."

With a little effort, and a lot of care, they helped Mrs. Brown to her feet and down the hall. As soon as Mrs. Brown was seated on the edge of the mattress, Dianna bent to remove her shoes. Dirk retreated towards the door.

"Please stay, Dirk," she said, setting aside the first of Mrs. Brown's sturdy low-heeled shoes to unlace the second. "I have to see to my unexpected house guest, and I need someone to sit with Mrs. Brown, until the doctor arrives. Would you mind?" She glanced at him as she put the second shoe beside its mate.

"Aye, Missus," he said. "I'll stay."

"Ach," Mrs. Brown muttered. "I don' need a grizzled old nanny. I'll be fine."

"You'll lie down and rest, and Dirk will keep you company, until I have the doctor's word that you will be all right." Dianna arched her eyebrows as she pushed to her feet. This garnered another decidedly Scottish and derisive sound from Mrs. Brown, but also her cooperation as Dianna guided her beneath the bed covers. "There," she said. "Now rest. And thank you, Dirk," she added offering him a grateful smile.

"Aye, Missus," he said, and moved to stand next to Mrs. Brown's bed.

∞ ∞ ∞

Sheriff Boone stared at Jimmy like the child was a Changeling. And then his blue stare turned on Dianna. "Carmen? My daughter. This is her boy?"

Dianna nodded. "She claimed he was. I see no reason for her to lie."

"Is that true, boy?" Boone boomed, turning back to the child. "Your mother is Carmen Boone?"

Jimmy ducked his head lower.

"Sheriff," Dianna murmured, and waved to the settee. "Why don't we sit and talk quietly, while we enjoy a glass of sweet tea?"

Boone shot her a startled look, as though surprised she would dare suggest he do anything, but exactly what he was doing. Fortunately, he remembered his manners, and the fact he was in her home, and swept off his Stetson. With an irritated scowl he lowered his massive bulk to the edge of the sofa where he sat, his hat trapped in meaty hands, wide elbows resting on his knees.

"Sit, boy," he growled.

Jimmy continued to stare at the patterned rug between his cracked and heel-worn boots. Dianna touched his shoulder, guided him to the settee opposite the sheriff, and sat next to him.

"Jimmy," she said gently. "I know you're scared, but I assure you the sheriff won't hurt you. He has a few questions he needs answered about your mother. Tell him the truth and everything will be fine. All right, dear?"

Jimmy gave no indication that he heard. Boone's slab-like face reddened.

A big, brash man, he was unused to being ignored, and when faced with resistance he usually resorted to intimidation. But Dianna sensed that wouldn't work with this child. Jimmy, she feared, was inured to bullying; his soul shielded by a heavy layer of indifference the way nerveless scar tissue built over the site of deep wounds.

She gave the sheriff a warning look she hoped he would heed. His scowl deepened, and he cleared his throat as though preparing to speak, but to her surprise he said nothing, only twitched his eyebrows indicating she do something.

"Mr. Boone is the local sheriff, Jimmy." *And your grandfather.* "He ensures the people of Douglas County are protected, and now you're in his jurisdiction, he's obligated to protect you. So, you see, you're safe here. We want only to help you, and will not permit anyone to hurt you. Isn't that so, Sheriff?"

Boone stared at her as though she'd accused him of murder, but he recovered.

Nodding, he looked at Jimmy. "That's right," he said gruffly. "No one's gonna hurt you, boy. I won't let them."

Dianna smiled. Boone squirmed, clearly uncomfortable with his supportive role. He was used to interrogation, not negotiation.

"Jimmy, dear," Dianna said, "will you let us help? Will you tell us about your mother, please?"

"Her name's not Boone."

The words were so softly spoken, Dianna wasn't sure if she'd heard, or imagined them. "Your mother's name is not Carmen Boone?"

"It's Hipwell."

"Hipwell?" Boone straightened, his eyes flaring as though an invisible rope had cinched around his beefy neck forcing him to lift his head and chest and align his spine to prevent his choking to death. Dianna half-expected him to grab at the imaginary noose. "Simon Hipwell?"

Jimmy hunched.

"Please, sheriff," Dianna murmured. "There's no need to shout." She pressed her lips together, held his gaze without flinching.

With a blustery exhalation, Boone jutted his jaw in the boy's direction. "Are you Simon Hipwell's son, boy?"

Nothing. Then a barely perceptible shrug.

Irritation rippled across Boone's florid features.

Afraid he would shout again, Dianna said, "Jimmy, darling, who is your father?"

"Don't know."

"But Carmen is your mother?"

He nodded.

"Where do you live?"

"Nowhere."

"Certainly, you must have a home? Where were you and your mother before you came here?"

115

"Arizona."

"Where in Arizona?" Boone demanded. More than a decade of believing his daughter dead, and she was living one state over.

"Flagstaff."

"What the hell, is she doing there?"

"Was." Jimmy looked at Boone. "She was singing. Like her Mama." Jimmy's tone was matter-of-fact. And icy cold. The air in the room filled with hollow silence, broken as Boone sucked for breath.

His big hands twitched, as though resisting an impulse to crush his Stetson. Or strangle Jimmy. Jimmy, in unnerving contrast, displayed eerie calm, his eyes—so much like Boone's in colouring—reflecting less emotion than a pair of glass marbles as he returned the elder man's stare. The similarities were startling: Bulky skulls, small eyes, flattish noses, and thick upper bodies lending each a bull-like appearance.

"Where are you and your Mother staying now, Jimmy?" Dianna asked to break the impasse. He didn't look her way, or even blink to acknowledge her question. "Jimmy, darling, I'm sure you'd prefer to be with your mother—"

"I'm not your darling."

Boone thrust up out of his seat. "How dare you speak to Mrs. Douglas—any woman—in such manner? You apologise right now—"

"Sheriff, please." Dianna gestured for the sheriff to sit. "There's been enough antagonism today—"

Jimmy said something so softly, she almost missed it. Frowning at him, she murmured, "What did you say?"

"I want to stay here," he whispered.

Dianna stared at the sheriff who looked as surprised as she felt. She looked back at Jimmy. He had dropped his chin so low it almost touched his chest. Heaven, what was the child's life like that he wanted to stay here, with strangers?

She couldn't keep him. Despite his mother's claims, he was not Jake's son. And there was Katie and Amelia to consider. *And JJ.*

Pain in her chest forced her to breathe deeply to counter it.

"Jimmy," she said, but before she could finish, he looked up.

"I'm not leaving," he said. "Don't make me leave."

∞ ∞ ∞

116

"Listen here, boy. You're my grandson, and you'll do as I say."

"Sheriff," Dianna said. "Could we talk in the kitchen?"

Boone glanced at her, his pugnacious expression hard. "There's no need to talk—"

"I believe there is." She stood. "Jimmy, I'd like you to go out to the stable, advise Dirk I sent you to help muck stalls."

Jimmy's head came up, his expression incredulous, whether with wonder at the prospect she might let him stay, or disbelief she would expect him to labour on her behalf.

"This is a working ranch, Jimmy," she said to dispel any doubt he might have. "If you're to remain here, you work. Period. We have no room for lay-abouts."

A faint blush filtered into Jimmy's broad cheeks, and then he stood and started out of the room. Boone stopped him with a hand on the shoulder.

"Where's your manners, boy?"

Jimmy scowled at him.

"Thank her, boy. Mrs. Douglas is showing you more courtesy than you've earned."

Jimmy's rigid posture seemed to harden, and then ever so slowly, relaxed just enough to permit him to face around, and rasp, "Thank you, ma'am."

"You're welcome, Jimmy."

"I'll see him to the stable," Boone said, and because she had no energy left to argue she sat on the settee as he steered his grandson out of the room. Crossing her arms, she stared at the window sheers.

How had her life come to this, her son missing, husband gone, and a child not her own abandoned on her doorstep refusing to leave?

"What did I do wrong?" she murmured.

"Nothing."

Dianna startled, and faced the entry. Eleanor offered a sympathetic smile.

"You heard?" Dianna asked.

Eleanor nodded. "Poor child, so angry and lost. Reminds me of Jake when he learned John was his stepfather."

"I know," Dianna said. "He's clearly hurting, and I've no idea what to do about it."

"There's little you can do," Eleanor offered a barely perceptible shrug. "You're not the source of his pain."

Dianna forced a smile. "I know, but I'll also not contribute further to his heartache. There must be something I can do to help?"

"You are." Eleanor smiled. "You're keeping him safe, until a more permanent solution is found."

Dianna shook her head. "I don't understand it, Mother. How could she leave him? She barged in here making false allegations against Jake, and then fled without so much as a word to her son."

"How do you know he wasn't aware of what she planned?"

Dianna blinked. "You think he knew she intended to leave him here?"

Eleanor's shrug was more definite this time. "It's possible. He isn't overly distraught by her absence. He asked to stay."

"He can't stay," Dianna exclaimed. "I've worries enough."

Lifting a framed portrait of Jake holding JJ from the piano, Eleanor nodded, but her gaze was on the smiling images of her son and grandson. Dianna's throat tightened. With a barely audible sigh, Eleanor set the frame back, looked at Dianna.

"If we can't find his mother, he'll become Hank's responsibility."

"I take no comfort from that knowledge," Dianna said. "The man's a brute."

Eleanor winced. "Hank comes on like a summer storm, but inside that big loud lummox, is a heart of gold."

"Well, he keeps it well hidden." Realizing how uncharitable she sounded, Dianna lifted her hands in supplication. "Oh Mother, what am I going to do?"

A knock resounded in the foyer.

"That's probably Hank now," Eleanor said. "Do you want me to talk to him?"

Yes.

"I think we should talk to him together." Dianna stood. "But first, I'd like to check Mrs. Brown. Do you mind taking the sheriff through to the kitchen? I'll be there in a few minutes."

"Of course," Eleanor said.

Mrs. Brown was fast asleep, quilt drawn to her waist, plump hands folded over her middle, lusty snores resonating from her partly open mouth. Elaina, curled in the armchair by the window, her stocking feet tucked under her, closed the book she was reading and set it on the lamp table as Dianna entered the room.

"Doctor's gone?" Dianna whispered.

Elaina nodded. "Pronounced her fit as a fiddle. Or make that an Oboe," she added with a grin. "Whatever he gave her for pain is strong. You could roll her bed out to the yard and jump horses over it and I doubt she'd change tenor."

"Thank you for relieving Dirk, though I'm sure he'll regret your coming to replace him."

"Oh?" Elaina frowned.

"I sent Jimmy out to muck stalls with instruction Dirk supervise him."

"Oh." Elaina nodded, and then sighed, a wistful sound. "He's quite handsome, isn't he?"

Dianna stared. "Dirk? Or Jimmy?"

Elaina laughed. "Heavens, no. Neither. I mean, not that they're unattractive. But I was talking about the doctor. Stanley."

"Stanley?" Dianna scowled. "Good heaven, Elaina, he's as old, if not older, than Dirk."

Elaina frowned. "What are you talking about? The man that was here was about your husband's age. Was he not the doctor?"

"What? Oh, yes. Perhaps." Dianna nodded. "I forgot. Dr. Stanley mentioned he was retiring and his son coming to replace him."

"So he *was* the doctor?" Elaina raised her eyebrows.

"I assume. I didn't see him. I was busy with—" Dianna bit her lower lip. "What a horrid day. What an awful, stinking day. I can't thank you enough, Lainey, for helping. For taking care of Mrs. Brown, and the girls. I truly hate to ask more of you, but would you mind staying here a little longer? I've unfinished business to attend."

"The boy?" Elaina's expression offered sympathy and concern, the former Dianna suspected for her, the latter for the boy.

"Yes," she said. "Jimmy. And his mother. And grandfather. I don't know what's going to come of it all, and as much as I'd like to stay here and spend time with you, I can't. Mother Eleanor and the sheriff are waiting in the kitchen."

∞ ∞ ∞

"Her ladyship is not receiving today." The butler regarded Jake with thinly veiled animosity.

Jake held his stare. "How about her husband? When do you expect him?"

"His Lordship's requested you not bother his wife again. Good day, sir."

"He's here?" Jake said, surprised. Hadn't she told him yesterday Marshall was in London?

Buckland closed the door. A bolt slid into place. Teeth clamped, Jake fought the urge to bust down the door, or smash through a window and dash up the stairs to that nursery.

Marshall was a British earl. With a cushy seat in the House of Lords. One of a select and formidable cabal with direct influence on the laws of the land. *"... the moment you step off the ship on to English soil, he will own you, if he chooses to."*

If the boy he'd seen yesterday wasn't JJ, he stood to spend a good portion of his life in a British prison for trespass, forced entry, and attempted kidnap of a powerful man's only son.

Heir.

He blew out a breath, faced around, glared at the Model-T. Pain clenched in his chest as his lungs, deprived of oxygen, spasmed.

Hiking a breath, he stalked down the steps, fired up the Model-T and hopped in. Ten minutes later he left the auto parked on the side of the road, and twenty-minutes after that, he zigged his way through the Oaks to within a hundred yards of the lawn where he'd seen the boy playing the day before. So focused was he on the manor, and his hope the boy might be brought outside again, he didn't hear the butler until he spoke.

"You were asked to leave, Yank. And told not to come back. So, now you're trespassing."

He started to turn, but not fast enough to prevent something hard and heavy connecting with his skull. He staggered. The second strike drove him to his knees.

The third, into darkness.

Chapter 10

Not Your Fight

hank you, Sheriff." Dianna dragged her gaze from the charred ruins across from the train depot long enough to offer Boone a smile as she accepted his aid to depart the No. 7 Express. She moved aside as he reached to assist Eleanor.

"Oh my," Eleanor said. "How dreadful. And recent from the look of it."

"It was and is damn dreadful." The speaker swept his hat from his head, offered Eleanor and Dianna a curt nod each, before turning to Sheriff Boone. "You must be Boone."

"And you must be Woods." The men shook hands, and then Sheriff Boone introduced Eleanor and Dianna in turn.

"Ladies," Sheriff Woods said with a smile. He was a slim dark-haired man with a thick moustache rolled to tips either side of his lean face. A man apparently impervious to the cold nipping Dianna's cheeks, as he wore only a thin black leather vest over a long-sleeved shirt tucked into dungarees.

The Navajo County sheriff's expression grew sombre as he touched a hand to the kerchief knotted around his neck, and then pistol holstered on his hip. The movements were quick, just long enough to assure him each was aligned as it should be, a ritual or nervous habit Dianna suspected he wasn't aware he followed. She shivered, as much from foreboding, as the chill September wind carrying ash, and the scent of scorched wood.

"Where is she?" Boone's speech was clipped, as though he too suspected something wrong and thought to right it with his customary brashness. He surveyed the tidy four-block square community that comprised Winslow, Arizona. "Your wire indicates she's working here, at a hotel."

The wire had not indicated exactly what the woman matching Carmen's description was working at, but Dianna had her suspicions, speculation confirmed when Sheriff Woods winced, and darted at look at her and Eleanor, before turning his gaze, reluctantly, to Sheriff Boone. Dianna maintained an expression of calm acceptance similar to that her mother-in-law projected.

If she was learning anything from Eleanor Douglas and Jake, it was that it was not her place to judge another's choices, until she lived their reality. She had only look back two years to see how different her life might be—and what choices she may have faced—if not for Maggie, and Jake, and others whom she now counted as beloved friends and family. They had helped her when she had not known how to help herself, offering the unconditional friendship, and love, Carmen had obviously never found.

Sheriff Boone and Mother Eleanor had cleared up the mystery of Simon Hipwell on the journey to Winslow: mean-spirited son of a pastor with fast fists around Jake's age, but who'd matured sooner, and routinely beat up Jake—and other boys smaller than him—until Jake knocked him senseless one afternoon earning Simon a whipping from his father. Not for fighting. For losing the fight. The family left town shortly thereafter, around the same time Carmen went missing.

"It never occurred to me he might be involved with Carmen," Boone had muttered, shaking his head. "I never saw the boy with her. Figured Pastor Hipwell left town because I had warned him if he ever whipped his son—or his wife who had two black eyes when I stopped in on them—again, I would give him a taste of his own whip."

It sounded like Simon Hipwell had inherited his tendency for violence from his father. And if he and Carmen had ended up married... *Don't make me leave. I want to stay.*

Poor child. Not a wonder he was so... damaged. His mother so angry. Who knew what they'd endured, or for how long?

Boone's inquiries turned up a Simon Hipwell, arrested and imprisoned a few months earlier after being found guilty of beating to death the man he'd found *in flagrante* with his wife. It didn't take a Pinkerton to deduce who the wife was. Or her reason for showing up at J-D Ranch.

Her husband in jail and no longer able to help provide for the family, Carmen had taken her son to the one place—the one person—she thought she might convince, or bribe, to take on Jimmy's care.

Boone's curt voice cut through her musing. "These ladies and I didn't travel all day to play guessing games." He scowled at Sheriff Woods. "Where's my daughter?"

The information gained about Simon Hipwell had been collected during Boone's outreach to every colleague's office in Texas and Arizona seeking information about his daughter and her potential husband. The information on Simon Hipwell had come in less than two weeks. But another week passed, before he received a lead from one of Sheriff Woods's deputies about Carmen. A long day's travel, and he was anxious to the point of belligerence. Eleanor touched his arm.

The gesture seemed to calm him. Or maybe it was the smile Eleanor offered him when he looked at her, because his humped shoulders levelled, his anger and tension releasing on a gruff exhalation as he brought a callused and freckled hand around to briefly cover hers. The admiration in his gaze scored Dianna's heart.

Jake had looked at her like that. Like she was the only diamond on a tray of coal lumps. The only rose in a garden of weeds.

She angled her face away, stared at the blackened husk of a building, until the urge to sob—and buy the first ticket out of Winslow to New York, and from there, on to England—passed.

Jake had left for New York on July 25th. She'd received a single postcard dated August 7th confirming his safe arrival in Liverpool, and plan to travel on to Ansmall the following day. If he'd sent anything in the month since his arrival in Britain, it was caught in the whirlpool of transportation confusion whipping much of the world to frenzy as Canadian and British Territorial forces from almost every corner of the earth commandeered available sailing vessels in a race to France to reinforce British, French, and Belgian troops on the ground trying to halt the German advance, while a counter-flow of non-resident citizens scrambled to escape countries impacted by the expanding ground war.

For the last few weeks, after the girls were abed, she'd sat in the kitchen with Eleanor and Lainey, Mrs. Brown, Dirk, and Garrett, and read what little news of the war found its way in to the most recent editions of the *Douglas Weekly* and *Amarillo Daily News*. Nothing she read helped assuage her growing fear. Or dissuade her belief she should have gone to England with Jake.

Had she gone, even if Elaina's suspicions had proven false, she'd know where her husband was, and even as she grieved her son, she'd be comforted with knowledge her daughters were safe far from the war and its deadly havoc. Instead, she was safe. Her daughters were safe. And the one person she'd counted on to keep her connected to those in England who might know something about Jake, was here too. Fortunately, Lainey had agreed to include in her most recent letter home to check on the family's welfare, a casual query to whether Jake had visited.

She'd have done it herself, less casually perhaps, but could not guarantee a reply. Though Mama and the earl had not overtly disowned her, Mama's infrequent and impersonal replies to her letters devoid of interest in Jake's well-being or conferred well-wishes from the earl, was clear enough. She only hoped they'd find it harder to be rude or ignore Jake's existence when all six-foot-four and seventeen-stone of him was standing right in front of them.

"Do you see your daughter anywhere in this group?" Sheriff Woods was holding out a daguerreotype.

Dianna sidled around to peer between Sheriff Boone and Eleanor's shoulders that almost touched, they stood so closely.

It was a portrait of more than a dozen women and half dozen men grouped in front of a long bar in the El Lugar saloon according to the reversed letters etched in the mirror on the wall behind them. The men wore suits and were seated on stools with their arms around the waists of women leaned into them from either side. The women's dresses were different colours, and all the same: low cut in front, with a hip-high slit on the side. Dianna skipped over the women's heavily made-up faces.

"There," she said and reached to touch the photograph.

Boone shot her a glare, and then squinted at the face Dianna indicated.

Clearing his throat, he nodded. "It's been a while," he murmured. "But I agree. That's her, third from the right. She has her mother's nose." A wistful note hollowed his normally booming voice.

Sheriff Woods nodded and glanced at the burnt building. "I'm sorry," he said and cleared his throat as he turned a regretful look on Sheriff Boone. "I'm afraid I don't have good news."

∞ ∞ ∞

124

The trip home was subdued. Dianna remained silent, staring out the train window at the dusk-shadowed countryside as much to offer a semblance of privacy to Eleanor and the sheriff as to control her fraught emotions fatigue and the train's bone-jarring pace threatened to rattle loose.

That Carmen had perished in the hotel fire not only grieved her for Hank Boone's sake, it exacerbated her sense of terror in not knowing the whereabouts of Jake. Or JJ. She wanted to cry. Pound her fists, and rail at the injustice of the sheriff's renewed loss. And her own. But she had no right, nor desire, to add to the sheriff's torment by burdening him with her anguish.

Though he displayed no overt signs of grief, his glossier than normal red-rimmed eyes, thinly compressed lips, and repeated squeezing of his right hand fisted on his knee revealed a man privately—and deeply— aggrieved. A man on the verge of explosive combustion contained only by the gentle touch of the woman next to him who dozed, her head against his brawny shoulder, small black-gloved hand clasping his large bare one. Anyone not familiar with the couple might assume they were married. At the least courting. But Dianna did know better. And though she supposed she should be shocked by their intimate tableau, she felt... proud.

She'd wondered why the sheriff, normally a private man, had invited her and Eleanor to accompany him. But seeing them together now, it was as plain as the seat vibrating beneath her.

On some level, the sheriff had sensed he'd need a friend. Support from the one person he knew he could trust to offer guidance, without judgement. Kindness without reproach. Solace without censure. He'd asked Dianna along, in part she believed, in recognition of the fact she was currently housing and employing his grandson. But in greater part, she suspected she was there to act as chaperone, insulate Eleanor's reputation against the chilling taint of gossipmongers. Tempering Dianna's pride in her mother-in-law's unwavering humanity, was sorrow, for she suspected Eleanor Douglas tilted into the sheriff as much to brace herself, as bolster him.

Life is so unfair at times.

They all ached for near identical reasons, mourning children and spouses lost to them. The only difference being she and Eleanor still maintained hope they'd reunite with Jake. Maybe even JJ. While the sheriff's hope had been snatched away, replaced with a tarnished pewter frame and the ghastly knowledge his only child had burned to death in a fire Sheriff Woods had described as, suspicious. *Poor man.*

His broad fingers were bleached white from the force of his hold on the framed photograph, the wiry hair on his knuckles bright as copper snips. He'd not put the portrait down since Sheriff Woods gave it to him and he confirmed the likeness within as that of his late wife, her black and white visage beneath the cracked glass remarkably preserved, having survived the worst of the flames and smoke under a body so badly burnt as to make it unidentifiable beyond gender: female.

Poor Hank.

Poor Jimmy.

With Boone's grudging agreement, she'd installed the child in McGuire's old bunk under the stern and constant supervision of Dirk and Garrett. Despite her initial misgivings, the boy had proven himself an eager and apt stable hand.

Though he lacked his predecessor's horsemanship and verbosity, he more than matched McGuire in brute strength, and surprisingly, work ethic. He set to whatever Dirk or Garrett assigned him—clean and polish saddles, repair broken bridles, restring girths, muck out stalls—without a murmur of protest. Guilt twined through Dianna.

Jimmy, like most everyone at the ranch, believed she and Eleanor had gone to Dallas for ranch-related business. Only Elaina and Mrs. Brown knew the true reason for their departure, and she'd sworn them to secrecy on the chance the trip proved fruitless. In an awful way, it had.

Not only were they returning without Carmen, they brought with them the horrific news she was dead.

"Oh, Jimmy," she whispered.

"I'll tell him."

Dianna jerked as if the sheriff had shouted, rather than growled the words.

"My grandson, my daughter," he added, his expression as beleaguered as it was obdurate. "I'll tell him."

Dianna nodded, offered a sad smile. "Of course," she murmured.

Eleanor didn't open her eyes or lift her head from Boone's shoulder, but her slim gloved fingers tightened on the sheriff's broad freckled hand.

∞ ∞ ∞

"Are you sure we shouldn't go with him?" Dianna asked.

"Absolutely," Eleanor said as they tracked the sheriff's progress through the kitchen window as he stepped off the porch and turned towards the stables. He moved slower than Dianna remembered, shuffling as though his boots were filled with bricks. He seemed less tall, too, an illusion created by his slouched posture. Dianna's heart ached for him.

He faced a difficult enough undertaking in trying to break through Jimmy's emotional resistance, without the added complication of being the one to inform the child his mother was dead.

She swayed as a sudden full-body flush, and rush of dizziness overwhelmed her.

"Dianna?" Eleanor grasped her elbow. "What is it? What's wrong?"

"Nothing." But she kept her eyes closed and head bowed, sink edge gripped with both hands, as she waited for prickly heat and resultant nausea to fade. "Just a little tired."

"Come, sit."

Eleanor directed her to a chair at the breakfast table, where she sat and obediently sipped the water Eleanor brought her.

Setting the glass aside, she smiled. "Thank you, Mother. I feel much better."

"You're sure?" Worry clouded Eleanor's gaze.

"Yes. Tired, but fine."

Eleanor sank to a chair and sighed. "I can't argue being tired. I'm surprised any of us are still standing. I swear I could sleep for a week without waking once." Though her tone was wry, a sheen of tears belied her true emotions.

The trip to Winslow had taken its toll on all of them. They'd spent the night in Amarillo, before catching the morning train to Douglas, but the break had offered no respite. Only more hours to wile and worry, while sleep lingered out of reach. It seemed her mother-in-law, with whom she'd shared the hotel room, had been no more successful in achieving the quiet mind necessary for slumber.

"Can we come down now?" Amelia's sharp face pressed between a gap in the butler door and frame.

Elaina had shepherded both girls upstairs the moment Dianna arrived home and quietly informed her of the tragic turn of events, whilst Mrs. Brown had hastened outside to find Dirk, advise him to send for Jimmy who was helping sort and separate the last of the calves and fallow cows bound for Fort Worth sales, under pretence other than the truth. That had been an hour ago.

"There's no harm can come from them knowing now," Eleanor murmured. "I'm sure Hank has told him."

"Yes, Amelia, darling. You may *all* come down now."

Amelia responded to the news of Jimmy and Sheriff Boone's mutual loss with her customary scowl. Tears purled in Katie's eyes. Charlie, picking up on the mood in the room, whined, and shoved her head between the chairs each girl sat on, earning a hug from each. Elaina hefted the kettle from the wood stove and poured the boiling water into a teapot, while Ms. Willow set out plates of quartered sandwiches.

"There you are," Dianna said as Mrs. Brown banged in through the porch door. "I wondered what happened to you."

The housekeeper set a bucket of potatoes in the sink. "I stayed out in the garden." She pulled a paring knife from a wooden block on the counter. "Figured Mr. Boone 'd be more comfortable not havin' me hoverin' about, while he waited for his grandson."

Dianna stood, crossed to the sink, and touched Mrs. Brown lightly on the shoulder. "He doesn't blame you. The disagreement with Carmen was not your fault. You ended up the injured party."

"Aye, well." Mrs. Brown kept her gaze on the knife she was using to deftly lift a potato's skin from its pale flesh. "I'm sure as the sheriff has his own opinion on that—" She broke off, as muffled shouts filtered through the partly open window.

"What in heaven?" Dianna ran out on to the porch.

Amelia blurted galloped past her.

"Amelia. Come back here."

Braid bouncing, Amelia disappeared around the side of the house. With an exclamation of frustration Dianna went after her, found her in front of the stable, amber eyes wide and hand clapped over her mouth. No wonder.

"Sheriff—Jimmy. Stop!" Dianna trotted toward the pair grappling and grunting in the dirt like a pair of enraged bears. Dirk stepped in front of her, shook his head.

"Not your fight, Missus."

She stared. Never in her life had Dirk given *her* an order.

"About time the pup learned a lesson," he added quietly.

"He's a child," she said.

Dirk lifted his snowy eyebrows. "With a man-sized chip on his shoulder needs paring down."

"He's right." Eleanor grasped Dianna's hand. "This was bound to happen sometime. The sooner they establish who's in charge, the better."

Dianna scowled. "You agree with this?"

Eleanor offered a resigned smile. "Not everything can be settled with words. Especially between men."

"He's not a man. He's a boy."

"I didn't understand it either when Jake was young, and he and John would occasionally butt heads like this. I even tried to intervene, once." Eleanor's smile turned wry. "John swiftly disabused me of that notion, made clear I had my way of working out problems with our son, and he had his. In all honesty, afterwards, when the dust settled, John and Jake were always... closer than ever. And by the time Jake went off to University, they were best of friends. So regardless my natural abhorrence for violence..." She shook her head. "I've come to understand that sometimes it's necessary. Besides, Hank is his grandfather. And the sheriff. He has the right to discipline, as he sees fit."

With an exclamation of disgust, and defeat, Dianna yanked free of Eleanor's hold to wave at Amelia. "Go back to the house—Elaina? Katie?" She glared in exasperation at her sister and daughter as they rounded the corner of the house. "Back inside. All of you. This is not your business."

Elaina shot her a reproving frown, but shepherded the girls away without comment, Amelia dragging her feet, Katie with silent grace.

Garrett emerged from the stable, dragged his hat from his head and gestured with it to the duelling duo. "Want I should stop them, Mrs. Douglas?"

She sighed, and shook her head, weary. "No. It's... not our fight."

"Not much of a fight anymore," Dirk said with impertinent cheerfulness.

Hank Boone was on his back. Jimmy was also on his back—on Boone's chest, immobilised by one of Hank's meaty arms around his throat and the sheriff's long legs wrapped around his torso, crossed at the ankles pinioning his arms. Eyes popped and face almost purple, Jimmy scuffed his boot heels on the ground, grunting as he attempted to wrest free. He'd have better luck shedding his own skin.

"You're right," Hank grumbled in the boy's ear. "I'm not your father. Or your mother. And I sure as hell didn't bring you into this world, but by God I'll take you out if I have to. No kin of mine is going to bring anymore grief, or disrespect to this world. It has enough as it is. Now you got a choice boy, and about one-minute to make it: are you gonna send your attitude packing, and pack up your belongings and come home with me where you belong, or am I gonna bury you next to your mother, and grandmother?"

"Sheriff." Dianna lurched forward, jerked to a halt when someone grabbed her hand. She whipped around to glare at the offender, clenched her teeth when her mother-in-law raised her eyebrows.

Leaning in, Eleanor Douglas whispered, "They must work this out their way. It's the only way the boy will ever respect Hank enough to trust him."

"Trust him?" Dianna hissed, incredulous.

"Yes," Eleanor said.

Pinching her mouth closed, Dianna looked helplessly at Boone and Jimmy.

The boy had stopped moving, but his body was stiff, his back arched, demeanour defiant despite what must have been incredible discomfort. The sheriff on the other hand, appeared relaxed, gave no indication having an audience bothered him. Clearly there were dynamics at work here which she did not understand. She would just have to trust Dirk and Mother Eleanor, the former being male, the latter having raised one, because they obviously understood men and boys better than she.

"You're damn stubborn, you know that boy?" the sheriff growled. "You get that from me. And like me, you'll find it only brings heartache. I lost your grandma because I was too much a fool to recognise she was dying inside. I might as well have put that gun to her head myself, 'cause my selfish ways sure enough killed her. And your mama? She's dead too, because of me. I wasn't there for either of them—" His voice broke. Then he closed his eyes, bowed his forehead to the back of Jimmy's skull. "But I'll be damned if I'll lose you, too," he rasped, and unlocking his arms and legs he went limp. "Go," he said hoarsely. "Go if that's what you want, boy. I won't force you to stay. But I will welcome you, if that's what you choose."

Jimmy, who remained oddly still while his grandfather spoke, abruptly rolled to his knees, glowered briefly at Boone, before surging to his feet. Dragging his forearm under his nose and smearing dirt with the blood that streaked across his cheek, he glared, warning everyone to keep their distance, before he charged into the stable. Hank staggered to his feet. Eleanor went to him. Dianna hesitated, and then turned to go after Jimmy, who was dragging his still saddled and sweat-dampened horse from a stall by its bridle reins. Dirk plucked her sleeve.

"Leave him, Missus," he murmured as Jimmy swung on the horse. "You'll only shame him further going after him."

"But... the horse," she said lamely over the echoing clatter of hoofbeats and anxious snorts from the stabled horses as Jimmy cantered out.

"Jasper'll be fine," Dirk said. "He's big an' tough an' quick to unseat anyone what treats him rough. Bloody hard to catch when he does. That's why I chose him for the boy. He'll learn quicker from being dumped in a patch of prickly pear or a fresh cow pat how to treat a horse, than he will the preachin' of an old man."

"You're not old," Dianna said.

"Aye, well, I'm not young. Not like this pup." Dirk hooked a thumb at Garrett.

Garrett laughed, and despite herself, Dianna smiled. And sighed.

Dirk was right. When she needed to grieve, she locked herself in her room where she was free to cry and scream into her pillow without fear of upsetting anyone else.

Jimmy deserved no less.

Chapter 11

Well-Matched

ou're getting married?" Dianna murmured, disbelieving. "When?"

"As soon as can be arranged, provided we 'ave your blessin'." Dirk reached for Mrs. Brown's chapped hand. The housekeeper's ruddy face darkened a few shades as she lowered her gaze. They sat shoulder-to-shoulder on the settee opposite. Dianna braced her hands on her knees, hollowed by relief.

When they'd approached her after the evening meal and requested a private audience, she feared they planned to give notice, and she'd not have blamed them if they did. There was no predicting what trauma might arrive at the front door next, fire, locusts...

Inhaling, she nodded. "Yes. Yes of course, you have my blessing. But you don't need it, you know. You're free to choose as you wish, but... thank you. Thank you for respecting me enough to ask. I am so... happy. Brilliantly happy for you both."

Dirk flushed so deeply his snowy eyebrows and whiskers seemed to glow pink. And then he glanced away, while Mrs. Brown bowed her head.

"What is it?" Dianna leaned toward them. "I thought you wanted my blessing?"

"Aye, we do." Dirk nodded. "It's just... We'll miss you."

"Miss me?" Dianna straightened. "Why? Where are you going? Don't tell me you're retiring?"

"Retiring?" Dirk scowled. "No. Well, what I mean is, now we're gettin' married, you'll not want us here, so we thought we might return to—"

"Not want you here?" Dianna said. "Why? Why would I not want you—unless you've no wish to continue working once you're married? That I understand. You're entitled to enjoy yourselves, after all."

Mrs. Brown looked up. "Are ye sayin', if we marry, you'll not require us to resign?"

"Heavens no." Dianna shook her head. "We're not in England anymore Mrs. Brown. Your status here is not contingent on your marital status. I don't believe love a suitable reason to fire anyone. But should you *wish* to go, if you have some place you'd rather be—"

"Nay, Missus," Dirk said. "We like it here."

"Yes." Mrs. Brown nodded. "We were only going to go back to Scotland, and my sister's ye see. Live with her, as she's alone. But if we can stay..."

Dianna willed a tremulous smile. "Of course, you can stay. For as long as you wish."

Hope charging her doubtful expression, Mrs. Brown glanced at her intended. He swallowed.

"Er, I wonder Missus," he murmured. "If we do stay on, where might you expect us to... stay?"

"Stay? Well, here of course—oh. Where will you *stay*?" She willed a smile. "I suppose, for the time being, you'll have to share Mrs. Brown's current room. Mrs. Stewart mentioned Mr. Sweeney is due in town next week for a visit. I'll invite them for dinner the Saturday when he's here and ask him about having a small cottage built that will be more suitable for a newly wedded couple."

"Oh, no." Mrs. Brown shook her head. "You'll not go to such trouble for the likes of us—"

"It's no trouble, Mrs. Brown," Dianna said firmly. "In fact, it will be a wedding gift. And yours to live in, even after you retire. Should you choose. It's the least I can do after everything you've each done for me." She hushed them with a motion of her hand. "Please, let me do this. I need something joyful to do, and there is nothing that could bring me more joy right now than to have you a home built, and show you how much you're loved, and needed in my life."

"Oh, boo," Mrs. Brown said, and burst into tears.

Dirk put an arm around her, gently teased her about her big heart as he handed her his handkerchief tugged from his shirt pocket. Mrs. Brown

133

accepted the white square without looking up, so she didn't see him drag his knuckles under his eye.

Dabbing her own tears, Dianna asked, "I'm curious..."

"Aye?" Dirk said.

"How long have you been... "

Mrs. Brown looked up, handkerchief crumpled in her hand. "Engaged?"

"Yes." Dianna frowned. "I never suspected a thing."

Mrs. Brown angled a faintly dour look at Dirk, before offering Dianna a wry smile. "Ye canna be blamed for not knowing when I didna know myself."

Dirk coughed, shuffled as though he was thinking of standing, though that would require him to unlink his arm from Mrs. Brown's, and Dianna suspected he'd have a fight on his hands if he tried.

"You didn't know?" she asked.

Mrs. Brown nodded. "Only jus' learned a short while ago 'ow he felt about me, though I'd set my cap for 'im first day I saw 'im. I was naught but twelve and come to work in the scullery for your grandfather, an' I was in the garden, collecting up the potatoes and carrots Cook sent me for, when I spied him walking the lordship's horse to cool it. It was another five years yet, before I summoned courage to tell him how I felt. Took him a wee-bit longer to finally get 'round to sharing his feelings about me," she added, angling Dirk a glare that might have been fierce if not for the merry glint in her eyes when she looked back at Dianna.

"Forty-five... years?" Dianna murmured, a lump rising in her throat.

"Aye, an' I'd still be waitin'," Mrs. Brown said, nodding. "If not for that bump on the head. Bless that girl," she added and made the sign of the cross over her ample bosom. "'Cause angry as I was wi' her I owe her. 'E asked me that day, after ye left him wi' me in my room 'cause he feared I wasna gonna live." She chuckled, an almost diabolical sound. "An' now 'e's in a pickle 'cause I survived, an' he 'as to marry me."

"Beth," Dirk said and squeezed her hand. "You know that's not true. I'm grateful to that poor girl. She helped me see that time was not mine to waste and that ye mean much more to me than—" He broke off, darted a glance at Dianna.

"It's all right," Dianna said. "I agree. Jobs and employers are like oysters, plentiful. But true love is as rare and beautiful as a black pearl, and infinitely more precious. I'm only grateful you decided to risk your positions here for each other. You deserve to be happy, and you have definitely waited long enough."

Forty-five years long enough. But had Dirk declared his feelings for Mrs. Brown at any time when employed by Mama's father or the earl, he and Mrs. Brown would have been dismissed. Neither could have afforded to lose such lucrative positions.

Clearing her throat, and blinking back tears, she started to rise. "Let me get Elaina and the girls—"

"Missus." The urgency of Mrs. Brown's tone dropped Dianna in her seat. Mrs. Brown glanced at Dirk, and when he nodded, she met Dianna's gaze as she leaned forward, whispered, "There's something else we'd like to discuss with ye, before ye invite in the others. Regarding Mrs. Stewart."

"Of course." Frowning Dianna tipped forward, raised her eyebrows. "What is it?"

∞ ∞ ∞

The first Saturday in October, and Dianna was again fighting tears despite her determination to display similar stoicism as the brides who advanced sedately toward their waiting grooms. Each was resplendent in her own way, but the transformation of Mrs. Brown was most remarkable.

Gone was the taciturn black and white uniform that had characterised her for fifty years. In its place was a long-sleeve gown of cream satin, overlaid with embroidered lace in a design of oak leaves and bell flowers paid for by Eleanor and Rosa, and altered by a local seamstress. Had Mrs. Brown had her way, she'd be now approaching her intended in low-heeled black shoes and one of her four out-dated, but almost new in appearance for how rarely she wore them, sombre-coloured dresses reserved for Sunday afternoon wear. Fortunately, she'd not had her way, because the corset, and cream-satin sash Elaina had gifted to enhance the ensemble, moulded a graceful hourglass in the housekeeper's sturdy figure.

Mrs. Brown's ever-present grey topknot had been converted, too, unwound and fluffed to a soft cloud of shimmering silver curls pinned under a wide-brimmed hat festooned with white silk roses, while the toes of white satin slippers peeked shyly from beneath the floor-length hem with each gliding step she took, a faint tremor of the pink-and-yellow-rose bouquet she clasped in white-gloved hands the only indication she was about anything more significant than her usual domestic duties.

Beside her, Maggie glowed like a sunrise in an off-the shoulder gown of flowing Citrine-Yellow satin edged with white lace along the neckline, her hair bound in a cascading waterfall of titian curls and pearl-encrusted hair combs, small white-gloved hands bearing a reduced version of Mrs. Brown's bouquet, better suited to her petite frame. She and Mr. Sweeney had taken some convincing, but upon learning it was Mrs. Brown and Dirk's idea—and greatest wish—that they double the joy of the day, they relented.

Dianna harboured a sliver of guilt she'd not stopped to consider her friend's wedding hopes. She hadn't realised Maggie and Mr. Sweeney had postponed their plans, unwilling to intrude on Dianna and Jake's grief. It was Mrs. Brown who'd gently reminded her the couple had intended to wed in the summer and suggested the dual-ceremony. Wise woman, Mrs. Brown.

The last three weeks' frenetic preparations had kept everyone, including Dianna, occupied night, and day. A whirlwind trip to Dallas to buy dresses. Fittings and alterations with the seamstress. Mounds of food to bake and baste. Casks of brandy and whiskey and tins of tea and boxes of cigars to order. Steer, hog, and chickens to butcher. Invitations to write, and send, the majority local.

Mrs. Brown and Dirk sent announcements, but no invitations, to England and Scotland, unwilling to delay the big day long enough to permit anyone they loved to travel over, especially in the midst of a war. Maggie had no family to invite, her parents and sister and known extended family having predeceased her. Mr. Sweeney, too, declined to invite family, reserving his contingent of attendees to his crew of builders that travelled with him. His foreman stood with him, and Dianna could not be happier for he and Maggie.

They were a well-matched couple, far better suited in Dianna's mind than Maggie and her first husband. Mr. Stewart had clearly loved Maggie, but he had been a haughty and unkind man—to Dianna, though she would never tell Maggie how he'd threatened her. Mr. Sweeney in contrast, was a dear to her. To everyone. Gentle, giving... *Like my dearest friend.*

Perhaps sensing Dianna's eyes on her Maggie glanced over, offered a faint teary-eyed smile, before mouthing, "Thank you". Then she looked back to the man in the dark-grey suit and white shirt and black tie who awaited her, his narrow back rigid, hands linked tightly in front of him.

Mr. Sweeney's hair was groomed one side and despite the parlour windows having been opened to permit a cooling breeze, perspiration sparkled like diamond dust between the thinning brown strands. If he sensed Dianna's gaze, he ignored her, having eyes only for his bride.

Dirk, in contrast, could barely see. He wiped at his eyes and brushed at his navy wool jacket with its crested pewter buttons so repetitiously, Garrett, slim as a broom handle in an ill-fitted suit loaned from Jake's wardrobe, bent to murmur in his ear. Whatever the young man said embarrassed or emboldened the elder man enough to impel him to draw up to his full five-foot-nine inches and hold his arms stiffly at his sides as he touched his polished brown brogues at toe and heel, like a soldier under inspection.

The red-and-green tartan of Dirk's kilt, and his off-white woollen knee socks, blurred to a whirling kaleidoscope forcing Dianna to close her eyes, pat them with her handkerchief to dry them. Next to her, Elaina sniffled, and grasped her arm. Dianna forced her eyes open.

Katie and Amelia, angels in white dresses with pink satin sashes and white knee-socks, either side of Elaina, clutched each other's hands, grinning in eager delight as Eleanor played out the final few chords of the Wedding March and the brides unlinked their arms in trade for their groom's. Justice Wardlaw cleared his throat. Eleanor rose from the piano and moved to the only vacant chair in the room, beside Sheriff Boone.

Upfront with Eleanor and the sheriff were Juan and Rosa. Behind them, friends, and neighbours, all of Maggie's students and their parents, and a few ranch hands in clean dungarees and freshly pressed shirts waited in quiet anticipation. Even Charlie had made the guest list.

Her golden coat washed to a glossy sheen and neck wreathed in fresh flowers, she sat between the girls wagging her tail so vigorously her whole canine body wriggled.

Happy, and surprised as Dianna was by the turn out, the presence of one person standing the other side of Garrett and looking just as awkward and uncomfortable in an ill-fitting suit, this time borrowed from Sheriff Boone, his big hands clasped in front of his hunched frame and face flushed to the short roots of his blonde hair, brought her special pleasure.

Jimmy had been gone two days when a wrangler from the Yellow House ranch showed up with Jasper, claiming he found the gelding mixed with his cavvy. Recognizing the J-D brand, he returned Jasper post-haste, concerned there was "trouble afoot". There was, but not as much as Dianna initially feared.

When the wrangler advised he'd found Jasper minus saddle and bridle in with Yellow House horses, Dirk pointed out that the gelding might rub off his bridle, but he could not shake the saddle without help, and therefore Dianna's assumption Jimmy had been bucked off and was lying injured somewhere on the vast rangeland was less likely, than Dirk's posit Jimmy had de-tacked the horse and turned him loose with the LFD branded herd.

Dirk's prediction proved out when, a week later, Sheriff Boone received a wire from Sheriff Woods that hinted at Jimmy's whereabouts. Dianna had not seen the wire, but Mother Eleanor shared its short message: *Big blond boy here. Not moved from outside burned hotel in two days. Know him?*

Boone's reply was even briefer: *Grandson. Keep safe till I get there.*

Jimmy returned to Douglas with Boone and together they rode out to the Yellow House Ranch to issue apologies and collect the gear Jimmy had hidden in some scrub, before continuing on to J-D Ranch where Jimmy mumbled his thanks to Dianna for allowing him to stay as long as she had, and apologies for disappearing so ungratefully, before advising her he was moving in with his grandfather.

Oddly enough Dianna discovered she was sad to see him go. Not because she again faced the prospect of replacing a hardworking employee. But because, despite his introversion and initial hostility, she'd grown fond of him. Perhaps because he reminded her of herself when she first arrived in Texas: alone, and lonely in the world.

Drawing a hitching breath, she looked around and realised that was not true of her anymore. At least, not entirely.

She was no longer alone. The room was fair to bursting with people she loved dearly, many of whom cared similarly for her. Still, as JT Wardlaw began the recitation of vows, she could not quell the sorrow undermining her joy. Because as much as she was not alone, she was desperately lonely.

Swallowing to soothe the dry ache in her throat, she willed her focus to the men and women of the hour, and away from the man and boy for whom her heart longed. She must have made a noise, however, because

Elaina slid her hand down her arm to grasp her hand, squeeze firmly, silent reminder to keep herself together. She did. Barely.

She clapped and laughed like everyone else when Dirk and Mr. Sweeney kissed their new wives to seal their unions. Smiled and made small talk for the rest of the afternoon into the evening, as she moved through the parlour and rest of the house to ensure her guests had what they needed, from cigars to brandy, and cake to tea.

At long last—after she saw all the newlyweds off on their way to town for the night before they caught the morning train to Amarillo for two more nights' hotel stay courtesy of Mother Eleanor, and the last guest to the door before tucking the girls and Charlie into bed—she staggered to her own chamber. Locking the door and not bothering to undress, she kicked off her shoes, crawled in to the big empty bed, and dissolved in disconsolate tears.

Part Two

Virtue rejects facility to be her companion. She requires a craggy, rough and thorny way.
~Michel de Montaigne

Chapter 12

We Will Visit

New York, New York
October 21, 1914

o you remember when I came to you?"

"Of course, *ma chérie*. I knew immediately you did not belong there."

Dianna dragged her gaze from the flat stone embedded in the earth to look at Mother Mary. "I was heavy with child. Like every other girl in the Home."

"*Oui*." The Mother Superior nodded, her handsome face sombre. "But even in your grief, and obvious physical discomfort, you were poised. Refined. Despite the single valise you carried, its sides hollow with emptiness, and even before I knew who you were, I knew you came from more. Much more. While the girls that most often came to me came from nothing. Would return, often, to less, their families having turned them out. I told you that, if you remember."

"I do." Dianna scanned the sunless wrought-iron-fence bordered plot squeezed amidst a tight grid of storied buildings from which laundry lines ran at cross-angles, damp clothing clipped by wooden pegs glittering with early morning frost. The grass was brown and short where it wasn't bare earth, but tidy and free of weeds and rodents, courtesy of the groundsman Mother Mary employed to maintain the cemetery. A couple clutches of withered cut flowers and a single-stemmed bloom indicated someone remembered at least three lives lost too soon.

She'd written Mother Mary the morning after the dual wedding to inform her of everything that had gone on, and the potential she might come through New York later in the month if she did not receive word from Jake by mid-month. Mother Mary wrote back immediately, admonishing her for not sending word sooner, and advising her in sternest terms that if she did come to New York on route to England, she had better arrive at least one day prior to her ship's departure.

I will meet you, ma chérie. We will visit. I will listen.

As promised, she greeted Dianna at Grand Central Station the day before. They shared a room at the Biltmore Hotel and spent the evening as the Mother Superior warned they would: Dianna talked. Mother Mary listened. Though she had, at Dianna's insistence, shared news of the nuns of Maywood Home now located in quiet rolling and wooded hills north of the city. Dianna took comfort in knowing the women whose kindness had comforted her when she'd so desperately needed it, were well.

"And Mitso?" she had asked, as intrigued by and fond as ever of the prescient black-and-white cat that ruled Mother Mary's heart, and office. "Is he still predicting births?"

"He is. Though with less vigour. A few persistent yowls, and head butts if I am tardy in my response, and he retires to the bed I made him by the fireplace. He spends more time there and less at the window, but that is to be expected. He's in his sixteenth year. Old bones prefer warmth, and require more rest."

Young bones required rest and warmth too, but so far Dianna's persistent insomnia, and the invasive cold of approaching winter, made both as fond a memory as Mitso.

Kneeling, she laid the bouquet in her arms on the ground, before rising to turn up the collar of her coat against the chill biting her neck along the edge of her scarf. "I remember well what you said, Mother," she said. "'*This place is for girls who have nowhere else to go, Dianna. It is a last resort. Not a first.*'"

"And I was right," Mother Mary said, her voice firm. "You did not belong there."

"But I did Mother." She offered her a rueful smile. "I belonged at Maywood, more than Charlotte belongs here. I needed to be there—"

"Only because you were uninformed, *ma chère*," Mother Mary said, her voice grave. "Once you knew who you were—"

"I don't mean because I thought Jake my half-brother," Dianna said. "Even when that proved untrue, I still needed to be there. With you. With..." Swallowing, she nodded to the plaque. "Her. Charlotte. I needed to learn, Mother. And Charlie... Charlie taught me. Even in her worst of days she shone. Shone with her goodness, her optimism. Her courage." She drew breath to strengthen her voice.

"Even as she was dying her thoughts were for her sisters. And the child. She begged me to help Katie and Amelia. Blamed herself for the child's death. She couldn't stop it dying inside her, Mother, but still she blamed herself. She wanted it. Wanted that baby, and even as I believed her naïve and nonsensical to think it, she birthed in me the possibility that I could. I could do what she could not, because she was too young. Still a child herself. But I... was not. I was a married woman and I wanted the child Jake had... helped me learn to love." She bowed her head to Mother Mary's bony shoulder as the nun moved closer, grasped her hand, exuding strength through the combined material of their gloves.

"I didn't love it Mother," she whispered. "I didn't love... JJ. Not at first. I never thought of him—it, if I could help it. My mind was only on the future. A future where *it* was part of my past. Unspoken. Unacknowledged. So deep in my forgotten memories to never be thought of again. But Jake changed that. He changed *me*." Clamping her lips, she fumbled in her pocket for her handkerchief, pressed it to her eyes.

Mother Mary said nothing, just stood there, strong, and unceasing in her compassion, while Dianna fought to collect herself. Inhaling, she straightened, cleared her throat, and stuffed the lace-edged linen back in her pocket.

"Jake taught me love, Mother. Charlotte taught me courage. And you... you taught me sacrifice. I have to do this," she rasped as she released the Mother Superior's hand and turned toward the cemetery gate, and the taxicab waiting at the kerb. "I have to. Love, courage, sacrifice. You all taught me that, and I cannot let fear and uncertainty tear me down, now."

∞ ∞ ∞

The motor carriage rolled to a stop. The driver got out, made to open Dianna's door. She stayed him with a hand. He withdrew and moved to unload the luggage. She stared through the begrimed windscreen at the New York harbour, and RMS *Olympic,* felt Mother Mary's concerned gaze on her.

Her throat tightened as Katie and Amelia's tearful pleas to travel with her echoed in her memory, grinding heartache soothed only mildly by Elaina's unsolicited decision to remain with them.

"Katie's becoming a woman," she explained after volunteering to stay. "She needs someone to talk to, someone who understands and can help her adjust to the changes she faces. And Amelia, well, she needs someone she cannot intimidate, or manipulate, and that is neither Mrs. Brown, nor your ever-patient mother-in-law. Mrs. Brown is much better at dispensing soup than she is intimate information and discipline. And Mrs. Douglas is far too indulgent, not to mention she has the ranch, and reconstruction of her home, to keep her busy. She does not need the added complication, or distraction, of a temperamental ten-year-old tyrant."

If not for the affection husking Elaina's voice Dianna might have taken offence at her description of Amelia, despite its accuracy. Instead, she laughed.

"And you believe you can control her?"

"It's not a matter of control," Elaina countered. "It's about negotiation. Every person has something they want, and every person is willing to trade to achieve it. Labour for shelter. Talent for recognition. Amelia wants independence. If she fulfils her end of the bargain, she'll get it."

"Really?" Dianna said. "What exactly is her end of the bargain?"

Elaina's smile was faint. "To complete her schoolwork, chores, and music lessons without fuss or reminder, and to comport herself with dignity and respect in all her interactions. If she shows me she's mature and trustworthy, I'll be confident in her ability to conduct herself appropriately outside my direct supervision, and therefore she'll earn opportunities to stretch her wings."

Elaina's expression had not invited joviality, or jest. And given her—their—upbringing, Dianna did not doubt the sincerity of Elaina's beliefs, or expectations. Only the potential to realise them.

Like Elaina, she had brought expectations to her role of adoptive mother to Katie and Amelia, confident she need only love and gently guide them, and they would fall obediently into line. She had since learned children, and parenting, were far more complicated, and messy, than a simple recitation of rules and consequences for breaking them. Quite frankly, the girls' emotions were fragile, and Dianna could only hope Elaina would see past each girl's very different front to their mutual heartache.

Steadying herself against resolve-weakening guilt, she reached for the door handle. Once out of the motor carriage, she folded a couple of bills in the driver's hand, and paused next to her luggage on the ground, closed her eyes as Mother Mary came to stand beside her, so close their shoulders touched.

Stillness settled over Dianna like someone had bundled her bodily inside a nest of soft clean wool or submersed her in a pool of warm sea water, even as the same bitter breeze whipping the *RMS Olympic's* flags tried to find chinks in the armour of her gloves, scarf, coat and skirts, and lined boots.

It had been a lot colder the night the *Titanic* sank. The air had pierced her skin like needles—

"Dianna, *ma mie*," Mother Mary murmured. "You shiver so—"

"I'm fine." Dianna locked her spine to compensate for her watery knees. "I'm fine." Forcing a determined smile, she added, "Let's go, Mother. Let's go and find out what's happened to my husband."

"Lead on, *ma chérie*," Mother Mary murmured. "The heart always knows the way."

∞ ∞ ∞

Threat of U-Boats in and around the English Channel forced them to a northerly route. It was as troubling and tense a journey as that Dianna had endured two-and-a-half year's previously, only this time everyone else on board seemed to share her mood. The subdued atmosphere was nothing like the jubilant environment that had charged her last ocean crossing.

Then, the fully-booked *Titanic* had launched to exuberant pomp and ceremony. The *RMS Olympic*, in contrast, slipped out of New York's harbour with little more than a hundred and fifty pensive passengers, and no crowds or well-wishers to see them off.

Where the *Titanic*—outfitted with the latest in electrical lighting—had blazed brilliantly as a shooting star as it raced through the night, and continued to glow even in its final hours, the *RMS Olympic* crept stealthily towards its destination its formerly distinctive black and white hues subdued by gunmetal-grey paint to make the ship more difficult to distinguish on the horizon by day; portholes covered and exterior lights extinguished to mask its presence at night. Six days on, and the rationale for such precaution became terrifyingly clear when Captain Haddock responded to a distress call from the *HMS Audacious*. The battleship had struck an underwater mine placed by a German submarine. It was sinking.

Most of the crew from the *HMS Audacious* ended up on board the *RMS Olympic* as the ships' combined crews spent the remainder of the day working with a naval destroyer to tow the floundering battleship. The joint effort ended abruptly when something on the *Audacious* exploded, and the ship sank. From there they'd been routed not to Gourock, Scotland as scheduled, but Lough Swilly. By order of the Royal Navy's Fleet Commander.

Four days. Four days they were held hostage on the *Olympic* because Admiral Jellicoe feared they would spread news of the *Audacious'* sinking, news the Germans could use to their tactical advantage. After a great deal of loud protest from all the passengers, herself included, beleaguered Captain Haddock was finally granted permission on the fifth day to sail to Belfast for disembarking.

Her joy at finally being permitted off ship was brutally short-lived, as they immediately returned to sea by ferry. To Liverpool. Where she booked a hotel so Mother Mary could rest, whilst she attempted to secure rail passage to Manchester, a feat complicated by the army's having commandeered the rail system for troop movement.

They had sailed out of New York on October 21st. She had expected to be at Ansmall before the end of the month. But here it was November 4th and they were only now shoehorned amidst a rabble of incongruently cheerful men given the men's ultimate destination.

Breathing shallowly against the pungent redolence of so many perspiring males confined in limited space she studiously tried to ignore talk that, like every conversation she'd heard or participated in since sailing out of New York, centred on the state of things across the English Channel.

Today's chatter focused on a battle at Marne. Though positive in suggestion that despite many lives lost, Britain and France would yet put an end to things quickly since they had not only halted the Germans advance on Paris but forced the Huns retreat, the discussion aggravated her fatigue. And anxiety.

Over ten-thousand brave British men and twenty-times as many French soldiers had died at Marne. An unthinkable number. At that rate, millions could potentially die if the war waged longer than a few months. And if the Germans weren't held back, and made their way across the channel... She shoved the worrisome thought from her mind, glanced at her companion as the train slowed on its approach to Manchester.

Mother Mary had not fared well. A greyish pallor darkened the thin skin under her eyes, a sickly colour exacerbated by the shadow cast by the black peak of her bonnet. She had her eyes closed, her strong face turned to the window. Perhaps sensing Dianna's gaze on her, she looked over. Smiled.

"You saved me, *ma chère*. I thought I was coming along to comfort you, and instead it is you who ensured I survived the journey. But I think I will forgo peppermint tea for a while. I drank enough on this trip. *Oui?*"

"I'm glad you're better," Dianna said. "Though your illness did help me. I was too busy fretting over you, to worry about myself."

Mother Mary chuckled. "Then my plan worked, and we are arrived safe. Where to next?" She glanced out the window as the train eased into the station.

"A restaurant. Hotel." Dianna glanced through the window at the lines of waiting men on the platform as the train chugged to a halt amidst a cloud of smoke. "Someplace warm and comfortable, until I can arrange transport for the next leg of our journey to Ansmall."

∞ ∞ ∞

The weathered manor and its moss and ivy-covered façade stood fast. It had for centuries. Though she didn't recall paint peeling on the shutters, and a general sense of... age. More likely she was comparing her former home to her current one with its gleaming columns, spacious front porch, and startlingly white paint. The house Jake had commissioned for her was a shimmering young bride full of promise, Ansmall Hall a withered crone stagnant with secrets.

Dianna suppressed a shudder. She must not allow her mind to wander dark paths. There was no good to be found there.

Starting up the steps, she halted when the front door flew open and a slender young woman bolted out on to the stoop to stare at her.

"Dianna? Oh my God, it is you." The young woman trotted down the stairs to grasp Dianna's forearms, stare at her.

"Lizzy?" Dianna murmured in disbelief.

Her memory of her youngest sister was of a thin and defiant child often outfitted like a boy in breeches and paddock boots, long red curls roped back in a tight braid, a good six inches shorter than the young woman looking her in the eye now. A young girl whose modest empire-waist gown could not entirely disguise budding curves, and showcased trim stocking-covered ankles as the hem stopped short above them.

Dianna touched the soft curling ends of Lizzy's hair, cut short in back and angled forward to curve under her chin. "Your hair," she said dumbly.

"I know." Lizzy flashed a wicked grin. "Isn't it brilliant? I had it done last week. Papa hates it."

Dianna blinked. And then laughed. "You can paint spots on a tiger, but you can't make it a leopard."

"What?" Lizzy frowned.

"Nothing. Come here." A sob escaped Dianna as she dragged her sister into an embrace. "Oh, Lizzy," she murmured. "I've missed you so much."

Lizzy mumbled, but the words were garbled.

"Oh, Lizzy, please honey," Dianna said. "Don't cry."

Lizzy shuddered, and clung to Dianna as though she feared if she loosened her grip, Dianna would vanish. Guilt twined through Dianna's heart, sharp and vicious as barbed-wire.

She opened her mouth, and closed it.

What words could heal the pain of her leaving in the middle of the night without a single word of goodbye? What sentence, or combination of letters, could mend the hole in a relationship ripped wide by two years absence?

She held Lizzy tighter, willed her to feel her regret, understand her sorrow, and accept that she had never meant her any harm. "I am so sorry, little one," she whispered. "Sorry, if I hurt you."

Lizzy jerked free. "*If?*" Her auburn eyebrows arched high. "You left. I woke up, and you were gone. Gone. No note. No letter. Nothing. It was like you never existed, like you never cared." She narrowed her eyes. "How could you? How could you just leave like that? How could you leave, and not tell me why? Why did you run away, Dianna? Why did you *leave* me?"

"I'm sorry, Lizzy. I never meant to hurt you." Dianna clasped her by the upper arms. "I... I wrote a letter—"

"Elizabeth." The name was spoken quietly, but with absolute authority.

Mama stood in the open doorway, her face grim. An even grimmer face hovered just above and behind her, and then retreated out of sight. *Buckland.*

Dianna's stomach twisted. She pressed her lips together, breathed through her nose. *Stay strong. For Jake. For JJ. For Elizabeth,* who despite the defiant set to her chin, trembled, whether with fear or anger, or some other emotion, Dianna couldn't tell.

Mama didn't look away from her youngest daughter.

"Come inside, Elizabeth, and go to your room."

"What?" Elizabeth glanced at Dianna, then at Mama. "No. Dianna's home. I'm not—"

"You'll do as you're told." Mama's voice was as hard as frozen steel.

Dianna bit her lower lip.

Mama had always lurked mutely in Papa's tyrannical shadow, pale and permissive, bending to his will the way a servant genuflected to a King. The regal woman with the unwavering green gaze was completely unfamiliar to her, though Dianna had witnessed minor demonstrations of inner strength the year before when the countess had arrived in New York accompanied by Lord Laxton, to inform Dianna of her inheritance and attempt to compel her return to Britain, flares of annoyance so quickly concealed behind a curtain of diplomacy, Dianna had discounted the countess's behaviour as staged. But some time since, the curtain had been raised, or torn away, to reveal the true act.

The change was unsettling. Like having a long-owned and docile Labrador suddenly curl back its lip and issue a throaty snarl.

How best to react? Firm and swift, as she would with a disobedient pet? Or placating and cautious as with an aggressive—and unknown—guard dog?

No. Neither approach was appropriate. She was not the Alpha. Nor prey. She was an equal. A woman and mother. Like Mama. And this was—had been—her home.

"Hello, Mama," she said, politely, but firmly.

Mama's gaze shifted to her. "Dianna."

Dianna waited, but Mama did not invite her in. She climbed the steps. "I've come to visit."

Without taking her eyes off Dianna, Mama said, "Elizabeth, now."

With a strangled sob, Lizzy raced past Dianna, nearly colliding with Mama who stepped aside to allow her past. As soon as Lizzy was through, Mama blocked the threshold.

"Are you not going to welcome me in, Mama?"

The countess lifted her chin. "Why are you here?"

Dianna shielded her surprise at her mother's aggressive tone, and decidedly inhospitable behaviour, behind a non-committal smile. "To visit."

The countess made no move to unblock the door.

"Really, Mama? Are you going to deny me welcome, especially when I've come all the way from America to see you?" *In the middle of a war.*

Do you have my son? Have you seen my husband? She stifled the words. Stifled the pain. Kept her expression curiously neutral.

So far, she had only questions. Suspicions. So many suspicions. And this was, as Mother Mary had reminded her on the journey over, her mother. Lady Laura Ellen Marshall. Countess of Ansmall.

Mama inhaled. "Why, did you come all the way from America?"

Dianna frowned. "What?"

"*Mon dieu Seigneur!*"

The countess tore her gaze from Dianna, looked toward the drive.

Mother Mary had exited the hired carriage. She marched up the stone steps, her Habit's hem swishing indignantly, and offered Mama a bruising stare equal to the one Mama had levelled on Dianna. The countess seemed to shrink, a conciliatory canine after a reprimand from its master. Dianna could almost visualise her ears flattening against her skull, invisible tail tucking.

"Mother?" Mama murmured. "I had no idea you were—"

"You were not meant to," Mother Mary said. "I promised Dianna I would remain in the carriage, until she called for me. She wanted to talk to you alone, but apparently, you are not as welcoming as she hoped you would be. And I 'ave travelled too many miles, over too many days, enduring rough seas and pro-longed confinement to be turned around now. This is your child, and she deserves answers regarding her child and

152

husband. If you have nothing to hide, Ellen, you will not mind our visit. *Non?*"

"Her child? Husband?" The countess frowned at Dianna. "What does she mean? I thought—" She caught her lower lip in her teeth.

"You thought, what, Mama?" Dianna said slowly.

"Nothing." Mama shook her head.

"No, you—" Dianna broke off when Mother Mary touched a gentle hand to her elbow.

"Let us go inside, Ellen," Mother Mary said, no compromise in her voice. "We've much to discuss."

Mama hesitated the space of a heartbeat, before stepping back, then stopped and angled a look at the carriage as the sound of crunching gravel signalled its departure.

"Your luggage?" She frowned at Dianna.

"We booked a room in town," Dianna said. "I wasn't certain what kind of welcome I'd receive."

The countess flushed, and then turned to lead the way across the polished-marble foyer, her heel taps sharp rejoinders of poised irritation. She'd regained most, if not all her composure, by the time they entered the drawing room.

The countess's acquiescence and incertitude immediately following Mother Mary's rebuke might have surprised Dianna was she not familiar with the role the Mother Superior had played that September night twenty-two years earlier, when twenty-three-year-old Lady Ellen Marshall entered a convent in France scared and in pain, convinced she would be leaving without the child she'd come to birth. Instead, Mother Mary persuaded the countess's new husband, Lord Edward Marshall, to let Lady Ellen keep her newborn daughter—her late fiancé's only child.

Mother Mary altered Dianna's birth certificate by three months, and waited until December to file it, so official record would show the female infant's birth landed a reputable ten-months after the Lord and Lady's February 22nd wedding date. In that moment, Mother Mary not only helped salvage the Lady's reputation and Lord's pride, she earned Mama's eternal gratitude and love. Awe. Child-like love and awe rooted in the stately nun's mother-like protection of a terrified and orphaned, bereaved, young woman wracked with pain and incapable of defending herself, let alone the child she was soon to birth, when the young bride's strong-willed and prideful husband would have seen the living reminder of his new wife's former lover handed off to strangers. *As I almost did with JJ...*

Clamping her teeth against want to race upstairs to the nursery, or demand why the countess had not responded to letters regarding the possibility Jake had visited, Dianna forced her knees to bend as she lowered to one of two settees faced to each other divided by a low oval table.

Mama was already on edge, seeming to want for any excuse to excuse Dianna from her company. And easy at it would be to excuse the countess's disaffection on nefarious culpability, Dianna had to allow for the possibility Mama was simply prickly with old-fashioned guilt at her role in attempting to shackle Dianna to matrimonial hell. Or retained anger at Dianna for failing to fall for the ruse.

"She is your mother, *ma chérie*," Mother Mary had cautioned. "But she is also human. And like all humans, weak, especially in the light of a mirror reflecting back one's sins. We must presume her, as anyone is presumed with respect to a crime lacking in evidence, as innocent. If she welcomes you and invites you to meet your brother, we can assume she is above reproach. If she acts otherwise..." She shrugged, offered a benign smile. "Reserve judgement, *ma chère*. Let her decide her guilt for you."

So far, the picture of innocence Mama was painting was dark. But hardly irrefutable in its guilt. So, she willed calm while Mother Mary eased to the wing chair at the end of the parallel settees. *The earl's chair.*

Dianna and her sisters, and Mama, had always sat facing each other like passengers on a train, while Papa, the conductor, orchestrated their lives. Or so Dianna had once believed. After learning last year Mama was the machinist behind Dianna's betrothal to the duke, she was less confident about her hierarchal assessment. Papa might be the conductor, but Mama was the coal fuelling the engine. Without her, the whole contraption would grind to a screeching halt.

When the Mother Superior finished arranging her voluminous habit's material and appeared comfortable, Mama lifted a bell from the sofa table, rang it, and reset it to the lace doily protecting the table's polished surface. She lowered to the settee opposite Dianna, her green eyes watchful, slender body tense, as though not sure from which direction to expect the next blow.

"Madam?" A maid curtsied in the doorway.

"We have guests, Gertrude."

"I'll arrange a platter, and bring tea, my lady." With a bob of her head, Gertrude backed out of the room.

Mother Mary gazed with interest around the room. "You enjoy a good life, Ellen." There was no criticism or condemnation in Mother Mary's tone; still, Mama's ears turned scarlet.

"I am fortunate," Mama said. "My husband ensures I want for nothing."

"I'm not judging you, *ma chérie*." Mother Mary smiled. "I merely observe the truth. I trust you will be as forthcoming."

Mama darted a suspicious look at Dianna, and reared back slightly when Dianna leaned toward her.

"What do you know of my son and husband?"

"Your son...?" The countess's frown deepened to consternation as she darted a look at Mother Mary. "I'm sure I don't know what you mean. I only know what your husband and Mrs. Brown wrote me about... the accident. And I... I am sorry, Daughter. I sent condolences."

Dianna inhaled against the grief ballooning in her chest. "Yes. I... read your letter." It was the only one of the numerous cards and letters received at the ranch in response to news of the tragedy inflicted by the tornado, she had read: *Thank you, Mr. Douglas for informing us of our daughter's injury and accept our sincerest condolences on the loss of your son. Mrs. Brown has also apprised me of what has happened and will continue to keep me informed. Regards, E. M.*

In other words, please don't write again. We'll get all our news from Mrs. Brown.

If Jake had found the countess's brush off hurtful, he said nothing. But then, he never did. Like his mother, he rarely had an unkind word for anyone. Unlike Eleanor, however, he was less forgiving when it came to confronting ignorance and arrogance. As though sensing Dianna's thoughts, Mama looked down. When she looked up, her expression was... remote.

"With regard to your husband," she said, her voice less gentle and more diffident, "I've not seen him since he was here in August."

Dianna straightened. "He *was* here? When exactly?"

Mama's frown deepened. "I told you, August—"

"What day?" Dianna inched ahead on her seat. "Last word I had he was in Liverpool on August seventh. He mentioned intention to come here, to visit. Did he see William?"

The countess scowled. "Why are you and he so interested in William?"

Dianna leaned forward. "Did he see him?"

Mama tilted away, her scowl deepening. "No, he didn't see him. He wasn't here that long. I... was unwell. Distraught, actually. Geordie and Alec had resigned just that morning, and Buckland warned many more were planning to go. To war. And I ... I had Elizabeth's birthday to think of. We'd originally planned to go to London. To the zoo. But then... everything changed. And it was all... very confusing. So, I'm afraid I was not at my best, and I encouraged your husband to leave after maybe... a quarter-hour. I watched him drive away myself. Honestly, Dianna." She hunched forward, her brows beetled with irritation. "What is going on? Why are you so anxious, asking such odd questions?"

Geordie and Alec were two of six footmen Dianna remembered, and if the others had resigned, that explained the oddness of Gertrude answering the countess's call for refreshments.

Swallowing, she stared at her mother. "If he was here, why didn't you write Elaina back, and say so? I've been wondering for weeks what's happened to him. I'm still wondering—"

"I received no recent correspondence from Elaina, or anyone your side of the water." Colour flared high on the countess's sculpted cheeks. "The last I've had from her came in... early August, to inform me she'd arrived safely at your house. And from you... March, I believe, was the last note I received. With your birthday wishes for Elaina."

Dianna sat back, shook her head. "Elaina wrote you at the beginning of September. When no reply came by mid-October, I decided to come over—"

"Which was a damn fool thing to do." Mama's brows pinched inward with prim bewilderment. "In case you haven't noticed, daughter, there's a war on. It's dangerous. And I don't know what it's like where you are, but nothing here is as it was. The overseas post is the least of our worries. We're losing staff. Horses.... " She exhaled. "I'm having trouble getting timely missives from your father—from London—never mind all the way from Texas."

Mother Mary's gaze narrowed on the countess. "Ellen," she said. "You are certain Monsieur Douglas was here, but the one time?"

Mama's expression changed from scornful annoyance to confused as she split a look between her mentor and daughter. And then she moved forward in her chair to focus solely on Dianna. "He's not been here since that first day," she said, resolute. "It was... four days after we entered the war. So ... August eighth. Have you not heard at all from him, since?"

"No." Dianna shook her head, tears welling. "Nothing. I've heard nothing."

Chapter 13

Why Would She?

Mama's cup rattled in its saucer as she set both on the table. "That's it," she said. "I told you everything there is to know. And I know there's nothing your father can tell you, that I've not already shared. He wasn't here."

"Then who was here?" Dianna asked. Mama's defensiveness needled. She seemed more interested in distancing herself from Jake's disappearance, than she did in helping sort out how best to find him.

"What do you mean, who was?" Mama said. "Everyone—"

"Everyone, who?"

"Everyone who's always been here." Mama heaved an exasperated breath. "Everyone that is, but your father, Geordie and Alec. As I said they resigned. And since then almost everyone else has resigned to go off to war in some capacity. Even some maids left for work in factories making bombs of all things. I've had to fight to keep who I have. Buckland wanted to tender his notice, but I convinced him that with your father away so much, he was needed here. I need someone to help run things." There was a desperate plea in her last words, as though she could not quite believe anyone would wish to trade their impeccable servant's uniform for drab military gear, and bombs.

The cold anger that had begun churning in Dianna almost the moment she'd sat down whipped to enraged fury upon hearing Buckland's name. Checking the urge to stand and shout her frustration, she bit out, "I'll go to London in the morning, see what my father might know, but first... I'd like to meet my baby brother and visit with my sister."

"I told you," Mama said. "Your father knows nothing. And your brother is sleeping."

Dianna fought the crippling urge to race up to the nursery. "How long does he nap?"

Mama's lips folded inward.

Dianna sighed. "Call for his nurse. Ask her."

With a huff of frustration, Mama rang her bell. A moment later, Gertrude appeared.

"Yes, my lady?"

"Tell Inverness I need to see her immediately."

"Master William is napping, my lady."

"I'm aware of that," Mama said coolly. "Certainly, you can relieve her for a few minutes?"

Gertrude tucked her chin, curtsied, and went out, her demeanour as stiff as her posture. A surge of gratitude for Mrs. Brown's bustling matronly affection warmed Dianna.

Mama and Papa's loss was her gain.

An awkward silence broken only by the sound of an occasional sip of tea held court in the drawing room until a dark-haired girl of about twenty entered, and inclining her head politely, murmured, "Ma'am?"

Girl?

Dianna suppressed a self-deprecating snort. She was only two-and-twenty herself. *But felt forty.* Which probably explained her assessment of her brother's rosy-cheeked nurse as a girl, when in truth, Inverness was old enough to wed and have a child of her own.

"Is my son feeling better?" Mama asked.

"Better Ma'am?"

"Yes," Mama said. "Is his fever relieved?"

Inverness appeared momentarily startled. But she recovered swiftly. "Uh... no, my lady. He's... still sick." Her tone was more question than confirmation.

Mama smiled apologetically at Dianna and Mother Mary. "Excuse me. I need to speak privately with Inverness."

"Mama—" Dianna broke off when Mother Mary waved a cautionary hand. As though deaf—or at least deaf to Dianna's voice—Mama departed, herding Inverness ahead of her. Dianna raised her eyebrows at Mother Mary.

"She'll be back," Mother Mary said and lifted a raisin tart from the tray delivered earlier.

"With excuses." Dianna exhaled. "I don't understand. If she has nothing to hide, why is she being so evasive?"

"Because she's scared." Lizzy sidled into the room, plucked a lemon bar from the tray, stuffed it in her mouth and speaking around it said, "First you ran away. Then Elaina went for a visit and never returned." She swallowed. "Then your crazed husband showed up asking questions, and snooping around—"

Dianna stared. "You saw him?"

"Spoke to him." Lizzy's smile was shockingly snide.

"What?" Dianna leaped to her feet. "You spoke to him? What did he say? Where did he go?"

"Go? I don't know. What did he want?" Elizabeth shrugged.

Dianna swatted Lizzy's hand when she reached for another lemon bar. "This is serious, Elizabeth. Jake's missing. If he spoke to you, I need to know what he said. It might help me find him."

Lizzy kept her head down, hand outreached, before slowly straightening to wipe a crumb from the corner of her mouth, her green-eyed stare as chill as the November rain that had begun to fall outside. "Mama thinks you blame her, and want to hurt her, by taking away everyone she loves."

"What?" Dianna frowned. "That's absurd. I don't blame Mama for anything." Which wasn't quite true. Mama had set in motion the catalyst that had temporarily ripped apart her world. But she'd rebuilt everything, and for the better in her opinion. "Lizzy," she said. "Please, this is not the time to be rude, or unhelpful. You know I've no intention of hurting Mama, or anyone. I just want to know—"

"Then why won't you come home?" Lizzy's eyes sparkled with tears. "And why did you take Elaina away from me, too?"

Dianna swallowed.

She'd believed—No. She'd *wanted* to believe Lizzy had adjusted to her being gone from Ansmall, as easily as she had adjusted to being gone. But Lizzy had not.

Why would she?

Just because her life had completely changed forcing her to run to keep up as she learned to love and discipline her children while she built a marriage and family, and stable of racing Quarter Horses, Lizzy's life

160

remained unchanged. Business as usual. She did as she had always done, lounge around the manse, sigh over text books, and hide from those who sought to tame her while waiting to grow up and escape the grim silence of hushed hallways. Dianna's throat tightened.

Lizzy used to crawl in bed with her after a nightmare seeking reassurance. On frosty winter mornings they'd lie abed, snuggled under heavy quilts, sharing dreams, or plotting a covert trip to the pantry for sweets. Now who snuggled and plotted with her?

"Oh, Lizzy," she murmured. "Please forgive me. I've been a fool. A selfish, selfish fool. I was—"

"I know." Lizzy's eyes narrowed. "Busy. Too busy to care about me. Too busy to care I'm all alone. Just like everyone else, you don't care about me!"

"I do care, Lizzy. I do—Lizzy!"

But Lizzy was gone, bolting from the room like a hare flushed by a hound. Dianna started after her.

"Leave her, child," Mother Mary said, tone soft if commanding. "You will 'ave better success, if you wait 'til she's calmer."

"I don't understand, Mother?" Dianna whispered. "First Mama. Now Lizzy. It's like they... hate me."

"Not you, *ma chère*. Who they are not without you."

"Who they are not?" Dianna swiped her palms over her damp cheeks. "That makes no sense."

"It's true," Mother Mary said. "You care. Deeply. Your energy lightens the dark corners of sad souls. Your passion, protectiveness... You make others feel worthy. When you are gone, they feel less so."

Dianna arched her brows. "You're suggesting they feel... unworthy?"

"Different," Mother Mary said. "In a way that is not welcome, as neither has learned to harness her power and shine without aid of your company."

"I don't think, so Mother," Dianna said. "Especially with Mama. She frequently accused me of causing her migraines."

"I did." Mama entered the room, a young boy in her arms, his chubby legs hooked on her short too-slender waist. His head was turned to her neck and all Dianna could make out of his face partially hidden by dark hair was a plump, and flushed cheek. Stubborn chin. Breath gasped from her as her chest squeezed.

Mama stopped short, gaze narrowing, forcing Dianna to lock her knees against the urge to rush over, verify whose child he was.

"I found your disposition challenging," Mama said. "I also found it invigorating. I admired and loathed you. You were everything I wasn't and wished to be: brave, independent... persistent. You never backed down when something or someone was important to you. You're a fighter, Dianna. I never was. Never will be. I miss that. Your spirit, and contrariness. You kept your father and I honest, forced us to examine our decisions, and though I know we rarely changed our minds, you must know you caused us to think. I didn't always like the thoughts your comments and arguments evoked, but..." She nodded slowly. "You made us better people, for your presence in our lives."

Dianna blinked, fighting tears as the countess resumed course for the settee, her voice soft:

"Mother Mary is correct when she says that we are not the same without you. The house is too quiet, everyone too polite. And now, without Elaina..." Mama glanced toward the open doors. "I never realised until today, hearing Elizabeth. But she's right." She sat the boy on the sofa, handed him a cookie. "William's too young for her and she's too young for the world. There is no one here for her. She's lonely, and I've been so wrapped up in William—" She touched his hair, eyes glimmering with rare tears, before she offered Dianna a regretful smile. "I am ashamed to admit that I was too involved in my own worries to notice how desperately lonely she was." She cleared her throat. "Inverness."

Inverness scuttled into the room. "Yes, my lady?"

"Stay with Master William, while he gets acquainted with his sister. I've some mending to do."

Mending? The countess was rushing off to sew? *No.*

She meant Elizabeth. She was going to make amends. To acknowledge— and hopefully help heal—her youngest daughter's shattered soul, apology and love Lizzy deserved to receive as much if not more from her eldest sister.

"I'll come with you, Mama."

"Later, Dianna," Mama said. "Let me talk to her first. Stay here and say hello to your little brother. Be careful he doesn't wipe his nose on you. He has the sniffles."

Chapter 14

Valour Is Stability

She'd known the moment Mama put him down, the little boy tucked in the corner of the settee, soggy biscuit clutched in one pudgy hand, was not JJ. His hair, though dark, was curly, and his eyes, though green, were lighter, almost turquoise, where JJ's had been more reminiscent of new moss. The boy on the sofa was built differently too.

JJ's square and sturdy frame Dirk often compared to a draft horse. The boy returning her gaze with a scowl had finer bones, sharp cheekbones beneath a chubby layer of baby fat. His nose and lips were similarly thin. *Like Papa's.*

Relief and despair writhed inside Dianna, each emotion attempting to gain the upper hand.

Papa had not kidnapped JJ. This was not JJ.

Not JJ.

She sank to the settee, legs giving out, as nausea and despair swirled up her gorge.

"Dianna?"

She turned slowly to regard Mother Mary, who shot out of the chair.

"Child—"

"I'm fine, Mother." Dianna planted a stabilising hand on the seat cushion. "I... I'm fine." *Liar.* She closed her eyes.

You always knew this was a possibility. Knew there was a chance Elaina was wrong, that in her haste to help, she muddled truths.

"Dianna." Urgency sharpened Mother Mary's voice.

Dianna snapped her eyes open to find her little brother leaned out for the goodies on the tray, a stream of mucus dangling from his nose. Blinking away her tears, she reached to block him with one arm, while tugging her handkerchief free of her pocket with her other hand.

"Hello, William," she said and waved off Inverness's attempt to pick him up, as she bent to kneel in front of the settee, obscure his view of the treats. "I'm your big sister, Dianna. How about I clean your face?"

"No," he pronounced.

When she maintained course for his nose, he pressed to the seat back, turned his head side to side and batted at her hands.

"Come now," she murmured. "A young lord must act politely, and be neat and clean, when hosting guests."

"Nooooooo!" A well-aimed kick caught her in the chin.

"You—" She lurched to her feet and scooped him into her arms, shook her head at Inverness, as she sat on the settee to pinion her brother's arms and hold him until his outraged screams, and vicious kicks, subsided to whimpering hiccoughs and feeble twitches.

When she was certain he was not going to resume the fight, she turned him on her lap, and with her handkerchief, gently wiped tears and mucus from his face.

"There now." She smiled. "It is better to cooperate, is it not, my Lord?"

He glowered at her, lower lip at full mast.

"If you aren't a miniature version of Papa."

"He is that."

Dianna looked over her shoulder. Mama was standing just inside the room. She moved to sit on the opposite end of the settee, offer Dianna an appreciative smile.

"You handled him well."

Dianna shrugged. "I've had some experience."

"*Oui.*" Mother Mary said. "Your grandson inherited his uncle, and grand-papa's volatility."

Dianna breathed in, didn't realise she'd closed her eyes, until someone touched her cheek.

She opened her eyes to find Mama gazing at her with compassion, tenderness.

"I am so sorry, Daughter. I should not have sent your husband away without allowing him to meet William, but I—" Mama pinched her lips together.

"Thought he was here to steal another child from you?" Dianna rasped.

Mama's eyes, a darker shade of green than her son's, glittered with unshed tears as her chin came up. "I don't know what I thought. All I knew, is he represented everything... everything I lost when you... stayed there. And now, Elaina's gone—"

"You didn't lose me," Dianna whispered. "You sent me away. And even though I understood then, as I do now, why I had to go, there is a difference. And Elaina will be back. She's only there because I'm here. She's looking after my daughters. As soon as I return... As soon as I know what's happened—" She hiked a breath, brushed a palm over William's hair, before using the same hand to dash at the tears spilling down her cheeks.

"Inverness," Mama said quietly. "Take Master William to the nursery and give him his bath."

"Yes, my lady." Inverness collected William from Dianna, and with a quick inclination of her head to her mistress, went out.

Mama shifted closer, grasped Dianna's hand. "I am sorry. Sorry about... everything. And I wish I could tell you more about your husband. But I can't. He left here, and I never spoke to him again. Did you check where he was staying?"

"Staying?" Dianna sniffled, wiped the moisture from her face with her free hand. "Where? Where was he staying?"

"In town. Poitras Inn, I believe he said."

"Poitras?" Mother Mary murmured, raising an eyebrow.

"Closest the train station," Dianna said. "We passed it on our way to the hotel." She stood. "I... I have to go there. He—they might know something."

"Just a moment, Dianna." Mother Mary raised her eyebrows, indicated Mama.

The countess was staring at her hands knotted in her lap. Her pulse fluttered wildly in her neck. Dianna frowned, and slowly lowered back to the settee.

"What is it, Mama? What else do you know? What haven't you told us?"

The countess slowly raised her gaze to Dianna's. "When... your husband left that day. I... went upstairs. To check William. But he and Inverness were not there. So, I went to check other chambers. I was in your old room when I saw something out the window. It was William and Inverness. They were playing on the front lawn. That was when..." She swallowed, and the next words tumbled out in a rush, "I saw your husband. And Elizabeth. At the end of the drive. They were talking. Then Buckland was there. And the gardeners. Then Lizzy came back inside. Your... your husband got in the motor carriage and drove away." She was as white as the doilies on the sofa table. "He returned the next day, but I... I had Buckland turn him away at the door. He never returned after that. I swear," she added emphatically. "I swear that is all I know. He never came back. And we never heard from him again. I assumed he'd gone home, or to Scotland to look at the cows he mentioned was his reason for being here in the first place."

"He talked to Buckland? You saw him talking to Buckland?"

"Yes." Mama nodded, her expression bleak. "About what, I've no idea. I never asked. And I honestly do not know what happened after he left here the second time."

"Ring him," Dianna commanded, her voice an octave below shrill. "Ring, Buckland."

"I can't," Mama said. "He's not here."

Dianna thrust to her feet. "Stop it, Mama. Stop lying. I saw him. I saw him when I arrived. He was right behind you—"

"He was here. He's not now." Mama pushed to her feet. "I am telling the truth, Daughter. When I went to check on William, I asked Gertrude to advise Buckland to send a note to London requesting my husband's return to Ansmall at his earliest convenience. She told me, Buckland had gone. Left me this—" She jerked a folded note from a pocket of her dress. "His notice. He's packed and gone, and no explanation. No request for a reference. And no," she added, pre-empting Dianna's question, "I did not ask Gertrude to inform your father of your presence here. I prefer him to return, sooner than later."

"Which he wouldn't do, if he knew I was here?" Dianna arched her brows. "Is he still that angry at me, Mama? Still so full of rage, he'll go out of his way to avoid me? Ignore my presence in his home—on this earth— the way he's done since the day I chose Jake over *your* and *his* preferred husband—" She broke off when Mother Mary grasped her hand.

"*Le courage est la stabilité, pas des jambes et des bras, mais du courage et de l'âme,*" Mother Mary murmured. Valour is stability, not of legs and arms, but of courage and the soul, her polite way of advising Dianna to lower her voice and treat her mother with respect if she desired her Ladyship's continued cooperation.

Dianna closed her eyes, imagined containing her emotions the way she might stuff live fighting snakes inside a drawstring bag and tug it closed. Exhaling, she opened her eyes.

"It's all right, Mama," she said in a voice so equable, if not for her frantically beating heart and roiling stomach, she might have convinced herself she was entirely at peace. "There's no need to send for Papa. We'll interview the staff together, see if any of them know where Buckland has gone. Then I'll stop in at the Inn and see if anyone there knows anything. If all else fails, I'll go to Papa. *Make* him see me. *Pas le fait d'être en mesure de gouverne des événements, je me gouverne.*" Not being able to govern events, I govern myself.

Mother Mary was not the only one who could use Michel de Montaigne's words to make a point.

$$\infty \quad \infty \quad \infty$$

The bedchamber was lit by a single sputtering candle, what remained of the late-afternoon light blocked by thick draperies. Frenetic shadows danced on the wall around the canopied bed, and it took Dianna a few minutes to distinguish Lizzy's russet head from the jumble of green satin heaped in the middle of it.

"Lizzy?" She didn't expect a reply, and so was not disappointed when none was forthcoming. Perching on the edge of the mattress she smoothed Lizzy's hair from her freckled cheek. No muscle-twitch or flicker of eyelid. "I know you're awake, Mouse. When you're truly asleep, you smile when someone strokes your hair."

Silence.

"I understand if you're angry with me. I'd be angry with me, too. What I did was unforgivable, though I hope one day you'll find it in your heart to forgive me. I truly did not mean to hurt you, Lizzy. I had to go. Had to. It seemed the best decision. It still does. Leaving, that is, not going without saying goodbye. Because if I had stayed, I'd not have fallen in love. I know I can't expect you to understand that. You're young, and you've yet to meet a man that makes your heart ache the way mine does for my husband, though I do wish you that. I pray you'll find love like the love I have with Jake—"

The bedding erupted as Lizzy sat up, her green eyes topaz in the candlelight. "You had love. I loved you, but apparently that wasn't good enough." Snapping the covers over her head, she hunched in a tight ball, a turtle withdrawing to its shell. Dianna brought a hand to her mouth.

Lizzy's depth of pain was greater than she'd imagined. How could she bridge the gap yawning depthless like the Atlantic, between their hearts?

The truth. It was the only thing that had ever worked for her.

Easing to her side next to Lizzy she put her arms around her. Lizzy stiffened, made to roll away, but Dianna refused to let her go. Closing her eyes, she whispered, "I was with child, Lizzy. Mama wanted to protect you and Lainey, so she arranged for me to go to America, until the baby was born. I was supposed to leave it there and come back here, but... things changed. The people who were to take the baby couldn't. He—Mr. Stewart—died when the *Titanic* sank, and his wife Margaret, who's now my friend, couldn't take the baby. Then I met Jake. Mr. Stewart's cousin. He was... good to me. Kind, and understanding. He didn't think me unworthy, or unchaste." She inhaled a shaky breath.

"He proposed Lizzy, and promised to help me raise the baby as if it was his own. I was... terrified. But I loved him. I didn't want to. I didn't mean to fall in love with him. I never planned to stay there, Lizzy. You must believe me. I planned to come home, to Ansmall, to you and Lainey but I... I fell in love. Oh God, I'm so sorry, Lizzy. I fell in love."

Lizzy squirmed around, until she was facing Dianna. With her sharp chin, and large eyes filled with tears, she resembled a woe-begotten ginger-coloured kitten.

"You really do love him?" she whispered.

Dianna nodded. "Yes, little one, I do. I really, really do."

"He didn't kidnap you?"

"Heavens, no. Where did you get such an atrocious idea?"

"Papa."

"Papa?" Dianna wiped at her eyes, scowled. "Why would he tell you such a thing? He knows I married Jake out of choice, not coercion. I told him." *Just moments before Jake busted his nose, because he refused to believe me. Was determined to drag me back here.*

That was a story best left untold. Lizzy didn't need all the gory details of the earl's transgressions. He was still *her* father.

Lizzy sat up, crossed her legs tailor-style, and said, "Papa said he was a charlatan who seduced you into staying with him."

Dianna pushed up to sit with her legs tucked to the side. "Papa said that? To you?" The comment wasn't truly surprising. But to speak in such a manner to Lizzy?

"Not me. Mama." Lizzy cleared her throat. "When Mama came back from America, I overheard her tell Papa that you refused to come back with her. That's when Papa said the American was a—"

"Thank you, Lizzy." Dianna inhaled and shook her head. "I understand. But Papa is wrong. Jake is not a charlatan. He's a good man, who loves me, and I him."

Lizzy nodded. "That's what Mama said."

Dianna blinked. "She did? When?"

"That same day. Papa made the comment about the charlatan, and Mama said that she did not think so, that she believed you were in love."

"Really?" Dianna leaned against the headboard. "Did she say anything else?"

"Just that your son looks like little William."

Shock almost stopped Dianna's heart. Fortunately, it continued beating, enabling her to ask cautiously, "Mama said JJ and William look alike?"

"Close enough to be brothers. Dark hair and green eyes, only William's hair is curly, and Mama said your little boy's hair is straight."

"As an arrow."

It wasn't a wonder JJ and little William looked so much alike. The earl and the late James Ramsay were close in appearance. Tall, athletic, dark-haired. Only their eyes were dissimilar.

The earl had eyes of blue-ice. The marquess, deep almost violet-blue eyes. Truths she knew not from the single photograph of the marquess and earl with her uncle she'd seen—it had been black and white—but from having faced the earl over the desk in his study, and at the dining table, hundreds of times over nineteen years. And in looking in her vanity mirror every day for almost as long, then having her uncle tell her how her eye colour matched her father's. That she looked *just like* her father. No wonder the earl had never warmed to her. She'd been, as he'd feared prior to her birth, a daily, painful reminder.

"Is it true? Did your little boy die?" Lizzy's voice was low, wavery with hesitant sorrow.

"He must have. I'd hoped—" Dianna brought a hand to her mouth.

"You don't really know for sure?" Lizzy whispered.

"No." Lowering her hand, Dianna shook her head and blinking back tears, told Lizzy about the tornado. "While I was... recovering, Jake and everyone, everyone in and around town, helped look. But... "

Lizzy's sharp features crumpled. "Oh Dianna, I'm sorry. So sorry, I was mean to you. And I didn't reply to any of your letters. But I was just so... angry."

Dianna hugged her. "It's all right, Mouse. I forgive you. Your feelings are natural. It's normal to think of yourself, when you're hurting. I know, because I did the same when I discovered I was with child. I was only concerned with myself, and my future. But Jake... he helped me realise that I was capable of so much more. He helped me understand what love is, and it's not regret, or resentment, Lizzy; it's acceptance and forgiveness. So please, I am not upset with you. And you must not be upset with yourself."

Sniffling, Lizzy pulled away, dragged a hand under her nose. "That's what Mama said."

"Mama?"

Lizzy nodded. "She was here before you, to apologise. She said she'd not been a good mother to me and wanted me to know she was sorry. She also said I should not be angry at you, that you were hurting more than me."

"Our hurts are different, Lizzy," Dianna said. "But your pain is as valid as mine. And you're entitled to it. Don't ever let anyone tell you that your loss is less than another's. It's not true. There is no way to quantify heartache."

"I missed you so much," Lizzy whispered raggedly.

Enfolding Lizzy in her arms, Dianna kissed her temple. "And I you, sweets," she murmured. "More than you know."

Chapter 15

Just Tell Me

*D*ianna tapped her toe impatiently. The repetitive clack resounded harshly in the cavernous octagon of Westminster Palace's central lobby.

During the day, the sound would hardly be noticed amidst the hurly-burly of parliamentary pedestrianism. But it was late, and the chambers vacant, so except for mosaics of St. George and St. David keeping watch over the south and north corridors respectively, and the Yeoman Usher who'd accompanied her, she was alone. She sighed, shifted position on the bench, and struggled to stifle her impatience.

The House had prorogued in mid-September and been called back on the twenty-seventh of October. Despite the break, the earl had apparently returned only once to Ansmall. Always focused on work according to Mama, the war had added a new level of intensity to the earl's engagement, which explained why even at this late hour when hushed shadows filled hollow spaces he was still within the hallowed chamber, instead of at Rosewood.

The townhouse's housekeeper had informed her that his lordship routinely returned after dark, and never before nine in the evening. Occasionally as late as midnight. Dianna puffed out a breath, curled her fingers into her palms.

Time was wasting, and she had no time to waste.

The innkeeper and his wife had tried to be helpful, and ended up filling her with more terror than she knew what do with.

"We ain't seen him," Mrs. Poitras said, her shrewd gaze hard as a pair of black stones. "Hired a room and our motor carriage for the week, then vanished the second day. Next morning, we woke to find the motor carriage parked out front. A few days later, a woman showed up for his belongings, said she was his sister-in-law an' he'd had a family emergency. I showed her upstairs and waited while she tossed his things in his carryall, and then away she went in a carriage."

Mr. Poitras, a gruff man, had even less to offer. He never saw the woman, or Jake for that matter after he'd hired out his Model-T to him.

"Paid it for the week," he muttered. "Never saw him again after. I work the bar every day, but Sunday." He indicated a hallway that led to the public house attached to the Inn.

No one else Dianna and Mother Mary talked to in town, accompanied by a police constable, remembered seeing Jake. And absolutely no one but Mrs. Poitras remembered a woman, though the Inn's ostler recalled the Brougham, if only for his appreciation of the perfectly matched pair of blacks hauling it when 'fine sturdy horse flesh like that' was being requisitioned and sent to France for officers' mounts, or to haul gun carriages'.

No one in Hereford seemed to know anything about anything related to Jake. And the only thing she knew anymore, was that her disquiet had reached a point she could barely contain herself.

The Yeoman said nothing, but his eyes gave him away. Every now and again he glanced at her tapping shoe in silent remonstration. She ignored him.

The earl could force her to wait, but she did not have to do so quietly.

Mother Mary had encouraged her to stay with her at Rosewood and await the earl's return, but she could not abide the townhouse's stuffy atmosphere. Two levels, with sleeping quarters below and living area above where windows overlooked Hyde Park, it was crammed with clunky furniture, gloomy portraits, and heavy patterned rugs all overlaid with the cloying odour of cigar smoke. But after three hours biding her time here, she was tired, hungry, and on the verge of screaming, wondering if she shouldn't have yielded to the older woman's wisdom.

The earl's voice preceded his appearance. The Duke of Blackburn exited the south corridor first, followed by another man, and then the earl, each man carrying an overcoat and hat.

"Papa." Almost two years of internal struggle on how to think of him, or refer to him, and relying heavily on formal reference to distance herself

172

from him when she did think of him, and *Papa* flew out of her mouth as naturally as a wild bird escaping a cage. She hastened forward.

If her presence surprised him, he gave no indication. His pale blue eyes slid across her face with the slow efficiency of a honed razor. The cutting sensation was so intense she was tempted to touch her cheek and check for blood. Shaking it off, she fixed a gracious smile, and bobbed a brief curtsy.

"Your Grace. My lord."

The duke merely twitched an eyebrow, but the other man smiled as he glanced at Papa.

"Papa?" he said.

To the uninitiated, the earl's lack of expression might be interpreted as impassivity, but Dianna recognised the emotionless mask for what it was: tightly controlled rage.

"Lord President," he said quietly, "may I introduce my daughter, Dianna. Dianna," he added in a parental tone that implied she would accord the adults respect appropriate to their positions. "I believe you're familiar with His Grace. And this is Marquis Crewe, Lord President of the Council."

"My Lords," Dianna said formally, and sank to a deeper curtsy. Rising, she flashed her brightest apologetic smile. "If you will excuse me, sirs, I have urgent business with my father and require a few moments of his time."

Her boldness was a horrid breach of protocol, as the earl's glacial stare attested, but she didn't care. The only man whose feelings concerned her, was Jake.

Papa opened his mouth to say something, but Crewe spoke first.

"Don't let us old men interfere in a matter of family urgency." He turned to Papa. "Ignatius and I will go ahead. If we don't see you tonight, we'll convene in my office at eleven a.m. sharp."

"No need, Lord President," Papa said. "Matters of State take precedence over personal issues. My daughter can wait until tomorrow to speak with me." His brutal gaze on her, and decision to use Lord Crewe's state title, rather than a less formal reference as Lord Crewe had used in regard to the duke, was intended to warn her that she had overstepped, and better retreat. Now.

She shook her head. "I'm afraid it can't wait, Papa."

The Yeoman's eyes flared slightly, and his cheek muscle twitched. Lord Crewe made no attempt to stifle his response.

"Matters of State are important, Edward," he said, clapping a hand on the earl's shoulder. "But never more important than a daughter's need for her father's guidance. I know. I have four who routinely test my sagacity. We'll catch up later, isn't that so, Ig?"

The duke nodded, though his scowl suggested he was more inclined to agree with Papa. "Goodnight Ansmall," he said gruffly, and turned away without acknowledging Dianna.

Lord Crewe remembered his manners.

"It was a pleasure meeting you, Lady Dianna," he said with a smile, and nod of departure.

She managed not to glance at Papa, but could not control the slow burn of a blush in her cheeks.

The duke's overt dismissal of her would reinforce the earl's displeasure at her unofficial abdication from Society, serve to remind him of the stature, esteem—political power—he'd yet wield had she not run away.

"Thank you. My Lords." Dianna dipped another low curtsy as Lord Crewe turned to follow the duke out, and gasped when a hand clamped on her upper arm.

"What are you doing?" the earl demanded in a quiet hiss, his long nose waving inches from hers like a dented blade. "And how dare you interrupt my session with the Lord President."

Her instinctive reaction was to freeze, peel back her lips in an ingratiating smile and beg mercy. She stopped herself, as the duke and Lord Crewe passed under the arch into the corridor and disappeared.

She had what she wanted: a private audience with her father. Except for the Yeoman. And she was not a child. Or a whipped dog. She deserved better treatment.

Shooting the Yeoman a withering look that made him flush and avert his gaze, she inflated her ribcage, met the earl's cool stare. "Let. Go."

"This is my domain," he whispered. "You'll watch how you speak to me."

"You'll watch how you *touch* me." She glanced pointedly at his hand still gripping her arm. "Please, Papa," she added quietly. "Do not embarrass either of us further."

A storm of emotion darkened his silvery-blue irises. As quickly, they regained their icy clarity. His fingers lifted slowly, stiffly, as though the physical retraction pained him. Perhaps it did.

He was unused to withholding his temper. At least with her.

"Thank you," she said. "I promise not to take more of your time than it takes for you to be honest with me."

"Honest?" The word rasped from his throat as though dragged out by his tongue against his will.

"Yes. Just tell me, Papa, where is my husband?"

Chapter 16

Of My Heart

Mother Mary was snoring softly in the depths of a wing chair, her head angled to one side, the Bible open on her lap. Dianna eased it from her fingers, lifted an afghan from the sofa back and draped it over her, unwilling to disturb her sleep.

She needed it, poor dear. A week on, and she was still not fully recovered from the debilitating illness that had kept her bed-bound on the *Olympic*.

The elder woman snuffled, wriggled deeper in the chair, but didn't wake. Smiling, Dianna straightened. Frowned.

When had such deep grooves developed around the Mother Superior's mouth, and so many silver strands infiltrate the narrow strip of hair visible along the edge of her slightly skewed nun's veil? Had her hair not been more cinnamon-coloured but two years ago? Her eyebrows, too, were heavily striated with silver. Feeling oddly bereft about the irreversible changes age was tolling on her mentor and friend, and mildly guilty for not having recognised it sooner, she followed the earl to his office. By the time she closed the study door with a soft click, and faced him, he'd poured a glass of amber liquid. She compressed her lips.

Could he not get through one night without the blasted stuff?

Jake rarely drank anything stronger than coffee. He believed in facing issues head on, with a clear mind. He had told her once, if the time ever came and he needed liquid courage, she should shoot him, because he would rather die than draw strength from a bottle. However, it was not the time for lectures. Even if it was, Papa would never listen.

He never did.

But he would this time. He would listen, or she would—

"Would you like a drink?" He gestured with the hand holding the glass. "This is Chivas, but I have sherry, or brandy if you prefer."

"I don't drink."

He blinked.

"I'm sorry. I didn't mean to be so abrupt." She willed a smile. "Thank you, but I never acquired a taste."

His forehead wrinkled, as though she had spoken an unfamiliar language. "Then what do you drink?"

"Tea, mostly."

"I'll ring—"

"No. Please. It's after eleven. Let the maid sleep. I'll be fine. I only want to talk—" She grasped the back of a chair facing his desk, struck by a dizzying flush.

"Dianna?"

"Sorry." She swallowed. "I've not eaten since this morning. Or slept well in days. I just... need a moment."

"Sit." Papa guided her to one of a pair of red-leather chairs facing the fireplace, an ivory chess set on a round table between them.

Eyes closed, and breathing slowly through her nose to disperse the heat and fatigue prickling below her skin, she tugged off her gloves and tucked them in a pocket of her coat, before wresting out of it. Leaned back, she opened her eyes to find the earl on his knees stoking the fire. The coals were red hot. The maid must have added fresh fuel before retiring for the night. It truly was the earl's habit to return late and sit up.

He stood, returned to the credenza, and a moment later a snifter of topaz-coloured liquid joined the glass of scotch next to the chess set. "Brandy. For you," he said as he settled in the opposite chair with a pop of joints. "I know," he added when she started to protest. "Consider it medicinal in its purpose. It will help ease the tremors."

"Tremors?"

"You haven't stopped quaking since we met up."

Quaking?

But it was true. She had her hands clasped in her lap, not because she was cold—she wasn't—but to still the palsy better-suited to someone four-times her age. Focused as she was on finding clues in Papa's facial expressions and mannerisms, she'd ignored her own conduct.

"Try it," he said raising his glass to his mouth. "You might discover you like it."

Another excellent reason to refrain. Yet, as though possessed by a spiteful spirit, her hand unlinked itself from its partner and took up the snifter.

The first sip made her cough and her nasal passages burn. The second was less troubling, perhaps because the first mouthful had numbed her palate. She exhaled, surprised how quickly the alcohol moved through her veins warming her blood, forcing another flush to the surface of her skin.

Setting the snifter aside, she swallowed a couple times to stretch her stunned throat muscles, and then asked, "Where is my husband?"

"I told you, I don't know."

Yes, he had told her, numerous times in the carriage over from the parliament buildings. Twice again outside on the street, before insisting they carry the conversation inside.

"You must know something, Papa. You must. Your man disappeared the very day I arrived asking questions. And then there's the woman—"

"You think Buckland's leaving was my idea? Or that I know this woman? Don't be ridiculous. I'd no idea you were this side of the Atlantic, until an hour ago. I only heard of your husband's presence this side of the ocean, after he'd visited with your mother. And I know nothing about any woman. How do you know your husband didn't meet her here, or arrange to meet her here, and go off somewhere?"

She stared, struck by his tone. Intimation. "Are you implying my husband... left me? For another woman?"

The earl shrugged. "It's been known to happen."

The constable in Hereford had hinted something similar, only with far more subtlety, phrasing his suspicion in the form of questions about the state of her and Jake's marriage, Jake's mental well-being, and their finances. She'd wanted to club him over the head with her reticule, but a sharp look and soft word from Mother Mary reminding her PC Good would be derelict in his duty if he didn't ask basic questions, had prompted her to contain her outrage enough to convince the officer she and Jake's marriage was strong, their finances more than adequate, and his decision to travel to England at her behest. She felt no differently, now.

She pushed forward on the chair. "He did not leave me. He came here for... business. And now he's missing. The last person he spoke to at

Ansmall was *your* man. Tell me Buckland never wrote you about his conversation with Jake. Mama said she saw him talking to him, and that she'd told Jake you were in London. Was he here?"

"Why would your husband come here when he told your mother he was bound for Scotland?" The earl arched his brows. "Cows. He claimed he was here to look at cows. There are no cows in London proper. Even if there were, I had no time in August to breathe, let alone entertain your husband."

"Jake. His name is Jake."

The earl lowered his gaze to his drink, pursed his lips. She glared at the fire, waited for the urge to cry to subside.

Two years, and he still clung to his abhorrence of Jake for protecting her from... him.

"We interviewed every servant left," she murmured. "No one seemed to know where Buckland went. Most claimed ignorance of his leaving. He never wrote you? Never mentioned Jake? Never hinted he was planning to resign?"

He continued to avoid her gaze by watching the contents of his glass which he swirled slowly with one hand. The perfect image of relaxed innocence if not for his other hand, which gripped his knee with enough force to turn his knuckles white. He tilted the tumbler to his mouth and finished the whiskey in a single swallow. Lowering his arm until his hand, still holding the glass, dangled over the end of the rest, he stared moodily at the flames.

"He sent a wire. About your husband's visit. Said he'd scared him off—"

"Scared him off?" She frowned. "Why? Why would he scare him off? He was there to visit."

"Was he?" He locked eyes with her. "Was that his only reason for showing up, to visit? Cows? Cows and a... keen interest in meeting his wife's family. Particularly, William. Why? Why would he be so interested in *my* son? What would drive a man to leave his wife, and family, to cross an ocean, and despite the outbreak of war in the country when he arrives, where prudence would urge him leave immediately and return home to safety with his wife and family, especially a family recently aggrieved after losing a child, he instead detours for an unannounced visit with people he knows look upon him with disfavour, and not only does he expect courtesy and hospitality upon his arrival, but he explicitly requests to see *my* son and daughter."

She stared. She'd not looked upon Jake's visit in such manner. She'd viewed it as a necessary deception, one she'd hoped Mama and the earl would view as she and Jake had decided he would play it: an attempt to breach the discord and resentment separating all of them. Which was a very real possibility, provided they did not have JJ. *Which they didn't.* Hearing now the earl's interpretation of Jake's unexpected sojourn to Ansmall, she could see her and Jake's plan for the disingenuous ploy it was. Understand the earl, and Mama's, unwillingness to engage.

Part of her wanted to cling to some justification for her and Jake's decision, convince herself she'd not have suspected the earl of nefarious intent were roles reversed, but... She'd suspected him, first.

Why believe she and Jake deserved enhanced consideration?

As though he'd heard and agreed with her thoughts, the earl shoved out of his chair, crossed to the credenza and with his back to her, poured another measure.

She remained where she was, limbs trembling with increased adrenaline charging through her. She lurched to her feet.

"Papa?"

He didn't move, did not lift his hand from the neck of the Chivas bottle. His other hand rested flat on the credenza's polished top, his head low as though he was contemplating a nick in the glossy surface.

"I'm sorry. I'm sorry I disappointed you. You and Mama. And that I... *we.* We lied to you." She stared at his image reflected in the window, angular face smudged to an indistinct oval by the desk lamp's illumination. She inhaled. "Jake came here to see if... see if you'd taken JJ."

With the jerky motion of a marionette he straightened, one vertebra at a time, and slowly spun to face her. His lips were white, ice-blue eyes brilliant with disbelief. "Why in God's name would you think such a thing?"

"I... It was me. I... I was mad with grief. Out of my mind with losing my... son." She brought a hand to her chest, hardly able to breathe for the pain. "I overheard Elaina describing how little William looked like my JJ, and I... I got it in my head. In my head that he... had to be here. Had to be... *alive.* So, I made Jake come and look. Look and see if—" She hunched as sobs tore from her, jerked when his hand closed on her arm.

"Sit," he said, and directed her to her chair. She collapsed in it and folding her arms around her waist, bowed her head, rocking as she fought for control.

"God's teeth, daughter," he whispered. "Why would you ever think I would take your son? I am deeply sorry for your loss. Deeply. And bloody appalled you'd think I'd have anything to do with it, though... I suppose I can, understand it." She heard a thump signalling he'd dropped in his chair. "I've not been the best... father. I... mistreated you, and for that I am sorry. I suppose I earned your distrust, but I can assure you, I have no idea what has happened to your son, your husband. Or to Buckland."

She stilled, limbs and tongue held hostage by shock of his apology, and, when she finally forced her head up, sight of a single glistening bead at the corner of his eye. *A tear.*

Anger, she knew. Disgust, reproach, criticism, these she was familiar with in him. Not this... sorrow. Regret. Recognizing it was paralysing. She knew not what to do: Look away and give him time to regroup and exhibit an emotion they would both find more comfortable, like anger? Or move beyond the past and offer solace and understanding? Her stomach cramped with either choice, so she did nothing.

He must have interpreted her silence as rejection, because he launched to his feet. "Go to bed," he said. "I'll try to locate Buckland. Find out what he knows, if anything. And I'll reach out to Chief Constable Richardson about the woman in the carriage. Ask him to have his men canvas the entire county for information. I can't say how long any of this will take, and I cannot guarantee even if found, Buckland knows anything. He was in service to the Queen once, and though I suspended his recall on the basis of age, there's every possibility his decision to decamp service to me was compelled not by deceitful purpose, but duty, in favour of lending himself to the King." He put his back to her, picked up the whiskey tumbler; silent dismissal.

She gripped the chair's arms.

She'd forgotten Buckland had served. Hoped to never see and certainly never speak to him again. But it seemed she'd have no choice but to spend at least a few minutes in his defiling presence if he was located, and she wished to learn anything more about what he and Jake had discussed. Whether Jake had mentioned going anywhere else, with anyone else, before leaving Ansmall for good. Because no matter the earl—or PC Good's—intimations, Jake had not left her for another woman.

She stood, stiffened her spine to control a palsy of exhaustion and anguish. "Papa?"

He stared at her reflection in one of the window panes. She held his gaze.

"Th—thank you."

His eyes lingered on her a moment, then he raised the glass to his mouth.

Swallowing disappointment she knew she didn't deserve, as she was no better in believing the worst of him because he'd always demanded more than was fair from her, she collected her coat.

In the hallway, she paused, face tilted to the ceiling, nose wrinkled as she fought a portent of tears.

Mother Mary's sonorous exhalations echoed from the front room. Silence throbbed behind the study door. But in the instant before she had eased the door closed, she could have sworn she heard the earl rasp, "For what it's worth, I *am* sorry Dianna, daughter of my heart."

Chapter 17

One Day Closer

Jake wiped his face with his sleeve. But instead of clearing the muck spatter, he only succeeded in smearing it. He exhaled, frustrated, tired of the filth and the wet, the bone-numbing cold that never left him.

His uniform and greatcoat were sopped and coated with mud. His feet numb, boots and socks soaked. Inner thighs burning with the chafe of his wet trousers. Every step sent pain shooting through his calf muscles as he staggered through the sucking muck. Yet, despite the rain and cold, his weeks' long simmering anger combined with the weight of his pack and the physical exertion as they tromped through knee-deep mud had sweat dripping off him like a lathered horse.

The field they slithered and slid across had once been full of crops, but heavy rain and artillery shells had churned the earth to a sinking quagmire fit for neither man, nor beast. Conditions were so bad, he'd had to shoot one of the horses that slipped off the road into a sinkhole up to its neck destined for a slow agonising death from dehydration and starvation, if it didn't drown first, when the lieutenant would have marched on after recovering the contents of the horse's saddlebag. He would have preferred to shoot the lieutenant.

Transferring the Enfield to his opposite hand he decided if he survived this nightmare long enough to make it back to Britain, he'd kill Edward Marshall. With his bare hands. Him and his bloody henchman. Who else could have orchestrated his kidnap? Forged military documents?

"Get moving, Chuck."

A shove from behind knocked Jake off balance. After he regained his footing, he briefly considered turning and giving in to his urge to shoot the lieutenant, and as swiftly dismissed the thought.

Phelps would love nothing more than an excuse to shoot back.

He's in on it. Has to be. Why else would he dismiss Jake's claim he didn't belong here?

"My name is Jake Douglas, not Jack McTeer. And I'm from Texas, not...Killevey? I don't even know where that is."

"Ireland," Phelps said. "And you're not the first to change your mind once you sober up and realise what you signed up for."

Sober up.

Buckland had slugged him good, with what, he'd never know. But guessed a bat, or oak limb, because the goose it had left on the back of his skull took almost two weeks to shrink to where he could wear his helmet comfortably. Three-inches lower and he'd be dead from a broken neck.

He had vague memories of coming partially to after that, only to have a canteen forced to his lips. The liquid contents were bitter and had soporific effect. The few times he surfaced enough to have any hazy memory, he recalled hearing male voices, but whoever was there was watching him closely, because the instant he flinched or groaned he was submersed again in the drug by force. At some point they allowed him to remain faintly conscious, longer, because he retained auditory echoes of a male voice excusing his incoordination and dry-heaving on drowning his sorrows at having to ship off not knowing if he'd ever see his wife and children again. His next fragmented and hallucinatory memory was being bundled along an echoing metal corridor.

When he fully awoke, violently ill but not as muddle-headed, the ship was docked at Le Havre and Phelps scoffing at his protests as he prodded him off the ship and into the back of a cattle truck.

"Lots change their mind, claim that there was a mistake in the paperwork," Phelps had muttered, angling his rifle, not directly at Jake, but in a way that left no question in Jake's mind he wouldn't hesitate to use it. "But I've seen enough of these—" He reached inside his coat to pull out a slim set of folded papers— "to know the real thing when I see it, and these, Private McTeer, are as real as any I've seen."

Jake had no doubt the medical clearance and attestation forms were authentic. As was the tag on a leather lace around his neck tucked under his tunic that, like the uniform he'd awakened in, labelled him: J. McTeer.

His father-in-law undoubtedly had access to all sorts of legitimate documents. He could only argue that the information contained on the paper work and around his neck was false. But Phelps was adamant: Jake was in his Majesty's army, and there was only one way he could get out before his tour ended—in a coffin.

The look in the lieutenant's eyes when he said it, his belligerent refusal to entertain Jake's claim... Co-conspirator with Buckland for sure. Marshall potentially, though at this point Jake could not directly link his father-in-law to any of it. He had only Buckland's word Marshall had warned him to stay away from Ansmall.

He wished he knew for certain it was Phelps's voice he remembered excusing his staggering and nausea on drink. Wished he could recall more details after he'd been hit, but everything between his last visit to Marshall's and landing in France was hazy, clouded with confusion. He felt a pang of guilt for having harboured doubt to the authenticity of Dianna's mental fugue. He'd apologise—profusely—when he saw her. And by hell he would see her again.

He had to cling to that belief, that he would see her and the children. That the carefully worded postcard he'd sent late-September when they'd stopped fighting and running long enough for anyone to pick up a pencil, had reached her. That Phelps hadn't torn up his last note like he had Jake's first two attempts.

All soldiers' communications were censored to ensure no one imparted information the enemy could use should they manage to intercept, or end up in deliberate receipt of, a soldier's letter home. Spies were ever a concern in any war. But more numerous and problematic was the enthusiastic or embittered soldier eager to convey his adventures or ordeals to loved ones back home. Phelps was the first in the line of communication defence.

He collected and read subordinates' mail before approving any for hand off to the Army Post Office where each letter or note was again reviewed for potential inflammatory, defaming, sensitive, secret, or coded information. Jake had managed to have one postcard approved, it, as required, vague on his whereabouts, only slightly more informative about battles he'd survived, and signed: *Always my heart, J.*

He had to pray Dianna understood his predicament, and was at that moment using her weight as Marshall's stepdaughter—or Marchioness Holderness—to get him back across the Channel. In the meantime, he'd soldier on. He had no choice if he wanted to continue dodging bullets in the back when shrapnel started flying again.

That's what had inspired him to shut up once they were on route to Rouen. Not Phelps's mocking, or threat to tie him to a post in view of his company, promise to shoot him if he tried to desert, but the looks he started getting from those who had volunteered. Stoically or eagerly signed up to kill, and potentially be killed, out of pride and loyalty to country—or the simple raw thrill some men found in battle.

He'd spent enough time fighting along the US-Mexico border with the Texas Rangers to know they, the men he marched with, posed the greatest threat to his safety—if they felt they couldn't trust him to have their backs. Cowards and turn-coats were the first to fall during the chaos of battle, and not by enemy fire.

Blowing out a resigned breath, he adjusted his grip on his rifle, scanned the scarred and pitted fields broken by patches of wooded areas.

They'd been marching since dawn and the sound of heavy artillery had grown louder by the hour. Ahead of him, Pte. Henry Sutherland struggled along, his tall narrow frame bent into the wind and rain, lifting his knees high with each squelching step, a crane stalking crawfish in a swamp.

He'd developed a tentative friendship with Sutherland, an easy-going talkative fellow who like Jake had a wife and three children at home.

Jake staggered, recovered, and dragging his booted foot from a slurry of black muck moved to the centre of the road away from the boggy shoulder.

Don't let your mind wander. Don't think about where you want to be. Remember where you are. If you want to get home, for God's sake, keep your wits. Remember where you are.

He would get back. God help him, he would get back to Dianna and the children if he had to kill a thousand Germans to do it.

"Quit your mumbling McTeer and move it," Phelps snarled.

Teeth gritted, Jake quickened his step.

One day closer to freedom. Just keep moving
Stay alive.

186

∞ ∞ ∞

Three days passed before Papa called her again to his office. She insisted Mother Mary accompany her. It was important that at least one level-head be present should Papa renounce responsibility for helping solve the mystery of Jake's disappearance.

Papa was gazing out the window, hands linked behind his back. He turned around, and paused, his polar gaze on Mother Mary.

She had been his guest for four nights, but it was the first time he had seen her. Awake. Though she rose with the sun, Papa was up and gone earlier, and he never failed to return until after she had retired for the night. Whether purposeful or not, he had managed to avoid the Mother Superior. Until now. His expression suggested he would have preferred to maintain the status quo.

"Mother," he said stiffly.

"My lord." Mother Mary inclined her head, ever so slightly. "I would say you look well, but it is a sin to lie."

She was right. Papa looked awful. Though he would never be described as robust, he was paler than normal. And thinner. The sharp bones of his face threatened to slice through paper-thin skin the colour of unwashed wool.

"Are you ill, Papa?"

"I'm fine."

No, he wasn't. And he would never admit it. To her, at least. She made a mental note to write Mama, ask her to exert whatever influence she had to sway the earl to consult the family physician.

"I've received word from Chief Constable Richardson," Papa said. "He had his men visit every business owner in town. Two others, besides the Poitras woman and her ostler, recall the carriage, but neither recognised it. None of the local or outlying residents they've managed to question know anything of use, either. As to Buckland, I've still not determined his whereabouts, so I've arranged your return to Ansmall. When I know more, I'll send word there."

Dianna shook her head. "I wish to remain here."

"That is a wish, I will not grant. The maids are packing your belongings as we speak."

"I—"

187

"If you want an answer, Dianna, you'll return to Ansmall at once." His words were precisely enunciated, his speech calm. Without compromise.

Was he threatening to recall whomever he had sent in search of Buckland, should she dare defy his command? Could he not understand she needed to be here, active in helping locate her husband, not twiddling her thumbs in Herefordshire?

"I agree with your father, Dianna," Mother Mary said. "There is more room at Ansmall and the air there fresher. And I'm certain Miss Elizabeth would welcome more time with her sister, and your mother time with her daughter, *non?*"

Dianna didn't look at her, and briefly considered advising her to return to Ansmall alone if she preferred it to the townhouse. Except she was there at Dianna's request, trusted to employ logic when emotion threatened to derail common sense. Common sense sometimes meant conceding to another's will if it meant retaining his cooperation.

"Of course, Mother," she said stiffly. "Ansmall's environment is... fresher."

A faint twitch of one of his black eyebrows was Papa's only reaction to her less than subtle censure.

He didn't want her around. The knowledge hurt. Which rankled her more. Like a blood-soaked dressing she'd thought herself incapable of absorbing more heartache. Yet her chest throbbed, the bloodied stump of her heart chafing against bone and gristle.

"I'll wait a week," she rasped. "If you've not sent word by then, I'll be back."

The eyebrow twigged again. "I would expect no less."

Chapter 18

Help Me

*J*ake clawed at his mouth and nose.
He couldn't breathe. He couldn't see.
Then he remembered.
Bombs.
Boche.
Sutherland?
He gagged, and coughed, scraped at the thick muck clogging his mouth.
Get up. Get help.
No, stay down. Stand up and you're good as dead.
Can't breathe. Need to breathe.
Stay down.
He forced himself to listen to the logical part of his brain, and kept his head down, barely above the cold puddle in which he lay.
Cough. Cough it up.
Drawing his knees under him, he rammed his fists into his midsection. Repeatedly. Just when he was certain he would suffocate, and his mind was ready to implode with the knowledge, his inner muscles contracted, and exploded like the bomb that had almost buried him under a storm of mud.

The clump of soil lodged in his throat shot out, along with questionable liquid. He coughed and gasped, dug the grime from his nostrils and mouth.

As sweet, smoke-filled air wound its way inside to his lungs, he dropped his head to his forearms, weak with relief. He sucked. And spat. Sucked and spat again, to clear the debris from his teeth and tongue. When he no longer felt grit, he slowly raised his head and tilted it one way, then the opposite. Stifled a moan.

No longer fighting to breathe, his brain could process other concerns, like the fact his head had been split in two, and his ears rang with a roaring tinny noise. Gently, cautiously, he ran his fingertips over his face and scalp.

His hair was wet and sticky, his fingers numb with cold forcing him to taste his fingers after each pass over front, sides, and back. Fortunately, he found no depressions, and tasted only metallic tainted muck. From the bomb he supposed. But no blood.

That was good. Vicious headache aside, he would live.

Rifle. Sutherland. As the two thoughts collided, Jake reached out, instinctively seeking both and found neither close by. He strained to think.

They'd been marching along a narrow track between muddy fields bound for a wooded area... He closed his eyes, visualised the minutes before the explosion.

His Enfield in his right hand. Whine of a whizzbang. Then face down in muck. He didn't remember the transition. Or what had happened to his rifle. *Where was Sutherland before the blast?*

Ahead. Ten yards ahead.

The smoke was so thick Jake could barely make out his fingers in front of his face. But he could feel and see enough to know he was chest down in a bomb crater. Fog mixed with black smoke capped the depression.

He was tempted to call Sutherland's name, but didn't dare draw attention. If he could barely see ten feet, the snipers fifty-yards out, could not see him. That increased the odds of him living another day. He slithered around the slick hollow using his hands to guide him, clasped something firm, moved his fingers over it to build a mental picture. *Rifle.*

He groped its length, jerked when his fingers encountered a hand gripping the stock.

"Sutherland?" he whispered and squeezed the hand. No reaction. No reflexive tightening. Nothing. He squeezed harder. Still nothing. *Dead or unconscious?*

Using his elbows, he dragged himself closer, ran his hand up the arm and recoiled when he touched mangled flesh. And bone. *No body. Just an arm.*

His first instinct was to put as much distance as possible between him and the limb, but he had to know if it belonged to Sutherland. Sliding the rifle closer, he examined the hand. Greyish-white skin smeared with mud, stubby fingers locked on the stock. Relief flowed through Jake.

Sutherland's hands were like the rest of him, long and narrow. This hand belonged to someone heavier, and likely shorter. Suppressing a shudder, he continued his search of the muddy pit.

Nothing. No sign—or parts—of Sutherland. With luck, he was alive and hiding in a similar muck hole. He might now be one of the gunners Jake heard strafing the surrounding countryside.

Heard.

He blinked. He could hear again. The rapid gunfire pinged off his ear drums like pebbles off a tin roof. He pressed into the mud, before realising the threat his instincts had recognised.

Voices. Foreign voices. And cries of the wounded.

The initial barrage of gunfire had levelled off to periodic bursts. In between, the congested air was rent by screams, moans, and men pleading for their wives and mothers.

Jake held his breath, strained to sort the English and French from the German, but they blended together, a seamless web of fear and anguish cast over the field like a trawler's net. He dug his heels in to the slippery earth, shoved himself further up the slope. Soon, he would be forced to pick a direction. Choose correctly, and find his way back to safety, relatively speaking. Choose incorrectly, and he'd end up in enemy hands.

Clouds, smoke, and fog obliterated the sun. He had no way to orient himself and would have to go on instinct. First, he needed a weapon.

The rifle had landed up slope from the arm, and except for the butt, was clear of the water. He dismissed the reality of what he was doing as he forced the stout fingers to release their hold and took the rifle part way up the slope. Shrugged out of his kit, he scrounged through the heavy pack until he found a clean, if damp shirt. After ensuring no mud clogged the rifle barrel, he used the shirt to clean the stock, paying careful attention to the trigger and firing pin. A knot of apprehension formed in his centre when he thought of using it.

He would prefer to fire it at least once, but so far, he'd escaped detection, and he wanted to keep it that way. He would forgo the test fire and pray the rifle worked when needed.

He pawed through his pack for another clean shirt, and a pair of socks. Then dug out his spare compass, extra canteen, extra boot laces, and a small metal container containing matches. He used one of the laces to hang the compass around his neck under his shirt, stuffed the canteen into one sock, the matches in the other sock, and rolled both in the spare shirt, before stuffing the bundle under the wet shirt he had on. The wrapped items were warm against his skin compared to his mud-soaked clothes. He shivered.

The cold was penetrating his bones. He would die of exposure if he didn't move soon.

Tearing the shirt he'd used to clean the gun, he fashioned a sling from it. Rifle cradled on his chest like a babe to its mother's breast he rolled on his back and using his elbows and heels wormed his way toward the crater's rim. Bullets sang overhead. To look out, was to invite death.

A breeze had picked up and was slowly, resolutely, dissipating the fog and smoke. He'd be an easy target soon. The wooded area and shelter it could provide was still a good quarter-mile away.

Spotting a dark hump of earth only slightly higher than the ground around it, he worked his way towards it. By the time he wiggled in behind, he was breathing hard, but only mildly warmer. He slipped the rifle free, rolled to his chest.

Mi Dios. The hump of earth was the mud-caked body of a horse, still in its leather traces, the wagon it had been hauling reduced to chunked, and splintered wood and metal.

Jake burrowed his fingers in the horse's shaggy coat. The flesh underneath was still warm. He watched the ribcage. No rise and fall. The horse was dead, but hadn't been for long, likely killed by the same shell blast that had tossed him in the mud hole.

"Help."

Jake froze.

"Help me."

Slowly, Jake turned his head.

Phelps was on his back in a shallow puddle about twenty feet away, left hand gripped to his right shoulder. Jake was careful not to betray the horror he felt when he noticed the shredded blood-soaked shards of tunic where Phelps's arm used to be, though his fingers flexed forcing him to consciously regain his hold on the rifle. *Phelps's rifle.*

He swallowed a rise of bile, ducked as spits of earth and mud exploded near Phelps's feet. Then again, left of his head. Either the shooter had a problem with his aim, or he was toying with Phelps, before he killed him.

"Help me," Phelps croaked, his gaze pleading. Behind Jake, the raised road provided shelter to English gunners firing from the far side, their bullets whistling overhead. Jake squirmed forward, peeked around the horse's body.

The enemy had taken shelter in the house and outbuildings of a farm. Muzzle flashes flared in broken windows, and from behind pieces of farm equipment, and mounds of earth Jake surmised were manure piles. Bloated cow and sheep carcasses littered the fields around the barns.

He and Phelps were stuck, literally, in the middle of a gun fight. He was hidden from enemy fire, behind the dead horse. Phelps was exposed. He couldn't get to Phelps, without exposing himself. He'd be dead before he got to Phelps. Phelps had to get to him. How?

The traces.

Jake dug in his pocket for his knife, cut the leather straps from the dead horse, leaving intact a ten-foot length. *Ten feet too short.*

He turned one end in on itself and rolled the leather, until it formed a tight coil. Then he smeared his face and body with mud, until he was the same colour as the earth. On his belly, he slid from behind his fleshy shelter toward Phelps, froze when a bullet embedded itself into the earth to his left, missing him by a yard or so. More bullets followed, each missing by a few feet.

Was the distance between he and Phelps, and the gunner, too great for an accurate shot?

Emboldened, he squirmed towards Phelps. When he was about twelve feet short, he snapped the leather trace loose. The coiled end landed inches from Phelps's left thigh.

"Grab on," Jake said. "I'll pull you."

Phelps stared at the trace, agony and hope waging war on his face.

"I'll be quick," Jake called. "Just wrap it around your wrist, so it doesn't slip."

With a visible intake of breath, Phelps let go of his injured arm and lunged for the trace, twisted the end of it around his wrist. Jake pulled.

Phelps yelped. Jake ignored him, and hand over hand hauled him close enough to grab him by the forearm.

"Use your feet man," he said, wriggling backward.

Phelps scrabbled weakly with his feet doing his best to propel himself in the direction Jake pulled, as bullets sang and whizzed, but thankfully—

miraculously—missed. By the time Jake had Phelps behind the horse, the lieutenant's eyes were closed, his mouth slack. Jake tilted an ear close to Phelps's lips, felt a faint exhalation, heard a gasping inhalation. Phelps wasn't dead. Just unconscious.

For now, anyway.

Cutting away the remainder of Phelps's shirt sleeve, Jake used it to tie a tourniquet on Phelps's arm a few inches above the stump. The stream of blood slowed to a trickle, but Jake felt his effort was too little, too late. Phelps's skin was greyish-green under the mud streaking his plump face. He'd be lucky to last a few hours. Definitely not the night. A sting of pain on his cheek, forced Jake to look up.

Rain clouds blackened by encroaching darkness had settled over the battlefield. Cold drops bit his cheeks, stung his scalp, stirred the already muddy earth to soup. He startled when a booming crack rent the air, remembered to breathe when he realised it was thunder, not another whizzbang.

The rain became a blinding torrent, needle-sharp and frigid. He pulled Phelps closer, tried to shield him best he could, as he glanced around for help.

It was too quiet. What happened to the gunfire? He peered through the blur of rain to the Menin road.

The mirage-like shadows could be men moving or could be curtains of rain blown by the escalating wind. He angled a look at Phelps. Every instinct told him to abandon the lieutenant and crawl for the road. Regain safety with his regiment. A deeper instinct, one born of experience in battle, forced him to remain where he was as long as no one was shooting at him. At least until it was dark.

Even the best sniper was blind at night without aid of a light beamed on his target.

When Jake couldn't see even shadows, and heard nothing but the steady splatter of rain bucketing into mud, he gritted his teeth, and anticipating a bullet in the head rocked to his knees. When a second later he was still alive, he grasped Phelps's arm and hauled him to a seated position, before getting his own legs under him.

Fifteen agonising seconds later he was on his feet, Phelps draped over his shoulders like a bloody awkward and heavy calf too sick or dead to walk. Rifle gripped clumsily in one hand, he started toward the road.

Every step was excruciating.

Nerves taut, buttocks clenched in anticipation of the bullet that would sever his spine, he staggered and stumbled, fighting to keep upright without losing the two-hundred plus pounds on his back. Every few minutes he paused to catch his breath, listen for Phelps's breathing. Miraculously, the lieutenant lived, his exhalations wheezing confirmation of his tenuous grip on life.

Chapter 19

Education and Lessons

*H*e made it a hundred yards inside the tree line, before hooking a toe on a root. Twisting, he managed to bend and slide Phelps to a carpet of wet leaves, before landing on his own hands and knees. He sucked for breath, and when he could breathe without gulping, he felt around. Finding Phelps, he slid a hand up to his neck, pressed two fingers to where the jugular should be.

Nothing.

Cupping his hands over his mouth, he blew to warm his fingers, hopefully lessen their numbness, and tried again.

Still nothing.

He bent an ear to Phelps's mouth. Not even a whisper of sound.

"Christ," he muttered and rocked back on his haunches, swiped at the sweat and rain dripping in his eyes, and froze when he heard voices.

German voices.

Double Christ.

He tried to remember if he'd thrown, or simply let the Enfield drop, and if so, where.

Forget it. Can't see to use it in the dark.

Easing upright he moved silently to stand with his back against a tree, slide his knife from his belt.

"*Wer ist da?*" came a whispered demand.

He tensed at the unmistakable sound of a rifle's bolt action being levered. Then reminded himself it was black as pitch and raining. The man couldn't see him. Only suspected someone was there.

"Otto, *bist du das?*"

Jake remained silent, barely breathing, as he prayed whoever Otto was answered.

"Otto," came the whisper again, this time more urgent. *"Bist du das?"*

Damn it, Otto, speak up. Tell him it's you.

As if guided by Gods a hoarse voice about thirty yards distant rasped, "*Ja. Ich bin krank.*" This was followed by the sound of retching.

The other German made a disgusted sound, then told Otto he should have left the wine where he found it, adding a derogatory statement about the French, and that the bottles left behind in the villa had probably been poisoned. Jake hoped so. That'd be one less German he'd be forced to kill if it came down to it.

As the first German moved off, he eased to a crouch, severed the lace around Phelps' neck to grab his identification tag, snicked off the label on the lieutenant's tunic too, before creeping deeper into the trees, away from the sound of retching, away from Phelps's body, away from other German voices now gaining volume through the hum of rain.

$$\infty \quad \infty \quad \infty$$

She was devolving into madness.

For a fortnight, Mother Mary and Mama had stayed busy catching up on years of news as they crocheted, or cross-stitched, their voices rising and falling depending on the intimacy of the conversation. Occasionally they burst into laughter, a pair of school chums sharing a private joke. Though they made no attempt to exclude Dianna, neither did she feel included. Her mind kept drifting to her daughters, her son, and husband. *Buckland.*

Who was the woman?

Papa derailed her plan to return to London the previous week by sending a detailed account of his and Chief Constable Richardson's vain attempts to locate either Buckland, or the mysterious woman, along with assurance that she was welcome to come speak to him in person if she felt it necessary, but he had no more to offer, than that contained in the report.

And so, she stayed at Ansmall, waiting, wondering... She tried to amuse herself by amusing little William, but his dark hair and green eyes proved painful reminder and she found herself cutting short their daily play time to wander alone.

Elizabeth attempted to humour her by recounting everything she'd missed since leaving home, but the enthusiastic divulgences fell short of intriguing. Not that the stories weren't interesting. They were. They just weren't as compelling as thoughts of the future. It was nearing the end of November, and JJ was still gone.

Jake still missing.

Where is he?

Who was the woman?

"Dianna?" Elizabeth bounded toward her. "What are you doing?"

"De-heading flowers." She bent to pluck the shrivelled orange husk of the closest Marigold.

"No, you're not. I was watching you from the window. You've been wandering circles out here for over an hour. Besides, it's too late in the season to worry about de-heading anything," she added surveying the brown grasses and bloom-less plants rimming the garden path.

"You were watching me?" Dianna queried embarrassed to be caught in a lie. "I thought you had lessons this morning?"

"I have lessons every morning, and they're boring. Ms. Harper drones like a monotonous bumble-bee." Lizzy sighed dramatically. "It's a wonder I stay awake."

Having spent more than a few hours at the mercy of uninspiring governesses and tutors, Dianna empathised.

But she did not condone inattentiveness in class.

"You need to listen," she said. "Learn everything Ms. Harper has to teach you."

"Why?" Lizzy scowled. "What does it matter the difference between an adverb and adjective?"

"The same as it matters the difference between subjugation and autonomy."

Elizabeth frowned. "What?"

"Education Lizzy," Dianna said. "Not the lesson, is what matters. An educated person has more choice. You do the lesson to gain the knowledge not because you recognise its immediate benefits—for the most part you don't. At least not right away. But later, when you're out in the world is when you realise you should have paid more attention, developed the skills when it was simpler to do so."

Lizzy frown deepened. "Simpler?"

"Yes. It's much easier to absorb and implement new information when you're not busy fighting."

"Fighting?" Lizzy grasped Dianna's arm, her gaze earnest. "Is your husband cruel to you?"

Dianna lifted Lizzy's bare hand to her lips, kissed the pale knuckles. "No, sweetie. I was not referring to Jake. I was referring to the inner fight. The war between dreams and reality. If dreams are the fuel, knowledge is the tool. Without it a dream is like a cart without a horse: nearly impossible to advance."

Elizabeth nodded, but Dianna suspected her philosophical homily was as wasted on her as Ms. Harper's English lesson.

"Do you want to go riding?" The appeal in Lizzy's green gaze sent a spear of homesickness through Dianna. *She's so much like Amelia.*

Forcing the ache aside and praying the letters she'd written and sent Katie and Amelia almost every day since her departure had found safe passage through the maze of German U-Boats hunting transport ships in the Atlantic, she smiled. "I'd love to ride, but... Are there horses left? Isn't the army requisitioning the good ones?"

"Not Papa's." Lizzy's tone suggested the earl was above commoners who'd have their horses trotted off to France willing or no. "At least, not all of them," she amended, perhaps sensing the arrogance of her statement. "We've still four breeding mares, and two stallions, a couple of yearlings Papa plans to train, and this year's foals. And mine and William's ponies. The foals are weaned. You can ride one of the mares."

An hour later, Dianna sighed with pleasure as she and Lizzy jogged their mounts single-file through the estate's woods, Dianna leading. The pervasive cloud cover she remembered as one constant when she'd lived here was absent, and the sun's bright barbs pierced the bronze foliage creating a kaleidoscope of gold light and shadow. And she was wearing trousers.

In Texas she'd learned to dress less for the time of day, and more for what was appropriate for a task. Given her only thought upon leaving America was to find her husband and learn if he'd found their son, she'd packed a wardrobe with social practicality in mind: tailored suits, day dresses, and evening wear appropriate to meet the standards of those from whom she planned to solicit help—or make accusations against. Like the earl. In amongst the fashionable wear, she'd squirrelled away her only pair of trousers, not with riding in mind; purely on sentimental impulse. Jake had given them to her Christmas last.

"You need something more practical for ranching," he'd said when she cast him a quizzical glance after opening the bright silver-foil wrapped box. "It's too easy to catch long hair and skirts on barbed-wire and scrub. Not to mention, it's hard to manoeuvre quickly on the ground around animals, if you're tripping over hems. Young, spooked horses, and ornery bulls, aren't known for being forgiving and if you're going to work with them, you need to be as light on your feet as possible."

To her surprise she found she preferred trousers to skirts, especially in winter, as she could tuck the trouser legs and warm leggings she wore beneath, into her boot tops, and thus keep out the snow and ice that usually formed a burdensome crust along her hems.

The trousers were similarly practical when engaged in tasks like gardening, and grooming the horses, shielding her skin from hair and dirt that never failed to wind its grimy way under her chemise. And despite their complete inappropriateness in her current location, she found she didn't give a fig what anyone else thought about her wearing them. Though in truth, Lizzy thought them brilliant, while of the two grooms left to manage the stable and remaining horses, only the young lad—Carl—gave her a second look. The older groom, Roy, a man she estimated close to Dirk's age, had gone about his duties with polite indifference.

"Let's go to the old church," Lizzy called.

A vaporous chill invaded Dianna's chest. "No."

"But—"

"I said, no, Lizzy." Dianna glanced over her shoulder. "And if you argue, I shall turn around and return to the manse."

Lizzy scowled, but thankfully, offered no retort. Dianna faced round, eased out a breath.

Lizzy now knew the reason she'd left Britain, but not the how, where, or by whom she had come to be in that condition. And she'd not revisit that place. Relive what happened there. What he'd done—She swallowed against memory of the handkerchief stuffed in her mouth, his empty stare as he'd dragged her to her feet afterwards.

Clinging to the horse's reins she stared straight ahead, spine and jaw locked, and concentrated on breathing as she forced her mind to seek out splashes of sunlight painting the path ahead. When her pulse slowed to normal and she could hear more than the rush of blood in her ears, she realised what she no longer heard: the clop of hooves behind her. She glanced back.

Yanking her mount to a halt, she braced one hand on the mare's rump to scan the rear trail.

"Lizzy? Elizabeth?" Her voice jangled off trees arousing reproof from incensed squirrels and annoyed jackdaws. It was what she didn't hear that upset her.

Tugging the near rein, she spurred the mare around, kicked her into a trot. *How dare she play such childish games?*

Turning the mare down a side trail, she spurred her to a gallop. A half-mile later she found Lizzy's pony tethered outside the derelict church. Relief mingled with a chilling sense of déjà vu.

"Lizzy? Elizabeth? Elizabeth Mary Grace!" Her outrage cracked the air and generated a muffled giggle. From the direction of the dilapidated structure. "Come out of there, Elizabeth. Right now. You know you're not supposed to be here."

"Why?" Lizzy appeared on a shelf of intact side wall where it adjoined the partially crumbled front wall, about twelve feet off the ground.

"Get down," Dianna demanded. "I told you I had no want to come here."

Lizzy made a face. "You're as stodgy, as Elaina," she muttered, before slithering out of sight inside the church. "Come on," she called, her voice a dull echo from within the moss-covered ruin. "The altar is surprisingly intact."

The altar. Where he'd forced himself on her—Dianna brought a hand to her mouth, closed her eyes, and swallowed, hard. When the sour bile receded, she croaked, "Elizabeth, please. Come out of there."

"What's wrong?" Lizzy stood in the jagged space where a door had once stood, her freckled features a mix of alarm and annoyance.

Dianna forced her head up, set her shoulders back. "I want to ride. Not waste time poking around this old fossil."

"You used to like poking around this old fossil. You said you found it fascinating." She plucked a leaf from the jungle of vines growing over the ruins. "Did you know Mr. Cooper joined the Navy?" She watched the leaf as she twirled it with thumb and forefinger. "Gwynny says he's in the North Sea." She looked up, her green gaze keen, as she let the leaf swirl to the decaying grass at her feet. "He never understood why you changed your mind."

Dianna swallowed, willed her thighs and hands to loosen their death-grip on the saddle and reins before the horse under her, already growing restless as it picked up on her anxious mood, escalated to unruly. "Because I did," she said. "Now let's—"

"You said you left because you were with child." Lizzy pursed her mouth.

Dianna stared, shaken by Lizzy's tone, the question in her gaze: *Was it Mr. Cooper's child?*

"No, no it wasn't!" she wanted to scream. But her throat had lost its ability to move, draw air, let alone thrust words out through teeth cemented together.

Lizzy had no clue what had happened. No notion that the plot they'd formulated together to foil Dianna's contracted marriage had gone horridly wrong. That someone other than Mr. Cooper met her here that day.

They'd worked it out so perfectly. Elaina had no clue. She was an unwitting participant in the day's deception as they headed out on horseback, chaperoned by Lizzy's governess Miss Ashton, bound for an afternoon's visit with Lizzy's best friend Miss Gwendolyn Cooper, and her mother Viscountess Cooper. Part way there Dianna feigned illness, convinced Miss Ashton and Elaina to proceed, escort Lizzy, and fulfil Viscountess Cooper's expectation of company, while she returned home. Alone. Once they were gone, she turned down the same path she'd galloped along just moments earlier... She forced her chest to expand enough to draw a shallow breath.

She'd told Lizzy she never made it to the church. Never met Mr. Cooper to discuss his brazen proposal they elope. Told her, as she told everyone else who'd rushed to her aid when she came limping home, that she'd fallen off her horse, had the breath knocked out of her, and once she'd caught it, and then the mare that had run off, her only thought had been to get inside the manse. Tend her injuries. Clean herself. *Oh, how she'd cleaned herself.*

Everyone, including Lizzy, believed her story. Believed her bruises and cuts, the filth on her riding habit, was caused by a tumble from saddle to earth when a hare burst from the undergrowth, spooking the mare. No one suspected the truth. Why would they? Buckland had been a faithful servant to the earl for twenty years at that point. His record was spotless.

So, a couple of months later when her... problem, became apparent, Mama, Mrs. Brown, Maggie... They all assigned blame to Mr. Cooper. He was the one she'd been caught corresponding with. The one she'd arranged through coded letters smuggled via Lizzy to meet. The one who, in those letters, expressed affection for her. But it wasn't his child. Mr. Cooper hadn't been within ten feet of her since they were children. He was just a kind man two years older who'd hoped to revive a childhood infatuation enough to satisfy them both he was a realistic, and potentially loving, alternative to an arranged marriage she desperately wanted out of.

Summoning strength, and moisture enough to speak, she said, "My husband is JJ's father. *Jake* is JJ's father. Now—" She tugged the far rein to turn the mare back toward the main track. "I'm going back to the manse. Are you—"

"I don't want to go back," Lizzy blurted. "I want to do something different. Fun. Not approved of beforehand. I'm so tired of having to do what everybody else wants. *I* want out of here."

Dianna halted the mare, scowled at Lizzy. "And go where? Where would you go, Lizzy? You're thirteen."

"I don't know. I don't care." Lizzy kicked at the leaf. "Anywhere is better than here."

"There are a great many places worse than here, Elizabeth." Dianna adjusted her grip on the reins, drawing them slightly to settle the antsy mare. "Trust me. You've no idea."

"Exactly." Lizzy glowered up at her. "I have no idea. Papa keeps me penned like one of his bloody horses, only let out on a fixed schedule to an appointed location."

Dianna compressed her lips, fought down the urge to kick the mare and gallop away from the memory of this place, the anger and frustration in her sister's voice pinging off similar emotions clawing around inside her.

It was this very attitude, the impulsive want to break free of Papa's controlling mannerisms, that had led her to believe she could escape. And nearly ruined her in the process. She could not let it ruin her sister.

Inhaling slowly, she affixed her gentle, but wise elder-sister expression, and said, "Promise to never scare me again by disappearing, and Friday, I'll take you to Manchester."

"Manchester?" Lizzy's eyes widened with wonder.

"Yes. We'll spend the night. The November Handicap is Saturday, at Irwell Castle."

"The races?" Lizzy exclaimed, excitement and hope flushing the brutish pout from her face.

"Yes. I overheard Mama and Mother Mary discussing how despite the war, some things go on as usual, including the races. At least at Manchester, they are. I understand Kempton has been temporarily converted for military barracks and training."

Lizzy's awed expression folded into one of doubt. "What about Mama?"

"She has Mother Mary to keep her company."

"And Papa?"

"He's in London."

"Mama will tell him."

She would. But after the fact.

"Sometimes, Elizabeth," she said. "It is easier to beg forgiveness, than ask permission."

Lizzy's answering grin was sly. "I know."

Chapter 20

Reconnoitring

izzy was positively pop-eyed as they strolled the racecourse grounds. "There are so many more people, than I imagined."

"Horse racing is a beloved sport of many," Dianna said.

Lizzy grasped Dianna's arm, dragged her to a halt and stared up at her. "Papa?"

Dianna stiffened as the ice-treat she and Lizzy had shared surged bitterly warm to her mouth. "Where?"

"That's what I'm wondering," Lizzy said. "Is he here, do you suppose? He loves horse racing."

Dianna exhaled, and managed a faint smile. "I shouldn't think so, sweets. He loves to watch when his horses compete, but I don't know he has any in this race. Besides, he's busy. Very busy. In London."

"But it's Saturday," Lizzy insisted. "What if he decided to come? Many of his friends are here."

Friends. What a strange word to hear in reference to Papa's political and social associations.

To Dianna, a friend was a confidant, someone with whom one exchanged personal information, secrets, thoughts, or experiences often troubling, occasionally naughty, and always designed to strengthen the bond of trust. She could not imagine anyone trusting the earl enough to volunteer a personal flaw or weakness. Though, to be fair, until she'd seen the daguerreotype of him with James Ramsay and Lord Laxton, she'd never contemplated the possibility he even knew how to smile.

Slipping her arm through Lizzy's and tugging her toward a booth, she said, "Forget about Papa. Let's see what the future holds."

Lizzy stopped so forcefully, pain shot through Dianna's shoulder. "I will not."

Dianna frowned. "What's wrong?"

"I will not speak to a witch."

"Witch?" Dianna glanced at the booth. "She's a Seer. A Gypsy. Not a witch. Besides, it's all in fun."

"They're witches. All of them. Give them a chance, and they'll steal your soul."

Dianna stared, surprised.

Lizzy was the bold one. The intrepid and daring sister. To fear something as harmless as a Fortune Teller? Only one person could drum such fright into her.

"It's Papa, isn't it," Dianna said, "stuffing your head with this nonsense?"

"It's not nonsense." Lizzy scowled. "And it wasn't Papa. It was Ms. Harper."

"Your tutor?"

"Yes. She told me about witches and how they mesmerise their victims, make them drink blood and do... awful things. I'll not go near, and risk losing my soul to the devil."

Momentarily at a loss for how to respond, Dianna decided against criticising Ms. Harper. She'd talk to Mama later, let her and the earl decide the tutor's future. For now, she needed to help her sister understand the value of expanding her knowledge outside that which was dictated to her.

"How about I have my fortune told," she suggested, "and you ensure I'm not mesmerised?"

"No. I won't—"

"Elizabeth, darling," Dianna said gently. "Do you trust me?"

Elizabeth tore her fearful gaze from the Fortune Teller's striped tent to frown at Dianna. "I want to."

Dianna managed not to reveal her immediate disappointment at the note of scepticism in Lizzy's voice. "You want to?"

Lizzy shrugged. "It's hard. I trusted you with all my heart before you left, but—"

"But I broke that trust." Heart sinking, Dianna touched Lizzy's cheek. "I understand, Mouse. And I am sorry. I also don't expect you to blindly trust me, or anyone, including your tutors, just because it's asked of you. You must make up your own mind, based on what you know of a person, or circumstance. Just... do me a favour. While I'm working hard to regain your trust, will you work as hard to question everything you've been told so far, ensure its... worthy of your firm belief? No need to answer me now, sweets," she added when Lizzy hesitated. "Just keep your mind open. Please? Don't believe everything someone tells you, especially if what you're told seems to serve the other person's interests, better than it does yours."

"You mean like now?" Lizzy raised an eyebrow. "When you're asking me to believe Fortune Tellers are harmless?"

Dianna laughed. "Yes, exactly like now. Tell you what, how about we forget the Fortune Teller, and go find our seats?" As though to applaud her decision to table the discussion a trumpet sounded warning of the first race's parade to post. Dianna entwined her gloved fingers with Lizzy's. "Come luv. Let's find our seats."

Once seated, she glanced at the racing programme, and froze when someone touched her shoulder.

"Miss Marshall?"

She leaned forward to angle a look backward. Lord Laxton returned her stunned stare with a smile.

"How good to see you, again," he said. "Are you here with your family?"

"Ah..." She cleared her throat, fought to keep her voice steady. "No, Mama and Papa were not able to come. I'm here with my youngest sister, Elizabeth." She nodded to Lizzy. "And I'm married now, Lord Laxton," she added with a faint rise of her eyebrows. "No longer Miss Marshall, but Mrs. Douglas."

"Oh, yes." He offered a bland smile. "I believe I heard something about that. Congratulations."

She narrowed her gaze, not enough to expose to Lizzy or anyone else the annoyance his words sparked, but enough to warn him she found his slight in poor taste. He ignored her, his banal smile warming as his gaze alighted on Lizzy.

"And how could I not recognise you, my dear? In my defence," he added with smooth, oily charm that further set Dianna's teeth on edge, "your lovely hat shields your glorious hair. More importantly, you no longer remotely resemble the grubby urchin I saw last. You've blossomed into a rare and beautiful rose, young lady."

Elizabeth's blush was a good three shades darker than her hair. "Th—thank you, my lord," she stammered.

"Elizabeth," Dianna said careful not to convey her agitation, "may I present Lord George Ramsay, Earl of Laxton. A friend of Mama and Papa's." *And my biological uncle.* Not that this was time or place to reveal something as sensitive as Mama's pre-marital indiscretions. Or her business to share it, even if it were. That was delicate information best left to Mama and the earl to disclose to their younger daughters.

"My lord," Lizzy said again, stronger, her flush fading to a pink glow beneath her freckles. "A pleasure to meet you."

"The pleasure is mine, Lady Elizabeth." Lord Laxton inclined his head again, before raising his gaze to Dianna's. Something shifted in the depths of his dark blue eyes, quick as the tic of muscle in his pale pouchy cheek, before it was gone, like the flicker of something long and slender disappearing around a corner that left one wondering if it had been a cat's tail or belonged to a squirrel. Or rat.

Snake.

"It is a pleasure seeing you again, Lady Dianna." The charming smile he'd given Elizabeth faded, replaced with a faint supercilious purse to his mouth reminiscent of the earl's haughty disdain for those who displeased him. "Please, do give my regards to your parents."

"I will, Lord Laxton. Thank you. And please," she added lightly, refusing to let his arrogance dissuade her from asserting her expectation of him, as she watched his eyes carefully. "I really do prefer to be addressed as Mrs. Douglas."

He hesitated, lips drawing inward a smidge, before he dipped his chin a fraction in assent. "Of course, Mrs. Douglas. Good day." He stood and made his way out along the row.

"My lord," Dianna murmured, and exhaling, turned in her seat in time to witness the first set of horses surge off the starting line.

He knew bloody well she was married. And who she was married to. But he, like the earl, despised Jake. Resented her. Blamed them both for blowing up the marital plans he'd helped Mama and the earl orchestrate with the duke that sent her running—eventually—into Jake's arms. Where she'd chosen to remain even after receiving her inheritance and all its requisite British, Canadian, and European residences. Laxton had initially—vehemently—opposed her decision. Until she offered him opportunity to remain on as figurehead of the Ramsay legacy—Her heart clutched, shooting pain that forced her to grit her teeth to contain a gasp.

Did he know?

Had anyone told him Jake was missing? That JJ was... She pressed gloved fingertips to her mouth.

She'd not sent word. It never occurred to her. Once her memory returned, she'd been too clouded by grief and preoccupied with other events and tragedies in short succession, to expend energy on anything not directly—persistently—in front of her. Unopened letters made few demands.

Mrs. Brown dutifully piled the post on the hutch by the kitchen door, she dutifully took it to her bedchamber and tucked it in her desk drawer. At least two envelopes bearing the Holderness seal and addressed to her as Marchioness Holderness, languished there. That was another reason she was rarely eager to open her uncle's missives—his refusal to acknowledge her written request that he use her married title on correspondence.

He'd acted in her stead for twenty years until signing over her inheritance, which had made it so very easy to convince him to remain on as her estate agent. But that had not stopped him conveying his disappointment in her choices with every quarterly report he sent addressed to the Right Honourable Marchioness Holderness, c/o J-D Ranch. She'd taken to asserting her authority the only way left to her: by replying only to exigent inquiries, and otherwise forgetting about him. But now that she knew for certain JJ wasn't in England... She fixed her eyes open, willed them to remain dry.

Not here.

Do not fall apart here. You'll upset Lizzy.

Later.

Back at Ansmall.

Cry there. Write him from there.

When the races ended, Dianna tried to hide her relief as she clasped Lizzy's hand and stood to leave. It had been a mistake to come. She'd hoped a day's distraction would ease the strain of waiting on word from the earl, but seeing Lord Laxton... A quick unobtrusive glance informed her he'd not returned to his vacated seat. Good. She was not disposed to talk to him again. Not disposed to raising more ghosts.

"Oh, Dianna," Lizzy exclaimed as they exited the seating area to join the mass exodus along the concourse. "Did you see the way Wardha ran? What a grand horse. I've never seen such beauty and speed!"

"That's because you haven't seen yourself ride," Dianna said clutching her sister's small hand more firmly, as they wound their way through a garrulous cluster of well-dressed people recounting their wins and losses.

Lizzy made a derisive sound. "Don't tease, Dianna. I'm serious. I want to ride like that. I want to race."

"I've no doubt you do, sweets," Dianna said. "Unfortunately, for you, Papa will never agree."

"Who says he has to know?"

Dianna glanced at her. "You wouldn't?"

Lizzy shrugged. "You did say it was easier to beg forgiveness, than plead permission."

"For some things, yes, but not in matters of life and death—Elizabeth." She frowned to reinforce her seriousness. "I won't counsel recklessness, so do not use my words as excuse to engage in dangerous behaviour. And don't roll your eyes at me. You'll make me regret this indulgence, and it's been such a wonderful day. I hate to end it on a sour note."

Lizzy had the grace to flush. "I'm sorry. I was teasing. I'd never dream to impair your relationship with Papa, by blaming you for my actions."

"Thank you, Elizabeth," Dianna said. "I value your loyalty and should hate very much to lose it." Allowing Lizzy to believe there was an amicable relationship to malign might keep her from acting foolishly. *Might.* She'd not missed the fact Lizzy had promised not to cast blame; she'd said nothing of avoiding such action altogether.

Knowing it folly to pursue the issue at risk of inspiring Lizzy's natural contrariness and thus, the very behaviour she sought to discourage, she said, "Let's get another flavoured ice, before we—" She jerked to a gaping halt.

"Dianna? What is it?"

She pointed. "That man."

"What man?" Lizzy turned her head to look.

"There. On that carriage—"

"Oh. I thought you meant Lord Laxton."

"Lord Laxton—" *Good God. It was him.* Focused as she was on the frighteningly familiar stocky coachman atop the Brougham, she'd not paid attention to the familiarity of the other form entering it. Her uncle.

"McGuire," she shouted, and broke into a trot. "Lord Laxton!"

McGuire met her gaze for an instant, and then he shouted something at the groom holding the door for Laxton. The man shut the door on Laxton who vanished inside the carriage without reaction to her shout. The groom started to clamber up next to McGuire and was almost tossed to the ground as the Brougham lurched forward, the attached horses responding instantly to McGuire's vicious snap of the whip.

"McGuire," she shouted. "Wait!" Hiking her skirts, she ran, caroming off bodies, heedless of startled exclamations and affronted retorts. "McGuire. Stop. Stop!"

McGuire never looked back, but expertly guided the horses around slower, and stopped carriages, as the groom made it safely to the seat next to him to throw a wide-eyed stare over his shoulder at Dianna as the Brougham shot out through the concourse gates, and turned on to the road. Dianna staggered to a halt, air rasping from her throat. Arms latched around her waist.

"Dianna. Dianna, stop. You're scaring me."

"He had my baby. He had JJ."

"What?" Lizzy demanded. "I didn't see a baby. Only Lord Laxton."

"McGuire," she said. "McGuire. Our groom. He disappeared when JJ disappeared. He—but. He's alive. With my... uncle."

"Who?" Lizzy said.

"Lord Laxton." She gripped Lizzy's hand. "And the horses were black. Come on. We have to go."

∞ ∞ ∞

"Will you please stop, Dianna? That pacing is driving me mad."

"Your stalling tactics are driving me mad."

Displaying uncustomary patience, Papa murmured, "I am not stalling. I'm reconnoitring."

That stopped her. Facing him, she waved a hand in annoyance. "We're not on a battlefield, Papa. We're in your office. In the heart of London. And writing letters is hardly reconnoitring."

"I am soliciting assistance, Daughter. What do you expect me to do? Laxton's not at his London residence, and I've not received word back yet on whether he's at or expected at Holderness. Even if he is, I can't exactly go haring up there and put a pistol to his head and threaten murder unless he reveals the nature of his association with this... McGuire? We must act with discretion, because regardless what you saw, or think you saw, Laxton is still a respected peer. And personal friend of Duke Blackburn. For all you know, the man you believe was your missing groom, wasn't—"

"He was." She hardened her stare. "It was McGuire I saw driving the carriage that I watched my uncle climb inside."

"Can you be certain? From what Elizabeth told me, you had a glimpse of a coachman from some distance, then took off like a crazed hound causing everyone within ten miles of the place to stop and stare. I can only pray that no one who knows me recognised you."

She narrowed her gaze at him. "Do I take that to mean you are more concerned with what your associates think of you, than you are in the whereabouts of a man that should know the welfare of your grandson?"

He threw down his pen. It bounced off a half-full tumbler of whiskey, before rolling toward the edge of the desk. Dianna caught it, handed it back to him.

"Thank you," he said stiffly. Laying it carefully aside, he massaged his face with both hands, before looking at her. "I *am* concerned with helping you, Dianna. Which is why I'm writing to associates of Laxton's who might know his whereabouts, a task better performed in silence. Why don't you get some sleep? I'll dispatch these at once, but do not expect a response before morning."

Jacketless, his shirtsleeves rolled to his elbows and tie loose, collar unbuttoned, and usually impeccably pomade-smoothed hair wrested to untidy black clumps, fatigue etched in the pale skin around his bloodshot eyes and humourless mouth; he looked as exhausted as she felt.

She and Lizzy had caught the last train out of Manchester—to London. Papa's astonishment at their late arrival was only outweighed by his outrage once he discovered their day's activities. Dianna had been forced to shout to quiet him long enough to tell him he could dole whatever punishment he believed adequate *after* he helped her locate her uncle and McGuire. Elizabeth, blessedly, had vanished into one of the bedchambers without argument after supporting Dianna's version of events, leaving

Dianna to fuss and fume while Papa scribbled. She glanced at the clock on the fireplace mantel. *Midnight.*

Papa was right. Tomorrow would be the earliest anyone was likely to respond to his inquiries.

"I need to write Mama, let her know—"

"That was the first note I dispatched."

She stared at his bowed head. She'd forgotten Mama and Mother Mary, until now. He had not.

"Thank you," she murmured.

He nodded and kept writing. She went to bed. When Lizzy shook her shoulder, she stared at her, temporarily disoriented, her body weighted with the residual effects of an exhaustive sleep hounded by spectral nightmares that pressed her deep into the mattress making it almost impossible to rise.

"What... time is it?" she croaked.

"Just after nine."

Dianna sat up, grappled for her robe. "I slept in—"

"The first reply just arrived. That's why I'm here. Papa sent me. Calm down, Dianna. You'll never get dressed hopping around like a flea."

A quarter-hour later, she found Papa where she'd left him: bent over his desk, his hair in disarray, shirt wrinkled. Tie askew.

"Didn't you sleep, Papa?"

He looked up. "There you are. Have you eaten?" When she shook her head, he gestured to the credenza. "It might still be warm. If not, I'll have Cook make something fresh."

The serving dishes were covered but odour in the room suggested scrambled eggs, ham, and toasted bread. Her stomach gurgled, but not with hunger. Just raw tension, anger, and... hope.

"Thank you," she said. "I'm not hungry. Elizabeth said you received a reply?"

"Yes. And you should eat." He dipped his eyebrows when she shook her head. "Starving yourself will not aid anything, Dianna. Certainly not you."

"What's in the reply? Who's it from?" she repeated quietly. Calmly. Adultlike, despite an overwhelming urge to shout.

He held her gaze, before easing out an audible breath. "I've still no conclusive information on Buckland's whereabouts. Or the woman. However—" He touched a sheaf of paper on his desk. "Lord Aldcliffe's informed me Lord Laxton's to marry on Thursday. Small, private ceremony, immediately after which he and his new bride depart for Canada. From there, on to South America for an extended honeymoon. They're not expected back in England, for a couple of years."

"He's getting married? I didn't even know he was engaged." Though it was possible one of the letters in her drawer at home communicated the startling news.

"No one did, apparently." The earl leaned back in his chair, steepled his fingers in front of him. "It's not a long-established relationship from what I gather, but a spontaneous love-at-first-sight sort of thing. Aldcliffe's note is short on words, but full of substance. He confides surprise at Laxton's sudden pronouncement, claims he and the rest of their coterie only received the news this past week. Aldcliffe's rushing out of London now. Seems he insisted upon hosting the ceremony and reception at his country house near Lancashire. Laxton's to meet him there this evening. The bride-to-be arrives Wednesday."

Dianna raised her eyebrows, pulse quickening. "So, we'll go there to confront him?"

"No." He shook his head, lowered his hands and sat forward. "I've arranged to have him intercepted."

She frowned. "You're bringing him here?"

"No. Ansmall."

Chapter 21

Any Relation

Gertrude answered the door.

"Any mail for me?" Papa said as he handed off his coat and hat.

"No, my lord."

"I'm expecting company," Papa said. "Send them directly to my study."

"Yes, my lord."

Dianna shrugged out of her wrap. "Where's my mother?"

"In Master William's chamber," Gertrude said, adding the wrap to the coat over her arm.

"And Mother Mary?"

"The Library."

"Come, Elizabeth. We'll apologise to Mama first."

Elizabeth emitted a pained sigh as she passed her coat to Gertrude. With another martyred sigh, she stomped up the stairs. Dianna followed, slowly, and was only half way along the upper hallway when she noticed her mother striding towards her, eyes narrowed on her like a hawk sighting a baby rabbit.

"I'm sorry, Mama—" Dianna gasped, and clutched a hand to her cheek, angled her head away to avoid a second slap.

"How dare you?" Mama snarled. "How dare you put my child in danger?"

"Danger?" Dianna scowled. "There was no danger. We went to the races—" She caught the countess by the wrist, before she could level further assault. "Don't hit me again, Mama," she said quietly. "At no time,

was Lizzy ever in danger. We went to the races, and afterward, to London."
I'm your daughter, too.

That detail seemed lost on the countess, as she scowled. "You were supposed to return here. You said nothing about London."

"We went, because I needed to ask Papa's immediate assistance."

"With what?" the countess demanded.

"Finding JJ."

"Oh, for pity's sake, Dianna," she cried. "Your father is not God. He can't perform miracles—"

"He's here."

"I know," Mama snapped. "I saw him come in—"

"Not Papa. McGuire, the man who was with JJ when he disappeared. I saw him at Irwell."

Mama blinked, frowned. "What?"

"It's true, Mama." Elizabeth approached with trepidation. "I saw him, too." Her gaze darted to Dianna's hand, and with a start, Dianna realised she was still holding the countess by the wrist. She let go.

Clasping the wrist Dianna had held with her opposite hand, Mama faced Elizabeth. "How do you know who you saw?"

Lizzy's gaze flitted to Dianna. She compressed her lips. She'd not be accused of coaching Elizabeth.

"Because, I saw him," Lizzy said turning her reluctant gaze to the countess. "On Lord Laxton's carriage—"

"Lord Laxton?" Mama rounded on Dianna. Accusation, horror, disbelief... the emotions surged across the countess's face like sheet lightning. "What did you—"

"I bumped into a family acquaintance, at a public venue, Mama," Dianna said. "After saying hello, Lord Laxton and I never spoke again. When the races ended, as Elizabeth and I were leaving, we saw him, Lord Laxton, getting into a carriage driven by the last man seen with my son."

Mama's eyebrows pinched inward. "You say that like somehow you blame Lord Laxton."

Dianna let her silence speak for her.

"No," Mama said, shaking her head. "You cannot possibly believe that your—that Lord Laxton, had anything to do with your son's disappearance?"

Again, Mama correctly interpreted her silence.

"Dianna," she said. "I'm appalled."

"Not as appalled as I. How else do I explain McGuire in his company? What else makes sense? None of this, has ever made sense, since the day I regained my memory. Why both my son, and McGuire, disappeared without a trace, save JJ's hat? Why no... bit of either of them, was ever found, during the clean up after the tornado. No sightings. Nothing. But all of a sudden, there he is. With Lord Laxton. One person, in all the world, that might have interest in my son, other than me and Jake." She fisted her hands against rage stoked when awareness flared in the countess's eyes, and was immediately snuffed out, replaced with doubt. Reproof. "If you'll excuse me," she rasped before her mother could raise further defence of Lord Laxton. "I have other amends to make." .

Mother Mary was more understanding of her detour, and appreciative of the reason behind it. Long hands folded atop the book she'd been reading and closed upon Dianna's entry to the Library, her greenish-gold gaze brightened as Dianna told her about seeing McGuire.

"This is good, no?"

"I don't know." Dianna shook her head. "He was the last one with JJ, but I... I can't get my hopes up." *Only to have them dashed again.* "We should know more soon. Papa's having Lord Laxton brought here." As if to confirm her assertion, the doorbell chimed. Dianna hopped to her feet. "That's probably him now."

Five minutes later, Lord Laxton, flanked by two burly men in black suits and bowler hats, glowered at Papa across the polished expanse of his mahogany desk.

"What is this, Ansmall? How dare you kidnap me? What kind of game are you playing?"

"One you should be intimately familiar with, George."

Lord Laxton's thick black eyebrows, striated with grey hairs, knotted over his faintly bulbous nose. "And now riddles? Seriously, Ansmall, this is a horrendous breach of friendship. If not for our relative closeness—" His gaze slid knowingly to Dianna—"I would be inclined to report this egregious event to Scotland Yard."

"Go ahead. I'm sure Basil will find the impetus for my momentary lack of good judgement interesting fodder." By whom, Papa meant Assistant Commissioner Sir Basil Home Thomson, head of the Criminal Investigation Department at Scotland Yard. Dianna only knew this because he was one of the first people to whom Papa had written requesting assistance in locating Buckland.

For the first time, Laxton displayed a hint of doubt, his haughty scowl tempered by flicker of uncertainty as he dragged his gaze from Dianna, to focus on Papa. Dianna stifled a frustrated growl.

Was he that arrogant he believed her impotent? Or did he, like Mama, assume his title and social standing made him immune from meaningful suspicion?

Of course, he did. He knew she'd seen McGuire at the reins of his carriage, and discounted her as potential risk the way he'd ignored her request he address correspondence to her as Mrs. Douglas. The knowledge stuck in her throat like a clot of sour milk. She wanted to cough it into her hand and smear it over her uncle's smug face.

The study door banged open.

"What is going on in here?" Mama's gaze bounced off each person in the room, before finally settling on Lord Laxton.

"Ellen. Thank God." He moved toward her but was jerked to a halt by the suited men who grabbed an arm each. "Let go, you buffoons," he snapped. When his order went unheeded, he looked to Mama. "Ellen—Lady Ansmall—please, talk some sense into your husband. He's lost his bloody mind, sending these gorillas to drag me here like a common criminal—"

"And why is that, George?" Mama advanced toward him. "What provoked my normally conventional and very private husband to such rash action?"

"I—" Lord Laxton fell silent. "I'm sure I don't know," he said after a tense moment.

"You do," Dianna cried, unable to contain herself any longer. "I saw him. Driving your carriage. Where is he? Where's McGuire?"

"McGuire?" Lord Laxton shrugged. "I know no one by that name."

"Dianna."

Dianna eased her gaze to Papa. He twitched an eyebrow. Slowly she unclenched her fist, lowered her arm, and stepped back.

Lord Laxton laughed. "Where was that unquestioning obedience when it mattered?"

She hit him. His head snapped back and then thrust forward like a striking snake as he attempted to break free of the men holding him. Fortunately, they were stronger.

"Bloody hell! Let me go." Laxton turned his glare on Papa. "Are you going to sit there, and let her get away with that?"

"If you are in any way linked to my grandson's disappearance," the earl said. "You'll be lucky if that is the worst you suffer."

Lord Laxton's upper body tilted back as though Papa had swiped at him. Dianna's heart leaped.

Grandson. He had called JJ, grandson, and was prepared to battle for him. Protect him.

Tears scalded her eyes.

"Tell us the truth, George." Mama moved around to stand next to Papa who was still seated behind his desk. She put a hand on his shoulder. "What do you know? How did you come to employ the man Dianna believes knows what's happened to our grandson?"

The show of solidarity astounded Dianna. The only other time she remembered seeing open agreement between her parents was when they joined forces to bully her into accepting marriage to the duke. Lord Laxton seemed to share her amazement.

The whites of his eyes stark around the indigo irises he stared at them, a purplish hue invading his jowls, bleeding into the grey-streaked black hair at his temples. "You can't really believe I would have any part in the kidnapping of a child? I'm about to be married—"

"Who said anything about kidnapping?" The earl's question was soft, but its implication resounded in the room like a thunderclap. Dianna's heart-rate accelerated.

Lord Laxton's too, from his rising colour as he blinked rapidly, eyes darting to look at everyone, but the earl. "I—I just assumed—"

"Answer me, George," the earl said in the same supple, yet entirely commanding voice. "Where is this McGuire?"

Lord Laxton cleared his throat, seemingly unable to meet Papa's chipped-ice stare. "I... already told you, I know no McGuire."

"Then what is his name?" Menace laced the earl's voice. "The man Dianna saw driving your carriage yesterday?"

"Oh. Him." Lord Laxton glanced at Dianna. "He... heard I was looking for a new coachman. Mine was called up—"

A scything sound rent the air as Papa yanked open a desk drawer, withdrew an envelope. He laid it flat on the desk, covered it with both hands and looked at the guards. "Wait in the hall," he murmured.

Mother Mary stumbled in when the first man opened the door. Despite the gravity of the gathering, Dianna had to bite back a laugh. Mother Mary looked as startled as a child caught with a hand in her mother's coin purse.

"I... was just—"

"Come in, Mother," Dianna said. "I believe my uncle may, very shortly, require the benefit of your counsel."

Mother Mary looked to her hosts. Both inclined their heads in assent. With a grateful smile, Mother Mary closed the door on the guards, and glided into position next to Dianna.

"Is there anyone else you wish to invite to witness this debacle?" Lord Laxton said. "A chambermaid, or groom, perhaps?"

"Mother Mary is a friend of this family," Papa said. "And of us all, the wisest." He peeled open the envelope, withdrew a folded piece of paper. "Read it."

With obvious reluctance, Lord Laxton accepted the note. His mild frown transformed to abject horror as his skin paled, and eyes roved the text. Looking up, he said, "Wh—where did you get this?"

"So, it is true," Papa said. "Making it well into your fourth decade unmarried, never being seen in public escorting a woman, is not proof. Many men of our rank enjoy extended bachelorhood, especially when birth order absolves one of need to produce the heir and spare, and some prefer to keep their private assignations private for fear of offending the wrong husband—or future wife. But, pending nuptials aside—congratulations by the way—your reaction confirms it."

Lord Laxton's mouth worked, but no sound came out. Finally, he sputtered, "You know about my—"

"Pending marriage to a mystery bride?" Papa nodded. "Yes. Even before you made mention of it a few moments ago. Why you thought to hasten, and keep such a momentous occasion secret I've yet to understand, however. Perhaps you can enlighten us on that right after you fill us in on Mr. McGuire?"

Laxton drew himself up, ripped the sheaf of paper in half. "My private matters are none of your business, Ansmall."

"That was a copy," Papa said, his tone bored, as Lord Laxton continued to shred the paper. "The original is locked safely in my office in London. It will remain secure—and thus your secret—only if you reveal what you know about this McGuire character. Once you have, I'll then decide whether to reinstate your travel privileges. Oh, excuse me." The earl angled the corners of his mouth in a hard smile. "I may have forgotten to mention, I had them revoked."

Laxton stood rigid and unblinking as a baby rabbit come nose-to-nose with a fox. When his hands started to lower, and his shoulders dropped, his visage taking on the sickly countenance of a man realising he'd not duck the hangman's noose today, Dianna knew her father had won. And remembered to exhale.

She sagged as the air left her lungs, straightened when Mother Mary grasped her hand, and squeezed in silent rejoice. She returned the squeeze, without looking away from her uncle.

"McTeer," Lord Laxton said, his tone dull. "I know him as McTeer."

"McTeer?" Papa frowned. "Why is that name familiar?"

"Because McTeer is Buckland's surname," Mama said. "He was born Peter Buckland McTeer, though he's used his great-grandmother's maiden name, Buckland, from birth, as did his father and grandfather when they worked at Ansmall."

Papa looked at her. "Buckland?"

She nodded. "Mrs. Brown kept a ledger detailing the backgrounds of all our employees, present and past. She gave it to me before she... left. I reviewed it, found it quite comprehensive, and in some instances, informative. I remember being surprised Buckland was Scottish. I thought him English to the core. But upon further reading, Mrs. Brown's notes revealed he's descended from the Irish branch of McTeers. Near Killevey. The ledger is in my boudoir, if you care to look at it."

Dianna sensed Mother Mary's gaze on her, but could not look away from her uncle's clenched hands from which bits of paper sprouted between his pale puffy fingers like marsh grass, her chest so tight she was forced to take shallow breaths.

"Is your McTeer any relation to ours?" the earl asked.

Dianna clenched her molars.

I have two sisters and nine brothers.

"Oh God," she moaned.

"Dianna?" Mother Mary grasped her arm. "What is it, child? You're white as goose down."

Covering her mouth with her hand, Dianna shook her head.

"Here." Mama thrust a wastebasket into Dianna's hands, just in time.

∞ ∞ ∞

A maid was summoned, the wastebasket carried out, refreshments requested, and everyone accepting of Dianna's excuse of her momentary discommode on stomach upset induced by long-held grief and anxiety aggravated by weeks of little sleep, though the countess's worried gaze lingered on her.

She avoided her mother's eyes as the suited men returned to rearrange the furniture, eventually resulting with Lord Laxton and the earl each seated in a wing chair facing the settee where Dianna sat chocked between Mama and Mother Mary like a leaflet buttressed by a pair of mis-matched but equally immovable bronze bookends.

She opened her mouth to demand her uncle tell how he knew McGuire/McTeer and if he knew where her son was, and choked off the question at the sound of a knock on the door.

Refreshments had arrived.

Two maids set out tea and accoutrements and a platter of edibles, before drawing the door closed softly behind them. No one moved to pour tea, or pick up a tart. All eyes were on Lord Laxton, behind which the suited men stood, stiff reminders that this was no social gathering.

Red-rimmed eyes pouched in an ashen face and red-silk tie canted, a small bruise blooming at the corner of his mouth where she'd struck him, Laxton looked like a man trying to account for lost hours after a long night's indulgence. With a beleaguered sigh, he said, "I received a letter. Late last May. From your steward, Ansmall," he added to the earl, "informing me Lady Dianna had, regrettably, passed in a tragic accident, but that her son... lived, and no one knew. He was believed perished also, victim of the same tornado that had claimed his mother." Laxton pursed his lips, cleared his throat. "He stated that for... a price, the child could be brought to me. In England."

Dianna leaned forward. "For a price? You received word my son was alive, and you—Where is he, uncle? And by God, don't lie to me and tell me you don't know where he is, or I swear by the blood that runs in my veins I will sell every Ramsay holding I can, board up those I can't, and give every liquidated penny of my fortune to my daughters."

"What?" He looked at her. "You wouldn't. You can't—"

"Can't I?" She glared. "I own Holderness Castle. I own you. You live there by my pleasure—"

"You don't understand." He started to rise and was immediately shoved down by a hand from each of the men behind him. He acted as if nothing had happened, and instead straightened in his chair to scowl at her. "You were dead. I was told you were dead. I believed you dead. And I... thought about telling you, Edward." He angled toward the earl. "I thought about telling you about the child, but then I... I realised he was Holderness's future. The only living heir, after me—"

"Well he's not," Dianna said through gritted teeth. "Because I didn't die. So, tell me where he is, right now uncle, unless you wish to spend the remainder of your life in Oakwood."

"Oakwood?" Laxton offered her a scornful look. "You think you can have me committed? On what grounds?"

"You're clearly insane," she said. "You have to be to do such a... cruel thing." She struggled to retain control, remain seated, anchored only by the calming hands her mother and Mother Mary each had on one of her knees. "Unless you'd rather be imprisoned for kidnapping? I'm sure Papa could arrange that as easily as he can a room at Oakwood."

Laxton darted a glance at the earl.

"That's right," Dianna said. "I may not have the authority to commit you to any place, but Lord Ansmall does. Now, once more, where is my son?"

"Truly, Edward," Lord Laxton said, his scoffing tone weighted with doubt. "You wouldn't dare imprison, or commit me? You understand. You understand I had no choice. I believed Dianna dead. The Ramsay fortune in need of a future heir. A boy must be on a ship to properly learn how to sail it. I know you understand that. It's the same reason you have kept poor Ellen in continued confinement all these years—"

"The only thing I understand," Papa said, "is that when you learned my grandson was alive, rather than alert me or my daughter—or her husband if you believed her dead—you conspired to kidnap him. How you possibly thought you could keep him, and introduce him to society as Holderness's heir without revealing your treachery, is beyond me. Perhaps my daughter is right, and you do belong at Oakwood." Sadness dragged Papa's words.

"Marriage." Laxton's chin rose in defiance born of knowledge the game was over, yet powered by desire to prove himself a clever player regardless.

"I'm to wed this week. Then go abroad. While away, my wife and I would welcome a son, who upon our return years later—"

"You thought to pass JJ off... as yours?" Dianna leaped to her feet, stomach a twisted knot of fury and revilement.

"I had no choice." Laxton tilted away as far as his chair back allowed. "It was that or he'd be sent back. Back to that bastard American you married. And I need him here. Holderness needs him here—"

"*I need him.* He's my son!"

"I didn't know you were alive, until it was too late. I'd already paid the money." He turned to the earl. "You must understand Edward, I—"

She lurched over the low table at Laxton, but Mother Mary grabbed her arm at the same time the countess grasped her skirt.

Rigid, quaking with want to unleash fury stoked by months of pain and anguish, weeks of fear, she rasped, "You're mad. *Mad.* And I want my son back. Where is he? Where is he?"

Lord Laxton still did not perceive her a threat, or he believed the suited men would stop her if she broke free of the countess and Mother Mary's restraint, because he never took his pleading gaze off the earl. She didn't need to take her eyes off her uncle to know her stepfather had already decided his fate.

The increasing panic pinching Lord Laxton's pasty face and beads of sweat purling on his brow confirmed he was in receipt of Lord Ansmall's customary icy resolve that foretold of no understanding, no forgiveness. Any time soon. Probably not ever.

"Where is my grandson, George," Mama murmured, her voice gentle counterpoint to the steel locking Dianna's spine and jaw, the chill radiating off the earl. "What did you do with him?"

Lord Laxton looked at her, his eyes wide, wary. And then his shoulders slumped, and he bowed his head to his hands.

"Holderness," he whispered. "He's at Holderness."

∞ ∞ ∞

"*Peux j'avoir plus d'eau, si vous plait?*" Jake raised the cracked mug the girl had given him and smiled. She smiled shyly back.

"What he said." The heavy-set man on the milk stool next to Jake laughed, a deep rumbling sound that seemed to rattle the barn rafters.

Dust and hay motes drifted down, shaken loosen not by Lieutenant Baxter's laughter, but by the percussion of artillery less than a mile away. A few other soldiers offered the girl smiles, but most sat quietly, their gazes flitting from Jake, or their CO, to the barn door, as though expecting it to burst open under an onslaught of German soldiers. The girl, in contrast, appeared quite composed as she gathered the empty pail and slipped outside.

He guessed her to be about fourteen, though she acted far older, serving as both nursemaid and mother to her ailing grandmother and brothers aged four and nine. He hadn't seen them—they were in bed asleep when he and Baxter knocked shortly before dawn requesting shelter in the barn until dusk—but she had told him about them as she shooed them to the barn, insistent that neither her grandmother nor brothers know of their presence.

"*Ils ont peur.*" They are scared.

Weren't they all? But rather than confess his trepidation at drawing her and her family into danger greater than that they already faced, Jake nodded, listened sympathetically as she explained how her father had gone to fight in the war, and her mother had disappeared over a week earlier.

"*Elle est allée trouver les vaches.*" She went to find the cows.

Before she left, she gave her daughter a pistol and six bullets, and made her promise if any Boche showed up she would spare her grandmother, brothers, and herself, humiliation, and degradation at the hands of the enemy. And though she made no mention of what her daughter should do should soldiers other than German invade the isolated farm, it seemed reasonable to expect her mother would want her to help anyone who was fighting the *Huns immondes*.

The girl had relayed the information with a practicality that made Jake shudder, and wonder if Katie or Amelia would be so self-possessed in the face of such a request, and whether Dianna—or he—could even ask it of them.

He had thanked her then, and complimented her courageousness, which she shrugged off, "*La vie doit être engagée avec le courage.*" Life is to be entered upon with courage.

His surprise at her eloquence must have shown, because she added, "*Alexis de Tocqueville. Je ne suis pas intelligent.*" But she was plenty smart. And brave. Brave enough to risk being shot for allowing British soldiers and one disenfranchised American to shelter in her grandmother's barn, within sight of German lines.

She returned with a fresh bucket of water. After everyone slaked their thirst, Jake thanked her, and advised her to go inside the cottage she shared with her grandmother and siblings and stay there, reassuring her that he and the others would depart at nightfall when odds were greater they could make it to their intended rendezvous undetected.

She looked at him, her deep brown eyes enormous. "*Nous emmener avec vous.*" Take us with you.

Inwardly, Jake winced. Outwardly, he regarded her with careful neutrality.

She had helped them. And was it only her, he'd not hesitate. But two young boys and an old woman presented a problem.

The twelve Scots Guards and their commander, separated from their regiment after a barrage of retaliatory artillery levelled the copse in which they'd taken cover after surprising a company of Germans, were determined to catch up to their unit the next day. To do that, they had to retreat a mile almost due north before turning northeast. But that mile was muddy farmland cross-hatched with water-filled ditches, near impossible to traverse in daylight with German lookouts, snipers, and artillery bunkers hidden in the forest.

Which was why they planned to go at night, when darkness made it harder for bullets to find targets. It also made it harder to negotiate the mud and water-pocked fields. With an old woman and two young boys...

"*St. Omer. Je connais le chemin.*" St. Omer. I know the way.

The girl trapped her lower lip in her teeth, stared at Jake, no longer stoic. Only afraid. Scared of being left behind to whatever fate felled her mother, because he could almost guarantee the woman did not get lost. Or run away. She'd followed cloven-hoofed tracks right into an enemy patrol. The girl, he sensed, knew it too.

"What'd she say?" Baxter, a stout florid-faced man with a thick red moustache and surprisingly deep brown hair, seemed amiable enough. Flexible. Able to think on his feet. At least for the four hours Jake had known him.

They'd run into each other—literally—in the woods where Jake had been trapped too long on the wrong side of the German encampment he'd stumbled into, living off what edible plants he could scrounge by

226

moonlight, and small animals he managed to snare using the laces of his boots. Just when he began to despair of finding a safe route past the enemy before he starved to death, along come the Scots Guards.

He'd watched from his hiding place, an abandoned animal den dug in beneath the roots of a fallen tree, as the BEF surprised their adversary shortly before dawn, driving them back with rifle fire and bayonets, scattering Huns in all directions, some running past so close he could smell them, the metallic scent of gun oil overlaid with the rancid reek of body odour and panic. When he could no longer see or hear Germans, he slipped out of his hole in the ground and wound up face to bayonet with Baxter.

"I'm one of you, Lieutenant-Colonel," he'd blurted.

"Are ye now?" Baxter pressed the tip of the bloodied bayonet to Jake's chest. "Ye dinna look like any o' mine. Ye dinna sound like any, either. What's your name? Who's your CO?" Enough suspicion and adrenaline buzzed in the big man's steel-grey eyes, his begrimed hands flexing on the stock and barrel of his rifle, tunic and face splattered and bayonet slick with grisly reminder of those he'd dispatched without bullets, Jake hadn't wasted time or breath trying to explain who he really was, but blurted the lie that matched the small disc on the lace around his neck and patch on his tunic.

"Private Jack McTeer. 13th Battalion. QO. And my... my CO's dead, sir. Lieutenant Phelps. Shrapnel. Bled out."

"Is that so?" Baxter's bushy eyebrows lifted. "Devil's Dozen, ye say?"

"Y-yes. Sir." Jake swallowed the sour taste in his mouth. By claiming the 13th Battalion of the Queen's Own Royal West Regiment of Foot, nicknamed The Devil's Dozen, as his unit, he had just committed himself to an indefinite amount of time in His Majesty's Army. Because he could not now accuse the same military, whose name he'd used to legitimise himself, of illegally conscripting him. But at least he would end up on the right side of the line.

Another moment's narrow-eyed consideration, thick eyebrows drawn thoughtfully, and Baxter muttered, "Ye dinna speak like a Hun. Then again, ye dinna sound much like a Brit, either."

"I was born and raised in America. But my mother's British. I... volunteered." Jake withdrew the lieutenant's tag from his pocket, handed them to Baxter, told him about the artillery barrage, dragging Phelps with the trace, trying to pack him out in the darkness and almost being caught by Germans, laying low in hopes they'd retreat or move on, so he could cross back to his own side.

"Good on ye for joinin' up on the side of ol' Blighty," Baxter said. "An' right sorry about your CO," he added, his expression genuinely remorseful. "But best we get on. There's a farm not too far back. We can rest there 'til dark. I expect when we get to Wipers ye'll be sent on to yer unit."

Despite his expressed thanks and sympathy, Baxter wasn't the trusting sort. He pocketed the tags, and kept his rifle trained on Jake, albeit subtly, the entire march to the farm, and barn they now sheltered in awaiting cover of darkness to make the journey to Ypres.

Jake said to Baxter, "She wants us to take her and her grandmother and brothers, to St. Omer. They have family there."

Baxter stared at the girl as though she had asked to use his gun to shoot him with. Then he shook his head. "Impossible. Me orders clearly state—"

"They can't stay here, in the middle of a battle ground," Jake said. "What if the Boche come back?" From the corner of his eye he saw the girl's hopeful expression fall.

She may not understand Baxter's words—hell, he hardly understood the man and he was well versed in English—but the LC's tone, and slow, negative shake of his head, left no room for argument.

Jake nodded. "Then I'll take them."

"What?" Baxter scowled. "Are ye daft, man? You're here to fight Huns like the rest of us, not to shuttle lads and lassies about like a blooidy ferryman. St. Omer is too far the wrong direction. The lassie an' her family'll just have to get themselves where they want to go, 'cause we're goin' on to relieve—"

"Respectfully, sir," Jake said. "I believe it was you who suggested I am better off with my own regiment. I'll have better luck at HQ in St. Omer finding out where they are, than I will in Ypres."

"Ooch, so that's it," Baxter growled. "Yer scairt, an' wanna use the lassie an' her auld grannie for protection—"

"I want to ensure they get someplace safe—" Jake lunged and tackled the girl, brought her down under his body just as the side wall of the barn imploded, firing mud and wooden shards in all directions.

Jake kept his head down and the girl pinned long after the debris stopped raining on his head, back and legs, and the immediate area around him fell eerily silent except for a few muffled coughs and low moans.

Where there was one, there were usually two. Sure enough, a second later, he heard the familiar whine that had alerted him to the first whizzbang.

The second shell exploded on the other side of the barn, near—or on— the small farmhouse, and it was all Jake could do to keep the girl under him. She was screaming, and shouting for her brothers and grandmother, trying desperately to break free of his hold.

"*Arrêt*," he said. "*Arrêt*! It's not safe. You'll be killed. Stay down." She went limp, and he prayed it was in response to his shouted demand, and not the result of a mortal wound.

Baxter was face down in the hay next to him, his helmet knocked off, head angled toward Jake, a broad freckled hand cupping his mouth. Blood seeped between his thick fingers, and ran from a gash above his ear, but his grey-blue eyes were open, if glazed.

Dazed, but alive and cognisant enough to know not to move. For now.

Others moaned, and there was some rustle of movement, but Jake dared not lift his head. Not yet.

The third missile landed short of its target, but close enough to fling mud, and other organic shrapnel on him and the others, and then a barrage of British artillery finally answered back, shelling the trees Baxter and he, and the Guards, had exited less than an hour before, repelling the Germans, harassing their gunners enough to distract them from their original target.

Jake pushed to his knees, helped the hysterical girl to her feet. She cried out in pain and fell against him. He looked down.

Mi Dios. Her lower leg canted in a direction it should not have been able to go.

He eased the girl to the ground, tore off his coat and laid it over her. Her teeth clacked with the force of her shivering, and she closed her eyes as what little colour pinking her cheeks vanished, and her exposed skin faded deathly white where it wasn't mud-splattered or beginning to bruise.

Baxter's men too, were on the move, shaking off dust and mud, wood, and other debris, as some secured the perimeter, and others checked on unmoving, or wounded comrades. One knelt over the lieutenant-colonel who was attempting to sit up.

The entire time Jake checked over the girl to ensure her broken leg was the worst of her injuries, she pleaded with him to help her brothers and grandmother, her voice tinny and distant through the ringing in his ears.

"*Oui*," he said. "*Je vais. Dès que je sais que vous êtes en sécurité.*" He hadn't the heart to tell her that even after he'd ensured her safety, he could do nothing for her family.

When he'd helped her up the first time, he'd had clear view over her head to the farmhouse owing to the majority of the barn's walls having been blown away. There was nothing left of the cottage. Only a smouldering crater, and few small chunks of broken brick to mark its place.

Chapter 22

Reserve Judgement

$\mathcal{A}$ medieval monstrosity with square turrets surrounded by an actual moat, Holderness Castle loomed at the end of a mile-long and winding tree-lined drive at the centre of a five-thousand-acre estate, near the coast of northern England.

"Squeeze any harder, and you'll pop a tendon child," Mother Mary murmured as the coach started up a low rise toward a wooden bridge linking the tree-dotted fields to the castle motte.

Mother Mary was right. Her hands were fisted so tightly the tendons in her wrists ridged the thin fabric of her gloves. She unlocked her knuckles, stretched her hands, and grimaced as pain shot up her arms.

"You must get control of yourself, *ma petite*," Mother Mary murmured. "Your *bébé* needs someone who is calm, at peace with herself, to help him find peace after what has no doubt been a very confusing and trying time."

"Courtesy of McGuire, and my *uncle*," Dianna muttered as she returned her attention to the window.

The earl shifted slightly on the seat next to her but remained silent.

"Your anger is making you sick, child," Mother Mary said. "It is like an anchor weighing you to the bottom of the sea. You are holding your breath, fighting an invisible foe, wasting valuable energy, energy you will need to repatriate your relationship with your son. Six months is a long time in the mind of a young child. He may not recognise you, and if he does, he may still be shy, attached to his new caregivers—"

"Attached?" Dianna stared at her. "Like... love?"

"Like," Mother Mary said evenly, "how all young children faced with chaos and circumstance enforced by the adults that control their lives do—

adapt. That does not mean your son loves anyone more than he loves you, *ma chérie*," she added gently over Dianna's sputtering. "It means children do what is necessary to survive. Emotional attachment, whether good or bad, is often part of the bargain. It is natural for a child—or any individual dependent on another—to accommodate the person with power, and thus gain protection by pleasing their *patron*. How young Jack has adapted will depend entirely on how he has been treated—"

"So, help me God, if they hurt him—I'm sorry Mother," Dianna said. "I'm sorry for using the Lord's name in vain—"

"He does not judge you, child. Nor do I." Mother Mary reached across, gripped Dianna's hand firmly. "You judge yourself, and too harshly at that. He does not blame you, for anything. And we must trust that the care the conspirators applied to the taking of the child, has in turn extended to the child, and he will be found intact, and unharmed."

The suited men had escorted Lord Laxton to London where he was to be held pending further investigation, under strict instruction he not speak to anyone, or dispatch a note. Papa dared not risk him alerting Buckland and McGuire, whose real name was Martin McTeer.

McTeer was Buckland's younger brother, and both men, Laxton had advised, were in hiding at Holderness with JJ until Friday, when they were to bring him to Laxton and his new bride in Liverpool shortly before they all disembarked for Canada, Buckland as Laxton's valet, McTeer as coachman.

As Laxton was borne east, she and Papa and Mother Mary went north to Manchester and on to Leeds, where six new suited men appeared and now followed in a second coach. The hours and anxiousness between had passed mostly in darkness, and small nibbles of food and drink at Mother Mary's insistence, but with the sun rising, summoning a pink-tinted mist over the tips of meadows and surface of ponds and lakes, exhaustion and irritability fuddled her. She could not adequately reason Mother Mary's convoluted supposition.

"I'm not sure I know what you mean," she said.

"What I mean," Mother Mary said, "is this Mr. McGuire, or McTeer, or whatever his name is, went to a great deal of trouble to earn your, and young Jack's trust, before absconding with him. You told me yourself he was good with the boy. Overly attentive in fact."

"Yes," Dianna said, if reluctantly.

"Then is it not more sensible to believe he would continue the same gentle treatment, than to assume he would change tactics, and terrorise the child?"

"But simply by taking him, he terrorised him," Dianna protested. "I'm his mother. He *needs* me."

"He, as all children, needs love, *ma petite*. You told me he received that from the man you knew as McGuire. Patience, kindness, attention—"

"Attention not his to give." Dianna flopped against the velvet-covered seat back, hiked a couple of breaths. "How can you defend that monster? He took my son. He took JJ away from me, away from his sisters, and father, and he had no right. He had no right to tear our family apart."

Mother Mary nodded. "I agree that what he did is wrong, *ma chérie*. And I do not suggest he should be excused for his most serious breach of trust. No, if anything, he deserves the full wrath of the law. What I am saying, is that you do yourself harm imagining terrible things, when by your own admission McGuire was nothing but good to the boy. It is better for you, and your son, if you believe in the best possible outcome. Children are very perceptive, *ma petite*. If JJ suspects you think him broken, or damaged in some way, he will believe it, and he will blame himself—"

"But—"

"But Buckland, his brother, your uncle... they're to blame. I know." Mother Mary sighed. "And you know from experience Dianna, children carry the weight of adult sin until they are adults themselves. Even then, there is no guarantee they learn enough or grow strong enough—like you—to shed what is not their burden to bear. And even if they do not hear the words, they sense the emotions. For your son's sake, Dianna, you must welcome him as though his absence was planned, a holiday if you will, a temporary trip from which he is greeted warmly rather than turned over and inspected for damage like a stolen museum piece returned to its curator. You can't embrace him in love, if your heart is hard with suspicion and bitterness."

Her mind railed against the Mother Superior's wisdom.

The nun had never birthed a child. Did not know the intimacy of feeling that child quicken within her body, or the agony and emptiness of separation as the child left the womb. She had never experienced the exquisite pain and scandalous pleasure as the child nursed, once more joined with her body, her soul. Yet...

Mother Marie-Jocelyn Claudine LeBlanc had many children. Every young woman that entered the home for unwed mothers she managed and every child they birthed, and she found a loving family for, were her children, her heart, her soul, because that was what she poured into making and keeping Maywood Home a welcome place for the wounded souls that entered it. *Like she did for me.*

Dianna scooted forward, brought Mother Mary's gloved hand to her mouth, kissed the soft suede with the same reverence she might the Pope's ring, and looking up, smiled.

"Thank you, Mother. Thank you for coming all this way to help hold me together and counsel me. I'm not sure I could have made it this far without you, at least not without falling apart, or making a complete horse's ass of myself. I will reserve judgement, until I see my son—What? Did I say something funny?"

"Oh, Dianna." Mother Mary clapped her free hand over her heart, as she wheezed. "You are ever one for bargaining. And surprising me with delightful vulgarity."

"I apologise if I offended you." Dianna released the Mother Superior's hand, and slid back on her seat.

"Not at all." Mother Mary swallowed, folded her hands on her lap. "Your honesty and candour refreshes. It is so different from the deference, or indifference, to which I've grown accustomed. With you, I never know what to expect. I enjoy that. Life can be boring when you're old. But with you, it is never dull. Never."

"Yes, well..." Dianna glanced at Papa whose pale cheeks held a spot of colour as he stared out the side window. He most definitely did not share Mother Mary's appreciation of Dianna's *candour.* Mute obedience had always ranked higher on his list of commendable qualities.

She managed a wry smile for Mother Mary's benefit. "I would prefer boring at this point, if it meant I was back home with my family intact, nothing more exciting to preoccupy me than thinking up ways to get JJ to eat his peas—" She broke off as the coach shuddered to a stop. A moment later, the groom opened the door.

Papa's face was grave, his movements rigid and precise as he exited. Dianna followed, and staggered as she stepped out on the step. She might have fallen had not Papa and the groom each grasped her by an elbow. When she was firmly on stable ground, the earl frowned at her.

"Are you, all right?"

"Yes." She attempted to ease her elbow from his hold, but he only tightened his grip, his gaze intent, worried. She smiled. "I'm fine Papa. Tired, that is all. Tired of this. I just want my little boy back—" She stiffened, stunned when he pulled her into an embrace.

"That is why we're here, daughter," he murmured.

She had never imagined him embracing anyone, especially her. Though of course, he must hold Mama on occasion. Forcing *that* thought from her mind, she struggled for composure as Papa released her and stilled as he and Mother Mary, who was head and shoulders out of the coach, locked eyes.

The Mother Superior continued her exit, released the groom's hand, and offered Papa a faint smile. *"Un acte rare et exceptionnel vaut beaucoup plus que mille ordinaires."* One rare and exceptional deed is worth far more than a thousand commonplace ones.

"St. Ignatius," Papa said.

Mother Mary's eyes flared in surprise. *"Oui, mon ami."* She inclined her head. "You are as full of surprises as your daughter."

"Even Atheists read, *mon ami sage.*"

"Touché." Mother Mary glanced at the stone monstrosity. "What now?"

"Now," Papa said. "We search my daughter's house. It's yours, Dianna," he added quietly. "All of it. From the smallest pebble to the tallest Beech, and every meadow and mortared stone, wooden crossbeam, floor rug, candlestick, and teaspoon in between. Holderness Castle and its lands are *yours.* You're not a visitor. You're Marchioness, and you do not need permission to enter."

She stared at the castle's high-arched main entrance inset with wide wooden doors so tall and broad a pair of elephants could pass through side by side with space to spare, and for the first time since the weight of her inheritance had been settled on her she felt empowered, rather than burdened. Drawing a breath, she squared her shoulders, and raised her chin, noted the earl's fractional incline of his head.

Approval.

Something warm flooded through her.

Gratitude.

Resolve.

With Mother Mary on one side, and the earl on the other, she marched up the flagstone steps to claim what was hers.

∞ ∞ ∞

"JJ? JJ? Where are you baby? Where are you?" Her voice echoed dully in the cavernous Grand Hallway, absorbed by a thick if worn floor rug and heavy wood-framed portraits of men and women ringing the curved walls of the domed room. Three hallways angled off it in different directions. A set of stairs to her left spiralled upward. She paused, uncertain which way to go.

"Is he here, *ma chérie?*"

"I don't know." She looked around. Not a footman or maid in sight.

"Good morning." A thin elderly woman in the familiar dress of a housekeeper emerged from the shadows of one hallway. She sketched a shallow curtsy, offered the earl a faint smile. "A pleasure, my lord. I'm Mrs. Rainbird. I've kept house here thirty years, and remember well your visits, though it's not as you might remember it when the marquis was alive. Everyone's been let go, save me and my husband. Lord Laxton gave everyone reference, sold the horses to the army, sent the cattle and sheep to auction. Said he'd be hiring new staff when he returned from his trip overseas—" She broke off at a noise overhead. "That's likely the new valet and—"

Dianna hiked her hems and took off up the stairs as fast as her feet would take her, Mother Mary on her heels, Papa and four of the six suited men, leading.

"Be careful," Mrs. Rainbird called out. "There's three of them."

The first-floor landing split into a balustrade walkway left and right, each curving round to form a ringed path overlooking the great hall below and hatched with doors along each wall. She moved to the railing, looked over, then up. Two more full-circle balustrades, one over the other, and, she assumed, dozens more doors leading to heaven knew where.

"I'll go left," Papa said. "You go right. The rest of you check the upper floors."

Dianna headed for the first door to her right as the suited men charged up the stairs, and Papa veered left.

Room after dusty sheet-covered furniture-filled room she searched, yanking loose protective covers, peering under beds and settees, up chimneys, and in and behind wardrobes and cabinets, any object of

236

sufficient size to conceal a small child. Mother Mary, who'd ascended to the first landing, remained along the balustrade near the stairs, relieving Dianna the added pressure of having to worry she or Papa might miss the stealthy departure of whomever had current custody of her son.

"Buckland!" Papa's voice rang out and was immediately followed by the sound of thudding footsteps.

Dianna raced out to the walkway in time to glimpse a blur of movement disappearing down a far set of stairs. Servant stairs. Papa gave chase, but he was still a good twenty feet behind on the other side. She started to run as well, stopped when she noted an open door.

"Did he have JJ with him?" she shouted.

"No," Mother Mary called back. She was half-way round on Dianna's side, her long quick strides tossing the hems of her robe. "He carried nothing. Just ran out of that room—"

Dianna darted inside, shoved open the drapes to flood the darkened room with light. "JJ? JJ?" She ran to the trundle bed, yanked back the quilt. Nothing. A large leather suitcase lay on the floor. She opened it, stared at a variety of ruffled white smocks, blue-trimmed sailor suits. She shoved to her feet. "He's here. He's got to be here."

"What about there?" Mother Mary crossed the room and reached for something on the wall. Dianna gasped.

A glass doorknob blended so perfectly with a white section of the gold and white-striped wallpaper, it was virtually undetectable.

"When you parted the drapes," Mother Mary said. "I noticed a wink of light where there should be none. But it's locked."

"Stay here in case someone tries to sneak out." Dianna dashed into the hall and pushed open the door to the next room.

A young blonde woman huddled in a chair, knees drawn under her blue skirt, regarding Dianna with open-mouthed fear.

"Where is he?" Dianna demanded. "Where is my son?"

The girl jabbed a panicked finger at the next wall.

Another cleverly disguised door.

Dianna cranked the knob. This one turned easily. She staggered into the next room, unprepared for the door's sudden give, and froze. Then slowly raised her hands.

"You can't possibly think to shoot me?" she whispered. "There are witnesses." She resisted the urge to look for JJ, but kept one eye on the pistol, the other on Martin McTeer. "Just tell me where JJ is, and you can go. I won't pursue charges—"

"Charges? For what? Looking after my nephew?" McTeer gestured with the pistol. "You were dead. I saw that twister lift you and send you flying. You *should* be dead."

She nodded, placating. "I was hurt. But I survived. But even thinking me dead, why didn't you bring JJ home?"

"I did. To his father."

"No." She shook her head, willed her tongue to remain moist enough to permit speech, her tone soft enough, to keep him from killing her. "Jake is his father—"

"My *brother* is his father. Oh?" he added. "You thought he didn't know? Of course, he knew. Had to, didn't he, when you took off instead of marrying the duke." His smile was as cold as the terror frosting Dianna's lungs. "He knew. Him and Laxton—"

"What?" She stared. "Lord Laxton?"

"Knows who really sired JJ?" McTeer raised his brows. "Who do you think put him up to it?"

"To stealing JJ? He told you to take my son?" He'd claimed to have no part in JJ's kidnapping. Only to taking advantage of the end result.

McTeer shook his head. "Laxton hired me to keep watch on him. Report back. But then... I saw what happened to you and started running the other way. Grabbed the wee Mac off the mare, and ran until I stumbled into a ditch. I threw him down in it and covered him with my body. Protected him." His chin lifted, eyes widening in defiance. "I protected him while things flew, and the wind howled... Then it was over an' I started to bring him back. I saw everyone gathered around you. You weren't moving. Katie was screaming. Screaming that you were dead. I was up on the hill. I could hear, but they... they didn't see me. So I turned around. Started walking. Ended up in the canyon. Ran into a man down there. I... I killed him. " His eyes widened more, taking on a wild look. The look of a madman. "Took his horse and clothes, and money. Rode to Amarillo, boarded the train—"

"You killed a man?" No, he couldn't have. But even as she resisted the idea, she knew it was true. He had murdered a man, and stolen her son. "You killed a man, and took JJ, of your own volition, because you... knew Lord Laxton would... pay for him?"

"Didn't know that." He shook his head. "But I knew he wanted the boy in England. Failing that, he sent me to keep an eye on him. And you. Make sure he was kept safe—"

"But how could he know about—oh, my God." She stared. "He was in on it."

"Ordered it." McTeer shrugged. "What better way to ruin your plans with that other guy and ensure you married who you were supposed to marry? Only you didn't, did you?" He jabbed the pistol at her. "You didn't marry the duke. You married the Yank!"

She held her breath against a scream, and the nausea rolling up her throat as she tried to grasp the enormity of what he was telling her.

Buckland hadn't acted alone.

He'd acted in concert with her uncle.

Lord Laxton had *ordered* her raped.

"Why couldn't you just leave things well enough alone?" McTeer rasped. "Grieve, and let your husband comfort you, give you another babe. It would have worked if you—"

"Mama?"

Dianna's heart almost stopped. She stared at the curtains encircling the canopied bed, gasped when the bedchamber's outer door flew open. McTeer started to turn and abruptly pitched back and to the side as a gunshot exploded Dianna's ear drums.

The pistol flew from McTeer's grasp. He grappled at the bed canopy in a vain attempt to remain on his feet, but the fabric tore loose from the frame and he tumbled to the floor, landing awkwardly on his back, green eyes wide and sightless, face splattered with the same blood soaking his shirtfront. Papa stepped into the room, pistol held expertly as Dianna, prodded by instinct, and noise barely audible over the thunderous echo of the gun's retort in her ears: a child.

Howling in terror.

"JJ." She scooped him free of the heavy quilts and kissed his sleep flushed face, brushed dark hair dampened with sweat from his small temples. "Oh, baby. Oh, baby. Oh JJ. My baby."

He clung to her neck, his chubby arms solid and strong; his whole body solid. Heavy. He was much heavier than she remembered.

"Mama," he whimpered and tightened his hold on her neck, as though afraid she might dissolve in a puff of smoke. "Mama."

"Oh, baby." She kissed his cheek, the fear she'd been afraid to even admit to herself—that her son might not remember her—washing away in a flood of relieved tears as she burrowed her nose in the delicate space between his neck and ear and inhaled deeply the familiar and welcome odours of warm milk, talcum powder, urine, and lye soap. A hand touched her elbow and the small of her back.

"Come," Mother Mary murmured. "We should go."

Dianna nodded, and adjusting JJ—with many words of promise she would not put him down so he'd ease his grip on her neck enough to enable her to prop him on her hip, silky head tucked under her chin—she sidled around McTeer's body careful to block JJ's view of the groom, and exited the chamber the way she'd come, while suited men poured in through the door Papa had entered.

The girl was still hunched in the chair, her hands over her ears. Dianna ignored her as she turned out into the hall and on down the stairs.

Part Three

If you press me to say why I loved him, I can say no more
than because he was he, and I was I.
~Michel de Montaigne

Chapter 23

Reste Fort

*D*ianna gripped Mother Mary's hand, tried not to let the fear she felt show on her face. Sergeant DeRosa, their escort, had been kind in his estimation of the horrors they would see.

Battered and filthy men exposed to damp treacherous conditions worse than most farm animals experienced, their expressions varying between stoicism, resignation, and indifference. Some without expression at all, their eyes eerily vacant.

A few smiled and tipped their helmets at the passing Red Cross wagon, their teeth startlingly white in filthy faces. Others stared as though unable to comprehend the presence of nuns on their battleground. But Sgt. DeRosa had assured them they were not near active battle.

The casualty clearance station was far enough from front lines to be safe from artillery and gunfire, close enough to treat seriously wounded soldiers before they were trundled off in ambulances bound for transfer to Britain for more intensive treatment and rehabilitation. Or burial.

The CCS reportedly also served as a layover for fresh soldiers newly arrived in need of supplies and tactical orders before being dispersed to assigned locations, and as respite for battle-fatigued men in need of rest and treatment of minor injuries and foot-rot, before they trudged back to resume the fight.

Dianna cringed as the motorised ambulance in which she and Mother Mary rode eased to one side of the narrow track to accommodate an oncoming horse-drawn ambulance, each driver fighting to keep their wheels from slipping off the road into the sloppy bog on either side. She glanced into the rear of the wagon as it passed, and faced forward again, closed her eyes.

Being warned she would see wrapped bodies stacked like cordwood for transport, and actually seeing it... DeRosa had said it was possible Jake had already left France, either as one of the injured, or in one of those wagons.

Was Papa, right? Was she on a fool's errand?

No.

If she had not looked for JJ, despite some people's insistence she had set herself a hopeless task, he would not now be safe at Ansmall becoming friends with his aunt and young uncle, getting to know his grandparents. She had to stay the course. She had to trust her heart.

Believe.

Jake was out there, somewhere, and by the grace of God she would find him and take him home. Fresh anger at Buckland's arrogance, and her uncle's corruption, flared under her breastbone.

Papa had promised to deal with them. How, he had not clarified. Knowing the earl, he would exact a penance equal to the crime, and though she should be outraged at the thought Papa would do to Buckland, as Buckland had done to Jake, she could not summon any feeling beyond satisfaction that Buckland would get his just dessert after his attempt to flee Holderness had been thwarted by Papa's phantoms.

It unnerved her, that part of Papa. Nineteen years in the same house with him, and no clue to his activities outside it. He had gone to London to work: Lord, peer, a father; politician and husband. No mention of covert operations involving sombre men in suits who skulked around in shadows.

Two had captured Buckland before he could make good his escape out the rear garden at Holderness. Two more marched the young blonde woman from the castle, whilst the remaining pair lugged McTeer's body out between them. In all, counting the first two, eight suited and unnervingly silent men, all of whom it turned out were under Papa's direct command. Something she and Mother Mary had been sternly advised against repeating to anyone on threat of imprisonment. If Mama knew of her husband's covert activities as overseer of a secret division within the War Office, she was as good as he at keeping secrets. The irony made Dianna smile.

Of course, they were good at keeping secrets. They'd concealed her parentage and birthright from everyone, including her, for twenty years. If they could withhold that information for two decades, they could conceivably withhold knowledge of political hijinks for longer.

What *was* surprising, was George Ramsay's misguided belief he deserved clemency, vociferously landing all responsibility for JJ's kidnapping on McTeer and Buckland. With McTeer dead and Buckland ill-disposed to answering questions, George Ramsay might yet be successful in casting attention away from his other illegalities. She hoped so.

She braced a hand and foot to keep from being jostled against Mother Mary as the truck's back end sloshed this way then that, before resuming a relatively linear course, and swallowed a rise of bile induced not by the rapid swerving, but by thought of what Papa and his suited phantoms might yet learn should they break Buckland's self-imposed silence.

Her gratitude for Buckland's adherence to the gentleman's code despite George Ramsay's total abdication from it, sickened her.

George Ramsay insisted Buckland had orchestrated everything after receiving word from his brother of Dianna's presumed death. Buckland neither confirmed nor denied the allegations. Nor did he admit to suggesting his youngest sister as Ramsay's conspiratorial-bride. Or explain how he and his brother came to approach George Ramsay in the first place. He said, nothing.

The sister, meanwhile, professed no knowledge of how either of her brothers had come to be involved with Ramsay, admitting only that she had been promised a wealthy life as a marquess's wife provided she claimed the boy as hers and Ramsay's.

Her name was Bridgett. She was the blonde girl in the chamber at Holderness. She was also, apparently, little William's former nurse, the one fired for suggesting his birthmark was a portent of evil, *and* the mystery woman who'd claimed to be Jake's sister-in-law. The Brougham and black horses were found in the stables at Holderness.

Mama had been horrified to discover Bridgett's involvement, while Dianna had been galled to know Buckland and McTeer had used a Holderness-owned carriage—*her* carriage—to facilitate their deceit. She'd also been thankful. Thankful Buckland had not revealed the depth of his treachery to his sister, maintained his customary non-communicative blandness when George Ramsay's allegations were relayed to him. Though she harboured no illusions that his silence was meant to protect her. It was his neck he hoped to spare the gallows.

She wiped her lips with her gloved hand, offered Mother Mary a quick, "I'm fine" smile when the elder woman glanced at her. Exhaling, she focused her gaze through the sleet and mud-spotted windscreen to the road ahead, but her mind swiftly returned across the channel to her encounter with Buckland out front Holderness.

"Where is Jake? Where is my husband? What did you do with him?" She'd been forced to keep her voice low, calm, as she clutched JJ to her, her body angled to prevent JJ seeing Buckland.

Silent, his long face as blank as that of the men who held his arms twisted behind his back, he stared at her. And then she saw it. A faint taunting gleam in his pale green eyes that sent a chill through her as he looked to JJ, and back again. She'd known immediately he enjoyed holding private the knowledge between them. Took pleasure in pressing it like a thin long-bladed knife to her metaphorical back, the tip struck through her clothes to stab soft flesh just above her hip, fully prepared to carve out her kidney should she raise her voice against him. Shaken, she'd stepped back, whirled, and handed JJ up into the carriage to Mother Mary, before clambering up to join her and reclaim her son, cuddle him all the way to London.

It was there, after private interrogation conducted by the earl and his phantoms, Buckland proved slightly more forthcoming. But only just.

She was mildly shocked to realise she revelled in the possibility they had tortured him. Equally appreciative of his stoicism as it related directly to her. Because if he conveyed anything of his association with Ramsay prior to JJ's kidnapping—of their conspired assault on her—Papa said not a word to her about it. But she knew the former steward hadn't. To do so would be to tie the knot in the rope that would hang him. Buckland was too smart for that.

He knew if he remained silent, the only thing he stood to be charged with was conspiracy to kidnap. With JJ found safe and well-cared for, he might even get a reduced sentence. While Ramsay would likely get off with public rebuke to go along with social ostracization now she'd stripped him of his title and access to her financial resources. But if either man confessed the other's part in the rape of Lord Ansmall's daughter...

Buckland would hang. George Ramsay's status as the late marquess's brother would spare him the noose, but he would end up in Oakwood or in prison—if Papa didn't arrange his premature death. Much as she'd like to see both men handed a maximum sentence, she could not stomach having her, or her son's reputation, dragged through the evil filth associated with either of them. She closed her eyes.

FRANCE. J. DEVIL'S DOZEN

POSTCARD SIGNED ALWAYS J. ASKS YOUR HELP

MRS. D CONFIRMS HANDWRITING

Dianna deduced, and Mother Mary and Papa agreed, the three telegrams Elaina had sent and Mama immediately dispatched to Rosewood upon receiving them at Ansmall, translated to Jake having sent word to advise of his whereabouts and request Dianna's help. His mother had confirmed the note as not a hoax, but written by him.

Presented with the three telegrams, along with his sister's admission she'd collected Jake's belongings in Hereford, Buckland finally confessed to paying the CO of his former battalion, a man named Phelps, to take Jake off to war in place of yet another of Buckland's brothers, Jack. He was the groom Dianna had seen opening the carriage door at Irwell, who, in possession of Jake's documents was to have gone cavorting off with the rest of the wedding party. But, Buckland insisted, he'd done it all on his lord's word, thus implicating the earl. Papa absolutely denied any part in it.

"When Buckland wired me about your husband's unexpected visit and the fact he'd booked into the Inn for at least a week, I told him if he came back to Ansmall, to run him off. Send him back where he came from. I said nothing about shipping him off to bloody war."

She tensed, and hung on as the ambulance's rear kicked out again, its engine revving as the tyres fought for traction.

That had been quite a row, and the first where she'd not capitulated, not backed down in the interest of self-preservation. They might have gone at it for hours instead of a half-hour had Papa not finally conceded his mistake in abdicating responsibility to Buckland, not promised her he would not sleep until he exhausted every avenue to getting her husband back to her.

"Jake," she had shouted, furious at his unwillingness to call him anything other than, *your husband*. "His name is Jake. And he's your *son-in-law!*"

Of course, the earl ignored her outburst in favour of immediately organising private meetings for himself with Lords Grey and Crewe, and Field Marshal Kitchener the newly appointed Minister of War. Within three days Rt. Honourable Kitchener was able to confirm that a J. McTeer had indeed gone to France with the 13th Battalion, but that the 13th's current whereabouts was unknown following "heavy artillery and fighting in the area of Ypres resulting in heavy casualties and stalled communications".

It had taken the remainder of that day to convince the earl to call in any and all favours owed him by people in position to help her get across the channel to look for her husband. That had gone even worse than the earlier row.

"Do it, Papa," she demanded. "Do it, or I *will* pursue legal action on Buckland's claim that you are responsible for my husband's kidnap and... illegal conscription. I'll start with Scotland Yard and the House of Lords, and end up in the street out front Parliament if I have to, shouting at the top of my lungs—"

"All right." He glowered, his lean face a blanched mask of fury. "I'll do what I can, God help me. For anything happens to you, your mother will never forgive me."

"I'll never forgive you if you don't."

He inhaled, the rise and fall of his narrow shoulders as close to defeatism as she'd seen from him, before he shouted for his coat and hat, and for the auto to be brought round.

It wasn't her threat of ever-lasting resentment that had swayed him she knew, but awareness of his precarious position with, not his peers or the authorities, but Mama.

The whole thing with George Ramsay seemed to have pushed the countess around a corner of some sort, for instead of resuming her normal pattern of passivity in the face of the earl's obstinance, she arrived at Rosewood with Elizabeth in tow, and ended up in the earl's office with Dianna berating Papa for his handling of Jake's visit, adding her voice to Dianna's cause, insisting the earl help rather than hinder Dianna's desire to find her husband.

"For once we are going to do as our daughter wants—*needs*—us to do, Edward," she said, green eyes narrowed and visage implacable. "Not what we think best for her."

When Papa finally returned from long meetings with the powers-be and called her into his office to advise her he had found her passage, and excuse to be in a war-zone, he was still furious.

"Sit." He pointed to the chair behind his desk.

She frowned. "Why?"

"I said, sit." He glared until she did so, if reluctantly, wondering why on earth he wanted her to sit at his desk, rather than before it as was her customary position. She found out soon enough when he placed blank paper and a fountain pen before her. "Your will." He swallowed, his Adam's apple sharp in his lean neck. "You will write your will before you go, and in it, you will grant your mother and I guardianship of your son should you fail to survive this enormously ignorant undertaking."

"But Jake—"

"Is missing. With no guarantee he'll ever be found." The earl's nostrils flared with his inhalation. "If you don't come back either, all of your children will be orphans. Your mother and I will see to JJ. You shall choose whomever else you feel best for your adopted children."

Angling her head to look out the ambulance's side window she willed the tears glazing her eyes to stop forming as she used the gloved edge of her thumb to wipe her cheeks. Mother Mary grasped her other hand, gave it a gentle squeeze.

"*Reste fort*," she murmured. Stay strong.

Dianna reciprocated the squeeze, but dared not look at her dear mentor for fear the grief and trauma she still felt, not only at memory of her father's words but with the truth in them, would dissolve her outward show of strength, reveal the fragility of her feelings.

She'd used her anger at the earl to help her control the tremble in her hand, hold back her tears, while she wrote the new will consigning to the dustbin, the one she and Jake had undertaken shortly after marrying and finalising their separate adoptions of the children. But now, the import of what she'd signed...

Per the earl's requirement, with Mother Mary as witness, she granted—upon her death—guardianship of JJ and all entailed property to Lord and Lady Ansmall, of Herefordshire, while Katie and Amelia would, should Jake turn up alive, remain with him in Texas. In the event he was not able to care for the girls for whatever reason, they then went—upon Maggie and Mr. Sweeney's agreement—to live with them, along with a generous annual allowance for the girls' care outside the substantial Trusts she also created for the girls, assigning Eleanor Douglas executor until Katie and Amelia each reached age of majority, and received her portion. She followed that gut-searing task up with letters to all parties involved, informing them of what she'd done, and why. She left London before the ink on the envelopes was dry.

Three days later, she and Mother Mary—who ardently and adamantly refused to be left behind—were nearing the end of another exhausting journey. Rather than feel vindicated, however, she wanted to scream at the injustice of it. Instead, she prayed she'd not only discover J. McTeer's whereabouts, but whether he was Jake. If so, she'd take him home. Alive or... not. She closed her eyes.

Please, please, let me find him alive. Let me take him home, where we belong.

It was the only way she could justify leaving JJ behind so soon after getting him back. Rationalise not returning home with him to America, to her daughters—She clamped her lips, fought a tsunami of tears as the ambulance grumbled to a stop.

Sergeant DeRosa hopped out, squelched and slid around to aid Mother Mary's egress, and then extended a leather gloved-hand to Dianna. His dark green eyes locked with hers. Her gut twisted.

Lowering her gaze, she stepped cautiously to the wooden walkway built to float on the sea of black mud that stretched as far as she could see, and as soon as she was stable pulled her hand free of the sergeant's, focused on normalising her breath.

Would she ever be able to meet a man's gaze and not experience a temporary spasm of terror if his eye colour even remotely resembled Buckland's?

"This way, Sisters," Sgt. DeRosa said. "The Lieutenant-Colonel will want to see you."

∞ ∞ ∞

Lieutenant-Colonel J. Wicker gestured to two of the three poured cups of tea, and took up the third in impeccably manicured hands, the fingernails trimmed square and short.

He was a compact dark-haired man with a thick moustache and piercing brown eyes. It amazed Dianna he managed to stay so crisp and clean, his uniform impossibly pressed with razor-edged creases, when everything and everyone around him was perilously close to being consumed by the muddy earth. Already the hem of her uniform was damp, the soles of her boots tacky with muck. The Lt. Colonel's boots were polished, black, and shiny, the soles free of debris.

250

He took a sip of tea, exhaled in satisfaction, and setting the cup aside looked at Mother Mary. His smile did not reach his eyes. "So, you wish to bring aid and comfort to my men."

Mother Mary nodded. "We wish to help, yes."

"It would help, if you turned around, and went back where you came from. I have enough concerns without adding to them a pair of do-good Sisters."

Mother Mary smiled, but like Wicker's, her gaze was firm.

He sighed. "You can tend the wounded and the sick but stay away from my soldiers. I need them focused on the next battle, and how to win it, not thinking about a hen and how to bag it." His eyes slid to Dianna.

She bit her tongue. Papa had pulled political strings to get her here, but here, the Lt. Col. held all the cards.

"Sister Dianna and I are here to offer only God's comfort," Mother Mary said. "I expect you will assure your men understand that?"

Wicker dragged his gaze from Dianna, pushed to his feet. Looking down his short nose at Mother Mary, he said, "I'll do my job, Sister. You do yours."

Mother Mary slowly rose to her full height forcing the general to look up. "Good day, sir," she said.

Outside, it was all Dianna could do not to shout. "How dare he insinuate such things?" she whispered after ensuring the office door was closed. "Has he no respect?"

Mother Mary took Dianna's hand. "Sometimes I forget how young you are, child," she murmured. "When you get to my age, little surprises you. Come now, do not waste energy on a man small as he. There is a greater man that requires your attention. Sergeant," she added, and waved to DeRosa who was overseeing the unloading of a supply wagon.

"Yes, Reverend Mother?"

"Could you have someone show Sister and I to our quarters?"

He nodded, and after speaking briefly with a young uniformed man holding a clipboard, he grabbed the two leather cases on the boardwalk outside Wicker's office. With a chin-gesture, he said, "This way, Sisters."

A short walk later he paused at the entrance to a small tent, indicated to Mother Mary and Dianna to enter, and leaning through the flap, he deposited the cases on the ground.

"With respect, Mother," he said, "but you should go to Rouen, or Calais. Or Boulogne. These tents are no place for women, especially those of the cloth."

"I go where God sends me," Mother Mary said.

"Trust me, Mother," the sergeant said. "God abandoned this place months ago."

Chapter 24

You're Not Alone

*J*ake's thighs quaked with the effort of squatting against the trench wall, his arms and back—every bone and muscle in his body—screaming in agony as he struggled to keep himself and his weapon below the top line of the trench and above the quagmire of blood and mud threatening to suck him under. Rain mixed with snow had fallen overnight, and though it had stopped, the damage was done.

He was bone cold, so numb he felt almost nothing. Or maybe his inability to feel had nothing to do with the weather, and everything to do with the carnage in which he steeped, grisly filth and brutal slaughter so incomprehensible death seemed a preferable alternative. At least some men thought so.

Three in the last week had either tossed their weapons and walked, weeping, into no man's land, or turned their guns on themselves. Two suicides by sniper, and one by his own hand. It was enough to rip the guts out of even the most stoic of men.

Jake kept his gaze fixed on the serpentine edge of razor wire barely visible about fifteen feet from the trench, a thin jagged and rolling black line puncturing the charcoal sky, careful to avoid Olsen's milky stare a few feet away.

The lieutenant's bloodied head hung over the side of the trench, his expression one of stunned wonder, as though questioning why he had died, and Jake lived.

Jake wondered that himself. How he had managed to escape a bullet or bayonet when Phelps—and now Phelps's replacement, and a full three-quarters of the 13th including all the officers, and Sutherland who he'd learned had survived the blast that killed Phelps but with shrapnel wounds, wounds that became infected and led to fatal septicaemia within the week—had not.

Lucky.

That's what Jake was. Like the French girl whose kindness in carting water to him and Baxter's men had saved her from the missile strike. Only her luck was a single stroke of fate, a case of being in the right place at the right time. Not that he said as much to her.

She hadn't wanted to speak to him after she learned the fate of her brothers and grandmother. His last image of her was of dark accusing eyes as she was loaded on a train bound for St. Omer. His only comfort came in knowing she would be safe there. And that she was still young enough to learn how to release the guilt, and maybe one day find peace—maybe even joy—in her survival, provided peace and joy ever reclaimed this Godforsaken place.

No, his luck was cumulative. Luck gained through three years with the Rangers under Wardlaw's gruelling tutelage where he learned to expect the unexpected, and to stay calm when it mattered. Luck in being big and strong. Big and strong enough, seasoned enough from years of ranching to endure long frigid nights and heavy work on short sleep and cold vittles. Luck found in the sharp fists of bullies at school, and in the tough wisdom of the man who raised him and taught him to fight back, instructed him in the art of hand-to-hand combat, how to move silently in darkness or daylight, and made him shoot round after round until he could knock a bullet casing off a fence post at two-hundred yards, who had taught him to listen, not only with his ears, but his senses, and recognise when things were too quiet.

Like now.

"Ready," he murmured and planted his feet a little deeper in the mud to ensure a stable launch. His words filtered down both sides of the line, carried in hasty whispers on the blue and trembling lips of thirty-two men, all that remained of what had been one-hundred and eighty-strong. He exhaled and adjusted his stiff hands on the gun's metal casing.

They would come, screaming and yodelling to frighten, bayonets and bullets plunging into soft tissue to kill. They would come because they had no choice.

Orders. Orders to retake the trench, regain the ridge—and the treasure it had given up—just as he and the men with him and those from other units in trenches further along either side, had had orders to take it from them, and not without consequence.

Hundreds dead and injured, trapped in razor wire, face-down in puddles and trenches: British, French, German, their cries and moans a common language falling silent as day broke and some succumbed to injury, the rest feigning death to avoid a sniper's bullet. Not a single stretcher-bearer could risk recovery until one side retreated. That was this morning's task. Repel the retaliatory strike, and drive the Huns from the woods.

Trees began to take shape about a hundred yards away, their skeletal trunks emerging black from the mist as they were forced to relief by the sun rising behind them.

Jake didn't need to see over the earthen dike running the length of the trench's edge to know the Huns were close. He could feel them. Smell them. Smell them over the blood and stench of gaseous corpses, the sharp tang of imminent danger mixed with fear roiling in the guts of the men crouched with him.

"Now," he shouted, and fifteen men lunged to thrust their rifles over the earthen bank and fire, low, just as he had ordered them to do—into the faces of the crawling Huns who were about a hundred yards out. Then, as he'd also instructed, those men dropped to change position while another fifteen leaped up from different points to fire, this time aimed higher, for the stomach of the enemy not hit in the first round who having lost the advantage of surprise, surged to their feet to close the distance. As the original fifteen popped up from new positions, Jake heaved the Maschinengewehr 08 over top of the trench, and scrambled after it.

"You want your machine gun, you can have it," he shouted. And opened fire. Beside him, Private Solomon fed the ammunition. He couldn't hear the screams over the gun's racket, but mouths opened, and bodies fell like wheat before a scythe. Solomon slumped next to him. Unmoving. The next round of fabric-coated ammunition lay limp next to him.

Hell.

Jake carved the machine gun side to side.

More Huns dropped.

The MG08 rattled to abrupt silence.

Jake grabbed a rifle. Aimed. Fired. Aimed and fired. Bullets whined and thumped with grisly precision as the BEF drilled bullet after bullet in rapid succession into the advancing Huns.

No. Not advancing.

Retreating.

They were turned around, running, their shadows shrinking in the smoky sun-lit mist filtering through the trees. Beside him someone stood, waved a fist, shouting in jubilant victory. He lunged to grab the man's arm, drag him down, and grunted as he collapsed in the mud, pain ripping through his chest.

∞ ∞ ∞

Dianna trembled as she scrubbed her hands.

Red. The water was red. Like her hands. She scrubbed harder. Faster.

It wasn't working. The blood wasn't coming off.

Yes, it was. No. No, it wasn't.

Her skin.

Her skin was coming off, sloughing into the water. She grappled to catch it, cup it in her hands, screamed when more fell away, and small chunks of bone dropped in the basin with bloody splashes.

The faster she tried to catch the falling pieces, the faster her hands fragmented.

Plink.

Splunk.

Sploosh.

"No." She staggered back, stared at the knobby bones protruding from her upraised arms. "No!"

"Dianna. Dianna, *ma chère.* Wake up. You're dreaming. You're dreaming, *ma chérie.* Wake up. "

Dianna lurched from sleep, stared without comprehension at the figure leaned over her.

"What is it child? What has scared you so? The wounded?"

Dianna gasped for breath as the nightmare receded, taking with it the paralysis, and horror. With a shake of her head, she dragged herself upright.

"No, Mother." As bad as the amputated limbs, sutured heads, and bandaged torsos of the men she saw in a day were, they were mild compared to the dream. She flexed her hands, grateful to find them whole and intact, if her nails uneven and knuckles dry, rough. "It was me. My hands. My hands melting away, until there was nothing left but bloody stumps. I was... useless." She swallowed, and met Mother Mary's worried gaze. "I couldn't stop them falling apart, Mother, any more than I could catch the pieces as they fell. They just disintegrated, and all I could do was watch. All I *can* do is watch, Mother. I'm useless." She shook her head. "I'm not a nurse. I can't stop their pain. I can't stop them dying. And I can't... I can't find Jake." She covered her face, burst into tears.

Mother Mary embraced her, massaged her back with one strong hand. "It was a dream, Dianna. A deceptive nightmare, because you *are* making a difference. You *are* helping. You give poor souls what the nurses and doctors cannot: time. You sit with them and listen. Write and post the letters they lack strength and ability to write and send. You read their letters to them, share jokes. You're treating their spirits, Dianna, and that is equally as important as mending their wounds. For those whose wounds are beyond repair... You give comfort, and compassion. There is no greater gift than to pass into the embrace of Angels from the gentle arms of an angel on earth."

"But Mother—" Dianna pulled away. "It's been almost a fortnight. I've talked to many men. So many, so badly hurt... None know of Jake, and I... I don't know how long I can do this. How any of them do this? The nurses, the doctors... The soldiers. It's awful. Awful what they endure. Have endured. The wounds. The wet and the mud. So much mud. And rats. Those filthy beasts—what are we doing, Mother? Why are we here? Why are we killing each other? Why is God *letting* us kill each other?"

"God is not letting us kill each other, *ma chérie*," Mother Mary murmured, her face grave as she cupped Dianna's face with broad palms. "We are killing ourselves, child. *He* gave us freedom. Freedom to choose, and light or dark, we choose the path; it does not choose us. When the collective will is great enough, chaos will surrender, and compassion prevail. Until then we must choose to remain on the lighted path, no matter how steep the going. No matter how easy it would be to sit and slide all the way to the bottom."

Dianna nodded as Mother Mary lowered her hands. "I know you're right, Mother. It's just, I'm..."

"Tired?"

"Scared."

Mother Mary offered a sad smile. "War is worthy of fear, Dianna. You've nothing to be ashamed of."

"I'm not ashamed, Mother. And it's not the war that scares me," she added, voice hoarse. "It's never seeing Jake or my children again, that absolutely terrifies me."

∞ ∞ ∞

"Ma'am. Miss. Angel."

The rasping cries and desperate stares of those that could see, started up the moment she stepped into the tent. Only the ones with heads bandaged to protect eye wounds did not seek her with their gazes.

Dianna did her best to answer each plaintive call, to ladle water into thirsty mouths, light cigarettes, spoon feed those whose hands, and in some cases, whole arms were lost to shrapnel on the battlefield. Cold compresses. Warm bricks. Bloodied bandages. Vomitus. Bedpans... How many she had collected, tucked, discarded, she lost count. The days had passed in a blur of instructions from Sister Nurses overwhelmed and thankful for the additional hands that freed them to tend wounds, change dressings, assist doctors with repairing more intensive, or delicate injuries. She was exhausted. Deeply. Literally. And losing hope.

Fast.

Jake could be anywhere. And nowhere near the battle lines that fed this casualty clearing station, though it was closest to where his unit was last known to be.

"Mum?"

Dianna grasped the hand waving uncertainly near her waist without thinking. Her heart constricted when she looked down. Drawing a shaky breath, she murmured, "How can I help?"

"I'm cold," he said. "Could ye cover me legs?"

She blinked a few times, and clearing her throat, said gently, "Of course. Let me get an extra blanket."

"Thank ye, mum."

As she gently released his hand, the young soldier lowered his bandaged head to the pillow. Thankfully his eyes were covered as well, and he'd not seen her face.

Truly, would she ever get used to the carnage?

The young soldier did not move, or respond, as she gently spread an extra blanket over his legless trunk. But when she touched his forehead—it was flaming hot—he groaned.

"Mum?"

"Shh," Dianna soothed, as she brushed back a lock of his sandy-brown hair that had fallen over his bandaged eyes.

"I want me mum," he whispered. "Can ye get her for me?"

The Nursery, as the ward for seriously injured soldiers was referred owing to the patients' infant-like need for round-the-clock care, was quiet. Only two Sister Nurses on duty, and each busy with a patient. After a frenetic few days, and a steady stream of wounded, she too should still be in her tent resting, catching up on much needed sleep, before another bloody battle kept them on the run for hours. If not days. But that dream...

She couldn't sleep. Or return to her tent, until she visited all the wards, read all the clipboards, scanned all the faces, or collarbones for a familiar notch if the faces were bandaged beyond recognition, hope flaring with each new intake of patients, and dwindling with each battered soldier she examined not her husband.

This young man was not Jake. The notes at the end of the bed identified him as Pte. Andrew (Andy) R. Frith, nineteen years of age, both legs amputated above the knee two days previous. And though she was worn out and still had two wards to inspect—the transfer ward where gravely injured but stable patients awaited transport to a base hospital, and the one she always saved for last—she sat on the floor next to his stretcher, grasped his cold hand in hers.

"I'm here Andy," she said softly. "You're not alone."

∞ ∞ ∞

Andy died shortly before dawn. Dianna bowed her head, let her tears fall freely.

I have a dog, Jip. And a girl, Heather. We grew up together. I asked her to marry me when I get back. She promised to wait for me. Is someone waiting for you? Did ye get my mum? She'll be sore at me. She didn't want me to go, not with me da gone. He died last year. Went to bed and didn't wake up, peaceful like. It's not peaceful here. Have ye heard from my mum yet?

In and out of coherence he went, one moment seemingly alert as she responded to his question about someone waiting for her and told him about the girls and their life on the ranch. The next muttering and moaning in pain, pleading for his mother.

"Ye've a kind heart, lassie."

Dianna started, and turned. A large broad-chested man with deep-chestnut-brown hair was sitting half-propped against the wall on the floor across the narrow expanse separating the two rows of twenty beds.

He grinned. "Lieutenant-Colonel Barnard Baxter, at your service."

Dianna sniffled again, and after pulling the blanket over Andy's still face, she pushed wearily to her feet. "You should be in the officer's ward."

LC Baxter shook his head. "I stay with my men. And Andy there was one of mine. Fine lad. Good boy. An' too blooidy young to die. I'm jus' glad 'e passed not knowing about his legs. Nothin' worse," he added, his tone a curious mixture of defiance and sorrow as he gestured to the foot of his bed.

"Oh, I'm sorry," Dianna said.

"Aye, weel, I got both hands, an' one good leg to stand on. Never did learn to shoot with my feet, so one less won't hurt my aim any." He laughed; a baritone rumble that made her laugh.

"You're in good spirits," she said.

"For a man wi' only one leg?" He laughed again, and then glanced at Andy's shrouded form. His grey-blue eyes glimmered with moisture that he wicked away with a rapid blink, as he lifted his head to look at her. "I'm alive, and the wound's clean. That's reason enough to celebrate."

She nodded. "It is."

"Is it true," he said, "what ye told Andy about ye livin' on a ranch in America?"

Again, she nodded.

"Funny," he said. "Almost fifty years I've had the pleasure of livin', an' spoke to mebbe three people from America in all that time, until I come to this Godforsaken place an' meet two—"

"What?" Dianna blurted. "Another American? Here?"

"Weel, not here," he said and stabbed a finger at the floor. "An' I can't say 'e was American, only he was raised there, an' British, least he claimed so, on 'is mother's side, though he didna sound like a Brit. More like one of them Canadians—" He broke off and jerked back as Dianna fell to her knees, grabbed his hand.

"Tell me," she said. "Tell me where you saw him? What did he look like? Was he tall and blonde, and big like you?"

"Aye, weel, 'e was no Jessie. An' fair-heided fur sure. Said his name was McTeer—"

Dianna slumped, dizzy.

Baxter grasped her by the upper arms. "Aye, lassie, what's amiss?"

"Where?" She swallowed, straightened. "Where did you see him? Is he okay? What did he say?"

Baxter manoeuvred to clasp her hands. He slowly looked her up and down, his gaze pausing momentarily at her waist. A frown dimpled his brow.

No doubt she had blood, or some other unsavoury stain on her white smock. Again.

When his eyes found hers, his expression softened, paternal. "Ye best take it easy, lass. Clearly the man's important to ye, but ye don' wanna go upsettin' the—"

"He's my husband," Dianna exclaimed. "And his name's not McTeer. It's Douglas. Jake Douglas. He's more than important to me. He's everything."

"Ooch, aye?" Baxter raised a bushy eyebrow. "He *is* important to ye. Tell ye what, last I saw 'im he was right as rain. Me an' my men had just plucked him from the arms of the enemy after he ended up on the wrong side of the lines, an' he returned the kindness by saving a French lassie from blowin' up wi' her auld grannie and two young brothers—"

"When? When did you see him?"

Baxter blinked, and then frowning, cast a look around as though looking for something. "A couple weeks past. Canna say for sure how long. What day is it now?"

"Tuesday—no, Wednesday. The twenty-third. December twenty-third."

"Aye weel, ah met yer lad on the fifth. I remember, 'cause I noted it in my report. An' the next day, we parted ways—"

She bent and kissed Baxter's freckled brow. "You're a dear, truly. Thank you. Thank you," she repeated as she scrambled to her feet. "Now I know it *is* him, and he is—was—alive, less than three weeks ago. I've got to find him."

Flashing the bewildered—and faintly blushing—lieutenant-colonel a grateful smile, she hastened out of the ward.

∞ ∞ ∞

"What do you mean, you can't?" Dianna scowled. "It's your job—"

Mother Mary laid a hand on Dianna's arm, but she shook it off, leaned her palms on Wicker's desk.

"He doesn't belong out there," she said. "He's not a British subject."

Wicker sighed. "Young lady—"

"Marchioness," she said and straightened. "Lady Dianna Ellen Louise Marshall-Douglas, Marchioness Holderness. My father is—"

"I know. The Earl of Ansmall, who's a close friend of Lord Crewe, who's chummy with the man I ultimately answer to, which is the only reason I bit my tongue when I received orders to receive you and ensure your safety." His brown eyes were almost black with anger. "But I'll not go baying like a mad hound at the moon, until I've irrefutable proof this McTeer is your husband, and that he didn't volunteer."

"He didn't. I told you. He was kidnapped and—"

"Bullyrag!" Wicker's eyes widened. "He might have been kidnapped, but he was *not* conscripted. No one's been conscripted into His Majesty's army. We've no need. Ours is one of the greatest and most-respected fighting forces on earth. Men volunteer—"

"Twenty-thousand men killed the first day," Dianna interjected. "The very first day they started fighting in this Godforsaken place." She compressed her lips. "The BEF is almost entirely wiped out. Fifty-five-thousand men. You've had to bring in thousands and thousands more of the territorial reserves. I know the numbers. I knew them before I left England. My father made sure of it." She swallowed, narrowed her gaze to match the threat in his. "And I'm not *asking* you, Sir. Because you've a duty to investigate whether the man Lt. Colonel Baxter met, is my husband. Whether he's wrongly serving in this bloody awful war. I deserve to know," she added, voice hollowing with fear, and longing. "*He* deserves. *My husband* deserves a chance to confirm whether he's a volunteer, or hostage, of your army."

Wicker's mouth opened, then shut, his lip curling in the shelter of his moustache as he glared. "I am under no such obligation, my lady," he

262

murmured. "We're a country at war, and you're becoming an impediment to my competent execution of orders—"

"I'm sorry." She heaved a steadying breath. Papa might be able, through his back-door access to the War Office, have Wicker ordered to have J. McTeer brought to the CCS, but that help would come later than sooner. And not at all if Wicker chose to ignore it and had her ushered out of Belgium. At his peril. But that would not help Jake now. "Please forgive my... forcefulness," she added. "I'm distraught. I've not seen my husband in almost five months—"

"And I've personally written letters to hundreds of wives who'll never see or hear from their husbands ever again," Wicker muttered.

"I know." Dianna bowed her head. "I know," she said again, and looked up to meet Wicker's bland stare. "It's not fair. It's not fair what any of us has to endure. I spent the night holding the hand of a young man who begged me to find his mother. All he wanted was his mother and I could no more give him that than I could give him back his legs, or prevent him dying there in front of me this morning, his hand in mine. His last words were, 'Tell Mum I'm sorry'." She sucked a breath, tears leaking from the corners of her eyes. "But you *can* do something. You can help me discover if my husband lives, or if I, like Andy Frith's poor mother, have to learn to live with my heart ripped out of my chest."

Wicker blinked. Shifted in his seat. Cleared his throat and tapped his manicured fingers on the wooden arms of his chair.

"My wife died ten years ago," he murmured. "They say time heals all wounds." He cleared his throat again. "It doesn't." He looked down, shuffled papers. Looking up, he said, "I'll see what I can do, but... no promises. I can't guarantee, even if it turns out it's him, he's still alive—"

"I don't expect you to guarantee me anything, sir. Whatever his... situation, I just want to know." She shook her head. "I simply need to know."

Wicker nodded. "I'll see what I can find out."

Word came sooner than she expected, and she hugged her middle as Wicker relayed the awful news: heavy shelling in the area where the 13th was reportedly dug in. Ambulances were due shortly.

They arrived forty-minutes later. There was no time to catch up on sleep, or do more than hop from one soldier to the next helping cut away mud-caked tunics and blood-soaked bandages. Retrieve fresh bandages.

Fill basins with boiling water. Press thick dressings to deep wounds when ordered. Step over and around stretchers on the floor containing dazed and unconscious men to offer words of comfort and reassurance. Smooth muddy and bloodied brows. Hold cold, cold hands when her immediate assistance was not required, while doctors and nurses decided who went to surgery now, who could wait a few hours, and who'd never make it regardless. The latter were moved to a separate tent, where she and Mother Mary were sent once the sorting was done, the tent she always checked last before turning in after each shift.

"Water," a voice rasped.

Dianna knelt next to a man holding his innards in by aid of the thick blood-and-mud-drenched bandage knotted around his waist. He still wore his tunic, though it was nothing more than shreds from mid-chest down. His uniform trousers were black, rips and tears exposing pale, blood-smeared skin. Mud clung to his boots and coated his hair making it impossible to gauge its natural colour. But his blue eyes shone unnaturally bright blue amidst the filth smudging his face as she dribbled water past his parched lips, careful not to let her knowledge of his fate show in her expression.

"Ah, you're dream, you are," he murmured. "An angel in blue-and-white." And he died.

She closed her eyes, breathed out. "I can't keep doing this," she whispered. "I just can't." She headed for the exit. Fortunately, no one asked where she was going.

Another horse-drawn ambulance churned through the dusk toward the CCS, orderlies already on the run to greet it and begin another round of triage. Dianna trotted after them.

"Jack. Jack McTeer?" She stumbled and slid alongside the wagon as it laboured toward the medical marques. "Private Jack McTeer?"

"Got no one here by that name," said a man hunched near the centre of broken and bleeding men heaped haphazardly in the wagon bed unconscious or moaning. "Maybe one of the others," he added with a jerk of his head.

She slipped and squelched to the next ambulance in line.

"No, sorry Sister, got none by that name." Same with the next two ambulances. "McTeer?" An orderly in the fourth—and last—ambulance in the train frowned as he scanned the mud-splattered and bandaged men. "I seem to recall that name. Lemme see. Uh, no," he said a moment later after examining the ID discs the soldiers wore on leather strings around their necks tucked under their tunics. "McIvor, not McTeer. Sorry."

Dianna staggered to a halt on trembling legs, and fighting tears of frustration and exhaustion she faced the direction from which the ambulances had come.

It was too dark to tell if there were more horses further on, head down and leaned hard into the traces slogging through mud so sticky it accumulated on spokes and axles preventing the wheels from rotating, turning the ambulance into an awkward and bloody heavy sled. A boom echoed in the distance. She crossed her arms, shivered.

The CCS was ten miles behind the lines. Not very far at all.

And too far.

She may as well be in Calais, or Canada, for all she could do to bring Jake home. She closed her eyes, gritted her teeth.

You will not cry. You will not. You asked to be here, and you will remain positive. You will continue to believe, until you have very good reason not to.

Hugging herself harder, she blinked against the sleet.

Her body ached with cold and fatigue. But if the soldiers could live, and fight in the ghastly weather and foul muck day in and day out, she could certainly stand a few more minutes.

"Sister? Sister Dianna?" A shadowy figure stood outlined in sallow light at the entrance to the marque she had left, the one she dubbed LC for Lost Causes as it was where soldiers with non-survivable wounds were sequestered. Where she and Mother Mary offered what little they could, to men destined to die in minutes, hours, and rarely, a day. Maybe two.

They wanted her back. To wash hands and faces. Cover trembling men with blankets and move on to the next poor soul. Occasionally offer sips of water, or like with Andy hold hands and listen. Sometimes scribble notes to transcribe later into more coherent form, something suitable to send on to surviving love ones. And it wasn't enough. It was not near enough.

The poor men in there would never see their wives or children or mothers and fathers again. Never taste another Christmas goose, or enjoy a pint at their favourite public house. The tickle of warm grass underfoot on a bright summer's day. *God how she missed that. Grass, and... warmth.*

Wiping a hand over her eyes she tried not to think of home, or of the men interred in the same mud in which they'd taken their last breath simply because there weren't enough stretcher bearers, ambulances, trains, and ships to transport them.

It was awful how many stayed where they fell. No cross. No grave. Nothing to mark their place, recognise their sacrifice.

*Please. Please don't let Jake be one of them. Bring him back to me. Don't let him die out there, alone. Don't let him be one of those poor men left behind—*She looked when the orderly shouted her name again, with more urgency.

"Quickly," he added, waving. "There's a soldier here Mother Mary thinks mebbe is your husband."

Chapter 25

It's Not Too Late

Mother Mary knelt beside a mud-covered soldier around whose chest wound a familiarly-ominous, blood-soaked bandage.

Dianna fell to her knees on the other side of him. "Jake? Oh my god, Jake, darling." She brushed his mud-caked hair back, clasped his face in her hands. He moaned. "Oh my God. Oh, my—Mother. Mother, what's wrong? Why is he in here, and not in the operating marque?"

Mother Mary shrugged. "I know not. I was washing the mud from his face, and... he looked familiar." Her gaze was bleak, her wide mouth flat with anguish. "I'm so sorry, Dianna—"

"No." Dianna shook her head. "No. It's not too late. He's breathing. He's alive. And I will not sit here and watch him die." She pushed to her feet. "Look after him. Keep him warm. I'll be back shortly."

∞ ∞ ∞

"You must operate."

"There's no use," Capt. Evans said. She had caught him as he was entering the operating marque after a short rest break. "We only operate on those we think we can save."

"You can save him. He's strong, a fighter—"

"I'm sorry. I feel for you. I do. But I have dozens of men I know I can save. I won't risk one of them to operate on one I'm sure I can't."

Dianna clenched her fists. "You have to—"

"I know what I have to do, Sister," he said, "and that's save as many lives as possible. I don't have time to waste on non-survivable injuries." He turned and pushed into the operating theatre.

"No, please—"

Matron Houser threw a solid arm out, blocking Dianna from following. "You heard him, Missus," she said gently, but firmly. "There's nothing can be done here for your man. The best you can do now, is be with him, comfort him—"

"No." Dianna shook her head. "I refuse to give up. Not after everything he and I have been through. I will save him." She whirled away and burst outside into the wintry night, tears hot on her cheeks. She was half way to the lost causes tent when she stopped, retraced her steps, and hastened into the nursery. A few minutes later she stopped a pair of stretcher-bearers.

"I need your help."

"Excuse me?" The taller of the two blinked as wet snow landed on his eyelashes.

"There's a man in there," Dianna said and pointed. "He needs to go to surgery immediately."

The shorter man glanced over his shoulder. "No offence, Sister," he said. "But any what's in there aren't fit for surgery."

"This man is. He's a lieutenant-colonel. I've been instructed to retrieve him, take him to operating bed three." Dr. Evans was on bed one. "Quick. There's no time to waste."

The men's breath fogged from their open mouths, and then the taller one shrugged.

"Why not? Lieutenant or latrine boy I'll pack him all the way to Tipperary if it means staying back from the lines awhile longer."

The other man hesitated for the space of a heartbeat, then nodded. "You got that right. No sense rushing back when we're needed here."

Three minutes later they deposited Jake on his stretcher on the ground inside the operating tent. Two minutes after that, a different set of stretcher bearers hefted him on to table three.

∞ ∞ ∞

The surgeon didn't look at the disc hung around Jake's neck. He simply cut away the bandages and bowed to inspect the wound. Dianna pressed her fingertips to her lips as nausea rolled up her throat, as the doctor palpated Jake's swollen abdomen and glanced at his grey-tinged face.

"B. Baxter. Scots Guard," a nurse said examining the stamped aluminium disc attached to the cord around Jake's neck. She scanned the blood-stained note pinned to the collar of his tunic. "CO. GSW. E. E. E.," she added frowning, and glanced at Jake as though suspecting him of authoring the shaky scrawl.

"Commanding Officer. Gunshot wound. Expend. Every. Effort," Dianna murmured, repeating the explanation Lt. Colonel Baxter had given her when he told her to add the three Es to the Dressing Station Medical Officer's notation after agreeing to loan her his ID disc. But she needn't have bothered. The doctor understood the acronym, because he immediately carved into Jake's blood-smeared chest.

She managed to contain an exclamation of joy, and almost simultaneous gasp of horror as she edged into a corner, well out of the way as the doctor barked orders and the nurses responded.

Surgical instruments clanked, blood-drenched dressings thunked into the empty petrol can or squelched underfoot if they missed their target, as nurses scurried about in answer to or anticipation of the doctor's next request. Despite what seemed absolute chaos, there was clearly a carefully orchestrated choreography in play, as except for minor bumps and the occasional curse, no one seemed overly flustered. Except her.

She had to keep reminding herself to breathe for the next thirty minutes, until the doctor suddenly straightened, rolled his head side to side, and blinked as though coming out of a deep trance.

He looked down, patted Jake's still shoulder. "I got the bullet and those bits you can live without out," he said. "Tidied up the rest. Now sir, it's your turn to E. E. E." And drawing a deep breath as though to brace himself, he added, "Next.".

Quick as that Jake was whisked away and another bloodied soldier slid on the table in his place.

∞ ∞ ∞

"Fight," Dianna whispered, and smoothed Jake's damp hair from his brow. "Fight. You must fight. For me. For Katie. For Amelia. For JJ. For yourself."

She dipped a cloth in cool water, mopped his brow and neck. His breath rasped, dry and hoarse. "Please," she begged. "Fight."

"How is he?" Mother Mary set a tray on a chair next to Dianna. Hot Bovril. Dry biscuit. Tea.

Dianna dredged up a smile. "Thank you. And... not well. His skin is flaming hot and dry, his breathing shallow, and his pulse fast. Much too fast."

Mother Mary's nostrils flared. "I will get the Matron."

"No." Dianna shook her head. "She was by already, just after reveille. She helped me change his bandages."

Three days since he'd been shot, and two since the bullet and a section of his liver in which it had lodged had been dug out, and his fever was climbing. Except to use the privy, she stayed by his side, spooning water and morphine past his parched lips, sponging him with cool cloths, sleeping on the floor next to his stretcher one hand on his hand in case he twitched a finger.

He hadn't.

Except for an occasional moan and the sporadic shallow movement of his chest, he was horrendously quiet. So was the ward.

The constant echoing assault of artillery barrages and sniping guns had gone silent. Truly it was the best, and worst gift, any of them could have wished for.

She'd awakened in the wee hours on the floor next to Jake's pallet, terrified by the unnatural quiet. So accustomed had she grown to the concussive booms and rapid-fire echoes of fighting that when the guns stopped sometime around midnight, she jolted awake, chest constricted as though it was her heart and lungs that had shut down. Even after she reassured herself Jake still breathed, she could not shake off the anxiety. It was not until she overheard the night nurse discussing the cessation in hostilities with a doctor—the Christmas Truce they called it—that she was able to connect her apprehension to its source. And realise it was Christmas Day.

That induced a new set of fraught emotion knowing the girls and JJ would wake up without her or Jake there, awareness not soothed by knowledge she'd left a list and money for Mama to buy and send gifts on her behalf. Especially as there was no guarantee the presents had arrived in time. The Post was being shipped on supply ships, but infrequently owing

270

to the U-boat danger. She could only pray the gifts made it without regard for timeliness.

"Matron and the doctors say it's up to him now," she said as she sponged Jake's dry skin. "There's nothing more they can do, Mother. He can't be moved, until his fever abates." Draping the damp cloth across his forehead, she stared at his face, hollowed by blood loss and fever. "If his temperature climbs any higher..." She met Mother Mary's sorrowful gaze. "He has to fight, Mother. He has to fight the infection, if he wants to live."

Mother Mary's expression hardened with resolve as she gathered her hems and eased to her knees the other side of Jake. Laying a palm on the cloth on his forehead, she extended her other hand to Dianna.

"It's not only up to him *ma petite*," she said as Dianna took her hand. "There *is* more you and I can do. We'll ask Him for help. Pray with me child. Pray with me, and trust in Him."

∞ ∞ ∞

"How is 'e lass?"

Startled, Dianna looked up.

"Lieutenant-Colonel," she whispered. Gently lifting Jake's head from her lap to the pillow she had scavenged from her bed, she scrambled to her feet. "You shouldn't be up. It's late—"

"Bah," Baxter grumbled. "I'm well past wearing knee-britches. I can do as I like, lass. Tis my leg, and my trouble."

"Then I'll get you a chair."

"I'm fine lass."

"My legs my trouble," she said. "Just don't fall on my husband."

A full twenty-four hours and the marque was still eerily quiet, heavy with shadow. A single nurse sat at a desk near the entrance reading by the glow of a low-lit lantern that outlined the colonel's bulky frame as he wobbled slightly on a single crutch, and muscular leg.

The nurse agreed to round up a chair, while Dianna prepared a fresh basin of cool water and clean cloths. She returned to find Baxter seated on the chair beside Jake, bent over talking to him in a low voice. A serious conversation from the look of it.

She hung back, unwilling to intrude. At her insistence Mother Mary had retired an hour earlier with a promise to return at dawn for Morning

Prayer, taking with her a promise from Dianna that she would send for the Mother Superior should anything change. So far, it had not.

Jake maintained his perilous hold on life, and Dianna had to wonder if it was her and Mother Mary's combined prayers, or pure stubbornness on his part keeping him alive, because according to the doctor who'd come around shortly before Mother Mary turned in for the night, he should have died in the trench. No doubt the good doctor made the statement in compliment of Jake's stamina, but it stung. Seemed to her an oblique way of the doctor telling her she was wasting her time trying to save her husband, because his death was all but a delayed formality.

"That's a fine lass ye got there, lad." Baxter's Scottish burr broke through Dianna's thoughts. "An' you'll do yerself an' her a great disservice ye up an' die now. So what's say ye dig deep an' find that stubbornness an' strength ye used to help Phelps an' that French lassie? Do ye hear me soldier? Ye dinna have permission to lay down and die. Sure, yer sare hurt. There's a lot o' good men hurt. An' that's good. Only the livin' feel pain. An' live ye will, soldier. Do ye hear me? Live, or by all that's holy I'll marry your lassie an' claim the bairn as my own."

Bairn? Dianna frowned. Had she told him about JJ? He'd overheard her tell Andy about Amelia and Katie, but did she mention JJ? Or did he mean the girls? If so, the correct syntax was bairns, not bairn.

"Aye, she's breedin' mac," Baxter continued softly. "An' from what I ken of her in the wee time I've had the pleasure of knowin' her, and by the way she's fightin' to keep yer sorry soul from the devil, I'd stake my good leg it's your babe. So, what's say ye stop with this lyin' about..."

Dianna missed what Baxter said next as she staggered. Tightening her hold on the basin that almost slipped from her nerveless fingers, she locked her knees to keep from sinking to the floor.

No. It wasn't possible. But even as she hugged the basin with one arm to lay her other hand on the taut swell of her abdomen yet disguised by the loose fit of her uniform, she knew it was.

Stress. Travel. Anxiety. Exhaustion. So many excuses. So easy to dismiss the absent when the present required so much care. To fall in bed at night too tired to do more than pray the next day brought word of her husband... She closed her eyes.

They'd made love the night before he left for England. *Five months ago. Almost to the day.*

She opened her eyes. Baxter's position blocked her view of Jake's face. All she could see was the outline of his idle lower body shielded by a wool blanket.

Hastening forward she sank to her knees beside him, and carefully set the basin and cloths on the floor, offered Baxter a grateful smile.

"Thank you," she whispered, and brushed her fingertips along Jake's cheek pale beneath thick whiskers of auburn and cinnamon. And grey, she noted with consternation.

He's not even thirty, yet.

"Jake, darling," she whispered. "Did you hear the lieutenant-colonel? You're going to be a father. Again. So please, you must fight. You must fight for us Jake, for our baby. Fight for our baby. *Your* baby. Please, Jake, live. For me. For our family. For Katie, and Amelia, and JJ." She grabbed his limp hand, pressed it to her middle. "Feel it Jake. Feel our baby. Feel your—" She looked down, startled when one of his fingers twitched. She stared at his face. "Jake?"

His burnished-gold eyelashes didn't move. Didn't lift to reveal the deep brown eyes glinting with devilish humour she missed so desperately. She looked at Baxter.

"He moved. I'm sure of it. I'm sure I felt his finger move."

"Ooch, aye?" Baxter inched forward on his chair, used the crutch to nudge Jake's ribs. "Wake up, ye lazy shite."

"Lieutenant," Dianna exclaimed, before glancing sharply at Jake. "He moaned. That was him, wasn't it?" She looked at Baxter. "Did you hear that? Or am I just—"

Jake grunted as Baxter prodded him again.

"Jake? Lieutenant stop that." She smacked the crutch aside. Baxter laughed, but she ignored him. "Jake?"

A sliver of brown iris regarded her from under one partly open red-rimmed eyelid.

"Jake." She grasped his face in her hands. He was warm, not hot, his colour more evenly pink, rather than mottled with fever.

"*Querida.*" The endearment sounded like a dehydrated toad's croak, but to her it was sweet, sweet music.

"Oh darling," she whispered. "You're awake. You're awake, and your fever's down."

"*Querida,*" he mumbled again as his eye closed.

She brought his hand to her mouth, kissed the coarse knuckles. "I'm here, darling. I'm right here with you. Lieutenant-Colonel Baxter and I are both here."

"Bastard."

"No, Baxter. Lieutenant-Colonel Baxter—"

"Bastard," Jake rasped, and with visible effort rolled his head to peer in Baxter's direction.

The LC hooked the edges of his chair with his fingers, hopped the chair forward to lean, and look Jake in the eye.

"Who ye callin' a bastard, ye blooidy skiver?" he demanded, broad hands fisted on his blue-pyjama clad thighs.

"You, you bloody Scot." Jake swallowed, gasped a pained breath. "Stay away from my wife you randy poacher, or I'll shoot off your other leg." And then he passed out.

Chapter 26

All The Way Home

*P*rentice, is it?"

"Yes, sir."

"Weel, Prentice," Baxter muttered. "Ye might notice I've not lost me hands, so' I'll thank ye to keep yours to yerself."

"Is there a problem here?" Dianna split a glance between the footman, and Baxter seated in a wheeled chair with a breakfast tray on his lap, over whom Prentice leaned.

The footman straightened. "Sorry, my lady. I was helping the lieutenant-colonel with his napkin."

"I dinna need help." Baxter stuffed the napkin into the collar of his pyjama top, flared it over his chest, and grabbed his fork. "I'm a grown man. I dinna need another grown man fussin' ower me like a blooidy wet nurse wantin' for a bairn to suckle."

Dianna inclined her head in Prentice's direction, silent permission for him to retreat to a less contentious area of the townhouse. Slightly red faced the footman—a boy really at fourteen, if tall for his age—offered a bow and slid a foot back in preparation of accepting her proposal. He stopped, glanced over his shoulder.

"Shall I assist Mr. Douglas, ma'am?"

"I don't need assistance." Jake scooped a spoon into his broth and lifted it, dribbling, to his mouth, feigned chewing.

Dianna stopped short of rolling her eyes, and offered Prentice a mollifying smile. "We're fine here, Prentice. Why don't you see if Mother Mary can use your help sorting supplies?"

Papa had ordered the parlour converted to a temporary hospital ward and arranged the assistance of a trained nurse, and delivery of requisite medical and food supplies to aid Lt. Colonel Baxter and Jake's recovery. Mother Mary was working with the nurse to organise the supplies, and together they were establishing a meal plan for Cook to ensure the men, mainly Jake, received easy-to-digest meals. Jake couldn't afford to enflame the perforated section of his intestine the surgeon had painstakingly stitched together.

"As you wish, Mum." Prentice exited, and eased the door closed. Dianna cast a baleful eye over her recalcitrant patients.

"Well," she said. "Aren't we a fine pair this morning? So chipper, and cooperative."

Jake scowled. "When do I get to see my son?"

"When do I get back to the front?" Baxter demanded at the exact same moment.

"As I told you yesterday," she said arching a brow at Jake, "JJ will be here this afternoon." Turning to Baxter, she forced a smile. "Secretary of State for War Kitchener plans to stop by later this week, but I expect only to extend his gratitude to you and Jake for your bravery and sacrifice for King and Country. I very much doubt he'll approve your return to the Front. At least not yet."

"Now who's the bright ray of sunshine?" Baxter shovelled a forkful of egg in his mouth, glared at her while he chewed.

"I'm sorry, Lieutenant-Colonel. I don't mean to toss a wet blanket on your hopes, but I know you despise canards as much as you detest laying *aboot*, and I respect you too much to lie to you. You have weeks, if not months of rehabilitation ahead of you. In fact, Papa's arranging for you to be seen by the Desoutter brothers and be fitted for one of their amazing, new duralumin legs."

His eyebrows shot up. "Dura-what?"

"A limb," she said, "to replace the one you lost, only made of a lightweight metal instead of wood. I understand the older brother lost his leg in a flying accident, but he still wanted to fly, so he, along with his younger brother who's an aeronautical engineer, fashioned his new leg out of the metal. It's supposed to be much easier to manoeuvre, as it's so much lighter, but as strong as any wooden prosthesis."

"Hrmph." Baxter's thick eyebrows bunched as he concentrated on forking up another mouthful of food.

"What time this afternoon?"

Dianna willed a patient smile as she faced her husband. "Soon. I'm just as anxious as you to see him again."

"Are you?"

She frowned, and glanced at Baxter, but he seemed completely focused on sipping his tea to the point his eyes were closed. She moved to Jake's bedside, lowered her voice. "Of course, I am. As much as are you."

Jake held her gaze, his dark eyes hard with accusation.

"What?" she asked. "Why do you seem angry?"

He set his spoon on his tray without taking his eyes from her. "You never should have left him. Once you had him back, you should have gone home, Dianna. To our daughters. You never should have come looking for me. You could have been killed."

Baxter coughed, shifted his position in the wheeled chair making it creak, and slurped more tea.

"This is not the time, Jake," she whispered fighting to maintain her smile. "We can discuss this when you are well, and we are alone. All that matters right now, is we are both safe, and our son will soon be reunited with us—"

"*Bonjour!*" Mother Mary swept into the parlour. "How are my favourite men today?"

"*Très bon, Madame,*" Baxter said. "*Et comment vas-tu?*"

Mother Mary laughed, so rare a sound to Dianna, she stared. More shocking, was the faint rosy glow in her mentor's cheeks as she returned the LC's smile.

"Your accent is almost perfect, *Monsieur* Baxter," Mother Mary said. "I will make a good French teacher yet, I think."

"Weel," Baxter said dragging out his Scots dialect, "my da used to say, 'Tis a canny man what learns to speak a beautiful lassie's language."

This time Baxter laughed with Mother Mary, and even Dianna couldn't help a smile.

Heaven, if she didn't know better, she would think they were flirting. She glanced at Jake. He did not exchange a knowing smile with her. He was not smiling. Nor eating. His spoon sat idle, a scowl contorting his face. Inhaling, she looked back at Mother Mary.

"You are a brilliant teacher, Mother," she said. "One of the best I've ever had the pleasure of receiving tutelage from."

"*Oui, oui,*" Baxter said and hoisted his tea.

"Thank you, *ma chère.*" Mother Mary looked at Jake. "And you, *Monsieur* Douglas, how fare you this beautiful morning?"

"Fine. Thank you, Mother," he added, grudgingly, his gaze on his fast-cooling broth.

Mother Mary's expression did not change, save a faint line that formed between her eyebrows. "Good," she said. "It is good you are feeling fine, because today you will stand up."

Jake pursed his lips. Dianna quelled a surge of anxiety.

It had only been two weeks since he'd been shot. Twenty-four hours since their arrival in London. Yet she knew from experience the longer he remained in bed, the further his musculature would waste, and the longer it would take him to regain his strength and stamina. His ability to withstand physical rehabilitation was of lesser concern to her however, than his mental state—and palpable anger directed at her.

Mother Mary exchanged a look with her, and then said to Jake, "How about we start now, as it seems your breakfast is not to your interest?"

"There's nothing wrong with my breakfast." He grasped the bowl, raised it to his mouth, his brown-eyed gaze obstinate over the white rim as he gulped.

"An' what exactly crawled up inside you an' died?" Baxter heaved his breakfast tray off his lap to a side table and began wheeling towards Jake's bed.

"Lieutenant—" Dianna started and stalled when Mother Mary grasped her hand.

"Come, *ma chère.*" She pulled Dianna toward the doors. "I think I hear Prentice calling for assistance."

∞ ∞ ∞

"Jake?" Dianna's voice was soft, uncertain.

He pushed higher in the bed, reached gingerly to turn up the lamp. Baxter, the wily old bastard, had finagled Prentice into helping him move to a cot on the ground floor where he could wheel his chair out on the stoop to enjoy his cigars under the assertion the smoke and odour seemed to irritate his ward mate. He was correct in stating Jake was irritated. Wrong in his reasoning.

It wasn't the odour or smoke that bothered Jake. It was watching the cagey bastard puff away as though he had not a care in the world, had never tasted anything sweeter than one of the cigars from Marshall's personal stock, luxuriated in anything grander than the gilded trappings and personalised service endowed upon them, when the minute anyone else was in the room he protested the very catering in which he seemed to enjoy wallowing when he and Jake were alone.

"I'm awake."

The door opened wider and she slipped into the room, turned to ease the door shut, before facing him. His throat constricted.

Her hair hung loose in ebony waves framing her pale face, exotic contrast to her ivory skin and white night dress. But it was the sight of her breasts, full and heavy, nipples dark halos beneath the thin cotton that sent a jolt of painful emotion through him.

Many nights in the last few months he'd lain sleepless in a frigid mud burrow carved in the side of a trench or ditch, or under that goddamn tree, trembling like a terrorised rabbit with cold and nervous exhaustion, unable to sleep for chill and constant threat of German patrols, the only thing keeping him partially sane the memory—and hope—of seeing her again. Holding her in his arms, hearing her soft sighs, and moans, as he traced the warm curves of her body, tasted her velvet skin—He clenched his fists, raised a knee to lift the bed covers off his growing erection as he forced his gaze to her face.

Lower lip caught between her teeth, she regarded him with round-eyed wariness. "I... came to say good night," she murmured.

He nodded, his larynx locked, and emotions too raw to permit him to speak.

"JJ will come around," she whispered. "He knows you. I know he does. He's simply unsure. He's experienced a lot of tumult. And eight months is a very long time in the memory of a young child."

Had it only been eight months? Felt more like eight decades. And JJ seemed to concur.

Dianna's attempt to lower him to Jake's lap earlier in the day had inspired JJ to lock his arms around her neck, shriek bloody murder until she finally carried him out at Jake's insistence. JJ's howls of terror had faded away behind the closed door long before the agonising concussion of his rejection eased to a painful echo inside Jake's chest.

"He's asleep?"

She nodded. "Papa had a trundle brought to my room, but he's splayed in my bed. I... propped pillows to stop him rolling off."

He nodded. "Your mother didn't stay?"

She shook her head. "She wished to get back to little William and Lizzy. We... we'll visit there, before... we go home. Did Papa stop by?"

Jake rasped his molars. "No. And he'd better not, or I'll rip every stitch holding me together tearing him apart."

"He's sorry, Jake. He... He never meant—never dreamed Buckland would do anything like this. And he's doing everything he can—has done everything possible to make things right. The only reason you're even alive—"

Don't." He stared. "Don't dare guilt me into forgiving him. Because I wouldn't need your guilt or any reason to forgive him if he hadn't told his goddamn henchman to get rid of me—"

"Yes. I know. I'm... sorry. I'm sorry for everything. I... I should have insisted on coming with you. None of this would have happened if only I'd been there to talk to him, to talk to Mama—what?" Her throat pulsed, eyes widened slightly. "Did I—"

"Go. Just go." He looked away, fists jammed hard in the mattress beneath the blankets. From the corner of his eye he watched her clasp her hands below the swell of their unborn child, twist her wedding rings as she forced a tremulous smile.

"All right then," she murmured. "Ah... good night."

He nodded, and waited until she was gone, and the door closed, to let all he felt and couldn't say loose in hot, silent tears.

∞ ∞ ∞

Chin braced on the heel of her hand she sat on the stoop, elbow on her knee, watching wheeled and pedestrian traffic pass. She sighed. "He's so angry. And still won't talk to me."

"He will. When he's ready."

280

She swivelled to look at Baxter. "What is it with you men? You talk to someone you barely know, and avoid even a single word of understanding with those who love you."

"Weel—"

"Yes, yes, I know." Dianna tugged her skirt firmly over her knees, the shawl tighter around her shoulders. "His other friend told me. He's afraid to be vulnerable around me, for fear I'll think less of him. But there's more to it than that. It's like he... blames me, for something. Or maybe all of it," she muttered.

Baxter exhaled a stream of smoke. "I'm sure he doesna know himself what's grinding between the wheels, only that he's crabbit as a bear wi' a thorn in his paw, and ready to swat and growl at anyone that gets too close."

She frowned at him. "He told you nothing?"

"Nay. Stubborn as a Scot, that one." Baxter tapped the cigar on the arm of his chair to knock off the ash tip and winked. Then his expression sobered. "I didna expect 'im to talk, ye understand? I only needed 'im to listen." He put the cigar to his mouth.

His stump had healed well, and the fitting gone even better. The Desoutter brothers promised to have his new limb to him by the end of February.

"'Twas his job to save the bairn an' return him to his mither's arms, ye ken?" he said, after letting a mouthful of smoke escape. "Instead, he ended up near deid, an' would be yet, had ye not been there to fight for him. You saved him lass, *an'* found the wee laddie to boot; the wee laddie he was sent to find what now shies away an' howls like a banshee when he gets too close. Leaves him fair raw inside, ye ken, knowin' the bairn is afeared of him. To feel he failed his family—"

"He failed no one," Dianna exclaimed. "None of what happened was his fault. And JJ isn't afraid of him. He's simply... shy. After all he's been through, that's to be expected."

"Aye." Baxter tapped the cigar again though there wasn't ash enough to warrant the action. "Shy. Scairt. Been through all, an' a lot more to boot. Like his Da. But knowin' it's not your fault, an' feeling it in yer heart, dinna always mash as smoothly together as turnip and butter, ye ken? 'Tis more like sand grindin' to glass inside him, an' that's not likely to change so long as yer cluckin' over 'im like he's a blind chick in need of hand feedin' and cartin' about."

"What? I—"

"I mean no harm by the words, lassie." Baxter transferred the cigar to his left hand, grasped her hand with his right and offered a gentle squeeze along with a paternal smile. "But ye asked, ye ken, how to get through to him. An' I'm tellin' ye, ye wanna get through to a man, leave him be. Let him find his own socks, fetch his own meals, an' answer his own questions. Show him ye trust him to take care of himself, and what's his to mind, lass. Let *him* find his way back to *you*."

Dianna blinked. "Are you suggesting I just—"

"Leave him alone? Aye." Baxter nodded, withdrew his hand, gestured to the floor above with the cigar. "That's what I told him. That he was a lucky man to have someone to fuss o'er him. I lost my sweet Ilene eight years ago, so I ken what I say. 'Tis a wise man what learns to speak a pretty lassie's language."

"Language?" Dianna repeated slowly. "I'm not trying to teach him French."

"Aye. He speaks it, probably better than you I'd wager. Naw..." Baxter's eyes crinkled at the corners. "Love, lass. That's the language I'm talkin' about. Every lass I've had the pleasure of known' spoke with her heart. When a man learns to listen, an' to heed what she's sayin', he's a rich man indeed. Me? I learnt too late. An' that's what I told him. When a lassie stops talkin' to ye laddie, when she stops seeking to mend what's broken an' starts building her own bridges, weel laddie, ye best hurry to dig those clots outta yer ears an' spit out that mouthful o' pride an' get to listenin' an' talkin' with a mind to forgin' a new path together, free of old haunts, afore she finds another man to walk an' talk with, an' leaves ye with yer pockets turned out."

"I would never—"

"Aye, lassie," Baxter said. "That's what my sweet Ilene thought. She meant it, too. Was no one more surprised than her when she told me. I can still see her face, bewildered like, as she told me she was leavin'. That she'd fallen in love." He shook his head, his voice hollow with disbelief, a faint cloud of breath unrelated to the smoke hinting at the potential of an overnight snowfall. "The butcher. She divorced me an' married the butcher. Good man, Taggert. Gentle despite his profession, ye ken. I allus thought him a wee bit soft, but he turned up a stronger man than me 'cause the last I saw my sweet Ilene, just this past spring, she still had that smile an' glow about her she'd had when she first told me about Taggert, an' I hadna seen in all our twenty years together."

"Oh," Dianna murmured. When he first mentioned losing his sweet Ilene, she assumed he had lost her to death. She scowled. "You threatened him? You suggested I would divorce him, if he continued to act so..."

"Selfish?" Baxter shrugged. "I suggested ye were human lass, with limitations, like the rest of us, an' he best get sorted out what meant more to him: his pride? Or his wife and bairns."

Dianna compressed her lips, faced the street.

"Aye, lass," Baxter murmured. "He's nay so block-headed as me, ye ken? He'll find his way back to you an' the bairns, but only if ye leave him to figure out how. Himself."

"But when I was hurt, he stayed with me," she rasped. "He forced me to get out of bed, and to exercise my limbs to regain their strength. He *refused* to leave me until I was well enough to manage without his help."

"Aye. You needed him, aye? You leaned on 'im. A man's used to that, others leanin' on him. It's what gives him strength, ye ken? Ye think we wallow in mud an' blood an' rats for the stinkin' fun of it? No. We do it, 'cause our country needs us. Freedom depends on us to uphold it. Our wives and bairns, mothers, sisters, aunts, grandmothers, and children and grandchildren yet to be born, rely on us to protect them from what the Boche would take from them, an' that's what keeps us goin' when we only want to curl up and cry like wee laddies rocked on our mithers' laps."

Dianna dashed a tear from her cheek. "So, I just... leave? Leave, him to get better on his own?"

"He'll no be alone, will he? I'll be here to make sure he eats his parritch, an' makes his bed proper."

"Is that not defeating the purpose of my leaving, if he learns to rely on you?"

"Who said anythin' about relying?" Baxter's brow furrowed. "Ye forget, lass, I've whipped sorrier men than him into shape for worse jobs than going home to a lass, an' bairns as beautiful as those he has to call his own."

She laughed, and more tears spilled. She wiped her cheeks. "I suppose I can go to Ansmall," she said smoothing her damp palms on her skirt.

"Nay."

"Nay?" She raised her eyebrows. "Then where? A hotel? Because I am most certainly not going to step foot inside Holderness."

The castle and its grounds might be hers in principle, but in her mind, it would always belong to George Ramsay. Even knowing her father had lived there prior to his death, did nothing to relieve the bitter surge of bile she experienced whenever she thought of the cavernous stone shell that had almost become her son's prison.

With the earl's assistance she'd hired a non-familial land agent to manage her holdings, many of which were unoccupied and overseen by two or three trusted servants, the majority of whom were elderly, like Mrs. Rainbird and her husband. Thank Heaven.

She had no time for interviews, and no body of qualified gardeners, footmen, grooms, maids, cooks, and housekeepers to draw from even if she did. Every available and able-bodied person was being diverted to the war effort.

One of her inherited residences had already been lost to the war: a French chateau currently in German-held territory. She planned to sell it when the war was over. Provided there was something left to sell. And Britain and her allies won. She breathed out.

That was not even worth consideration. The Allies had to win. The alternative was... unthinkable. As were Baxter's next words.

"Home, lass," he murmured, the teasing light that had brightened his gaze when he mentioned whipping Jake into shape dimming to sober certainty. His thick brogue too, faded to memory, as he clarified with ruthless clarity: "Your home, lass. Not your parents. Not the castle. Not anywhere here in jolly ol' England." He dipped his chin, his gaze stern. "If you want your husband to return to you whole, then he needs to make the whole journey home. To Texas. Without you."

Chapter 27

You Are My Heart

ama?" The fear in Katie's voice lifted the fine hairs on Dianna's neck. She dropped the mixing spoon in the bowl of cookie batter and whipped around.

The kitchen door was open, the screened porch door closed to keep flies out and permit the heat from the stove to escape, blurring the man's features. Still, she knew him. Instantly. Intimately.

The door squeaked as he pulled it open.

"It's all right, Katie, luv," Dianna murmured when Katie moved to stand behind her. "It's only Papa."

"Papa?" Katie said, sceptical.

"Yes. Go upstairs, but don't tell Amelia. Not yet. And don't wake your brother, or let Charlie come down. Keep her in your room with you."

"What about—"

"Ask Elizabeth to stay with her."

Pain flinched around his eyes as Katie, with a wary backward glance, vanished in the direction of the stairs. He watched her until she was gone, and then swivelled to face Dianna. After a long, silent moment, he cleared his throat.

"You look well."

She could almost feel the effort it took him to not look down, to not question the flatness of her abdomen. "You look like hell."

A corner of his mouth quirked within the heavy russet beard, not a smile, but close. "They say you spend enough time somewhere—" He staggered, shot a hand out to brace himself against the wall.

She grabbed his other arm in time to help him slide to the floor. "You're hurt?"

He shook his head. "Over did it." He shifted to sit with his back against the wall. "Probably should have accepted Mother's offer to bring the auto. Or borrow a horse."

She crouched. "You walked here—wait. She knows you're here? Your mother knows you're here?"

"Not all the way," he said. "I sailed a goodly distance, and then took a train—" His teasing smile vanished. He nodded. "Yes. Mother knows I'm here. She picked me up in town. Took me to her house at my insistence. I'm sorry I didn't warn you. Or let her warn you. I wanted to surprise you. You and the children."

"Surprise us." She swallowed, and straightening, moved to lean against the far counter, fold her arms over her chest to contain a surprising jumble of tumultuous emotions ranging from relief, to rage.

Mr. Sweeney and his crew had finished rebuilding Eleanor's house, and Dirk and Mrs. Brown's cottage, a fortnight earlier. Within two days, her mother-in-law, housekeeper and stable master, had moved into their respective new homes. When they were settled, Maggie and Mr. Sweeney and his crew, departed for Florida, where Mr. Sweeney had taken on a new contract, leaving Dianna alone to help the children adjust to yet another new routine, this one without Elaina or their grandmother, with whom they'd grown quite attached in the months she was away. She was in no mood for surprises.

With a deep inhalation, Jake gripped the counter, struggled to his feet. "I'm sorry, Dianna," he rasped, one hand on the counter for balance as he reached out with his other hand. "I'm a fool. I..." He closed his mouth, eyes brightening with tears when she kept her arms crossed. Lowering his hand to his side, he shook his head. "I'm a goddamn fool."

She leaned back, resisted the urge to throw her arms around him, tell him she forgave him and that everything would be all right.

Let him find his way back to you. He needs to make the whole journey home. Alone.

"You saved our son," he murmured. "You saved me, and I... I was ungrateful."

She bit her lower lip.

He bowed his head. When he looked up, his eyes were dry, his expression determined. "I made a hash of things, Dianna. I was arrogant, and... bitter. Bitter that I had failed where you succeeded. Bitter that your father—stepfather's arrogance nearly got me killed. He apologised, by the way. And I..." He angled his jaw up, eased out a breath. "I accepted his apology." He offered a wry smile. "I didn't want to. I really did not want to forgive him, but... I didn't deserve it. I didn't deserve to let my anger at him poison the rest of my life. Poison me. Any more than you deserved my venom."

She nodded, then hiked a breath. "So... that's it? You've apologised, and..."

"And nothing," he said. "I ask nothing more from you, than hopefully, one day, your forgiveness."

"All you want is my forgiveness?" She raised her eyebrows. "You came all the way here just to apologise, and ask my forgiveness?"

"No. No, *Querida*," he said, his voice the strongest she'd heard since he spoke his first breathy words in France following his surgery. "I didn't come only to apologise, and ask forgiveness. But I thought it appropriate to start there."

"Start there? Start there, and go where, Jake? Where do we go from here?" The tears she'd been fighting broke free. She made no attempt to stop them.

Too long she had restrained her emotions, along with the loneliness and fear that had plagued her over a year since awakening to find her life in a million tiny shreds. Since then she'd managed to stitch together a fraction of the remnants. A single sweater from what had once been a beautiful full wardrobe. Even that was pocked full of holes.

Small holes in her memory. Larger ones in her children's hearts created by first the loss of their brother, and then father, and then mother. Yes, they'd eventually been reunited, four of them at least, but not without lasting scars.

Katie, ever her shadow, was even clingier, hardly leaving her side to permit her to use the water closet. Amelia, always a tempest in a teapot erupted in louder and more frequent outbursts than ever, despite Dianna's concerted effort to expend as much energy and attention on her as she did any of them. And JJ... He was too quiet. Far too quiet. Much more subdued than the child McGuire—McTeer—had spirited away. The only one not affected by the changes was—"May," she whispered. "Jocelyn May Ellen Anne, for Mother Mary, your mother, mine, and Charlotte."

Jake frowned.

"Their middle names," she said. "I gave her their middle names."

His eyes widened, and his gaze dipped to her waist, before returning to her face. "A girl?" he whispered, his eyes awash with tears. "We had a girl?"

She nodded. "She's almost four weeks old. Born April 16th."

"A daughter." He clasped a hand to his face. His sobs struck like whip lashes to her heart, cutting the tight cord of anger binding it. Warmth flooded through her, love and forgiveness cleansing the cold acrimony she'd nurtured in the empty moments between seeing to her children's needs, and neglecting her own.

She touched his arm. "Would you like to see her?"

He dragged his hand from his face. "Please," he rasped. "I want to see her. I want to see all of them."

"We're here." Katie's soft voice was oddly firm. Confident. She and Amelia stood either side of JJ, each of them holding one of his little hands.

The girls returned Dianna's stare without expression, their features blank canvases awaiting the fickle artist's muse, a skill Dianna once believed exclusive to cultured drawing rooms and studies—as that was where she'd mastered it—and now knew it for what it was: instinctive expertise acquired as a matter of survival.

JJ, in contrast, scowled, his flinty gaze, sleep-reddened cheeks, and tousled hair lending him the air of a plump rooster roused from his roost long before the first light of dawn. Behind them, Elizabeth cradled May, her expression, like JJ's, reproving, though with slightly less ferocity.

She had fought and argued to be allowed to journey home with Dianna, JJ, and Mother Mary. The earl and Mama had, predictably and reasonably, refused to grant their permission. Lizzy, predictably and completely unreasonably, refused to heed it. A prolonged argument ensued, argument that ended in massive uproar when Lizzy posited England could be invaded by the Germans and she'd be safer in America.

At that point, Mama gave up. Threw her hands in the air and told her to go, just go. The fight fizzled out of the earl then, too. The pair of them deflating like a couple of windless sails.

Dianna's attempt to reason with Lizzy also failed, though she'd not put much effort into convincing her to remain in England. Especially after Elaina sent word, she would meet Dianna and Elizabeth in New York with Amelia and Katie, where Elaina would say her goodbyes before stepping on a ship home. And so, in a tearful exchange, Mama and the earl had traded two daughters for one, and a rosy-cheeked grandson for a pale and angry son-in-law.

The son-in-law in question pressed a hand on the counter as he made effort to stand tall, his gaze never once leaving the children.

He was naught but skin and bones, the broad shoulders and burled biceps of her memory now sloped and shrunken with disuse and illness, his white shirt, and dark trousers baggy when once they'd moulded to solid musculature. She had to draw hard on her childhood tutelage to maintain an impassive expression.

"Katie," he whispered. "Amelia. You're each as beautiful as I remember." His voice caught, hoarse with awe and regret, but he made no move toward them. Instead, he held his arms out, permission for them to come to him. If they chose.

Amelia was the first to break. Dropping JJ's hand, she flew into Jake's embrace.

"Papa," she cried. "Oh, Papa. Where have you been? Why didn't you come home with Mama?"

"I told you, Mia," Dianna said. "He was hurt, too hurt to travel—" She broke off when Jake dropped to one knee and grasped Amelia with one arm, bowed his head to hers.

She had explained his absence to the girls, and everyone else, on his precarious health and need to convalesce in England until he was fit to travel. In truth she hadn't known if he would return to the ranch. Or have her served with divorce papers.

Tears cascaded down her cheeks as Katie shuffled towards Jake, stopping only when JJ balked. Elizabeth, astute as ever, shifted May to one arm.

"Go," she murmured taking JJ's hand. "I've got him."

Thus freed, Katie glided forward, a doe alert for the faintest whiff of danger on the wind. Jake extended his hand. The moment she accepted it, her reserved shattered, and she folded into his embrace, sobbing.

He held the girls close, stroking their heads as he murmured profuse apology that he'd not come home sooner. JJ leaned against Elizabeth's legs, his green eyes filling with tears, lower lip pushing out as he dragged his gaze from his stepfather and sisters, to Dianna.

Her first instinct was to hasten over, lift him up and reassure him. Instead, she lowered to the floor and put her arms around her husband. And her daughters, best she could.

"Mama," JJ demanded. "Mama."

Let him come to you... "Come on, baby," she murmured, holding a hand out. "Daddy's home. Come see your daddy."

"Go on then, you little Bufflehead," Elizabeth said. "Quit your nonsense and greet your father proper." She released JJ's hand and to Dianna's utter surprise, crossed to gently place May in Jake's arms. Jake stared at her in utter shock. Then smiled in pure gratitude.

"Thank you," he whispered.

She nodded and strode swiftly from the room. JJ gazed after her, his expression as disbelieving as Jake's had been. Then he darted a suspicious glance at his mother and sisters. Dianna kept her face averted, watched JJ from the corner of her eye as Jake fawned over his daughters.

"Oh, here we go again," Amelia muttered when May squawked. "She cries all the time—"

"She does not," Katie protested. "Well not as much as she used to. She slept three straight hours last night."

May loosed a howl, arching her small back to emphasise her displeasure with competing, and rather noisy attention, especially when it did not include breakfast. Jake chuckled, and holding her securely in his big hands, lifted her to look at him.

"What's wrong, *hija?*" He smiled tenderly. "Are you hungry, or wet?"'

"Both, probably," Dianna said. "But she can wait a little longer."

The rapid clickety-clack of nails on wood heralded Charlie's arrival. She burst into their midst, brown eyes wide as she skidded to a stop, staring at their huddle, before glancing at JJ. She whined.

"It's all right, Charlie," Katie said extending a hand. "You can come. She can, can't she?" she added, looking up at Jake.

"Of course," he said.

But rather than accept Katie's invitation, Charlie retreated to stand with JJ. He grasped her ruff with one pudgy hand and with the other hand pointed at Jake. "My baby," he said.

When Katie started to get up, Dianna stopped her.

"Let him come to us," she whispered. "He must want to be a part of this. We can't force it."

They settled in around Jake, Amelia and Katie tucked in against his sides, May braced on his upraised knees, Dianna leaned close to Katie.

"I have my own filly, Papa," Katie said. "Moonlight Princess. She's the best filly in the barn."

"She's not," Amelia said. "My filly is the best. Crimson Rain. That's what I named her, Papa. She's Diablo's step-sister and bright red, like Aunt Maggie's hair."

That was something else Dianna had worked hard, and swiftly, to rectify upon her return home to discover J-D Quarter Horses' second crop was beginning to hit the ground and she'd yet to name the previous year's foals. Or let Katie choose her filly.

Amelia was not to be left out, and true to their natures, Katie chose Firelight's weanling, a delicate creamy-gold filly, while Amelia instantly fell for Rain Dancer's spirited sorrel yearling.

"Not stepsister, Amelia," Katie said. "Half-sister. Crimson Rain and Princess have the same sire. We're stepsisters, because we don't have any of the same blood as JJ and May—"

"No," Dianna said firmly. "No one here is a step, or a half, or a portion of anything less than a full-fledged family member. Do you understand me?" She touched Katie's cheek, then Amelia's. "We are a family. All of us. Together. You and your sister were born to different parents, but you are our daughters and JJ and May's sisters."

"Your mother's right," Jake said quietly. "Family is not what blood runs in your veins. Family is what love grows in your heart." He glanced at May, then Amelia, Katie, and Dianna, before finally looking at JJ who had gravitated modestly closer, but remained well outside arm's reach. Sweeping his gaze around once more, Jake smiled. "I love you all, with all my heart."

"I love you, too, Papa," Katie murmured and bowed her head to his shoulder.

Dianna bit down on her surprise, chest swelling with joy at Katie's first, ever verbal expression of affection. Love. Oddly, Amelia, the first to run to Jake remained silent, but bowed her head to Jake's other shoulder. JJ stuck a finger in his mouth, his gaze no longer suspicious, but curious.

Charlie whined again, took a hesitant step forward and looked questioningly at JJ, as though pleading with him to go with her to join the family muddle. Jake gestured for Dianna to take May. The girls, reluctantly, lifted their heads and eased away permitting Jake to fold his legs cross-wise, lift his hands in invitation.

JJ glanced at Dianna. She smiled.

"Daddy," she said. "This is your daddy, and he loves you."

JJ pulled his finger from his mouth. "Daddy?" He turned a doubtful look on Jake. As one, the girls moved closer to Jake and again, rested their heads on his shoulders. The display of unity, and Charlie's encouraging yip as she strained her body forward without moving her feet, proved too much.

JJ let go of Charlie. "Daddy?" he murmured.

"Son," Jake said with soft conviction.

"Daddy." JJ eased in to pat Jake's beard. "Daddy 'ere."

"Yes, *hijo*," Jake said. "Daddy's here."

JJ threw his short arms around Jake's neck. "Daddy."

Dianna alternated between sobs and laughter, and comforting her youngest child as her older children revelled in the return of their father, and Charlie the reunification of her flock. When they all eventually quieted, JJ on Jake's lap, the girls leaned into him, Charlie curled contentedly against his leg, Jake kissed the tops of the children's heads in turn and stroked one of Charlie's ears, before looking at Dianna in whose arms May had fallen asleep.

"You are my heart," he whispered. "Each and every one of you." He touched their faces in turn, his smile almost bereaved, his gaze tender. "My family, my future, my own."

Epilogue

You Are My Own

Douglas, Texas
May 1915

S unlight through the Oak's budding limbs dappled the girls' bonnet-free heads and Charlie's coat as they regarded the stone in silent contemplation. Even JJ seemed to appreciate the solemnity of the moment, as he remained quiet, looking down from his perch in the crook of his father's arm, green eyes curious as his sisters spread the blanket Katie had carried up from the carriage while Amelia untied Charlie's leash. With a quick look to Jake for permission—and upon receiving it—Charlie bounded off down the hillock, to sniff and explore.

Dianna waited for Amelia to get settled on the blanket, before handing her May. Katie accepted the picnic basket from Jake, so he could put JJ down long enough to join them on the blanket, drawing JJ back in his lap as Dianna reclaimed May. Katie looked over. Dianna nodded, and together Katie and Amelia opened the box.

One by one they fit sixteen candles into the icing on the cake. Jake withdrew the matchbox from his coat pocket and gave it to the girls, cupped a hand to help them light the candles, careful to keep JJ angled away though thankfully the day was warm and breeze faint, so flames flared to life with little trouble. Dianna's throat tightened as the last small taper was lit, and Katie and Amelia faced the stone.

Katie started out first, the words of the song soft, wavery, quickly reinforced by Amelia's surprisingly harmonious lilt. Dianna and Jake added their voices.

By the time they reached the final chorus, tears streamed from Dianna's eyes, her voice reduced to a rasp as she murmured, "Happy Birthday, to you."

Jake reached for her hand, squeezed as the girls opened the gifts they'd brought for their sister and propped them against the marble headstone, a framed portrait of just the two of them, and another of them with their new family.

Dianna closed her eyes as the letters engraved in the stone she had ordered in New York on her way home, and had delivered along with the new casket containing Charlotte's exhumed remains, blurred to unreadability. Not that she needed to see them. They were forever etched on her heart:

Charlotte Anne Harney
May 18th, 1899 – November 15th, 1912
Beloved sister. Dear friend.
Love. Courage. Sacrifice.
Forever, our own.

Author's Note

My Own is a work of fiction. Its storyline, characters, and settings are from my imagination. Interspersed in this work of fiction are mention or appearance of real-life people, entities, and events of the time like Lords Crewe and Grey, the Right Honourable Secretary of War Kitchener, and activities surrounding the loss of the HMS Audacious on October 27, 1914, including Admirable Jellicoe's decision to detain passengers of the *RMS Olympic* four additional days.

Irwell Castle in Manchester was the site of the Manchester Handicap on November 28, 1914. The BEF (British Expeditionary Force) suffered grievous losses (as did all armies involved in the war). Conditions on the front lines and in the Casualty Clearance Centres were horrific.

My research, however, turned up no existence during WWI of a 13th Battalion in the Queen's Own (Royal West Kent Regiment), so I took advantage of creative licence to add it. Phelps's dishonourable activity is also complete fabrication born of this author's imagination, however, his censure of the soldiers' letters home was not a stretch. The British Army Post censored mail to prevent inadvertent or deliberate revelation of military resources or activity the Germans might have used to their advantage had they come into receipt of any letters.

The Queen's Own (Royal West Kent Regiment) raised a total of 18 battalions during the First World War and was awarded 79 battle honours and 3 Victoria Crosses during the course of the war. The 1st Battalion landed in Le Havre on August 15, 1914 and participated in a number of battles including The Battle of Marne briefly mentioned in the story; their travails inspired my fictional Devil's Dozen whose nickname was born of unlucky superstition associated with the numeral 13.

My Own is written in homage to the strength of the human spirit. Our ability—given a willing heart—to rise above misunderstanding and differences to find common ground, merge paths toward better understanding and improved well-being by lifting another's need ahead of selfish, or fearful want. It's also written in respect of those who have, and do, put themselves on the line in service to others so that people like me might enjoy the privilege of sipping tea in our cosy warm homes, while we spin tales and craft stories honouring love, loss, and redemption. Courage, commitment, and sacrifice are the universal stardust that puts the sparkle in Love, Freedom, and Democracy.

∞ ∞ ∞

For more information on what inspires me and my stories and shapes my writing, or to learn about other novels in this or other series, and to sign up for my newsletter to receive advance notice of future releases, and time-limited sale prices on my books, visit: www.deborahsmall.com

If you enjoyed My Own, I would really appreciate it if you left a review on Goodreads and on the website of the retailer from whom you purchased your copy. It truly means a lot. Thank you.

∞ ∞ ∞

Author's Note Resources

-**Crewe, Marquess of** (UK, 1911-1945):
http://www.cracroftspeerage.co.uk/online/content/crewe1911.htm?zoom_highlight=Crewe
-**Forces War Records**: https://www.forces-war-records.co.uk/units/3554/queens-own-royal-west-kent-regiment/
-**Lord Horatio Kitchener** (1850-1916):
http://www.bbc.co.uk/history/historic_figures/kitchener_lord_horatio.shtml
-**Merriam-Webster Dictionary**:
https://www.merriamwebster.com/dictionary/devil%27s%20dozen
-**Sir Edward Grey**, 3rd Baronet: https://www.britannica.com/biography/Sir-Edward-Grey-3rd-Baronet
-**Sporting**. Timaru Herald, Volume CI, Issue 15517, 30 November 1914:
https://paperspast.natlib.govt.nz/newspapers/THD19141130.2.14
-**The Imperial War Museum Book of 1914**, The Men Who Went To War. Brown, Malcolm. 1st Ed. 2004 Sidgwick & Jackson. Edition used: 2014 by Pan Books, London.
-**The sinking of the HMS Audacious**: https://www.royalnavy.mod.uk/news-and-latest-activity/news/2014/october/27/141027-hms-audacious-sinking

*For a more comprehensive list of resources used to help guide the writing of this novel, please go to: www.deborahsmall.com

My One True Love

It's when you're not looking, true love finds you...

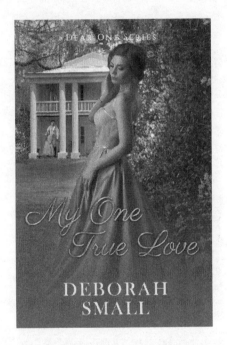

Book III in the Dear One series
Coming in 2019

For more information, visit:
www.deborahsmall.com

My Dear One

Love, born out of tragedy...

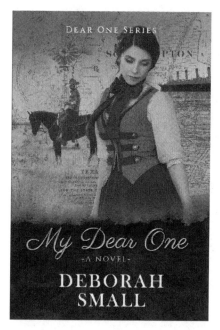

Book I in the Dear One series

Published in print June 2018

For more information, visit:
www.deborahsmall.com

Made in the USA
San Bernardino, CA
29 November 2018